THE
PREDATORS

TONY J FORDER

A DS Royston Chase Novel

Copyright © 2023 Tony Forder

The right of Tony Forder to be identified as the Author of the Work has been asserted by him in accordance Copyright, Designs and Patents Act 1988.
First published in 2023 by Spare Nib Books

Apart from any use permitted under UK copyright law, this publication may only be reproduced, stored, or transmitted, in any form, or by any means, with prior permission in writing of the publisher or, in the case of reprographic production, in accordance with the terms of licences issued by the Copyright Licensing Agency.

All characters in this publication are fictitious and any resemblance to real persons, living or dead, is purely coincidental.

tonyjforder.com
tony@tonyjforder.com

Also by Tony J Forder

The DI Bliss Series
Bad to the Bone
The Scent of Guilt
If Fear Wins
The Reach of Shadows
The Death of Justice
Endless Silent Scream
Slow Slicing
Bliss Uncovered
The Autumn Tree
Darker Days to Come
The Lightning Rod

Standalones
Fifteen Coffins
Degrees of Darkness

The Mike Lynch Series
Scream Blue Murder
Cold Winter Sun

The DS Chase Series
The Huntsmen

Psychopaths are social predators, and like all predators, they are looking for feeding grounds. Wherever you get power, prestige, and money, you will find them.

—*Robert D. Hare*

This book is dedicated to Dorothy Laney, Kath Middleton, and Lynda Checkley, whose eagle eyes and editorial bent have steered me well for many books now. I really don't know how I managed without them before they started beta reading my work.

ONE

IN DETECTIVE SERGEANT ROYSTON Chase's opinion, there were three different kinds of dicks in the world. Dicks who behave like arseholes. Arseholes who behave like dicks. And the third – and by far the most despicable of the trio – the kind of dick that forces you to leave the warmth and comfort of your own home to attend a scene of crime on your day off when the weather is doing its best to break the spirit of even the most enthusiastic abominable snowman. Today, Superintendent Waddington was that dick.

The storm blew in hard across Cherhill Down. Thick clumps of snow the size of small rocks obscured vision beyond a dozen yards or so. A dense copse provided some respite at least, its skeletal branches garbed in white winter apparel. The detective leaned into a boisterous flurry as he picked his way between the scattering of trees, head down, gloved hands rammed deep into the pockets of his fleece-lined jacket. He'd pulled the hood up and drawn it tight around his face the moment he stepped out of his car, not caring if he looked like Kenny from *South Park*. His thoughts were focussed more on his reason for being out in such unpleasant weather than the freezing wind doing its damnedest to force a brass monkey to strike out in search of a welder.

Aristotle once suggested that to appreciate the beauty of a snowflake, it was necessary to stand out in the cold. Chase wondered if the Greek philosopher had ever frozen his arse off on a Wiltshire hillside in a blizzard prior to summoning up that particular piece of free-thinking bullshit.

Following a path denoted by a series of green flags whose tall poles strained beneath the force of the squall, Chase entered the area with caution. He didn't want to stumble blindly outside the permitted boundary lines. Other than the route in and out and the scene itself, there was clearly an awful lot of the thicket yet to be searched.

Scott Buchan, the crime scene manager, waited for him beneath a wide awning attached to a crime scene tent. The canopy was three-sided, shielding those who ventured inside from the worst of the weather. Buchan had also snuggled into a heavy winter jacket, which he wore over his forensic suit, its hood pulled down, an elasticated cap wrapped over his head. He stood alongside DC Claire Laney, Chase's colleague. The CSI looked up at his approach, face grim and flushed the colour of raw liver from the biting chill.

'Don't tell me,' Chase said through chattering teeth. 'Dog walker discovered the body, yes? They're a hardy bunch.'

'Oddly enough, no.' Buchan's voice was cultured, with a vague Scottish lilt. 'A soldier on leave who'd set out to yomp a small part of the trail came into the wood to escape the worst of the snowstorm, and pretty much stumbled over our corpsicle.'

Chase flashed him a questioning frown.

Buchan nodded, pushing back his thick-rimmed spectacles. 'Virtually frozen solid, the poor wee thing. My guess is she'd started thawing out as the daily temperatures rose, but then last night's frost and now this sorry mess began covering her up and freezing her again.'

'I won't bother asking for an ETD.'

'I wouldn't if I were you,' Laney said curtly as she stamped her feet to keep her circulation flowing. 'Our esteemed SOCO here reacts like a bit of a twonk when you ask stupid questions.'

The crime scene manager greeted this with a grunt and a shake of the head. 'I'm sorry, but as I told you not five minutes ago, an estimated time of death is a little out of the question given the circumstances. This bonnie lass is going to take a couple of days to reach the point where I can do anything with her. We are looking at her body having been here several weeks, possibly a month or two.'

'Cause of death is suspicious, though, right?' Chase observed. 'Otherwise neither me or DC Laney would be here.'

'Aye. My initial examination suggests she was beaten and perhaps strangled. Judging by the position in which she was found, and the disarray of her clothing, I think it's likely she was also sexually abused. I wouldn't want to pre-judge in what order those three things occurred. Frankly, given her condition, it's hard to say with any degree of confidence what happened here at all.'

Chase exhaled with a groan, filling the space between them with a cloud of misty breath. 'Shit! I don't suppose there's any chance of sperm surviving, is there?'

'Not enough to swallow,' Laney muttered.

Ignoring the comment, Buchan ran a hand across his unshaven chin, weighing up his response. 'Healthy sperm can survive for up to five days. Frozen sperm might last for years. However, for that length of time we're talking cryostorage, certainly not the kind of temperature or conditions we have here. But if this poor girl was killed shortly after being ejaculated into, and froze soon afterwards, then it may be possible to find some of those sperm cells thawing out along with her.'

'But we shouldn't count on it.'

'No, you most certainly should not do that, Royston. How are Erin and Maisie, by the way?'

Chase smiled the smile he usually gave when asked about his wife and daughter. 'Both good, thanks.' He didn't return the question; Scott Buchan was single, gay, celibate, and childless.

'Good to hear it. Listen, if you want to get up close and personal with our corpsicle, I still have to ask you to suit and boot. Exposure and weather created a chaotic scene, but since we got her beneath canvas it's also become a rapidly evolving one. We had no option but to move her into a clearing large enough to put a tent over her, so you might be better off running your expert eye over the spot where she was actually discovered. Just look for the red flags.'

'Thanks. Makes sense. I'll do that.' He preferred to see the victim in situ, but in this case he would have to make do with the photographs and video footage taken before the CSI technicians moved the body.

'I'll stay here with Scott,' Laney said. 'I've already had a look at the actual crime scene. Let me know what you make of her possessions. I've formed my own opinion, but I'll be keen to hear if you agree.'

Nodding, Chase moved on. Ahead he saw tape being mauled by the wind, forensic staff and police officers huddled close by. This was no weather to be out in, but partially protected by the beech trees those gathered at the scene would continue to do their very best for this poor young woman. He nodded at everybody, though they were all pretty much wrapped up as he was, and it was difficult to tell who was who. As he made his way around a knot of trees, he immediately understood why Laney had asked him about the victim's possessions.

To begin with, he had not expected the tent.

The green Night Cat was, he knew, designed for hiking and camping. Its presence caused Chase to alter his entire impression of the suspected murder. He'd imagined the victim had been lured into the copse by her attacker, possibly even snatched somewhere close by and dragged under cover and out of sight. Now he realised she had probably been hiking, camping out for the night rather than paying for lodgings. An error in judgement she sadly did not live to rue.

CSI had erected a separate forensic tent, its flaps pinned back to provide a gaping entrance. Inside stood a foldout table upon which lay a large empty rucksack and its previous contents, each labelled, numbered, dated, and initialled ahead of being packed away in suitable containers. Chase took his time browsing through the items. The clothing, toiletries, and personal possessions were as expected. He was, however, intrigued by a few things he found and one he could not. He asked one of the techs if they'd already removed a mobile from the scene, but was told no phone had yet been recovered.

The lack of a phone suggested a robbery, and the purse on the table was also empty. Chase wondered about that. Why go to all the bother of removing its contents? Why not take the purse and toss it away later? Had the person responsible for this simply wanted to ensure they left no identification behind and decided to help themselves to their victim's cash at the same time?

CCTV, mobile phone data, and GPS locating were some of the most prominent tools major criminal investigations had come to rely on in recent years. But there were no security cameras anywhere nearby, and it looked as if whoever had murdered the young woman had enough wits about them to take her mobile away with them. If so, they'd probably broken the SIM card, tossed the battery if it was replaceable, and smashed the rest of the phone afterwards, discarding the separate pieces in different locations.

It's what he would have done if he were so inclined.

He removed his own lined gloves, pulled out a pair of nitrile replacements from a nearby box, and wriggled his hands into them before picking up a crumpled hiking guide. He had no idea what the *Wessex Ridgeway Trail* was, only that according to the pamphlet it ran between Wiltshire and Dorset – Marlborough to Lyme Regis to be more precise. It wasn't the only such leaflet among her possessions, the other being *The Ridgeway National Trail* between Overton Hill at Avebury and the Ivinghoe Beacon in Leighton Buzzard. In contrast to the other trail map, this one was in pristine condition. If their victim had started off in Wiltshire, it was unlikely that she would make camp here on her first night. Considering the state of the guides, his best guess was that she had taken the Wessex trail in the opposite direction, beginning in Dorset.

Chase turned to look back outside. Red flags twisted and flapped a good half a dozen paces from the tent. He wondered why whatever had happened to her had taken place outside in the cold air when the tent was there to provide shelter and comfort away from potential prying eyes. The area itself would surely provide them with no real evidence in respect of footprints or DNA, so it would all rely heavily on the body itself in addition to the young girl's belongings.

Collecting his thoughts, he looked out at his surroundings. The Cherhill white horse lay beneath a carpet of fresh white snow, completely hidden from view. The continuing snowfall partially obscured even the Lansdowne Monument, a soaring 35 metre obelisk. The normally attractive landscape had become bleak, an opaque two-dimensional vista that made him feel chilled to the marrow just looking at it. Remote and frigid, the crisp white terrain defined its slick, sparkling surface with indistinct shadows. Other than voices, the only sounds were those of crunching footfalls.

'What do you think?' Laney asked, startling him as she popped her head inside the tent.

'I think I'd rather still be curled up on the sofa at home. But if you're referring to this tragedy, I'm curious as to why she wasn't found inside the tent. I think it's likely that she camped here alone, and some predator stumbled upon her, which makes me wonder if there's a fellow hiker out there somewhere who saw or heard what happened. Judging by the flyer I just looked at and the kit she was carrying around with her, I'd say she hiked here from Dorset. It's going to be a couple of days before we have any update on the body, and with no phone or ID, we can at least begin with misper records and see what we can come up with.'

'I had the same thoughts and questions. If she had a fire going, and used a torch at night, she'd probably not have been hard to see even here inside this copse. She might have drawn unwanted attention from locals. Have you seen her yet?'

He shook his head. 'No point. She won't be telling me anything now that SOCO have removed her from the spot in which she was killed. I know what to expect – partial decomp, blackened flesh, all that awful stuff.'

'Decomp was more advanced than you might imagine. Looks like the daytime temperatures rose just enough to begin the thawing process, after which the flesh froze up again and then the snow came back with a vengeance. That activity could have happened a couple of times if you think about how the weather's been since the turn of the year.'

Chase could only imagine the ravages time and exposure had wrought upon their victim, her features almost certainly unrecognisable. He knew he had that to come, but would wait until the poor girl had been completely defrosted. Either way, it wasn't going to be a pretty sight.

'Come on,' he said. 'Let's have a quick word with the first responders and then we can get out of this bloody awful storm.'

'That may be the smartest thing you've said since you got here, cupcake,' Laney replied.

'You and smart are mutually exclusive, so how on earth would you know?'

Laney took a step back. 'Woah. Is there a glitch in the filter system today, Royston?'

Chase shook his head, squinting in the face of a snow flurry. 'Not where you're concerned,' he said, grinning as he turned to walk away. 'I've no need for excuses when it comes to speaking my mind about you, Claire.'

TWO

'Did I tell you about my pussy?' Claire Laney asked over the rim of her mug of hot chocolate. 'Short haired, warm and fuzzy, beautifully groomed. Surprisingly still flexible – albeit well-worn – with just the occasional leak and embarrassing odour.'

Colleagues sitting within earshot in Swindon's Gablecross police station break room appeared horrified. Stunned into silence, each of them was at pains to look anywhere but directly at the detective constable, who casually leaned against a small fridge.

'It's all right,' Chase said with a knowing smile. 'She's talking about a cat.'

Everybody exhaled at the same time, relief etched into their faces. A couple of officers chortled and held a hand to their chests. As their laughter subsided and the room began to settle, Laney said with perfect timing, 'Cat? I don't have a cat.'

Caught unawares, Chase coughed up some of his own hot drink. There was a collective gasp of shock, which caused Laney to smirk and say, 'You lot are so bloody easy. Of course I'm talking about a cat. She's a sweet old puss on the downhill slope. A charity I work with provides elderly moggies in their final few years on earth to kind and considerate owners. And when they can't find any kind and considerate owners, they let us have one instead.'

Chuckling to herself, she turned and breezed out into the

corridor, making her way to the office allocated to the small team of three. Chase followed in her wake, still recovering from having spat out his drink.

'Do you really have a cat?' he asked. 'Or did you just want to do a pussy joke?'

Glancing back over her shoulder, she grinned and said, 'Of course I have a cat. You really think I'm that shameless?'

'All right, then. So what's its name?'

'Merkin,' Laney said, with barely a pause.

This time, Chase found himself attempting to wipe sprayed tea from the wall, his partner laughing it up. He swore beneath his breath and then said, 'You don't have a sodding animal at all, do you?'

'I'd tell you, but it might send your filter issue into overdrive. We wouldn't want that at the start of a new operation, now, would we?'

The concern Laney spoke of referred to a problem Chase dealt with on a daily basis as a result of a tumble he'd taken in the course of duty. He'd fallen and struck his head hard on solid ground, the injury requiring emergency surgery which had left him with the occasional inability to control his mental filter. This resulted in him not always making allowances for his audience when speaking, and unintentionally being condescending and rude to people. Since acquiring Claire Laney as a partner, he'd played on the condition and left her guessing which of his utterances were genuine examples and which were a case of him toying with her.

She'd mentioned a new op. He wondered about that. From the first two police officers on the scene they'd learned that the soldier who'd discovered their Jane Doe had offered nothing more than they already knew. He confirmed he had not touched the body, halting his approach the moment he realised she was dead. Chase asked his uniformed colleagues to email him the man's details as soon as they returned to their local station. He and Laney then drove separately to the regional operations centre at Gablecross on the outskirts of Swindon.

In the aftermath of a serious case he, Laney, and PCSO Alison May had investigated in the autumn, the village-based station they worked out of had subsequently fallen into disrepute. The tiny hamlet of Little Soley owed much to the local estate owned for generations by the Webster family. Despite the most recent occupier and former area Chief Constable, Sir Kenneth, having brought disgrace upon himself and his reputation, the incumbent senior police officer for Wiltshire had decided to maintain the presence as a gesture to the past and out of respect for the current inhabitants of the village.

Chase had negotiated with senior leadership a role for the three of them to play in the more rural communities of the county. As part of that deal, the more serious crimes were run from Gablecross. PCSO May had applied for a direct entry route to becoming a detective constable, which was quickly approved. An enthusiastic and diligent officer, Chase had taken her under his wing. In his view, the young woman had the talent to go with the ambition and he was keen to nurture her natural aptitude for the job. As for Claire Laney, he was still coming to terms with her abrupt manner and odd sense of humour.

'Is it still horrid out there?' May asked as the two of them walked into the tiny office. CID Rural was printed on the door nameplate, though some wag had added the words *Carrot-crunching Idiots Department* beneath in indelible ink.

Laney spread her hands and looked herself up and down. 'No, I always dress like Scott of the bleeding Antarctic. Allow me to introduce Sherpa Tensing here,' she said, gesturing towards Chase.

'You're getting your explorers mixed up,' he pointed out, climbing out of his own heavy jacket.

'All right, so Shackleton and Tensing, then.'

'No, it's Tensing you've got wrong. He's not famous for the Antarctic.'

Laney rolled her eyes and groaned. 'Well, the sodding Arctic, then. Same thing.'

'They're really not, Claire. In fact, they're poles apart. Literally. And I don't mean the modern meaning of the word, which apparently embraces figurative usage. I mean the proper meaning, the original one, way back when literally was literally literal.'

'Don't confuse matters, cupcake,' Laney begged him. 'You do that far too often for your own good. Still, at least I now know Tensing is famous for something other than just being a bloody sherpa.'

Chase finally managed to heave his jacket up and over its hook on the back of the door. 'He is, indeed. He was the first, along with Edmund Hillary, to reach the summit of Everest.'

'Ah, of course. There you go. I knew it involved some English explorer. I wasn't too far off.'

'Quite. We could even call it a near miss. Except for the fact that Hillary was a Kiwi, you're a whisker shy of being spot on.'

Laney's gloves were heavy, but she managed to comfortably show him the middle finger of her left hand. 'Don't stand there being a pedantic plod over shit nobody cares about, Royston, not when you could be getting the biscuits out. Trudging through all that snow has given me an appetite.'

Stripping off his hat, which also found a home on the same door hook, Chase eventually muttered, 'It's not pedantry if you're completely right and the other person is entirely wrong. It's called stating facts. We used to revere it in this country, but we live in a time that appreciates rumour and hyperbole over truth and facts.'

'Okay, well, here's a fact for you: I'm freezing my bollocks off and I need this hot drink inside me. But I also need to chomp on a Hobnob at the same time. And don't,' she snapped, raising a warning hand this time, 'waste your breath telling me I don't have any bollocks. I'll have you know I have a mighty fine collection of plums in a jar right next to the one containing Eleanor Rigby's face. You get that biscuit drawer open and stop wasting time.'

'I wasn't going to say a word,' he said, stooping to retrieve the packet from his desk. 'Besides, I wouldn't mind betting your balls are bigger than mine.'

'Oh, believe me… they are.'

'Actually,' May said, stretching languidly in her chair, 'some people believe George Mallory and Andrew Irvine reached Everest's summit almost twenty years before Hillary and Tensing.'

'For fuck's sake,' Laney chided, staring her down. A mouthful of glove muffled her words, but she peeled it away before finishing. 'Enough with all this crap. My brain cannot handle such banality.'

May gave a disappointed shrug. 'I'm just saying. Anyhow, I don't care who got there first. I just always thought it was amazing that Tensing was named Sherpa and later became a sherpa.'

This time, the groan of complaint came from Chase. 'That's enough from you, *Dora the Explorer*. My brain might actually explode if I hear another word about it.'

Ten minutes afterwards, the three of them were satiated and plunging back into the job. Laney was still cold and wore her ugly leather jacket with tassels running up the outside of the arms. Chase filled May in on the crime scene. He outlined his discovery of the trail guides, explaining the logic of his assumptions.

'I think that's sound reasoning,' she said with a firm nod. 'I know those hiking trails, and you can walk them either way. Sounds to me as if our Jane Doe was intent on doing both parts. If she began down on the coast, that first stage is around 140 miles. The second is only 90 or so. She could easily have set up camp to shelter from the first snowfall on her way to completing the final leg – she was on the right route to take her down into Avebury and then on to Marlborough.'

'How do you know so much about it, my love?' Laney asked, both hands wrapped around her bulbous heat-retaining mug. She had slipped into a chair behind her own desk, spitting biscuit crumbs as she spoke. 'Sounds like the kind of old tosh that would bore me rigid. You wouldn't catch me walking anywhere by choice other than in and out of buildings I need to be inside or outside of.'

'I have a couple of friends who are keen hikers,' May explained. 'They've done that walk several times before, and in both directions. They aim to walk the PCT when they're ready.'

'What's that when it's at home?'

'The Pacific Crest Trail. If you hiked the full length, it would take you from Mexico to Canada, more than 2,500 miles, including deserts and mountains up the west coast of America.'

Chase puffed out his lips. 'Makes my strolls around Nightingale Wood close to where I live sound tame.'

'Those Ridgeway trails are looking a bit pathetic, too. But it fits if we're looking at why our victim might have been there.'

'It does. And that could buy us a jump on this in terms of identification. If she lived in Dorset or nearby and was reported missing, then we may be able to narrow it down.'

'True,' Laney said. 'But just because that could have been her starting point doesn't mean that's where she lived. She might've travelled to Lyme Regis in order to start there at the end of the trail.'

Deflated, Chase agreed. 'So what counties bordering the trail do we have? Somerset and Hampshire?'

'You may want to include the Isle of Wight as well.'

Chase snapped his fingers. 'Devon is in the mix, as Wiltshire has to be.'

'Okay. So expand the misper search to include those counties as well. Any and all girls and young women who went missing shortly after the turn of the year.'

'We don't know exactly when she died, do we?'

'No, but let's go back eight weeks to begin with. We can always work backwards from there if we have to, but if I'm remembering correctly, December wasn't too bad weather-wise so I'm betting she holed up where she did to shelter from that snow, which began the first week of January.'

'It was bloody freezing at one point just before Christmas, but I don't recall it snowing that month, either. Do you want me to follow up on that?' May asked him.

'Yes, please. But tread carefully. Just obtain the records and sift through them. Set aside any of interest and we'll take a look at the results together.'

'Which leaves you and me doing what in the meantime?' Laney asked.

Chase scratched his chin. 'That's a good question. We'll stay here for the rest of today and then back over at Little Soley nick from tomorrow. First thing I need to do is meet with the Super to report in and have him make arrangements to set up a team. Which reminds me, Alison, how do you fancy shadowing the exhibits officer?'

The ex-PCSO's eyes glimmered. 'That would be great, Royston. I'd be honoured. Are you sure about it, though? I mean, it's a responsible post, especially in a murder enquiry which this probably will be.'

'Let me put it this way: you either know what needs to be done or you can quickly learn from an experienced officer. But it's not all about bagging and tagging. You're going to have to get out there on that hillside and work closely with the officers on the ground and the CSI team. You might even have to attend the post-mortem. Are you up for all that?'

'Absolutely.'

'Willingness goes a long way with me,' Chase said. 'Look, Alison, you know the fundamentals. An exhibits officer will take appropriate precautions when handling exhibits, having first identified the relevant items. You keep good records of everything, you secure everything, you manage access to each item, you liaise with all appropriate parties. Update HOLMES at regular intervals so that the exhibits record runs parallel to our own investigation. Remember, you may have to attend court if this results in a trial, so if you have any doubts whatsoever, tell me now. I'm throwing you in at the deep end, but I don't want you to drown.'

'I understand. I can cope. I'm thorough, I manage my time well. I rely on my common sense and organisational skills. All of which means I was born to do this job.'

'Okay. It may only be for a couple of days. By then our victim will have thawed out and we might be able to ID her. Until then, if I can get you in with exhibits, Claire and I will run the searches instead.'

'When is the Super expecting you, Royston?' Laney asked.

Chase checked his wristwatch. 'Ten minutes ago.'

'Well, you'd better run along then. Don't keep him waiting. Oh, and please do give him my love.'

'Aren't you better equipped for that?'

'I don't know. Isn't he gay?'

'Not as far as I'm aware, no.'

'Maybe you're just not sending him the right signals.'

'And maybe you're just a mad old bag with no sense of right and wrong.'

Laughing hard, Laney said, 'Oh, Royston, my little cupcake, you are much mistaken. I do have a sense of right and wrong. I just don't care enough to pay them any heed.'

'Are you two sure this is the right training environment for me?' Alison May asked, grinning as she looked between them.

'Not if you want a long and illustrious career, no,' Chase replied.

'That's what I was thinking. It's not exactly a safe space.'

'Too bloody true it isn't,' Laney added, rubbing her hands together as she spun around in her office chair like a child. 'And it never will be while I'm crowding it. But you will at least have some fun along the way.'

Chase shook his head and stood to leave, keen to have the last word as he fled the office. 'Don't pay any attention to her, Alison. And take comfort from the fact that, no matter how deep you might sink, you'll never get lower than Claire.'

THREE

THE SUPERINTENDENT HAD BEEN an orderly man for as long as Chase had known him. Fastidiously so, some might say. But although his desk was permanently tidy, the office was observably a busy working environment, which helped remind Chase of the kind of senior officer Waddington could be. The two had enjoyed a cordial and collegial relationship until the accident. Since then, however, the DSI had seemed unsettled when juggling with the differences between the detective sergeant he had previously commanded and the one he currently had to deal with. Almost as if Chase embarrassed him these days, and as a result had put distance between them.

As he entered the Super's office, Chase noted a flicker of alarm pass across Waddington's features. He had long since overcome the hurt feelings caused by his boss's reaction to his presence, and while he continued to regard the man as a good copper, what was missing between them these days was respect. Something neither of them was ever likely to regain.

'You're late,' Waddington decided to open with, making a point of checking his watch.

Chase took a seat at the desk, dismissing the jibe. 'I wanted to quickly establish some initial thoughts with Claire and Alison before speaking to you, sir. The scene was so unusual I felt it warranted further discussion.'

'And the result of that conversation…?'

'The Crime Scene Manager, Buchan, is leaning towards murder, with the possibility of some physical and sexual abuse. He says it might take a few days for our victim's body to thaw completely, but he hopes to start gathering evidence as the remains begin to soften. They won't remove her from the scene for a while yet, so a delay is inevitable. Our thinking is that we react as if this will be a murder enquiry. We'll need an SIO, and an exhibits officer out there as soon as. I'd like to have Alison shadow exhibits until we have a firm strategy in place. Meanwhile, Claire and I have some groundwork to focus on; among Jane Doe's possessions were a couple of hiking guides, and we suspect she had completed the first part of that trail. A trail which most likely began in Dorset.'

Nodding along, Waddington said, 'That's a good start based on what you had to work with, Royston. We'll need confirmation on COD of course, but if we can get a head start on this then so much the better. Will you work out of your office here for the duration?'

'No. We'll attend as and when necessary, but I'd prefer to be closer to the scene. Also, we're supposed to be doing more than paying lip service to the notion of manning the station in the village. The more people see us come and go, the better their perception.'

'Very well. And COD?'

'Cause of death will hopefully become more obvious as the body thaws out. I wouldn't like to speculate.'

'Understood. What's the scene like at present?'

Chase considered his words carefully. 'Chaotic. The recent thaw exposed the body enough to be stumbled over, but the latest snowstorm blew in not long afterwards, leaving us to deal with a complete whiteout. Being halfway up Cherhill Down complicates matters because it's difficult to get close to in this weather. The trees offer minimal protection, so until I see the crime scene photos and video footage, I'm finding it hard to get a feel for it. The fact that she was discovered yards away from her tent has me wondering why she died unprotected, which again steers us towards murder or suspicious circumstances at the very least.'

'Very good. Sounds as if you have a handle on it for the time being. After sending you out there, I gave some thought to operations should it prove to be a murder. Given everything we have learned since, I'm bringing in DCI Knight as SIO.'

'I'm not familiar with the name.'

'Nicole has been with us for just shy of a year. A strong leader.'

Chase would rather have heard Knight described as a decent copper, but nodded amiably all the same. 'If you think she's right for the job, then I'm sure we'll make it work.'

'Good. I'd do the job myself, but I'm snowed under… no pun intended. Officially, we don't yet have a murder, of course, but I agree that we must still launch our investigation. Better to begin and have to stop than start the process later than we could have. You carry on with the tasks in hand while I put together a team. Major Crimes have their hands full with court appearances and the gang murders in Swindon town centre at the weekend, so I'd rather not distract them from an ongoing op.'

'Sounds good. And TDC May?'

The Superintendent frowned for a moment before realising who Chase was referring to. 'Sorry, yes. I can't quite get used to this Trainee Detective Constable role.'

'Hardly surprising,' Chase said. 'She's the first of her breed in this authority. But she'll also be an inspiration to those who follow.'

'I do hope so. You fought hard for acceptance of the post. As for your request, if you can spare May then of course she can shadow whoever DCI Knight assigns to exhibits. You are May's mentor, but experience in specialist roles is all part of the training programme. Let me speak to Nicole and together we'll make the necessary arrangements. I'll have her contact you just as soon as I have her briefed.'

'Thank you, sir. The three of us will crack on until I hear from her.'

Waddington sat back, interlacing his fingers and resting them against his white-shirted chest. 'Speaking of the three of you, how are things with DC Laney?'

Chase frowned, curious. 'Absolutely fine. Any reason why they shouldn't be?'

'No, not at all. It's just that… well… don't you find her a little… fractious? Overbearing at times?'

Chase allowed himself a smile. 'Oh, I see what you mean. Yes, sir, she's both of those. But we make it work.'

'I'm glad to hear it. However, if you end up having to inform family members about our victim, DC Laney may not be the best person to have alongside you. Another job for May, perhaps. Just a thought, Sergeant.'

'I'll consider it, sir. But you have to remember, Claire held a rank higher than mine at one point, and for quite some time. She's seen it all, done it all. Yes, she can be crass at times, but I think she also understands there's a time and a place for her nonsense.'

'If you say so. Use your best judgement.' Waddington frowned and then offered a weak smile. 'Who knows, perhaps Laney has a touch of what you have.'

Chase shook his head, returning the gesture. 'No, I don't think so, sir. She's just generally unpleasant.'

Leaving Waddington to contemplate his rejoinder, Chase returned to the office. 'It's a go,' he said as he took his place at the desk set aside for the team leader of this merry little band. 'The boss is putting together a team. The SIO is somebody I haven't worked with before, nor do I know her by reputation, but provided we all behave ourselves…'

'Why are you looking at me?' Laney complained.

'Why would I look anywhere else?'

She glanced at May, back to Chase, then shrugged. 'Okay. Fair enough. I'll play nice. Is that what you want to hear, my love?'

'It's not about me, Claire. DCI Knight may be happy for you to call her Nicole, but probably not to be referred to as a cupcake or anything else along the lines of baked goods or tasty treats.'

Laney raised a hand and hooked her little finger. 'Five minutes,' she said. 'That's all it will take for me to have her wrapped around this. Just like I had you.'

Chase shook his head dismissively. 'Your charms were lost on me, Claire. Still are, if I'm being honest. But let's crack on and get stuck into mispers. I'll take Devon and Dorset while you two fight it out for the remaining counties.'

'Any idea at all of age range?' Alison May asked.

'None. It was impossible to tell. Given the camping gear, we may be able to rule out a stroppy early teen taking off with the hump. Let's err on the side of caution, though. Limit your age-range search to between 18 and 30 to start with. We can always go wider if you get no hits.'

'We'll probably get tons of hits.'

'You'll be surprised.'

May regarded him quizzically 'You think? I heard a stat suggesting someone in the UK is reported missing every 90 seconds, of which around 170,000 individuals a year actually are.'

'Close enough, and it sounds bad, but taken out of context they're misleading. The long-term figures for mispers reduce dramatically as time passes, with less than 3,000 remaining missing for more than 28 days. Given on average only 40 per cent of those will be female, each county will have a much more manageable number for us to consider.'

Chase understood they could place no reliance upon bare statistics, especially considering the nature of human beings. But he also knew that stats provided an approximation, which often made a task appear less daunting. And once you were able to swap percentage figures for actual numbers, assignments took on a completely fresh perspective. Half an hour later, he was happy to be proven right when his own search of the records for Devon revealed fewer than 5,000 individuals having been reported missing over the past year, of which 147 were aged between 18 and 30. This figure reduced further still to 65 females, and massively so when analysing those who were still recorded as being missing for longer than 28 days. His search left him with only three females within the search criteria he had established. Sadly, for a whole variety of reason, of those initial missing persons reports, around 100 ended up being recorded as fatalities. He wondered if one of the three names he had on his screen was their murder victim.

He jotted down a few basic details before sending the individual documents to the centralised printer. He made his way along the corridor in a trance-like state, his thoughts drawn to the officer about to become his SIO. It had been quite some time since he'd had a direct line manager working closely alongside him. His stint in the tiny village of Little Soley on the border with Berkshire had provided him with an autonomy he'd enjoyed. Chase had his own way of working, and although he could be a team player, he preferred to lead from the front. Nobody said it out loud, but his accident had all but put the kibosh on further career advancement. For a time, he'd been treated like a pariah, but he realised that was more out of fear of the unknown on the part of senior officers than any resentment or lack of respect for his abilities. In being formally associated with Gablecross once more, he felt the need to prove himself all over again.

If he was up to it.

For misfits like him and Laney, the Swindon police HQ was hardly the best of environments. On the downslope as if she were taking a run on the luge, his relatively new partner claimed not to care about perceptions or internal politics because she was on her way out as soon as she hit fifty-five and could grab her pension. Chase thought that might have been true at one point, but since the case that brought them together, she seemed to have taken a fresh interest in her work. He hoped part of that was due to him, but sensed much of her change in attitude had arisen from a new appreciation of what it meant to be a police officer. Even so, the freedom to return to their familiar village surroundings on a regular basis suited them both.

In the print room he used his swipe card to retrieve the pages, and moments later he carried hard copies of three missing persons reports back to the team's office. Before collecting them, he'd sent the digital file to Scott Buchan, the crime scene manager. He didn't hold out much hope for facial recognition, but the sooner they could obtain an ID the better. In his view, it was worth trying everything.

As he walked into the office, he heard voices and saw a woman standing in the centre of the room speaking with both Laney and May. Tall, upright, dressed stylishly, she had long red hair that flowed over her shoulders, and wore just the right amount of makeup to accentuate her eyes and prominent cheekbones. As her gaze fell upon him, Chase was immediately drawn to the effervescent smile and outstretched hand.

'And you must be DS Chase,' she said as they greeted one another.

'I'm not at all sure I must be, but I am. Royston, please.'

'Royston it is. I'm DCI Knight, but please do call me Nicole. It's good to meet you. I was just telling Claire and Alison that the rest of the team are waiting for you all in the major incident room. They're raring to get stuck in.'

'As are we,' he said, a little taken aback by Knight's overt friendliness. The cynic in him wondered if it was all an act. The professional in him decided to give her time to prove him wrong.

FOUR

The major incident rooms were on the third floor of the Gablecross building, the largest of them additionally used for media briefings. The inaugural meeting of the Operation Silverback team took place in the second MIR. First up from DCI Knight came a brief introduction.

'Because this is not a crime in action, we have a relatively small gathering,' she explained. 'However, I've selected people I know well and who are the best at what they do. You'll get to know each other well as time goes on, I'm sure, but for the time being we'll make do with roles and responsibilities. How does that sound?'

When she received nods of agreement and positive murmurings, Knight continued. 'DI Howard Fox, or plain old Foxy to us here at GC, is this team's most experienced Investigating Officer and my right-hand man. DS Jude Armstrong is our case officer, and worth his weight in gold. If anybody needs to know the current status of this operation, seek him out first. Family Liaison Officer, DC Natalie Mann, is kind, caring, compassionate, and above all else, shrewd and insightful. If there are skeletons to be found, Nat will root them out. Then we have DC Efe Salisu, an exhibits officer with a mind like a database. Running CCTV and Communications jointly, we have DC Reuben Cooper, who also happens to be a whizz at interviewing and seldom emerges from the room without a good lead. Finally,

DC Paige Bowen has a handle on intelligence and disclosure, and tends to team up with Reuben to dissect our suspects.'

Each of the team members either nodded, held up a hand, or stood as the DCI introduced them. Knight explained that the head of the Crime Scene Investigation unit was unavailable, otherwise she would also have been in the room to discuss the work being carried out on Cherhill Down.

Chase then introduced himself, Laney and May. The role of TDC was an unknown quantity, as was May herself to these colleagues, but clearly everybody had heard of both him and Laney. Without any conscious thought he added, 'Whatever you've heard about me is almost certainly exaggerated. Due to a minor brain injury, I have a habit of blurting things out when under pressure, so at times I might come across as blunt or even downright rude. I promise you it is seldom intentional. When Claire does the same thing, however, rest assured she means every word of it, and it's always premeditated. She really is as spiteful and disagreeable as you've heard.'

He was delighted to hear laughter echoing off the four walls. Laney shot him daggers, but she was also smiling along. 'We're here for the rest of the day,' he continued. 'Tomorrow morning we'll return to Little Soley, but we'll keep in regular contact throughout this investigation. I'm happy to liaise directly with Nicole, and all three of us will keep apprised of events through Jude, your case officer.'

'*Our* case officer,' Knight reminded him without obvious rebuke. 'We're all one team for this op.'

'Of course. Did the Super mention having Alison shadow your exhibits officer? Sorry, *our* exhibits officer.'

'He did. I've already mentioned this to Efe.'

DC Salisu shot a glance in May's direction, her wide smile displaying an immaculate array of gleaming white teeth.

'There are to be no elephants in this room,' DCI Knight said after a slight pause. She turned to those colleagues with whom she was most familiar. 'Yes, our Little Soley contingent were responsible for outing this county's ex-Chief Constable following his sudden death.

But their hard work also brought about an end to suffering and misery for so many. What they did had widespread ramifications in this authority, but it was necessary. More than that, it was the right thing to do. So, if you feel unable to welcome them unreservedly, tell me now and I'll have you replaced for the duration of this op.'

Nobody said a word, but Chase was grateful to Knight for having raised the matter. Not everybody inside the Job was happy with him and Laney for having investigated one of their own, but the vast majority of fellow officers had changed their minds once they knew exactly who and what Sir Kenneth Webster had been.

'This is Operation Silverback,' the DCI said. 'Now, let's get on with it.'

Chase filled them in on the direction he, Laney, and May had taken the case so far. He concluded with the information they had pulled from various databases.

'That's impressive,' DI Fox said with a nod of appreciation. 'Something out of nothing always is. I assume you three will want to pursue your own leads?'

'Want to and will do, even if it means a fight to the death,' Laney said unequivocally. 'We're the ones who froze our arses off on that hillside.'

Fox smiled. 'Of course. No argument here. I'd be equally determined if I'd already put in the hard graft.'

Laney crossed her arms and scowled. 'Damn! You're not all going to be this pleasant and reasonable, are you, cupcakes?'

'I won't deny there are strong egos in this room,' DCI Knight admitted after the resulting laughter had died away. 'But we all have the same objective. I find the best way to achieve that goal is to work together. We set personalities aside and we operate as a team. Agreed?'

'She agrees,' Chase said quickly. 'You'll have to excuse our village porcupine. Her quills may be barbed, but in the main they are there for the purpose of defence.'

Once again, his humour pierced the tension like a bullet. Everybody in the room seemed to relax, and chatter broke out between colleagues. Chase waited for a lull before continuing. 'Look, I'm the first to admit that Claire and I are an odd couple as partners. We've not known each other for very long, but we appear to rub along just fine. I think Alison is the glue holding us together, the sane one, if you like. We have our own styles, and we enjoy steering the ship. But we're also fine being deckhands. Us working out of the village station shouldn't be any kind of barrier. We needn't be in the same room together to function as a unit, not with today's technology.'

Knight cleared her throat. 'Superintendent Waddington did mention something about the mobile phone signal not being reliable at your station.'

'I think that's an issue with his phone rather than mine,' Chase said, suppressing a grin. 'Often he can't reach me when others can.'

Laney's snort of derision was unsubdued. Unlike everybody else in the room, she knew he had an illegal signal jammer in his jacket pocket. Using such a device carried a maximum two-year sentence if caught, but after moving out to take charge of Little Soley's police station, he'd decided it was a useful ploy and one easy to explain away if he wanted to remain out of touch. Waddington had demanded he carry an Airwave at all times to maintain contact, but Chase often left it in his desk drawer, citing memory lapses due to his brain injury. Another ruse he was happy to exploit.

All ten members of the team spent the next hour ensconced inside the major incident room. DC Paige Bowen offered to open a case file on the HOLMES database, suggesting she begin by logging the work completed so far by Chase, Laney, and May. Knight gave her the go-ahead and said she would start the policy book.

'I'll make a note of the progress made so far,' she said. 'I'll also itemise you three following up on your misper lists as the first operational decision.'

Chase glanced over at DC Reuben Cooper. 'Obviously we have no timeline as yet, but even once that is established, I think CCTV is going to be thin on the ground. Possibly a complete non-starter.

Once we have our victim identified, however, her phone is likely to be important.'

'I'll have a RIPA request form all set to go,' Cooper responded. 'I have a good relationship with all the major providers.'

The Regulation of Investigatory Powers Act of 2000 allowed the police access to phone data provided an officer at the rank of inspector or above authorised it. Critical evidence could be found in an individual's phone records, and often proved crucial in advancing an investigation. Chase hoped this op would prove no different.

'Does that not cover email access as well?' May asked.

Cooper grimaced. 'Good question, but no. Emails are an entirely separate thorn in our side. Most of the servers they reside on are located outside the UK, mainly in the States. Different set of rules altogether. We apply under the Mutual Legal Assistance Treaty, but in reality, we seldom bother. It's a lengthy process, it can eat up physical resources, and by the time they deliver we're often way beyond the point of needing it. Usually we get what we need from phones or other devices and set about MLAT only as a last resort.'

Chase concurred. 'If we reach that stage, then the case is probably dead,' he confirmed, then swiftly turned to Fox. 'How do you want to handle the victim's family as and when we know who and what we're dealing with?'

'I'll have Nat on standby for when you ID our victim,' the DI assured them. 'As family liaison officers go, DC Mann is at your disposal and is as good as they come. You need have no concerns about that. She knows what's required of such a pivotal role.'

Chase was pleased with the cooperation and apparent eagerness of the officers who formed the nucleus of the team. If the op proved to be a murder investigation and a major enquiry launched as a result, the team would likely expand two or threefold. But as a core, he liked what he had seen and heard. DCI Knight came across as both professional and open to ideas, leaving him feeling positive about the prospect of working alongside her. Or for her, if it came to it.

When the meeting was over, Chase asked his new DCI for a private meeting. She had her own comfortable, spacious office on the same floor. On a tall bookshelf placed against the far wall stood lines of requisite protocols and procedure manuals in thick binders, though he guessed they were seldom required. He spotted an array of silver frames on the desk, their backs to him; family photos, he imagined. As the two of them took chairs facing each other, Knight raised her eyebrows and said, 'You have concerns, DS Chase?'

'Please, make it Royston. And yes, I do. Not in terms of the team, or having you as SIO, more about your take on me and my team. I wondered if what I heard in there was genuine or said mainly for the troops.'

Knight's eyes narrowed as she smiled. 'I'd heard you were forthright. Good. I prefer that. I'll respond in kind. You don't know me, Royston. Nor do you know about my career. I spent four years working for the Met. In London it's quite common for officers to be begged, borrowed, and even stolen from other nicks when there's a big op running. So in terms of organisation, it won't be a stretch for me if you three base yourselves in Little Soley. As case officer, DS Armstrong will be your main point of contact, but I'll always make myself available. Myself and Foxy will run the show, but day-to-day communications go through Jude. If this ends up being what we think it is, then I'll ask you to attend the occasional briefing. Otherwise, provided Jude knows what you're doing, and you also take on your share of actions, I don't foresee a problem.'

Chase gave a nod of approval. 'I'm pleasantly surprised to hear it. Our esteemed leaders were quite happy to cast me out into the back of beyond. That was before Sir Kenneth, of course. But you and I have never worked together before, so your endorsement feels genuine.'

Knight narrowed her gaze just a little. 'Don't get me wrong, Royston. I can be riled, I can get pissed off, and I can be demanding. But only when the circumstances dictate it. This working relationship won't succeed or fail because your office is elsewhere.'

'Good to know. And the Sir Kenneth investigation? Excuse me for asking, but other than a handful of colleagues, I have no idea who else regarded him as a friend.'

'Then rest assured, I wasn't one of them. And even had I been, that would no longer have been the case once you exposed the truth about him. Him and a whole host of others. The higher echelons felt the sting of it for a while, but ultimately, we're all better off when these kinds of monsters are weeded out.'

'Fair enough. And you're confident the rest of your team feels the same way?'

'I can't speak for them individually, but if there are any lingering resentments, they won't get in the way. And I'll remind you again… they're your team as well for the duration of this case.'

He took the hint. 'In that case, thank you, Nicole. Last autumn seems like a very long time ago, and the three of us have pretty much worked as a trio since Alison decided to step up. I didn't know what to expect from the Gablecross of today, but you've gone out of your way to make us feel welcome.'

'Which you are. You had friends here at GC long before you accepted the transfer to Little Soley, and nobody I spoke to had a bad word to say about you. Claire is a relative newcomer who came with a reputation. Some negative reports, but mostly positive ones. You vouching for young Alison is good enough for me. Don't worry, what you see here is what you get. I meant it when I said we're each here with a single purpose.'

Chase was happy to hear it, though he continued to harbour doubts. 'DCS Crawley and DSI Waddington have their reservations about me. I can't say I entirely blame them. They're both decent men, decent coppers. But they have rank and status to protect, and my big mouth is like having an unexploded bomb waiting to go off.'

'That's them. I'm me. If you embarrass me, I'll live. Getting results is what we're all here for, and I think you may be surprised to learn that the investigation you believe others have doubts about only enhanced your reputation. So, are we good?'

'We are.' There was no caution in those two words. 'One final matter.'

'Go ahead.'

'The media. By now they'll know something's going on at Cherhill. I'd like us to drop a veil over Operation Silverback until we know where we are with an ID. If somebody reported our victim missing, then her DNA will be in the Missing Persons database. Given the condition of her body, it could take a couple of days to make that comparison and identify her. Can we hold out for that long when it comes to our friends from the Fourth Estate?'

'You mean am I willing to plead with the DCS to approve doing so?'

Chase shrugged and allowed himself a thin smile. 'I suppose I do, yes.'

'In this instance, I happen to agree with you, Royston. Even if I didn't, I'd give your request due consideration. I assume you want it that way to prevent parents all around the country having to needlessly speculate rather than for purely operational reasons?'

'To be honest, I hadn't yet considered operational reasons for holding them off. I realise we're going to have to tell them something. I just want to make sure that when we do flesh it out, we know as much detail as possible and that the poor kid's family have been informed.'

She nodded. 'Absolutely. Consider it done.'

Chase was impressed. DCI Nicole Knight was already proving to be everything he had hoped for.

FIVE

'Twelve possibles,' Chase muttered idly, looking up at the information written on the narrow whiteboard screwed to the wall behind his desk. 'What are we to do about them?'

Alison May had travelled to Cherhill Down with DC Salisu, the exhibits officer. He and Laney had re-examined the list of mispers pulled from neighbouring counties. The question was how to move on that intel, considering they potentially had a further thirty-six hours before being able to identify their victim. Less if Scott Buchan could take an earlier sample of DNA and they found a match, but Chase wasn't banking on them being that lucky.

'Getting our hairy arses out of here and back to civilisation would be a good start,' Laney said with a curt snarl.

'Ah, how sweet. You want to be all cosied up and intimate in our quaint old village with just little old Royston for company?'

'Not especially, no. But I prefer there and you to here and them.'

'It's colder there,' he pointed out.

'So we'll throw a passing yokel on the fire. They're fifty percent peat, so I hear.'

He chuckled at that. 'We can rough it here for a bit longer. How about we flesh out our list? All we have at the minute are the bare statistics. If we pull their misper records, one of them might stand out as the most likely candidate. Assuming somebody somewhere carried out an investigation, we speak with whoever ran it. How does that sound?'

'Why can't we do that back at the ranch?'

Chase shook his head, firm this time. 'It's the first day, Claire. They're happy for us to work our own way where we feel comfortable, so I agreed we give them the rest of the afternoon here. Even you can manage that, can't you? Tell you what, I'll buy you a late lunch.'

Laney seemed to perk up at the thought of stuffing her face. 'Where? My choice?'

'Why not?'

'How about Eddie's?'

'Eddie's?'

'Yeah, Eddie's Grill. They do a tasty Philly cheesesteak melt.'

'All right, that sounds good. Let's work through these names first, though. I'd like to feel we made some progress today.'

Less than thirty minutes later, Chase thought he'd struck gold. 'How about this?' he said, turning to his partner. 'Grace Arnold. Twenty-two. Reported missing on Saturday 14th January. She set out to hike on New Year's day and was supposed to call her parents when she arrived in Marlborough. By that stage, she was between a day and possibly three days late, depending on how tough the hike was. It's not far off 140 miles if you follow the Wessex Ridgeway trail.'

'Our victim had the map for that, didn't she?' Laney said, swivelling her chair to face him. She tapped the chewed end of a Biro against her teeth, a habit he detested.

'Yes. According to her parents, she was doing the Wessex Ridgeway, taking a two-day break in or around Marlborough, and then going on to tackle the Ridgeway National, which runs from Overton Hill to Ivinghoe Beacon in Leighton Buzzard.'

'She an experienced hiker?'

Chase read through the comments on the statement made by Grace Arnold's father after reporting her missing. 'It doesn't say. Maybe nobody asked her parents the question.'

'She has to be our victim, doesn't she?'

'I wouldn't be surprised. I mean, this girl could have come unstuck in any number of ways walking that trail and camping out, especially at that time of year, but she's a good fit and I'm not seeing any other misper mentioned in connection with hiking.'

'She from Dorset?'

'Actually, no. Her trail began in Lyme Regis, which *is* in Dorset, but the Arnold family live a few miles further down the coast in Seaton, which lies over the border in Devon.'

'It's her, Royston. It has to be.'

He nodded stiffly. 'I think so. There's no way we can have her parents ID the poor girl in her current condition. But we could move things along by having a word with them. We can arrange to have crime scene photos of her belongings sent over so's we can show them to Mum and Dad.'

Laney puffed out a long, slow breath. 'What a shit job.'

Chase gave a reluctant nod. 'I know. I don't like it any more than you do, Claire. But we can't hide behind the fact that we believe it's her. Not if we speak with them. They have to know our line of thinking, though we must also stress the lack of formal identification.'

Running both hands through her hair, Laney said, 'What a great start to the year for those poor sods.'

'You never know, they might be the sort of people to find some relief in knowing. She's been missing for six weeks, so they have to fear the worst every time they wake up to a new day.'

Laney checked her phone. 'It's a five-hour round-trip even in the best of weather conditions, so today is out of the question. Is there anything else we can do in the meantime?'

'There's a note in the misper file to say the NCA were called in to offer specialist advice. The agency's Missing Persons Unit is dedicated to the task, so they have the expertise and experience. I'm only guessing, but I doubt they will have searched every inch of both trails. Grace Arnold was overdue in making contact by day fourteen, but for all they knew, something could have happened to her before she even got out of Lyme Regis. If this is her – and we agree it probably is – then we know she made it to the end of the first trail. Neither the Devon and Cornwall police nor the NCA could have been aware of that.'

Chase made the call. The officer he needed to speak with wasn't at his desk, but he called back less than twenty minutes later. Investigating Officer Gordon Fellowes was unsurprised to learn of the discovery of a frozen body.

'The kid had a warm, loving, and supportive family as far as we could tell. She was taking a gap year after completing a degree at university. No financial worries, no problems at home or with a boyfriend. She was evidently an active young woman and was an experienced hiker and camper.'

'So, not a runaway,' Chase remarked.

'Didn't feel like it. We advised the locals how to proceed, especially in terms of the search.'

'I was saying to my DC a short while ago that for all anybody knew, she could have come to harm within minutes of starting out.'

'Of course. We had to consider that. We began there with calls for information from the public, explored CCTV, but the trail itself takes the hiker away from larger towns. It's a strange route, and really doesn't touch anywhere significant until it reaches Warminster. We looked hard there as well. Then both Devizes and Marlborough. After that we started looking at the second trail but got no joy.'

'How about social media photos and GPS taken off her mobile?' Chase asked, curious as to why Fellowes hadn't mentioned it.

'No good, I'm afraid. She wanted to see what it was like being off the grid. Against all advice, the girl left it at home. Told her parents she wouldn't, but when they called her, they heard it ringing in her bedroom. Found it sitting on top of her charging unit.'

That explained its absence from the property SOCO had found in the copse up on that hill. Still, Chase was intrigued by what he had learned. 'What did you make of this going off the grid business?' he asked. 'Anything there concern you?'

'At first, yes. But then her mother explained Grace's fascination with the Chris McCandless story. You know the kid I mean? The one they made a film about after he was found dead out in the wilds of Alaska having gone off the grid himself?'

It rang a faint bell, but Chase decided to fill in the blanks at a later time. 'Okay, Gordon, thanks. Given we know she reached Cherhill Down, it's likely she also made it to Marlborough a day or two earlier.'

'I'd say so. You're wondering what investigators did to try to locate her, right?'

'I am.'

'Okay, so at that point we reached out to your own area force. One of my colleagues was involved in that, and I recall his report suggested pretty much every communication was via email. We advised the usual calls for public information, and our understanding was that local officers hit pubs, restaurants, and coffee bars asking questions and showing Grace's photo. As far as I can tell, they got nothing from it.'

Chase grimaced. With so many people being reported missing, trying to trace them consumed a lot of police time. With this particular person, the fact that she could have disappeared at any point over the previous fortnight along a 140-mile trail, suggested officers would have considered it routine. The one thing that took him by surprise is that he had not been aware of it, prompting him to say as much to his NCA colleague.

'I spend most of my time working out of a station just a few miles from Marlborough. I pride myself on my local knowledge, but this seems to have passed me by.'

'Is that really unusual?' Fellowes asked. 'A misper enquiry by the book. Short and sweet. Your area HQ in Devizes will have handled it. I think you'd have to have been right there in the mix of things at the time to know about it.'

Chase conceded the point. Devizes often forgot all about his tiny village station when sharing information. Equally, he was lax in perusing the internal bulletin boards. In retrospect, it was easy to see why something like this could have eluded him.

'What was your assessment?' he asked.

'Just another sad misper we'd probably never hear about again until her body turned up, I'm afraid. As I said before, I didn't see Grace as a runaway. The odds were good that she'd come to harm at some point during her hike, though at the time I thought it could just as easily have been by accident. Seems I was wrong.'

'I can call with the result of the ID if you like,' Chase offered.

'That'd be good. Thanks. You going to want our assistance on this, Sergeant?'

'I don't think so, but I won't rule it out completely. We have our body, most likely a murder victim. If her DNA tells us it's Grace Arnold, and the PM indicates murder and possibly rape, then she's no longer missing and we'll have major crimes to focus on instead. Should it not be Grace, then we may ask for your help in identifying who she is.'

Chase closed the call with a heavy sigh, resting the phone against his forehead.

'You okay, my love?' Laney asked, her brow crinkling.

'You're enquiring after my health?'

'I'm not a bloody monster, cupcake. I may lack class, I may be bordering on the feral, but I do do compassion… when it's called for.'

He nodded and raised a placatory hand. 'I'm all right, thanks. Just thinking about poor Grace Arnold. More specifically, her last moments alive. There she was, great things ahead of her. Then some predator comes along and out of lust, or rage, or simply because he could, he blows out her candle.'

'Then let's hope we get to meet him. And if there's any justice in the world, it'll be looking down into his own cold grave rather than an interview room.'

Chase eyed his partner for a moment, his gaze first narrowing and then widening. 'You wouldn't rather see him nicked?'

'No.' DC Laney's face clouded over as she grew serious. 'If we grab him up, we might charge him, a court might find him guilty, his sentence might be what we'd all like to see, but none of it is guaranteed. On the other hand, dead is dead, and whoever did that to our victim doesn't deserve to live.'

'Food for thought,' Chase said with a nod.

Laney grunted. 'I can only hope it's more filling than the lunch you promised but failed to provide.'

He smacked his head and apologised. 'Sorry, Claire. I got distracted.'

'No worries. Work of this kind is never a bad thing to be sidetracked by.'

SIX

Later that evening, distracted by the case stirring pots inside his head, Chase reflected on Claire Laney's point of view. The first investigation he had worked with her the previous autumn was the most sickening, heart-wrenching, operation of his entire career. When it came to how he calculated the scales of indecency, rape was right up there close to the top. Murder was not. He understood how taking another life was one of the worst things a person could do, and yet the impulse was intrinsically human. A moment of untamed rage, jealousy even, murder often the result of a temporary loss of mind. Never to be repeated. Those who killed for pleasure or gain were in a different league.

During that op with Laney, he'd questioned his own moral fibre, his sense of right and wrong. He'd witnessed a cold, sober, intentional murder and had done nothing about it afterwards. The victim had been inhuman, vile, an odious man who, had he lived, was entirely capable of carrying out further atrocities in the future. Chase had not pulled the trigger, and he could not have prevented it from happening. But the thing that bothered him most in the days and weeks to come was that he also wasn't sure he'd wanted to.

His commute from Gablecross that evening had been a much shorter and more pleasant one than he was used to. He considered himself fortunate enough to be able to turn a switch inside his head when he went home. He was no longer Sergeant Chase, the detective. He was Royston Chase, the husband and father. His eight-year-old daughter greeted him in her usual excited way, charging at him and leaping into arms she took for granted would catch her as he scooped her up and held her aloft. Erin, his more languid wife, was also there to welcome him with a kiss, a hug, and a cold beer.

Before dinner, he played *Catch the Crook* with Maisie, a board game that was both a treasure hunt and a mystery. When he carried his daughter up to bed afterwards, he read her the *Gruffalo* for about the hundredth time. There was no getting away with skipping pages, not with that book. Chase couldn't imagine how reading to your child could ever be regarded as a chore. For him, it was one of life's great pleasures, and while he encouraged her to try other stories, the tale of a clever mouse who invented a monster to protect himself against all enemies, real or imagined, was her absolute go-to bedtime favourite.

'You'll have something new for her any day now,' Erin told him when he mentioned having dreams about a giant Gruffalo eating up all the remaining hours of his life.

He cocked his head. 'It's almost ready to go on sale, is it? That's great news.' His wife's business produced personalised books for children, and she'd been unusually stressed lately over the company's latest release.

She puffed out her cheeks and feigned wiping sweat from her brow. 'It's one thing having your author miss a deadline, but when your artist does so as well…' Erin shuddered, but then smiled. 'Just life getting in the way. The main thing is, we'll have a new creation out there by the end of the month.'

'I'm so pleased to hear it, sweetheart. I'm excited to know what adventure our daughter will be going on next.' He rubbed his hands together.

'It's called *Maisie Goes to the Moon*. Believe me, the two of you are going to have so much fun with this one.'

His wife's enthusiasm for the project was so infectious, Chase quickly forgot all about his own problems. He sat back and relaxed as they discussed a weekend break to visit his parents, in addition to making plans for a holiday over the summer. Later still, with a second beer in one hand and the other dipping in and out of a tub of cashew nuts, he and Erin watched repeats of *Mandalorian* on the Disney+ channel. That was the point at which his mind wandered, and his wife didn't take long to notice.

'Quite a day, huh?' she said, muting the television. 'Were you out long in that snowstorm?'

Raising a feeble grin, Chase arched his eyebrows and said, 'Long enough. In any other season, up there on that hill with those views, I suppose it might not be the worst place to lose your life. But in deep winter, in these conditions…?'

Many of his colleagues envied Chase's ability to switch off from the job when he arrived home. What he didn't tell them was how it all came flooding back the longer the night wore on. Erin leaned across the large sofa to wrap both arms around one of his, nuzzling into his shoulder. 'Do you know the cause of death?'

He shook his head and told her about the frozen body discovered beneath the gnarled and snow-garlanded branches of the thicket. 'Scott referred to her as a corpsicle,' he said with a second shake of the head. 'I appreciate the need for gallows humour at times, but that seemed a little on point. If it's who we think it is, she was just twenty-two. That's only fourteen years older than Maisie is. Can you imagine it?'

Erin shuddered. 'I don't want to, thank you all the same. I know you occasionally can't help but think of Maisie when you have a young female victim, Royston, but I never want to hold that image inside my head.'

Chase understood his wife's reticence, but he had his reasons. 'Sometimes it helps focus my mind. It gets my juices stirring. Makes me want to nail the bastard responsible all the more.'

'I know,' she said, squeezing his arm. 'It's part of your process. I hate it, and I wish it didn't have to be that way, but if it gives you an edge, then so be it.'

He took a long pull on his bottle of beer. 'I think I just want to see it from all sides. Not just the victim's, not just the killer's, but through the eyes of those left behind to grieve. It's as much for them as anyone.'

'So, are you going to base yourselves at Gablecross?'

'No. Tomorrow we're back at Little Soley. If things don't change, Claire and I are driving down to Devon.'

'You're going to speak with your victim's parents?'

'Yes. Actually, we'll be delivering the bad news. Not that there's much to tell, only that we believe we've found their daughter.'

'Is Alison not going with you?'

'No. I arranged for her to shadow the team's exhibits officer. Goes by the name of Efe Salisu.'

Erin pulled back to look up at him. 'How exotic.'

'That's what I thought. All I know about her is she's Nigerian born, but moved here with her parents when she was a toddler. Tall woman, shading six feet I'd say. Seems nice enough. Actually, they all do. And this Nicole Knight might be the real deal as DCI, too.'

He spoke about the delay in making a positive identification, and how Waddington had been keen to open up an investigation at an early stage. He also mentioned the National Crime Agency's involvement. Like him, his wife was surprised he'd not heard of the appeal for information when the Devizes police visited Marlborough.

'Mind you, we were away for a week,' she reminded him. 'When would the appeal have happened?'

'Third week of…' He pushed back his head and groaned. 'Of course. We were in Dubai with your mum and dad.'

'There you go, then. Asked and answered.'

Chase pecked Erin on the forehead. 'Completely slipped my mind. Mystery explained. If every other question is as easy to answer over the next few days, I'll be one happy chappy.'

'I can make you a happy chappy later if you like.'

He glanced down to see her feline eyes glimmering suggestively back at him.

'I love it when you channel your Michael Corleone,' he said. When Erin reared back and frowned silently at him, he laughed and cupped her chin with his hand. 'From *The Godfather*. He also liked to make offers people couldn't refuse.'

SEVEN

Overlooking Lyme Bay on the Jurassic Coast, the seaside town of Seaton had become a major focal point of the East Devon Area of Outstanding Natural Beauty. Its long, curving grey pebble and coarse sand beach stretched for more than a mile. Chase had bored his partner senseless with these details and more during their road trip, having read up on it prior to leaving Little Soley. A little over two hours after setting off, they found the tidy detached bungalow owned by Mr and Mrs Arnold a short walk from the tramway. In the far distance, beyond the curve of the road, snow-capped peaks rose hundreds of feet where the town gave way to countryside. It had avoided the worst of the bad weather, but hadn't missed out entirely.

Chase blew out a deep sigh. Laney followed suit. Theirs was an unpleasant task, one which no amount of experience prepared them for. He turned to look at his colleague. 'Does it need saying that I should do most of the talking?' he asked.

'Does it need saying that I find that offensive?' she replied.

He couldn't read her. Four months working together, and he had yet to figure her out. Laney had a fiery tongue, but also a wicked sense of humour. She seemed to take great pride in keeping him off balance. He decided to call her bluff.

'Yes. Not that I'm bothered either way. Fact is, with your attitude and your gob, these people could end up traumatised if I let you loose on them. It'd be like letting Jaws run amok in a swimming pool.'

Her hard stare wavered, giving way to a wide grin. 'Fifteen-love to you, Royston, my dear. Seriously, though, I'll follow your lead. If you want me to keep the mother out of the way making a cuppa in the kitchen, just give me the nod.'

They exited the car and trudged through the slush before making their way up a path cleared of all melting snow to the front door. Chase pressed the bell. They'd come a long way, so the larger part of him wanted the Arnolds to be at home. A smaller part prayed to some unknown deity that the couple would be anywhere other than here.

Seconds later, a man who looked to be closing in on a half century pulled the door open. He would have stood tall and wide had it not been for the burden he carried. Clearly encumbered by his daughter's continued absence, Jack Arnold stood bowed and shrunken by heartache. Whatever light that still flickered in his eyes was snuffed out the moment Chase introduced himself and his colleague.

'You've come about Grace,' he said, following a sharp intake of breath. His voice cracked on the third syllable.

'Yes, sir,' Chase said with genuine regret. 'We have.'

'She's dead, isn't she?' The hand he'd kept on the door tightened its grip, fingertips whitening.

'May we come inside, Mr Arnold? This is something we really ought to discuss with both you and your wife.'

Grace's father stepped to one side, allowing the two detectives to pass through into the hallway. 'I'm not sure how much my wife, Ruth, will be involved in whatever discussion is required,' he said, closing the door behind them. 'I'm afraid she is quite heavily medicated at the moment.'

Chase nodded as he paused to allow the man to shuffle past and lead the way. The interior of the bungalow was as neat and tidy as the outside had appeared from the car. Warm, comfortable, without any lavish flourishes. Jack Arnold showed them into a spacious lounge whose French windows led into a bright conservatory. One wall hosted a collection of framed photographs highlighting the day of Grace's graduation from university. Beneath them stood a sideboard, its top littered with standing frames, each revealing a family photograph. Happy, smiling faces taken on better days during better times.

'Where is your wife at the moment, sir?' Chase said, remaining on his feet.

For a moment, the man looked faintly embarrassed. 'In the kitchen. I'll try to persuade her to join us. I apologise in advance if she refuses. She's not… not quite herself these days.'

'That's understandable.' Chase's choice of words was deliberate. Early on in his career, he'd made the mistake of telling people he understood their grief and their loss, leaving him fully exposed to retorts suggesting he couldn't possibly understand if he'd never been in their precise situation.

When he and Laney were alone, he turned to her. 'You might have to join Mrs Arnold out in the kitchen after all.'

She gave a tight nod as she unbuttoned her coat. He was happy that her attire today was more befitting of the grim occasion than her usual abomination of a leather jacket. 'Let's see what he says first, Royston. If she won't join us, there has to be a good reason. This may be something she will accept more if it comes from him rather than a stranger.'

'So, you do have a beating heart beneath that armour.'

'Up yours, cupcake. You do your job and leave me to do mine.'

Moments later, Mr Arnold came back into the room, accompanied by his wife. The hollows of her cheeks and bruises of neglect and sleep deprivation around her eyes told their own story. The sallow complexion and unkempt short mousy hair with a heavy central line of darkened roots only emphasised this poor woman's state of mind.

'Please,' her husband said, his hands trembling, 'say what you came to say. I wish I could tell you this isn't something we've been expecting.'

Chase nodded and did as he was asked. 'Mr and Mrs Arnold, we're here to inform you that the body of a young female was discovered yesterday in a Wiltshire copse. I must emphasise at this point that we have not yet been able to identify the remains. We hope to do so within the next forty-eight hours. However, having studied relevant missing persons data and analysing the scene for ourselves, I do have to tell you that we strongly suspect the body to be that of your daughter, Grace.'

He paused, taking in their facial expressions. Jack Arnold's features remained solemn and dejected, while his wife seemed so unmoved by the news that she might well have not fully understood the words.

'I realise this will be devastating for you both,' Chase went on. 'And again, I need you to understand that the lack of a formal identification means we are not here to make an official pronouncement. But given the information at hand, and the potential for media intrusion, it is something we felt we needed to pursue. Would you both feel better sitting down? My colleague here will be happy to make drinks for us all. Also, is there anybody we can call for you?'

'I'll make the relevant calls myself, thank you. But I think we could both do with taking a seat.'

Watching Arnold steer his wife across to an armchair by the window caused Chase to swallow thickly. The couple moved and reacted like they were in their sixties, decades abandoned to the misery of loss without closure. With Ruth lowered into her chair, her husband turned to shake his head at Chase. 'We're all right for drinks, thank you. Help yourselves to one if you like; clearly, you've come a long way.'

Chase gave Laney the nod. 'Add two sweet teas,' he said more softly. 'Just in case.'

While they waited for their drinks, he walked the couple through the first stage. 'Our information is that Grace set out on the first of

January to walk both the Wessex Ridgeway Trail and the Ridgeway National Trail, with just a short break in between. Is that correct?'

Jack Arnold nodded. 'Yes, it is. Grace has a will all of her own, officer. Strong of mind, body, and spirit. We cautioned her against hiking on her own at this time of year, especially as weather predictions were not in her favour. Grace believed she'd complete the first stage before the snows blew in, that she'd rest up during the worst of it, but wasn't bothered if it came earlier or later. She considers weather and terrain to be part of the overall experience.'

Chase noted how the man spoke about his daughter in the present tense. 'I have to say, one of the reasons we think we've found Grace is the presence of hiking trail maps and sheets of route notes. Of the missing persons matching the relevant miscellaneous details, only your daughter came close.'

'And when will you know for certain? You'll need me to formally identify Grace, won't you?'

'Let me tackle that by informing you that we have issued a report to the coroner, so if the victim is your daughter, Grace is in their capable hands. We would hope to have a forensic identification within the next forty-eight hours. When you reported Grace missing, you provided materials giving the police her DNA. We'll test against that sample, and if we have a match, then we will obviously confirm.'

'I assume you've already taken a sample from the body?'

Chase just about stopped himself from squirming. This was the one question he didn't want either parent to ask. Now that it had been, he was presented with a dilemma. He didn't want to lodge the image of their daughter's frozen body in their heads. His mind sought the right response, and this time he thought it best to deflect.

'Both the pathologist and our forensic team will be handling that side of things. They'll notify us as soon as they have the results back in. There will have to be a post-mortem carried out to ascertain the precise cause of death. If the COD remains unknown or is judged to be from unnatural or violent causes, then a coroner's inquest will also be required, which is why they've already been informed.

I'm sorry to sound so formal, but it's my duty to inform you of our procedures. Obviously, the first thing we need to do is confirm ID.'

'Whatever you think best,' Jack Arnold said. He seemed to grasp the importance of Chase's words. His wife continued to sit in numbed silence, but even so, her eyes clouded over.

Chase took a set of photos from his inside jacket pocket. He handed them over to the couple. 'Would you take a look at these for me, please? They show the tent and backpack we found close to the body. Please tell me if you recognise them.'

They tried their best, but eventually the father handed the photographs back and with a shake of the head he said, 'I'm sorry, Sergeant Chase. I've never laid eyes on the tent our Grace uses. As for the backpack… I can only tell you that it looks familiar, but I can't say for sure that it's hers.'

'I want to see her,' Ruth Arnold said abruptly, her voice raised as if convincing herself first and foremost. 'I want to see my Gracey.'

DS Laney was the first to respond as she entered the room with drinks in hand. 'Of course you do, my love. Any mother would. And you will. However, at the moment, our pathology team is taking care of her and we need to let them get on with their work.'

'But you said you needed to identify her. We can do that, surely? Who better than her own parents?'

Laney handed a mug to Chase before sipping from her own. 'I won't argue with you there, Mrs Arnold. But the circumstances of the death are currently unexplained, and unfortunately that automatically sets in motion a set of protocols and procedures. Please believe me, the moment we can allow you to see Grace, we will.'

Having briefly exploded into life, the woman turned her head away and shrank so far back into the armchair that she might well have become part of the upholstery. She was both with them and absent once more.

'I appreciate everything you've told us so far,' her husband said softly, his fingers flexing around the mug of tea he was holding. 'But

I think my wife has a point. If this is Grace, then we ought to be the ones identifying our own child.'

Chase sucked in a breath. Here they were, then, despite his best efforts to conceal the awful truth. There was no avoiding putting ugly thoughts inside their heads. It simply could not be avoided. He regarded the couple with a slight bow of the head. 'Forgive me, Mr and Mrs Arnold, but the victim in this case was discovered after being exposed to the weather for several weeks. Visual identification is impossible at this stage. To be blunt, if we can avoid putting you through that ordeal we will.'

The following silence hung between them, cold and merciless.

'I don't envy you,' Arnold eventually said, regarding both officers affably. 'Having to deliver such awful news to complete strangers.'

'It's never a pleasant task,' Chase responded, his face suitably grim. 'But it comes with the territory. It might well have been local uniformed officers, but we felt it was on us to break the news. We also wanted to speak with you, to get an idea of the kind of girl Grace was, and also to confirm our suspicions that she is indeed our victim.'

'I understand. Tell me, did she suffer?'

The question took Chase by surprise. He gave himself time to consider his answer, determined not to allow his lack of filter to speak about the probable strangulation, the likely rape.

'I wish I could give you a straight answer,' he said instead. 'When we were at the scene yesterday morning it was during the worst blizzard I've witnessed in many a year. Our forensic team struggled through it as best they could. Whatever the outcome, sir, I urge you not to think along those lines. I realise it's only human nature – I have a daughter of my own – but nothing good can come of imagining Grace's demise.'

Arnold nodded, glanced at his wife, and then rested his gaze upon Chase once again. 'I've heard and understood everything you've said. I appreciate how difficult this must be for you both. I also accept it when you tell me you cannot officially confirm if this body you found is our Grace. But father to father, it is her, isn't it, Sergeant? I see no doubt in your eyes.'

Chase took a breath. 'I believe it is, sir. Yes. I wish I could be definite, and I could still be wrong. But you're right… I'm convinced the body we found is that of your daughter.'

Before his words could settle, Laney took a small step forward and said, 'We have a Family Liaison Officer on the way. However, earlier on DS Chase asked if there was somebody we could contact on your behalf. Somebody who might be able to come over to keep you both company after we've gone. We want to spend some time finding out more about Grace, Mr Arnold. So, I think now would be the perfect time to make that call.'

EIGHT

By mid-afternoon, Chase and Laney were back at the station in Little Soley, which huddled against the river Kennet. The old stone building could get draughty and was cold more often than not, but he loved working there. Gablecross was corporate, Devizes austere and remote, but here he felt at one with the tiny community. Whether the public dropped by to report sheep loose on the road or alien-crafted corn circles, it always felt like a duty well done and one to be shared.

A number of outside broadcasting vans sporting large satellite aerials lined up at the kerb close by. A group of TV and newspaper journalists, together with a handful of photographers and camera crews, gathered in a pack on the pavement. Chase let out a groan the moment he laid eyes on them, while alongside him, Laney stiffened. Both climbed out of the Volvo as soon as he'd set the brake, walking briskly through the throng who demanded to know if police had yet confirmed the identity of the body as that of Grace Arnold.

Chase stopped so suddenly that Laney bumped into him. 'Where did you get that name from?' he snapped back.

A couple of reporters close by reacted with derision. 'It's not exactly a secret, Sergeant Chase,' one of them said. 'Her name and photo have been all over the news since mid-morning. Grace was reported missing in January, and haven't you just got back from speaking to her parents?'

'We have nothing for you,' Chase said, eyes front but head up as he moved on. *No reports of police officers scurrying today.* 'My colleagues at Gablecross will issue a statement later on.'

'So, get your parasitic arses back over to Swindon,' Laney suggested as she brushed past. The pair clattered through the door, leaving the clamour behind.

They had used the drive back to re-examine their exchanges with Mr and Mrs Arnold. They'd left the coast with a greater understanding of the couple's daughter, together with a sense that whoever had attacked and murdered the young woman was more than likely unknown to her. Before she embarked on the hike, at least.

'I wonder how many other hikers were on that same trail in January,' Chase had wondered aloud at one point. 'Grace might have encountered many, even at that time of year.'

'Perhaps, but Cherhill Down isn't on that specific trail,' Laney reminded him.

The location of the body had taken Mr Arnold by surprise. He pointed out that neither of the two trails his daughter had chosen to walk threaded across Cherhill. He told them the downs had its own small circuit, often used by dog walkers.

'The white horse might have attracted her,' he'd muttered, almost to himself. 'But not with snow on the ground. What would be the point?'

Chase thought about that part of the conversation as he slipped in behind his desk, a mug of steaming hot chocolate in hand. Irrespective of the foul weather, the likes of Avebury, Silbury Hill, West Kennet Long Barrow, and Cherhill, might have interested their victim enough for her to venture out to visit these historical landmarks ahead of embarking on the second leg of her walk. She had to set up camp somewhere for the night, so why not atop Cherhill Down itself?

Once again, the question he asked himself was what had drawn a predator to Grace Arnold on this occasion? Had the light from her campfire drawn them in like a flapping moth? Was it the girl herself – had she been spotted? By another hiker, perhaps? Or had somebody followed her from another part of the trail? Also, Grace had to eat and drink, so where had she shopped? If she'd completed the first stage of the hike, then she'd been to Marlborough and had possibly stayed overnight there. But the town of Calne was closer to where her body had been discovered. There was also the inappropriately named Black Horse pub, just a short walk away in the foothills of the downs.

Still furious that the connection between their victim and the missing Grace Arnold had been either made or purchased by the media, Chase was eager to be doing something more pro-active.

'Fancy another trip out?' he asked, glancing across the room to where Laney sat with her boots on the desk, her own drink cupped between both hands and perched on the swell of her chest. The purple sweater she wore looked thick enough to ward off the liquid's heat.

The DC narrowed her gaze in suspicion. 'You admiring my temporary cup holder or my puppies?' she asked.

'Isn't there still room in the world to admire both?'

Laney looked down at herself, creating multiple chins. 'It must be my uplifting bra that provides the necessary support to rest a mug on. It's certainly not my saggy old funbags.'

Chase laughed, though he wasn't about to take the discussion any further. He didn't think it was possible to offend Claire Laney, but these days it wasn't beyond the realm of possibility for somebody to overhear their conversation and take offence on her behalf. 'So, trip out or not?'

'Where to this time?'

'It occurred to me that our girl might have bought herself some rations before bunking down for the night. Calne is the closest place to Cherhill. She may also have nipped into the local pub for a livener, so we could call in there on the way back if you like.'

She gave him a weary thumbs-up, despite groaning theatrically as she lowered her feet back down on the floor. 'You're a fiery ball of energy today, cupcake,' she said. 'You been hitting the Red Bull behind my back?'

Chase laughed off the suggestion. 'It's pure adrenaline. If this poor kid suffered the way we think she did, I want the bastard who did it off the streets. The sooner the better.'

'I'm with you there. So, whereabouts in Calne are we going?'

'Sainsbury's. Grace probably couldn't have arrived before the eleventh of January, which is ten days after she set out. She might have stayed close by or even in a B&B who take cash, which is why there were no charges to her debit or credit cards. She will have wanted to have a bath or a shower and a hot meal before setting off on the second leg of her hike, I'm sure. Her parents seemed to think that was likely. So, let's find out which staff were on duty between the twelfth and, say, the fifteenth, to allow for her completing the hike in a slower time due to the weather. We can widen the search afterwards if necessary. We can also have them pull security camera feeds for those dates, which I'll ask them to send over to DC… Cooper.'

Laney nodded, winding a long scarf around her neck. 'That's a good shout. When you're not being a complete dummel, Royston, you occasionally reveal yourself to be a half decent copper.'

He frowned as he pulled on his coat. 'A dummel?'

'Uh-huh. It's Wiltshire slang. You know me, I like to insult people in their native tongue.'

'I've never heard the word before.'

'Well, get used to it. You're going to hear a lot more of it before we're finished.'

Laney hooked her small backpack over one shoulder. Chase nodded at it. 'What's with that?' he asked.

'I'm not using my bag anymore,' she replied.

He frowned. 'You had a bag?'

'Of course I had a bag. You probably never noticed it because of the camouflage pattern.'

He snorted. 'If you say so. Why did you stop using it?'

'I put it down somewhere and couldn't find it again.'

Chase couldn't tell if she was joking or being serious, so he let it slide. Before opening the door, he peeked out of the closest window, relieved to see that the media had moved on. Good, he thought. Let them be Gablecross's problem, not ours.

What should have been a forty minute drive took closer to fifty due to heavy traffic going in and out of Marlborough, but within ten minutes of arriving at Sainsbury's, Chase knew their journey had been worthwhile. Upon arrival, they showed their warrant cards and asked to see the manager. Sally Phelps was young and smart and all business. Once he'd explained what they were after, she wasted no time asking superfluous questions, keen to help in every conceivable way. The first piece of good news was that the store retained internal security camera feeds in the cloud, so providing footage from the specified week would not present a problem. Secondly, only twelve employees worked the floor area, including cashiers, and of those dozen people, eight were currently on shift. Phelps pulled up a list of employee records on her computer and sent them to a printer in a nearby room for later collection.

'I can pull them off duty one at a time for short periods,' she suggested helpfully. 'I take it this is about the body found on the downs?'

'Word gets around quickly,' Chase observed, eyeing the woman shrewdly.

'That much police activity attracts attention. I saw it all still there when I drove in earlier today. What with that and them not allowing anybody close to the area, assumptions were made. People tell me they mentioned a name on the news, showed a picture of the poor mite.'

'I can't comment on speculation. There will be a media briefing later on today, I'm sure. We'll be asking for help from the public, but we thought we'd get a jump on it.'

'We'll do what we can to assist you in any way, Sergeant Chase. But we get all kinds passing through here, so you may not get what you came here for. I'm not sure your girl will have stood out is what I'm saying.'

Chase thought about that. As they were already there, it was tempting to interview the staff, but he and Laney would be dealing with largely unfocussed minds. If Grace Arnold could be located on the security footage, a precise date and time would surely engage the memory.

'Do you get out on the shop floor much?' Laney asked during the lull.

'As often as I can.'

The DC leaned forward and took her phone from the inside pocket of her coat. She flicked through a few images before turning it to show the store manager a photo of the young girl presumed to be their victim. 'Ring any bells?'

After a few seconds, Phelps shook her head. 'Sorry. No. Would she have looked this good, though? I mean, she's a pretty girl, but after a long hike and probably wearing bulky clothing and a beanie or something like that…'

She wasn't wrong. It was a long shot. Her response helped persuade Chase about what to do next. 'Tell you what, let's leave staff interviews for the time being. Our colleagues will go through the security feed you're going to send across. If we can narrow it down, I'm sure it'll help your people, and we can also eliminate anybody who wasn't on duty at the time.'

'Or times,' Laney said. 'For all we know, she came in more than once.'

It was a point they discussed as they headed back to the station. Chase drove as far as the Black Horse pub, before pulling into its car park. He reversed into a space from which they could stare out of the windscreen at the hillside rising up to meet the copse. A few lilac-coloured forensic suits still flitted about alongside the day-glow yellow of police officers manning the crime scene. Fortunately for them, not only had the snow blown itself out the previous evening, but the sun was shining and the wind had backed off to a gentle breeze with occasional gusts to stir the branches.

Chase took it all in and breathed deeply. A snowy winter landscape was the most beatific of sights. When it wasn't smacking you in the face with heavy clumps of the stuff. Or when it threw a blanket over a corpse.

'Where did you meet your attacker, Grace?' he whispered to himself.

'She's not up there anymore, cupcake,' Laney said from the seat beside him. 'The pathologist has her in his lair.'

'I know. But this is where she took her last breath. Had her final thoughts. I can't help feeling that where she met her killer is going to prove crucial in catching him. If he left traces of himself behind, they're either long gone or of no use to us. But if they first interacted somewhere other than that hillside, that's how we'll find him.'

'You sound ever so sure of yourself, Royston.'

He turned to face his partner. 'That's because I am. I have to get a hook into something, Claire. At this moment, it's all I can see.'

The pub was not yet open for business, but the man who answered Chase's persistent knocking introduced himself as the landlord. 'I thought you were those bloody journalists again,' he said. 'Came in here last night and this lunchtime asking questions but not buying any sodding drinks. I told them where to go. Bloody vultures.'

He shook his head when he saw the photo of Grace Arnold. 'We get all sorts in here,' he said. 'Some come for the ale, some for the food, others for the entertainment when we have live bands. We get ramblers and hikers, too. Can't say I recognise this girl, though. That her body you found on the downs?'

Ignoring the man's understandable curiosity, Chase said, 'How many other people work in the bar or wait on the tables?'

'Depends. Me and the wife do a lot of it ourselves, but if we're busy we can have between two and four staff on of an evening.'

'I don't suppose you have security cameras, do you?' Laney asked him.

'No. No call for it around here.'

'Is your wife available to talk to?'

'She's with chef in the kitchen, but I can fetch her.'

'And the staff you mentioned?'

'Just two on tonight, but they won't be in much before six.'

The two detectives spent ten minutes with both owners before Chase was convinced Grace hadn't entered the pub. Even so, he sent the photo to the landlord's phone and asked him to show it to his staff just in case. Both refused the offer of an early drink before they left. On their way back to the car, Chase paused to look back up the hill once more. The snow was thawing fast. Soon the white chalk horse would be visible again. Cherhill had history, but from this point on it would forever be tainted.

'Were you aware this pub was once a watering hole for an infamous bunch of highwaymen?' he said to Laney.

'No. Should I be?'

'I thought you might. They robbed coaches coming through on the London to Bath road. But the reason they stood out – if you'll pardon the pun – is because they carried out their attacks while they were completely naked.'

Laney gave a great bellowing laugh, coughing as she reeled it back in. 'You're kidding me, right?'

He shook his head. 'Not at all. They claimed it scared the passengers into handing over everything they had. Also, that it made them more difficult to recognise because people wouldn't focus on their faces.'

'That would be some line-up of suspects, eh? Never mind your faces, lads, drop trou and tighty-whities and let's take a look at your cock and balls.'

'Sounds like a great remake of the *Usual Suspects*.'

'Yeah. Spacey would enjoy that one, I reckon. Except if it's in the winter.'

This time it was Chase who laughed. It went on a little too long, but he needed it. Peering up at the crime scene had filled the pit of his stomach with dread. Not so much because of what had taken place there, more the churning fear of not solving the case or being able to obtain justice for Grace Arnold.

NINE

Gary Elder could not shake the feeling that he was being followed. Oldbrook wasn't one of the more pleasant parts of Milton Keynes to live in, and like most similar districts anti-social behaviour was on the rise. But having been born and raised in and around the area, it did not intimidate Elder in the least. He would never describe himself as immune from danger, nor part of the darker deeds planned behind closed doors and inflicted upon the community. But these were his streets, and he could sense the mood of its inhabitants. Today his radar was pinging as he bustled along the street, and although the pavements and alleyways were well-populated, he was unable to identify any specific reason for his unease.

He had never been sure at which point twilight became dusk, but he was quietly confident that the day was rapidly approaching that moment. The last natural light faded into the west as numerous rolling clouds chased the weakening sun over the horizon. A sudden and unwelcome urge to race home threatened to overwhelm him. Soon the rats would be out there in the dark; rodents and human dross both. His usual route home had him cut through the narrow alleyway between South Eighth and South Ninth streets, but so intense was his sense of apprehension that he stuck to South Row until he reached his turning.

There, his gait became more casual. The road was less busy, but he put on a front in case he encountered friends or neighbours. No way he wanted them to witness the anxiety threatening to overwhelm him. Nonetheless, he remained wary of the brick and concrete corridors that criss-crossed the grid pattern of streets and dwellings. He walked on the side of the road that provided him with the best perspective of each junction as he approached them. A couple of alarms as he spotted groups of young men gathered together, hoodies pulled up to obscure faces. Relaxing when he recognised the crew as local dealers peddling their cheap rocks and pre-rolled joints. He felt them checking him out as he kept his head down. Despite himself, he felt his legs pumping faster, hoping not to hear footfalls heading his way from behind.

With a heavy sigh of relief, he reached his own home, turning the key in the lock and entering quickly, slamming the door closed and slipping the deadbolt across.

'Sammy? Sam, you here?' he called out.

No answer. The girl he lived with, first as a roommate and later an occasional fuck-buddy, seldom left the house when she didn't have to. She made an absurd living through her YouTube channel, and while he didn't know precisely what she did to earn money, she was never late with the rent on her room, so he paid little attention to it. She had a cracking body, and he enjoyed it when they got together. He doubted he could raise a hard-on at that precise moment, but if she was in the mood for a cuddle and a bit of heavy petting, that might make him feel a whole lot better.

In truth, the impression of being followed had dissipated during the day. But it had returned during his walk home, unsettling him to the point where he had become paranoid about it. He had no idea why anyone might be interested in him or what he did, but that prickly sensation at the back of his neck refused to go away. Dread had shadowed him from the time he left home that morning, and he was more than usually glad to have arrived back home safe and sound.

He switched the kettle on to make a cup of tea. He wondered if Sammy was filming, perhaps live streaming, which was why she hadn't answered him. He took out two mugs and made her a hot drink as well; one of her Mocha mixes, to which he added a little hazelnut syrup. If that didn't earn him at least a tug job later, then nothing would.

Elder had polished off half his own drink before he thought about Sammy again. He called out her name once more. Still no reply. Sighed as he heaved himself off the stool at the kitchen breakfast bar. He knocked on her door before pushing down the handle and entering the room.

His girlfriend's hands were in her lap, wrists bound together with a thin strip of cloth. There was something silky stuffed into her mouth. Her head jerked up in alarm as he stood looking down at her supine figure on the bed. His first thought was that a paying customer had asked her to do something kinky, yet she was fully clothed and not dressed up as she usually would be when displaying herself on web cam. His second thought was to wonder why her wild-eyed gaze went beyond him… behind the door he still held open.

The figure, wearing a dark balaclava over his face, stepped out in front of him. If the head covering took him by surprise, the weapon the man held almost made Elder soil himself. The rectangular-bladed hatchet looked shiny and new, its thin blade stalling his breath.

'Gary Elder?' the figure asked in a deep growl. Other than the ski mask, the man wore a midnight blue roll-neck sweater, black jeans, and black work boots.

'Y… es?'

The man turned his head and pointed at the girl lying on the bed. 'You stay there,' he told her. 'You move before I tell you it's okay to move and I'll chop you both into tiny pieces. Slowly and painfully. You understand me?'

Sammy nodded furiously, her forehead beaded with sweat, cheeks wet with tears.

The man looked back at Elder. 'You and me are going to have a chat,' he said.

'Whatever you say. Please, just don't hurt her, okay?'

'I won't need to provided you come with me and do as I ask.'

'Are you… are you going to hurt me?' Elder asked the man. He felt weak asking, sickened by his cowardice. But fear was a great leveller. He had no idea who this man was, nor what he wanted of him, but it could not be anything good.

Pausing, perhaps for effect or to intimidate further, the man eventually sighed elaborately and said, 'That largely depends on the answers you give to the questions I have to ask you.' His featureless head bobbed up and down. 'But to be honest with you, Gary, I don't fancy your chances.'

TEN

DS CHASE AND DC Laney were both at Gablecross police station the following morning when news came in from the pathologist, Ray Petchey. With the victim's body thawing gradually under controlled conditions, he'd managed to secure a DNA sample and had already sent it off for testing and analysis. His request for an urgent turnover had been answered with a promise for results by the end of business. But there was something more significant he had to share with them, having asked to be put on speakerphone.

'This is going to go down as one of those atypical cases,' he began uncertainly. 'In lieu of the postmortem that I'm still unable to perform, I examined the remains as closely as possible. I had strangulation down as the most likely cause of death. However, overnight, a large clump of frozen snow slipped away from her head, revealing a part of the poor thing's cranium that hadn't been accessible beforehand. I immediately noticed her hair was matted with something dark and thick that looked a lot like dried blood. When I parted the clumps, I spotted two significant lacerations made to the scalp just behind the ear with what I believe to be a bladed instrument.'

'So you're thinking sharp force trauma as the COD,' DI Fox said, wrinkling his nose in distaste.

'It's the leading contender, yes. I'd venture she sustained both injuries in a single frenzied attack.'

DS Cooper, the case officer, was the first to react by raising a hand. 'I'll give Nat a bell to warn her,' he said. DC Natalie Mann was the team's designated Family Liaison Officer, who the previous afternoon had travelled down to the coast to be with the Arnolds. 'If our victim is Grace and we have proof of that before we all go home, then we need to inform her parents ASAP. We can bring in a local by the end of the week, but it's good that she'll be with them to begin with.'

'They called Mrs Arnold's sister as well as their son while we were still there,' Laney said. 'Both were due to visit last night and may still be in the home today.'

Fox thanked the pathologist, killed the connection, then faced the two detectives from Little Soley. 'Cheers. If we get DNA confirmation this evening, will you want to deliver the death notice yourselves?'

Before Laney could react, Chase leaned forward in his seat and nodded. 'Definitely. I will, at least.' He turned to his partner. 'With DC Mann there as FLO, you needn't tag along if you don't want to, Claire.'

'If you're going, cupcake, I'm going,' came Laney's firm response.

'Your report suggests both parents have come to terms with their daughter's loss, is that right?' DI Fox said, reading from a notebook.

Chase had written up the document late last night. He recalled every word, and was adamant. 'Mr Arnold is fairly stoical, his wife bereft but not fooling herself. He's somewhat detached, while she has not coped at all well. I wouldn't say either has come to terms with it, but they have both accepted Grace is gone. For them, I'd say the past few weeks has been all about waiting for the doorbell to ring.'

'I have to agree,' Laney chipped in. 'But I'll add this: neither are going to react well to having their worst fears confirmed. Mr Arnold is nowhere near as strong as he'd like to be, while his wife will fall to pieces, I'm sure.'

'What if we don't get a COD today?' DC Bowen asked. As the intel and disclosure officer, she was responsible for gathering and disseminating intelligence as well as controlling and preparing evidence for the resulting case. The cause of death was a vital component in any investigation, even down to how and when it was first revealed to those outside the investigating team.

'We should still inform,' Chase said, no doubt in his mind.

'I understand why that would be your preference, Royston,' Fox said. 'But have you considered how they might cope with a double blow extended over time? Say they are told this evening that their daughter is our victim, but then have to wait perhaps another day to learn she was raped and strangled as well as having her head smashed in with a sharp object. That's more awful news piling in on top while they're still reeling from having received the death notice. Might it not be better to delay until you can provide all the information in a single conversation?'

Chase understood the dilemma. There was no doubt that discovering Grace had been raped prior to being murdered – if indeed that was what happened – would be a bitter blow. But his sense of both parents was that learning of their daughter's death was something that would simply confirm what they already knew, and that this, as opposed to how she met her untimely end, would be the most devastating aspect.

'It's a fifty-fifty call,' he conceded. 'No way is the right way. What I'm thinking at this moment is if we get ID confirmation today, then we inform them. If we also have COD then fine, but if not, we go ahead anyway. But I might well change my mind and do as you suggest. My call, I think, unless DCI Knight overrules me. Where is she, by the way?'

'In with the Super,' Armstrong said.

'And Alison?'

'Glued to DC Salisu. Actually, they are both down in exhibits categorising and logging evidence.'

Chase nodded. 'Is that working out? I spoke to our TDC last night and she said it was, but hinted her partner for the day was a little tight-lipped.'

The Gablecross team laughed as one, which alleviated the air of despondency in the room. 'That's our Efe. Takes a while to warm up, but even then, she seldom says something just to fill a silence.'

'The more I hear about her the more I like.'

'You were right about CCTV, Royston,' Reuben Cooper said. 'Bugger all help from the crime scene. We're obviously going to consider bus and taxi dashcam footage, but that's going to take some time to amass, let alone go through. But great work with Sainsbury's in Calne. That was a good thought. I haven't looked at it yet, but I got several large files in my mailbox overnight, so I'll be on it as soon as we're done here.'

'I did have one idea,' DI Fox offered. 'We could look up hiking and walking groups, ask if anybody was out on the downs mid-January. They might have seen Grace camped up there, or even met her during their walk.'

'Absolutely,' Cooper said. 'I'll search for local groups and get in contact. I did check out Grace's social media. She's on Facebook and Instagram, but the last posts on both were on New Year's eve. She mentioned how excited she was to be going on the trails and how she was looking forward to being off the grid for a few weeks.'

'Which is why she left her mobile behind.' Fox shook his head. 'I understand the urge, but you'd think she would have taken it with her if only for emergencies.'

'Too tempting, Foxy,' Paige Bowen said. 'You'd tell yourself it's there only for when you have problems, but then the temptation is to keep a record of milestones and take snapshots. I've heard ridding yourself of all communications is part and parcel of the thrill.'

'There's another angle for us to consider when it comes to social media,' Laney said, shifting in her chair. 'Anybody who saw Grace's feed would have known her plans, her approximate route, and that she was out of contact with the rest of the world. Somebody out there might have regarded that as an invitation. We ought to take a hard look at her online friends.'

'Her page isn't private,' Cooper told them. 'It's open to all public scrutiny. Literally anyone could have seen it and taken note.'

Fox slapped both hands against his legs. 'I despair at the way some kids leave themselves wide open.'

'I hope you're not implying it was her fault,' Bowen said quickly.

'Of course not.' His face became a scowl. 'You should know me better than that, Paige. I'm simply saying there has to be more common sense used. By everybody, not just women. I'm all for a free society, but the fact is there are bad people out there who wish us harm and we should all do our best to avoid them. We lock our doors at night for good reason.'

Chase agreed with Fox. Some people became agitated by the mere suggestion that vulnerable people could help themselves be less susceptible, but it wasn't a question of blaming the victim. Rather, a conscious effort to navigate a society that had become more violent and angry in recent years. It wasn't sexism or misogyny, either; there was nothing he would say to a woman that he wouldn't also advise a man.

He sat for a while, considering their current status. Comms was an essential tool in modern investigations, and although security camera footage might yet tell them Grace Arnold was in Calne shopping on a specific day, the girl not taking her phone with her onto the trail ensured they had no way of tracing its daily movements. It was a setback, but by no means a decisive one. Plenty of alternative avenues were available to the investigation team; though it just might take some old-school policing.

That and a whole lot of luck.

*

Having collected Alison May from the exhibits area, Chase drove his colleagues to Little Soley. For a second time, they'd had to barge their way through the media gathering, sparing them no words at all on this occasion. The three of them now sat in his office which was barely large enough for one, the trainee detective squashed up beside Laney on the other side of his desk. Throughout the journey and in the five minutes since they had arrived back at their village station, May positively gushed about her experiences working with Detective Constable Efe Salisu. It had been hard out there on the hillside the previous day working in collaboration with the CSI techs, she admitted, but declared herself feeling all the better for the experience. After bringing her up to speed on the status of Operation Silverback, it was Laney who voiced her abiding concern.

'I'm worried that at the end of this the best we're going to have is an ID and COD but nowhere to run with either. Our girl died up there on that hill. That likely rules out anybody from her life down there on the coast. The most likely scenario is that she crossed paths with her killer along the way, probably close to or even on Cherhill Down. After five or six weeks of winter temperatures, with frost and damp, snow and wind and rain, we all know we're not getting great forensics from the scene. With no surveillance and no mobile data, either, you have to ask yourself what else is there for us to grasp at.'

Chase wanted to disagree but found himself unable to. He liked to take a positive approach, but nothing Laney had said was incorrect. Instead of debating the subject, he turned to May. 'This is how it goes sometimes, Alison. By and large, we tend to gather a huge amount of evidence in the first forty-eight hours. But as you've already seen, these are unusual circumstances. Not only are we delayed in obtaining a legit ID and cause of death, but we have no tech and very little science to work with. It's a challenge, and the reward for solving this one will be all the greater for it.'

'He's being polite, my love,' Laney growled, her smoker's voice deep and chesty. 'Most of the time it's a shit show, but we wade through it in our wellies hoping for a break.'

'Working hard to create that break,' Chase argued.

'Fair enough. I'll accept that if you accept it's a shit show.'

He kept his eyes on May and shrugged. 'Claire may be right. But we still do it. And for all the right reasons.'

THE PREDATORS

'I'm not expecting rainbows and unicorns,' May said, her gaze flitting between them. 'I'm a realist. And four months of working alongside you two has left me with no illusions. Efe was telling me how difficult this case is going to be considering the state of the body, so I'm ready. I don't need the sugar coating and I don't need the crap. I'm as prepared for failure as I am for success.'

Laney widened her eyes. 'Bloody hell! One day without being tied to my apron strings and our little girl has blossomed into a woman.'

'You'll do, Alison,' Chase said with a nod of respect. 'You'll do just nicely.'

Smiling, May took a breath. 'Efe and I logged nothing else of consequence – nothing you hadn't already seen laid out on the table. CSI was keen to remove exhibits from that specific scene, and made it clear they'd be opening the packaging again to check for blood, fibres, prints, etcetera. We were entering the details into the system when you came to fetch me.'

'It's a vital piece of the overall investigation,' Chase reminded her. 'Especially when it comes to the CPS and an eventual trial. Good experience for you, too. Now, let's get back to our own part in this op. DC Cooper has a lot on his plate with several days' worth of surveillance footage to wade through, so I'm thinking we ought to take some of that off his hands. Agreed?'

He was encouraged to see both Laney and May nod.

'Excellent. I'll have him send across days three and four. They have enough people to cover the rest. It'll give us something to do, because there's bugger all else we can be getting our gnashers into until we get that ID and COD confirmed.'

'And what then?' May asked. She hooked one leg over the other, settling to the task at hand.

'We go back to the beginning. Only this time, we'll know who and what we're dealing with.'

'Okay. But how does that help? I'm not being negative, Royston, but how will having those details help us find whoever did this to her?'

'They probably won't.' Chase stared hard at her. 'But you'll be surprised at how galvanised you can become once you know for certain who your victim is and how they died. How they were murdered, in this case. It focusses the mind more than it already was, makes you work that much harder, and as I said before, you somehow find the break you need.'

'And what happens if you don't?'

'You eventually move on to the next case.'

'What, and just forget all about this one? Forget all about Grace Arnold, if that's who our victim is?'

Chase heard the dismay in his colleague's voice. It carried a certain cadence he'd heard many times before. He softened his tone when she spoke next. 'No, Alison. We never forget what happened, and we never forget who it happened to. But when you've exhausted all your ideas and run down every lead and you still have nothing to show for it, you have to move on. But believe me, if you're the right kind of copper – and you are – you'll carry failure around with you no matter what else follows this one. When you least expect it, the stench of it will pucker your nostrils. You'll taste it like a coating on your tongue, and the memory of it will eat its way into your brain like a worm. Prepare yourself for that eventuality, because it will happen to you one day. That's why we're going to make sure it's not one day soon.'

ELEVEN

Chase was on the phone to DCI Knight when Alison May first spotted Grace Arnold. Laney watched the Sainsbury's footage through with her again just to be certain, but the two of them agreed the figure was indeed their victim. He looked on eagerly as May played the video back once again. The moment he laid eyes on Grace he checked out the time and date stamp.

'Friday the thirteenth,' he said. 'That fits our timeline. Allows her to have reached Marlborough, spend a night in a B&B getting clean and warm and fed, before laying up somewhere waiting for the storm to pass ahead of setting off on the second leg of her journey. Immediate thoughts, Alison?'

May cleared her throat and spoke as they allowed the film to run, their victim popping up every so often casually filling a wire basket as she made her way around the store. 'First of all, there's no sign of her backpack, and she wouldn't have left it outside. So, either she took a room in Calne, or she set up camp on the downs before walking or bussing into town for provisions.'

'Good. Next?'

'Well, obviously we can narrow it down as far as store staff and security are concerned because we have the exact time. We can perhaps also identify what she bought. Oh, and she's clearly alone.'

Laney patted her on the shoulder. 'Nice one, my love. She's on her own here for sure, but was she buying for two? If we can make out a few of the items she puts in the basket, the store manager might be able to find the matching till receipt for somebody paying cash at that time on that day.'

'Fast-forward to the footage showing her at the till,' Chase said. May did so and then cocked her head at him. 'Hmm. I'm not convinced that shopping shows Grace re-stocking her supplies for the hike ahead. Seems more like her buying a few odds and sods to last the rest of the day.'

'I wouldn't expect her to buy her hiking provisions in Calne,' May said firmly. 'Following that specific trail, she'd pass through Marlborough on the way between Overton Hill and Ogbourne St George. That's where she'd do a full shop, in their Waitrose. It makes more sense, because why carry the extra weight further than necessary?'

Chase scratched his chin, his frown deepening. 'Good point. We still need to check additional footage to see if Grace returns to the Calne Sainsbury's the following day, but we also need to acquire surveillance from Waitrose in Marlborough.'

'But we don't think she made it off that hill,' Laney pointed out. 'If she never returned to Marlborough, she would never have stopped off there to restock.'

'You're probably right. But let's have it anyway. Can't have too much evidence. Even nothing will be helpful to firm up on our estimated time of death.'

'I'll get on it right away,' May said. 'You want me to speak to the manager at Sainsbury's as well, see if I can get hold of the till receipt?'

'Yes, you do that,' Chase told her. 'Claire and I need to put our heads together. Perhaps we can form a hypothesis based on this fresh information.'

'We should canvas B&Bs in and around Marlborough, that's for sure,' Laney said as May left them to begin tapping away at the computer behind the front desk.

'You want to have a crack at that? Narrow it down by distance first, then price. We can perhaps pay them a visit later on today.'

He called DCI Knight while Laney got to work. He told her about their breakthrough with the supermarket security film. 'Alison is searching through the following day's footage – that's the Saturday. We don't believe she made it back to Marlborough, but we will follow that up as a matter of routine. We're also checking out B&Bs close by to see if Grace spent the night in one on either the Wednesday or Thursday. Narrowing all this down may lead nowhere, but I still prefer the days and dates even if only in my head.'

Knight was enthusiastic. 'I know what you mean, Royston. It's a good shout. If you can find out where she stayed, then perhaps whoever runs the place can tell us who else was there at the same time. Might give us a name or two to follow up on.'

'I was thinking the same thing myself. Who knows if that's where she first attracted the attention of the person who killed her?'

'*If* she was killed.'

Chase noted the unspoken reminder to be cautious. It was one thing believing a murder had taken place, and another altogether knowing for certain. 'Of course. I'll rein myself in a bit before I go all out. Still, decent paths to follow.'

'Absolutely. And better to be pro-active. You already have a grasp of this one, so run with it. I'll let you know as soon as ID comes in. I've spoken to pathology, and they confirm COD won't now be until tomorrow because the post-mortem won't be completed today. The poor mite is still partially frozen, otherwise she'd already be under the knife. However, because Petchey requested a rush on DNA and the Cellmark lab is only in Abingdon just outside Oxford, he had the sample couriered there. And just to add, we've contacted as many hiking groups as we could find. Most only have email addresses, but we're on it. Meanwhile, have you given any more thought about how you'll deal with Grace's parents?'

Chase had, but while he remained cautious, he'd made up his mind. 'I think you were right to raise the possibility of a more circumspect approach. However, we tell relatives all the time about the death of loved ones without also knowing the COD. I realise this situation is unusual, but I don't see any reason to delay.'

'On the whole, I'd say you were probably right to go ahead, Royston. There's no making this appear to be anything other than what it is. When it gets this ugly, you just have to rip off the plaster.'

Happy to have the DCI's support, he ended the call and turned back to Laney. 'What have you got?'

'Surprisingly few B&Bs in Marlborough. Ten in the town itself. I'm thinking we drive over and split the list up between us rather than do them together.'

'Print off the names and addresses. I'll let Alison know where we're going.'

'Here's a thought,' Laney said to him, her lips twitching. 'How about we pretend we live in a technological era and I pop the details over to you in an email?'

'And if my phone dies?'

'Okay, so here's another suggestion: check your bloody battery before we go out.'

It wasn't an argument he was going to win. Instead, Chase huffed and did as he was told. Less than five minutes later they were in the car and heading west. Speaking to Bed and Breakfast proprietors, showing them Grace Arnold's photograph, and requesting guest information, was all part of the early grind. When asked about investigating serious crimes, Chase always said there were four parts to consider: the initial drudgery of evidence gathering, identifying, locating, and arresting a suspect based on that evidence, charging and taking that suspect to trial, followed by the result. Depending on the verdict, a case could be three parts bad to one part good, but at best it was usually fifty-fifty. This early stage was often matched by putting the case through the CPS and bringing it to court, each element equally painstaking in its own way.

He was grateful to find a parking space in the central strip running through the town's main road. While Laney's five premises were spread out along the High Street, his formed a rough circle concentrated at the end furthest away from the college. He struck lucky on only his second, the clean and beautifully presented Lamb Inn.

'Oh, yes, I remember her,' the owner said immediately upon seeing the photograph. Joyce Tompkins stood little more than five feet in slight heels, but she possessed a dynamic and forceful personality. Her nod was firm and brooked no debate. 'She came in… ooh, must have been mid-January. If it had been in season, I'd probably have taken little notice, but the poor thing looked exhausted and clearly in need of a rest, a long hot bath, and some good warm food in her belly. She got them all here.'

'Did she tell you she was on a hike?' Chase asked. The two sat around a small circular table in a room described by Tomkins as the 'parlour'. He'd already called Laney to let her know she could end her own visits.

'Didn't need to – you could tell just by looking at her and the gear she carried. But she did say she'd completed one part and needed to gather her strength before taking on the second. She mentioned the trails she was walking, but I don't remember what they were called.'

'That's okay, we know her route. We believe she must have stayed here on the night of Wednesday the eleventh or Thursday the twelfth. Most likely the latter. Would you mind checking your records for me? Also, if you can identify any other guests who stayed here the same night, that would be of enormous help.'

'That part's easy enough. We had two others booked in at the time, a young couple from Leicestershire down to visit Avebury and the like.'

'When you say "young", how old roughly…?'

'I should say they were in their late twenties or early thirties. Young to me, that is. I can get you their names as well if you like, you know, while I'm checking my records.'

Chase thanked her and said he'd take any and all information connected to the night in question. Mrs Tompkins disappeared for ten minutes or so before returning with a broad smile plastered across her face. Both cheeks seemed to glow with pleasure. She held out a sheet of A4 paper, saying, 'Here you go, Sergeant Chase. The young woman, calling herself Grace Arnold, stayed on the Thursday night. She arrived late afternoon or early evening. It was dark outside but not fully, if you know what I mean.'

He heard himself sigh as he took the information from her hand. As evidence to further police enquiries, it was golden, but it also added further confirmation that they had correctly identified their victim. 'I do,' he said. 'And this is extremely helpful. Tell me, did she seem nervous to you at all? Anxious about anything?'

'No. To the contrary, I thought she was astonishingly upbeat for somebody who had walked for many days, especially with the weather having turned so nasty. To be honest, that young lady didn't have a care in the world, if you ask me.'

'And she stayed here for just the one night?'

'She did. And if you're about to ask if she said where she was off to next, she told me she was getting ready to tackle the next stage of her hike by camping out again and was going to visit a few of the sites before she left.'

This made sense to Chase. Grace had recharged her batteries, got herself clean and rested, and had then acted as a tourist for the day before setting up camp on Cherhill Down. It fit the narrative and timeline he was piecing together inside his head.

'How about the young couple? When did they leave?'

'They were booked in for the whole week, their last night being the Saturday. I have their contact details if you need to speak to them.'

'Thanks. I dare say we will. Back to Grace… do you know if she went out that night at all? Perhaps to another pub?'

'Oh no, once inside, she didn't budge. She had dinner here after cleaning herself up, a couple of drinks with her meal, and then went up to her room. She never even popped her head into our bar.'

'So as far as you're aware, she met nobody and spoke to nobody.'

Tompkins shook her head. 'Not between checking in and back out again, no.'

'Do you have phones in your rooms?'

'No. No call for them these days, not with everyone carrying a mobile around with them.'

Chase gave a wry smile. What he'd learned gave them a fixed time and position, but yet again nothing to suggest who her killer might be. He thanked the woman and went to meet Laney, who sat nursing a Mocha in Caffe Nero. He ordered one for himself and joined his partner at a table for two, shrugging off his coat before sitting down. Over their drinks, he related the essential details of his conversation with Joyce Tomkins, Laney nodding along as he spoke.

'At least we're narrowing the window,' she said, seemingly upbeat about the new development. 'That can't be sneezed at with a case like this.'

He agreed. 'If we can lock it in with a bit more CCTV, I'll be happier, but I'm clearer in my head as to the dates we're looking at. I'm pretty sure Grace was murdered the same day she went shopping in Calne. The Friday night. But we'll check to see if she turns up on camera anywhere afterwards, just to be sure.'

He sat back to mull it over. They knew where, they almost certainly knew when. The what and the how would arise from the post-mortem. From this point on it was all about the who, because the reason why seemed obvious: either Grace was killed deliberately or otherwise during an attempted rape, or shortly afterwards when her rapist decided to cover his tracks. Much of this was still to prove, including the murder and sexual abuse, but as an experienced copper, Chase felt his deductions were logical.

'What's up, cupcake?' Laney asked, frowning at him. She blew over her mug to help cool the steaming liquid inside.

He gave her an uncertain look. 'I'm not sure. I just have that nagging feeling about this op. You know, the one that makes you doubt your ability to find answers.'

Following another blast of air over the surface of her drink, Laney said, 'I reckon we've done bloody well so far. Certainly better than that forlorn look on your fizzog would suggest.'

Chase waved her veiled complaint aside. 'We have. No doubt. But when I look ahead, I'm left to wonder how we'll make any further progress. Other than asking for help from the public, it's quite possible that the only person who knows who was on that hillside with Grace Arnold, the only person who saw her attacker, was Grace herself.'

'Then you'd better hope you're wrong, because that poor thing isn't about to tell us anything.'

'Not unless she has their DNA under her fingernails, and in the unlikely event that it's been preserved. Then she might tell us everything we need to know.'

Laney arched her eyebrows. 'That's you all over, Royston. You're an optimist at heart. You have all the fears and doubts we pessimists experience, but somehow you find a way to look on the bright side. Frankly, it makes me sick.'

Chase drained his mug and set it down. He chewed over her words before saying, 'Maybe I need those inner doubts and fears to challenge me, Claire. Without them, I might see no light at the end of the tunnel.'

'Like me, you mean?'

'If the cap fits.'

'Hmm. Not that there always is one. A light, I mean, not a cap.'

'I don't agree,' he said with a defiant shrug. 'A light is always shining somewhere, even if we can't always see it. Sometimes you just have to work harder to find it.'

Before Laney could add anything further, Chase's phone rang and when he saw Ray Petchey's name on the screen he answered it immediately. He listened intently to the pathologist without saying much in reply, thanked the man before saying goodbye. Then he looked across at Laney.

'DNA results are in on our victim. It's a match for Grace Arnold.' He heard the dull monotone of his voice. While the forensic evidence proved what they already believed, it was not a truth that set them free.

His colleague nodded. 'I take it that's not the light you were referring to, Royston?'

'No,' he replied softly. 'It's a step forward, but confirming the identity of our victim is no cause for celebration. Not in this instance. Sorry, but I see only darkness still.'

Laney's head continued to bob up and down. 'Sadly, I know exactly what you mean,' she told him.

TWELVE

By the time he arrived home that night, Chase realised his mood had become more sombre. On the way back from the office he'd stopped off at Swindon's Great Western Hospital to visit the mortuary. There, his first sight of Grace Arnold's remains made him feel both nauseous and miserable in equal measures. Riven with blackened patches of flesh – the result of prolonged exposure to freezing temperatures – in addition to recent putrefaction, the young girl's swollen body was a grotesque assault on the senses. He hadn't needed to see their victim, but felt he owed Grace and her family the dedication and respect.

He remained sitting in his car outside the house, unwilling to bring his current frame of mind into his home life. Not that Erin would chew him out for it; over time, she had become accustomed to the emotional peaks and troughs and the valid reasons for them. But since their daughter had been born, he'd worked hard not to impose the darker elements of work on Maisie. He cleared his thoughts for a quarter of an hour before heading inside and submitting to the usual rambunctious greeting in the form of the cartoon Tasmanian devil that was his daughter.

Over a customary chilled beer, he listened eagerly to Maisie's in-depth commentary on her day. His daughter's enthusiastic narration held him transfixed as she barely paused between scenes, hurriedly gathering her breath and moving on each time as if afraid to stop even to gather her thoughts. In a constant stream of words she told him about her choice of breakfast cereal, the walk to school, each lesson and every conversation, the after-school club, Erin collecting her, their walk home discussing the class project, and everything she had done since coming back through the front door. Her excitement was infectious, and for those precious few minutes he was able to cast aside his troubles.

Inevitably, as the evening wore on and with Maisie asleep in her room, his day at work and the investigation began to intrude into his thoughts once again. Chase realised he was being more subdued than usual, but their frozen victim stalked the corridors of his mind and refused to be budged.

'Penny for them,' Erin said to him at one point as he struggled to keep up with the storyline unravelling on an episode of *Blue Bloods*. She flashed a tentative smile. 'Or am I going to need more money than that tonight?'

'A tenner, maybe,' he replied, raising a feeble return smile. 'And even that won't get you too far.'

'That bad, eh?' His wife put aside her newspaper crossword. 'You want to talk? I'm stuck, so I could do with having my brain unclogged.'

Typical Erin, he thought. Trying to make it seem as if him spilling his guts would help her most of all. 'There's not a lot to tell,' he said. 'Which probably explains why I'm not quite myself tonight. Sorry. I don't mean to dwell on it.'

'Then tell me what you can. How much further did you get today?'

Chase took a deep breath before responding. 'We have an ID. DNA confirmed what we already knew: the body was that of Grace Arnold. I went to see her on my way home.'

His wife cringed. 'No wonder you've been so quiet. That can't have been easy, Royston.'

'Easier on me than it will be for her parents.'

'Even so. I understand why your mood is so low tonight.'

He nodded. 'We also know she stayed at a B&B in Marlborough for one night, before preparing for her second long hike. Tomorrow we'll flood the town with Grace's photo asking the public for information. There'll be a TV and newspaper appeal as well. But that won't happen until after Claire and I have informed the Arnolds.'

'Ouch. What a horrible job.'

'Yeah. Not quite as horrendous as having your worst fears confirmed, though. And as yet, I can't even tell them precisely how their daughter died. The best we can hope for is to get the PM result tomorrow afternoon, but currently all I can confirm are the suspicious circumstances of Grace's death. I'll leave the more horrific details out until we know for certain.'

'No wonder you're distracted. Those poor parents. Did your victim have any siblings?'

'A brother. Supposedly no boyfriend, but we'll need to talk to her friends and perhaps find out one way or the other. Parents aren't always in the know.' He grinned this time, remembering how Erin's mother and father were clueless about their daughter dating him for the first four months of their relationship.

'I take it you still have no suspects?' she said.

He shook his head. 'No idea where to even begin looking for one, either. With the crime scene itself so spoiled by time and weather conditions, we'll be fortunate to obtain any leads there. She wasn't with anybody when she was captured on security cameras, and she met nobody throughout the evening she stayed at the B&B. We can't place her with anybody at all since she left home. So far.'

'So far?'

'Well, it's still a long shot, but since we've narrowed the time window, we can start placing her in certain locations on specific dates. Once again, we'll be relying on the public for their help.'

'I'm sure the media will be interested.'

Chase knew what Erin meant, and he felt the same way. Following the serious case he'd exposed the previous autumn, journalists had swarmed all over him and Laney in a futile attempt to make celebrities of them. Neither had been remotely attracted by the possibility, and both had fended them off as best they could. Eventually the furore died down, but Chase had a sense they were merely biding their time, waiting for the next major crime of interest to seize upon the opportunity to raise spectres of the recent past. This time, however, he was one of several detectives working the case. He'd leave it to DCI Knight to keep them at bay. He'd rebuff those who sought him out directly, and anybody doorstepping the family home would find Erin to be even more forceful and determined to dismiss them.

'I have more of a buffer this time,' he said. 'An SIO, IO, and case officer stand between me and those vultures.'

'Even so. They'll corner you at some point. They'll bring up the past and hope your filter isn't in place. And we all know how they twist words around, Royston.'

He held out his hand, interlocking his fingers with hers. Her concern was obvious. 'Hey, don't worry about it. They'll find a story no matter what, even if I say nothing. This brain damage of mine is a curse at times, but there are occasions when it works in my favour. You know better than most how often I've said what I wanted to say only to later blame it on my lack of filter. Sod the media, Erin. Their focus needs to be on Grace Arnold, and I'll bloody well make sure they remember that.'

His wife shuddered as her lips turned downward. 'I keep wondering what it must be like. To have your own child disappear like that. To not know where she is. And to then have the police turn up at your front door.'

Chase had been on the other side of that too many times not to know the most likely reactions. 'For some it's a relief, because far too many parents never find out what happened to their children. They'd rather get that knock from us than not. As for Mr and Mrs Arnold, they clearly still held out some hope. Him less so, but even he was still open to the thought that she might be found safe and well. You could tell the mother had never given up, which was why she was so distraught and worn down by the past number of weeks. It's only when you give up hope or learn the worst that you can move on.'

'If you can. I'm not so sure I could, Royston.'

He thought of Maisie, sound asleep in her bedroom. Warm, fed, secure, and loved. He couldn't imagine losing her, his beautiful and precious daughter suffering the same awful fate as Grace. He didn't need the extra resolve, but he determined there and then to find the man who murdered that young girl and to make them pay for robbing the Arnolds of any meaningful future.

THIRTEEN

Chase and Laney returned from Seaton late the following afternoon. Confirming the death of Grace Arnold in person to their victim's parents was as tough as Chase had imagined. Both broke down and had to be consoled, though in reality no amount of comfort could ever offer solace to parents grieving the loss of a child. It was a long drive down and back to utter a few miserable words, but both he and his partner had agreed it was only right that they were the ones to deliver the sad news.

While they were at the Arnolds, the family was doorstepped by a particularly aggressive journalist. Following his third knock in as many minutes, Chase excused himself to open the door. Before the man who stood there could talk, Royston reached out to grab him by the scruff of the neck and pull him in close. In a voice lowered so that nobody else on the pavement could hear, he said, 'I won't bother to ask if you have a conscience, because clearly you don't. But you knock on this door again and I will do everything in my power to make your life miserable.'

As the reporter made to protest, Chase squeezed tighter and drew him six-inches closer. 'I'm a man of my word. Now walk away and leave this family to grieve, you absolute disgrace of a human being.'

When Laney quizzed him about the incident, he said he'd carried out some pest control. He refused to tell her anything else.

They arrived back in Little Soley to find a woman waiting in the reception area to speak with them. Alison May was at her usual post behind the front desk. She introduced their visitor as Mrs Beth Hutton.

Chase nodded a greeting and showed the woman into the office. He gestured for her to take a seat, before easing himself into his own chair. Laney had followed them, but remained standing on the threshold, leaning against the door frame.

'What can I do for you today, Mrs Hutton?' Chase asked.

She was a stern-looking woman with shoulder-length curly brown hair. Other than a deep shade of pink on her lips, she wore little makeup and had a youthful glow to her skin. When she spoke, her cultured voice carried with it an anxious trill.

'I'm here about my son, Sergeant Chase. He's been absent from home these past two days. I haven't heard a word from him, and neither can I reach him on his mobile. None of his usual friends have been in contact with him recently, and he's not been at work, either.'

Chase immediately gave a nod to Laney, who took out a notebook from the backpack nestled by her feet. He returned his gaze to the woman seated by his desk. 'What's your son's name, please?' he asked.

'Neville. He goes by *Nev*.'

'Same surname as yourself?'

'Yes.'

'And you live here in Little Soley?'

The brown curls shook. 'Sorry, no. We're from just outside Leighton Buzzard.'

A Y-shaped crease forming over his nose, Chase exchanged puzzled glances with his colleague, before saying, 'I'm terribly sorry to hear your son may be missing, Mrs Hutton, but I'm not at all sure why his absence brought you to our door.'

'I understand, but if you'll give me a minute I can explain. My son is twenty, so a couple of days away from home without reporting in to Mum is nothing to worry about. Or so I thought. But then I happened to catch a news item on my phone about the body of a young girl you found down here the other day. Pretty little thing. Blonde and slight. I probably wouldn't have thought twice about it other than to feel desperately sad for her parents, only the more I stared at the photograph the more I thought I recognised her. So, I read the article more fully and one or two things jumped out at me.'

Chase leaned in, intrigued by where this was headed. 'Please go on,' he said.

'Well, other than her looking familiar, I thought there had to be a connection between what happened to her and my Nev.'

'How so?'

'Because he was also walking that trail in January. And then it clicked. The reason I recognised her is because she was in a photo my son showed me when he returned from that hike. He also posted it online. On Instagram.'

Chase felt his stomach lurch and his heart skip a couple of beats. 'Okay, so I'm starting to understand why you came to us. But how did you end up at this station? Who told you to speak with me?'

'The article I read mentioned you by name, and it also gave your location. I recognised both from that horrible mess you were involved in last year. I could have called ahead, but I just assumed… well, I'm sorry, but I assumed I'd be fobbed off on the phone.'

'That's not the case, I assure you. But now that you are here, let's talk more about your son and this photo. So, you're telling us that he hiked one of the trails and at some stage during that hike he met our victim. Do I have that right, Mrs Hutton?'

'Yes, that's correct.'

'Do you know where their paths crossed?' DC Laney asked, moving from her spot by the door to stand in the woman's line of vision.

Hutton shook her head, her wan face showing the strain of the past couple of days. 'Not exactly. But I can tell you that the selfie was taken in a pub close to the downs where they discovered the girl's body. It may be nothing, but even to me it seemed like too big a coincidence.'

'Understandable,' Laney said with a comforting nod. 'But our victim went missing back in January, whereas your son clearly returned home from his hike. The chances of the two events being linked are unlikely.'

'I realise that part. Even so, the girl's body was discovered only three days ago, and I last saw Nev the morning after it was reported on the telly. That doesn't seem quite so remote if you ask me.'

Chase assembled the new information quickly, his mind seeking further avenues to explore. 'Mrs Hutton, we'll want to see the photograph, but before you show it to us, please tell me more about your son and our victim. Did he talk about her much? If so, what did he have to say? Did he come to realise she had been reported as missing?'

She put her head down for a moment, hands fumbling together. Then she looked back up, clearly trying to keep her emotions in check. 'He didn't talk about her specifically. He mainly spoke about the trail and the hiking experience itself. When he showed me the photo, he didn't even mention her then. I had to ask who she was.'

'Okay. And what did he tell you?'

'Only that they'd come across other mad hikers like themselves, all walking the trails in the dead of winter. A few of them ended up in the same pub one evening and got together for a group photo, and she happened to be one of them.'

'When you say "they'd" come across other hikers, who exactly do you mean? Was Nev with other friends?'

'Yes. He was with four fellow hikers. They didn't really spend time together other than when they hiked. I wouldn't call them close friends, exactly, but they enjoyed each other's company. Perhaps it's better if I just show you.'

Beth Hutton took out her phone, opened up the Gallery app and turned the device to show Chase and Laney the photo. She flipped the phone sideways. 'Nev is standing next to the girl… your victim. To his left are his four friends. To the right of the girl is another female and a male. Nev said they were a couple of students. The girl was the only one hiking on her own.'

Chase studied the photograph, then said, 'Tell me, Mrs Hutton, when did you see the news item and recognise the girl?'

'Wednesday afternoon. Lunchtime, it would have been.'

'Was Nev at home with you at this point? Did he also watch the news?'

'No, he was already out by that time.'

'Okay. Going back to the evening when the photo was taken, is that the only time your son saw this girl, do you know?'

Hutton shook her head vigorously. 'Oh, no. This entire group spent the evening together and then they all camped up on the downs overnight.'

'You do know that's where Grace Arnold's body was discovered, don't you?' Laney said, a little too vociferously for Chase's liking. He recognised the significance of what they'd learned, but laying into this distressed mother wasn't going to help matters.

If she'd noticed Laney's abrupt tone, Mrs Hutton didn't mention it. 'Yes. I do. But as I said before, Nev never really spoke about her, other than mentioning the fact they all had a few drinks and then camped out together. It never came up again afterwards.'

'Was she still there when your son and his group left the following morning?' Chase asked.

Hutton's eyebrows knitted together. 'I… I have no idea. I don't think it came up. Like I say, if I hadn't mentioned her after seeing the photo, he probably wouldn't have commented at all. I got the impression it was just a bunch of fellow hikers getting together before going their separate ways.'

Chase wanted to pursue the lead, but he was acutely aware that the only reason Beth Hutton was in Little Soley was because of her missing son. 'Tell me,' he said, 'can you think of anything your son said or did either on Tuesday or Wednesday morning when you saw him last which, now that you know about Grace Arnold, sheds a different light on anything he brought up? Did you perhaps notice a change in his behaviour?'

'No. Not that I can think of. What are you suggesting, Sergeant?'

'I'm not suggesting anything, Mrs Hutton. But in light of what you just told us, I do think your son's disappearance coming shortly after the discovery of our victim's remains has to be more than coincidental.'

As if for the first time, the awful reality dawned on the woman and her face became all the more ashen. 'Oh, my God! You think my Nev had something to do with this girl's murder, don't you?'

'I'm not suggesting anything of the sort,' Chase replied sharply. 'But I do have to wonder if he knew more than he said. If you can't think of a good reason for his continued absence, then some connection to this find on Cherhill Down is a decent starting place.'

Hands to her face, Hutton leaned forward and began to sob gently. 'My son had nothing to do with what happened to this poor girl. He wouldn't have. He couldn't. He's just not that kind of lad. He's not capable of harming anyone. I want him back. I just want him back.'

Neither Chase nor Laney made any initial move to comfort the woman. Often it was best to allow people to vent their anger or dismay before reacting with sympathy. Eventually, Chase came around from his side of the desk and crouched down, taking Hutton's hands away from her face and holding them in his.

'Listen to me,' he said gently. 'If your son came home from that trip and behaved as if nothing out of the ordinary happened, then the chances are good that he didn't know anything about Grace Arnold's murder. In fact, him showing you that photo in the first place tells me how unlikely that is. Being involved in the death of another person takes its toll, so I'm sure you would have noticed a change in Nev's behaviour over the past month or so if he'd been aware of it. In truth, it sounds to me as if he learned about it before you did, and the news came as a shock to him. It's perhaps unsurprising if he's reacted badly.'

Hutton's moist eyes took him in. 'You really think so?'

Chase didn't. Not with any degree of certainty. But he said so anyway. 'The thing is, if Nev had no idea, then perhaps his friends did. Them, or the couple you say camped out with the group that night. So, we're going to have to trace them if possible, and we will need to speak with your son's friends as a matter of some urgency. Before we do so, however, I'd like to have Nev's mobile phone number.'

Sniffing and regaining some composure, Hutton said, 'But he's not answering. He won't accept my calls and he hasn't replied to any of my messages.'

'That's okay. We'll try again, anyway. But the important thing is, if we have his number, then we can gain access to his phone records. From that data, we may get a better idea of where he is, where he's been, and who he's been in contact with these past couple of days. We can put that in motion at the same time as we speak to his hiking friends. Is that all right with you, Mrs Hutton?'

Uncertain and mostly distraught, the woman nodded. Chase patted her hand and sat back. After such an emotional start to the day, he hadn't anticipated a similar situation blooming when they got back to their station.

Earlier, having informed the Arnolds of their daughter's death, they'd spent some time with DC Mann discussing her role as Family Liaison Officer. The couple had reached the point where they were comfortable having the officer with them in their home, yet it was time to ease a more local FLO into position. They'd also asked to take Grace's mobile phone for evidence, which Mr Arnold had readily agreed to. Following the exchanges with Beth Hutton, Chase was hoping that a thorough forensic sifting of data would find communication between the two phones, providing the investigation team with another lead to follow.

He thought back to their conversation with the grieving parents. A harrowing experience for all concerned, confirming their daughter's death nonetheless appeared to settle the couple. Chase believed knowing was better than not knowing, because while hope could be a force for good, it could also consume a person from the inside out. With the parent of another missing person in front of him, he knew he had to find the right words.

'You were right to come to us today,' he told her. 'I could offer you meaningless platitudes and promise you everything will turn out all right in the end, but when I look at you, I don't think that's what you want. In all honesty, I think you need to prepare yourself for any and all eventualities. But – and I must stress this, Mrs Hutton – one of those outcomes is that your son may well arrive home at any minute having no idea how much concern he has caused you. My advice to you is to return home after we've taken a statement and obtained the information we need. I take it you've reported all this at your local police station?'

'Yes. They were kind, but I got the impression they were humouring me. Like you, they expect Nev to come walking through the door oblivious to all the fuss. It was only because of this connection to your victim that I decided to travel down here.'

'And we're glad you did. A member of our team will be in touch with your locals and will keep lines of communication open from this point on. We'll notify you as soon as we learn anything – if we learn anything. You return the favour if he does turn up. As for any connection Nev may or may not have to our murder victim, that's not your concern at this moment. That's for us to investigate. And we will, but without prejudice. Please believe that.'

It probably wasn't enough, and yet Hutton visibly relaxed. Taking the opportunity, Chase asked her to send him the photograph and gave out his email address. She obliged, and moments later he heard the chime of an incoming mail. He thanked the woman for her co-operation, offered his best wishes and then nodded at Laney. 'Please show Mrs Hutton back out to reception, Claire. Have Alison take a statement. Names and contact details first, at which point she can run the usual searches. Meanwhile, I'm going to chase up the PM and take a look at Grace's phone. With any luck at all, we'll have made significant progress before the end of the day.'

A couple of minutes later, when Laney returned to his office, Chase looked up and said, 'Did you recognise the pub in that photo?'

'No. I don't think so.'

'We were there just the other day. It was the Black Horse. They were in the Black Horse that night, Claire.'

'But the owner claimed not to have seen her,' she said, scrunching up her face.

'He did, indeed.' Chase got to his feet. 'I think we need another word in his shell-like.'

FOURTEEN

THE NUMBER OF COLLEAGUES attending the office meeting the following morning took Chase by surprise. It was Saturday, and he'd anticipated seeing only those who were on duty. DCI Knight had not sanctioned overtime, yet the room was full and the team complete.

'My thanks to those of you giving up your own time today,' DS Jude Armstrong said. 'We felt this was a pivotal briefing, given the progress made yesterday and the information we received late on. Let me begin there. PM report confirms Grace Arnold was not murdered by manual strangulation as first presumed, but as a result of the sharp force trauma she received to the head. Sadly, the poor girl was also most likely raped, but the condition of the body makes it impossible to be certain. I called Nat, who subsequently informed Mr and Mrs Arnold. She stayed with them last night and will hand off to a local FLO later on today.'

'What about the brother?' Laney asked. She leaned back against a wall by the door, arms folded beneath her chest. 'When Royston and I paid our first visit, I got the impression his parents were going to ask him to join them. He wasn't there yesterday, though, when we confirmed our victim's identity, but they did say he'd turn up.'

'I don't have any word on that,' Armstrong replied. 'I'll be in contact with Nat throughout the day, so I'll find out more. She says the couple appear to be handling the news well, having had a few days to live with the very real possibility. Yesterday's confirmation hit them as hard as you'd expect, but perhaps not quite as badly as it might had it been our first visit. So, if there are no objections, I'll go around the room and if you have something you can tell us all about it. Let's start with you, Reuben.'

DC Cooper stood and cleared his throat. 'Calne Sainsbury's gave up nothing more by way of additional footage of Grace. Having isolated the days she arrived and left Marlborough, we've put in requests for private and business security feeds, and we'll obviously scrutinise anything picked up by our own street cams. We'll hit those today, but probably won't get other film through until Monday. We have a local TV appeal going out this evening. If you're not sure why the Black Horse pub is important, Royston will fill you in. Late on yesterday, I made a formal request for CCTV for the night of Friday the thirteenth of January. They got back to me first thing this morning, but sadly only to confirm what they told DS Chase: they don't have security cameras.'

Chase swore beneath his breath. He'd hoped they were lying.

'As for the mobile phone data,' Cooper continued, 'Royston and I went over Grace's phone yesterday evening after using the manufacturer's backdoor to circumvent the password. We found no suspicious texts or voicemail messages, and certainly nothing related to this Neville Hutton lad, whose name you'll see in your briefing notes. More about him later. I put in a RIPA request with the provider for any deleted files still retained in Grace's backups. We concluded this was unlikely to yield anything significant, but it's a box ticked. However, Grace did exchange texts and calls with one young man close to home who may have been her boyfriend. We've also asked the company for call logs, and of course we'll be following up with the lad himself. I've already asked Nat to ease him into her conversations with the Arnolds, see what they know about the relationship.'

He paused to gather his breath. 'Any questions before I hand over to Royston? No. Good.'

Chase stroked his chin as he pondered where to begin. The unexpected visitor to Little Soley seemed ideal. 'Neville Hutton is a person of interest,' he said, eyes scouring the faces of his colleagues. 'No more than that at this stage, and there's a good chance his hiking buddies will join him. The fact is, these young men spent time with our victim on or around the time of her death. Our understanding is that they first met in the pub; a bunch of trail hikers grouping together. They then camped for the night on Cherhill Down. Now Mr Hutton is missing. That's where our information stops. According to his mother, Neville showed no sign of agitation or discomfort, no sour moods or anxiety after returning from the hike. All was well, apparently. Until Wednesday. Around mid-morning he left the house without saying a word to his mother – not unusual, it seems – but he has not been home since, and neither has he made contact. No response to her calls. I tried the number, but it went straight to voicemail, so either it's switched off or the battery is dead. Long and short… I don't believe the discovery of a body in that specific location on Monday, and Neville Hutton's absence from his home these past few days, are unconnected.'

'You think he could be our killer?' DI Fox asked.

Chase pursed his lips and shrugged. 'I think we'd be right to put him in the frame. But perhaps no more so than any of the other men camping on the hillside that night. When he returned from his trip, he voluntarily showed his mother the photo taken of him and his pals together with a couple of students and Grace. Personally, I don't see him doing that if he'd killed the girl.'

'Do we have the names of these other hikers?'

'Only one so far. A Gary Elder is a known friend of Neville's. The other three members of their group and the couple who joined them remain unidentified at this time. Tracing them is a priority. Hutton's phone contact list might give us more, but we probably won't get that until tomorrow at the earliest.'

'Agreed. Let's start the process by scouring social media accounts for both Neville Hutton and this Gary Elder. If the Hutton boy posted updates on Instagram, then we can hopefully identify his followers and friends, including those fellow hikers. What about our approach regards this lad, Elder?'

'I'm thinking we ask him to attend for interview without caution,' Chase suggested. 'Same for all of them once we have them identified. Purely as witnesses. We invite them in to tell us about that day, and to glean what we can about Neville himself. If they refuse, then we pay them a visit.'

Fox appeared satisfied. Meanwhile, DCI Knight jotted something in her notebook. She then fixed her attention on Chase. 'Interview strategy?' she asked. 'Let's begin with Gary Elder.'

'Like I said, we treat him as a witness having spent time with Grace. We want to know how they met, what they did in their time together, details relating to the other couple, the lads whose names we don't yet have, plus of course our missing boy himself. If I remember correctly, Reuben and Paige are your two nominated interview specialists, right?'

'They are, yes.'

'Same duo with respect to witnesses rather than persons of interest?'

Knight's eyes widened. 'I'd say yes, but I think all of us can throw our hats in the ring for those.'

Chase nodded. 'Okay. Good. I suggest that once we have the other names, we pull them in and interview them all at roughly the same time. The less they get to talk to each other the better.'

'I don't like to pour cold water on your ambitions, Royston, but if your intention is to get these done over the weekend, then I'm going to have to ask Superintendent Waddington for additional budget. There are six of you, plus Nat, to cover.'

'This has become a bloody murder investigation,' Chase snapped. 'If everybody here is happy to put in the time, you make the right decision and ask for permission afterwards.'

'And what if we're denied the funds afterwards?'

'Don't allow that to happen. Do your sodding job!'

He felt a hand on his arm, Laney's voice speaking his name. He closed his eyes and took a breath. Then he looked up at DCI Knight. 'I'm sorry. Please forgive me, Nicole. Look, I'll forgo any claim if it comes to it. I'm sure others here will do the same.'

Chase felt heat rising in his cheeks. His filter had failed him miserably, but with Laney's help he had reeled himself in to make a calmer plea. He hoped Knight hadn't taken offence.

'What if we can't persuade them to provide witness statements at the same time?' she asked, seemingly unperturbed by his outburst. 'What if we're unable to locate them all? It is the weekend, after all. They could be anywhere other than at home.'

His shoulders slumped. He was getting carried away, running before they'd barely started to walk. 'That's true enough. On the one hand, it's better for us if these lads don't confer in between interviews. On the other, their pal is missing, and even if they don't know where he is, any of them could be in contact with Neville. Your call as SIO, Nicole, but reluctantly I think we must err on the side of caution. Let's start with the lad whose name Mrs Hutton gave us. Once we have the others identified, we see who we can get hold of and who can make themselves available, then we'll divvy them up to those on duty or willing to chance the overtime call.'

This time, the DCI nodded. 'I agree it's less than ideal having to interview these lads at different times, but with Neville Hutton currently missing, we have to consider his welfare above all else. If we're able to speak with Mr Elder, then we really have to begin the interview process. We all want to nail Grace's killer, but our possible misper has to be our priority for the time being, especially given the connection to our own case.'

Nodding, Chase finished his part of the briefing. 'Regards the Black Horse, it's important because we can place our victim there on the night we currently believe she was murdered. She spent the evening there with those other hikers before they joined her on that hillside. We actually visited the pub on our way back from Calne the other day, at which time the owner said he had never seen Grace

Arnold before. Claire and I paid him another visit yesterday, and this time he realised that on that particular night he and his wife were in London seeing a show. They were able to verify that, so we have a satisfactory explanation for why he didn't recognise our victim. That's it from me.'

The back and forth continued for several minutes, after which others in the room updated the team on their progress and weighed in on the policy decisions and actions. Chase regarded Knight closely throughout. She hadn't seemed at all fazed by his raised voice and clipped tone, and was equally even-handed when it came to disagreements. She listened, sometimes approving sometimes not, before making their next moves clear to everybody. DCs Paige Bowen and Efe Salisu were given the task of making initial contact with Neville Hutton's friend.

No more than ten minutes had passed when DC Salisu turned and made a plea for silence in the room. 'I have news,' she said breathlessly. 'Though I don't know what to make of it. My call to Gary Elder was answered, but not by him. It was the police at Witan Gate station in Milton Keynes. They have the boy's phone because he was the victim of a crime. On returning home from work on Wednesday evening, Gary Elder found his girlfriend bound and gagged and a masked man brandishing a cleaver of some kind. When questioned later that same night, the girlfriend told officers she had heard nothing the two men discussed, but she was not in a good way emotionally and may not have remembered events clearly.'

'So, what happened to Elder?' Chase asked, fearing the worst.

Salisu shrugged. 'That's just it… we don't know. He and this stranger left the house together and Elder hasn't been seen since.'

FIFTEEN

Having allowed time for the fresh information to sink in, Chase was the first to respond. 'What just happened?' he asked, looking around the room. 'Did we go from the murder of a young woman out on a hike to something else entirely?'

DCI Knight blinked at him, her features contemplative. 'It certainly looks that way, Royston.'

He scratched behind his ear. 'Eight people, so far as we know, camped up on that hill back in January. Now one of them is dead, and two of them are missing. What the hell happened on Cherhill that night?'

'More than we initially thought, that's for sure.'

Chase's mind whirled, blitzed by the news DC Salisu had delivered. 'We need a complete overhaul of our thinking,' he said. 'Because everything we thought we knew, other than Grace Arnold having been murdered, is wrong.'

'I agree. So, let's examine it again. Grace was not, as we first assumed, camping out alone on the night we think she was killed. Both Neville Hutton and Gary Elder were there as well. As were three of their friends, plus another young couple.'

'According to Hutton's mother,' Laney pointed out. She shrugged. 'I'm not suggesting she's telling porkies or is wrong, but she got her information from him. As yet, we have no corroboration.'

'But we're able to place them all in a pub just minutes from that location on that same night,' Chase reminded them. 'A lot of the finer details are missing, but I think we can afford to go along with that as a sound thread to pull at.'

Knight nodded. 'I agree. We're currently lacking the names of five principal characters who were also there, but this is a good place to start.'

'It is. Despite there being so much we don't yet know.'

'Including which of them – if any – murdered Grace,' DI Fox said, sourly.

'Neither do we know who took Gary Elder from his home in Milton Keynes,' DC Bowen pointed out. 'Nor why the Hutton lad is missing.'

DCI Knight exhaled heavily and raised a hand. 'Okay, let's agree that we're short on facts and big on speculation. On the other hand, all lines of enquiry have to begin somewhere. So, we do what we do best, people. We record what we know, we action in order to find answers to the things we don't know. We investigate and rule things in or out. If we limited ourselves to what we know for certain at this stage we'd have no direction at all.' She glanced across at Chase. 'Your thoughts, Royston?'

'This begins with a young woman by the name of Grace Arnold being murdered on Cherhill Down in mid-January. We know from the pathology report that there was an attempt to strangle her, but that she died after receiving two savage blows to the head with a sharp weapon. We have evidence that Grace spent an evening with a bunch of fellow hikers, and anecdotal but entirely feasible evidence telling us those hikers spent the night camping on the same hillside as Grace. All of that ties in with the last time Grace was seen or spotted – as best we can tell from our searches. That, to me, is a decent lead to pursue.'

'And if we're right about this, there are two distinct paths to follow,' Knight said, standing and walking across to the board. She picked up a marker and began to write. 'First, we put into motion

TIE actions on those unknown hikers. And so's we're all on the same page, here that means Trace, Implicate, Eliminate. Some of you might have used Interview in other force areas, but that's how we roll. Second, two of those hikers are missing, one of whom may have been the victim of an abduction. Now, their misper cases are being dealt with by officers local to where they lived, but we need to evaluate them as well in order to understand what their disappearances mean for our own investigation.'

'The names of the three remaining friends should be easy enough to obtain,' Chase said. 'Our social media trawl will hopefully provide results. Then there's the data from the Hutton lad's phone, and of course, Gary Elder's girlfriend and his phone data as and when we can have access to it.'

'Reuben,' Knight said, looking across at DC Cooper. 'Throw the group photo of our hikers up on the eboard, will you? Everybody, your thoughts, please.'

Moments later, all officers in the room were facing the huge screen, eight smiling faces staring back out at them.

'First thing I noticed was that's not a selfie,' Salisu said confidently, her voice gentle and measured. 'Nobody in that shot is taking the photograph. So either they asked a stranger to take it for them, or there's another member of the group on the other side of the camera.'

'Mrs Hutton was firm about there being five lads, including her son, in the group of fellow hikers,' Laney insisted. 'Her son also mentioned only two student hikers, who were a couple. She was equally certain about that.'

'She may be misremembering. Either that, or her son was.'

'Or they both got it right and somebody else in the pub that night took the photograph.'

'Okay, okay,' Knight said, stepping back from the board. 'Let's have a think about actions and roles. Other than Grace Arnold, we have two additional names to work with. Mrs Hutton pointed out her son, leaving us to identify which of these other lads is Elder. We, of course, need the names of those friends. Royston, you were already on that, so you might as well continue. Then we have our two student hikers to TIE. Let's face it, they could have travelled to the area from anywhere. Plenty of people do. Finally, I want to know who took this photo.'

Chase shook his head, having spotted something familiar in the image. Knight picked up on it and jerked her chin in his direction. 'You have something to add?' she asked.

He nodded. 'Only that I don't think our young couple travelled far at all. Look closely at the beanie the girl is wearing.'

'That's the blue and gold Marlborough College crest,' said the case officer, DC Armstrong. 'I see what you're saying, Royston, but her wearing one of their hats doesn't mean she goes there. She could've borrowed it from a friend.'

'She could have. But check out the scarf the young lad holding her close has wrapped around his neck. Blue, claret, and white. That's from the college's Marlburian collection. Nobody loans those out.'

'Are you sure about the scarf, Royston?' Knight asked him.

'I am. Seen enough of them around in my time working out of Little Soley. I'm betting the pair of them either attend or only recently left the college.'

'That's a good spot. It gives us something solid to work with.'

'It does, and that has me thinking. Although Claire and I dealt with Mrs Hutton, we had no time to build a rapport with the woman. Certainly not enough to count for anything. I'd like to suggest you send somebody else to talk to her further, leaving myself, Claire, and Alison to focus on the young couple. It makes sense, given our station is so close to Marlborough.'

He looked on as the DCI turned his request over in her mind. He knew she'd see the logic of his suggestion, but to smooth the way he spoke up again. 'Given the stature of the college, there's every chance we'll get bogged down with their legal department. If we get held up, we can take on a share of the other actions. There's plenty for us to get stuck into.'

Reaching a decision, the DCI gave a slow nod. 'Very well. See what you can get done today. Get the ball rolling at the very least. I want you to attend the briefing here on Monday morning, though. Claire and Alison can work out of Little Soley while we all get ourselves up to date.'

Chase nodded. He was happy enough with the arrangement. Nonetheless, he was concerned about extracting personal details from the college. The kind of place that had educated the current Princess of Wales didn't give away its information easily. He felt certain that he and Claire were going to have to jump through a whole variety of hoops, but hoped for some luck. Often it depended on who you spoke to first, their willingness and flexibility to provide assistance. In this case, he expected internal safety and welfare measures to throw up additional barriers. And depending on who these kids were, perhaps even personal security.

After he and Laney had returned to their rural team's smaller working space within the Gablecross building, he outlined his thinking to both his DC and trainee investigator. Alison picked up on his concerns immediately. 'A friend of mine once dated the son of a minor royal. She and her family were vetted as if they were a terrorist cell. She said the whole time they were together she felt watched, under constant surveillance and close observation. It was all terribly cloak and dagger.'

'I don't doubt it,' Chase said, immediately thinking about the case that had bonded the three of them, and the view he had glimpsed through the door into precisely how far the establishment and their outriders were prepared to go to keep secrets secret. 'The children of some extremely influential people attend Marlborough.'

'Let's hope we catch a break and discover our couple are the offspring of relative nobodies,' Laney said with a snort. 'Though nobodies with money, obviously.'

'I imagine the college provides scholarships, so let's not prejudge these two kids or their parents.'

'Oh, come on,' she scoffed. 'You attend a place like Marlborough, you're bound to think your shit doesn't stink.'

'Yeah, I know. But the fart gives you away, right?' Chase grinned.

'Besides, you have a self-proclaimed prejudice, Claire.'

Laney clamped a hand to her chest. 'Me? I'm as tolerant as fuck, you ignoramus.'

'Of course, but you do have a thing about people with money.'

'Oh, and you don't?'

'No, I do. I can admit to that. But I regard that as my problem. As I mentioned when we were working Sir Kenneth's case, I've known privileged people who were the salt of the earth and working-class heroes who were pure scum. I'm just saying, let's give this young couple the benefit of the doubt.'

'What do you want me to do while you're both at Marlborough?' May asked.

Chase gave that some thought. Continuing to shadow DC Salisu was a constructive way for May to occupy her time, but sensing the struggles he and Laney might have in front of them, he had a different idea. 'Tell you what, Alison, just in case we hit a hard dead end, it might be worthwhile you doing some research on our behalf. Have a word with a legal advisor to find out what we may need by way of warrants to compel Marlborough to identify our couple and provide next of kin contact information.'

'You really think we're going to need it?'

'I think it's possible. Forewarned is forearmed, and all that guff...'

'So why not wait to get the answers you need first and then go tooled up with everything you have?'

'Because as soon as you start trudging through the legal quagmire, progress is like walking with bags of cement strapped to your feet. It's going to take some time to scrape together, especially as it's the weekend. I want to start rattling cages right away. Today.'

May frowned. 'I don't mean to talk out of turn, Royston, but is provoking these people really the best approach? Don't we get more with sugar than vinegar?'

Laney let out another snort, this time a concerted effort designed to project how risible she considered that little homily. Somehow, she kept her lips pressed together. Chase didn't think it would last long.

He gave a shrug. 'That I don't know for sure. Sometimes you need to make people aware that you'll take any path necessary to obtain information. Even if they clam up and demand we go through channels, as I assume they will, it won't hurt to let them see how seriously we are taking the matter. You never know, it might help us at some point in the future.'

'And besides all that,' Laney cut in, eventually unable to keep her mouth shut as he had surmised, 'Royston is way too impatient to wait for paperwork to be processed. He's all action is our boss, Alison. All balls and bluster, codpiece thrusting forward.'

'Thanks for that little mental vision,' May said. 'Now I need to go and scrub my eyes with wire wool.'

Chase gave a weary shake of the head as he peered at Laney. 'You still off the cigarettes, Claire?' he asked.

'Yeah. Why d'you ask?'

'No reason. Just that it hasn't exactly smoothed out your gruff exterior.'

Laney shrugged dispassionately. 'Talking of gruff, my old man said he'd leave me if me stopping smoking altered my voice. Reckons he's got used to me sounding like Barry White wearing a Darth Vadar breathing mask. He told me if I start sounding like Joe Pasquale, he's packing his bags and walking.'

'I don't know who that is.'

'You must do. The comedian with the high-pitched, squeaky voice. You know: "I've got a song that will get on your nerves, get on your nerves, get on your nerves…"'

'Yeah, me too. Any Barry White song.'

Rolling her eyes, Laney groaned and said, 'I sometimes forget how much younger you are than me. Not that you look it most of the time.'

Chase bit his tongue as an interesting thought crossed his mind. 'Tell you what, ladies, I've changed my mind. TDC May, you're with me. DC Laney, have a fun time with legal.'

'You can't do that,' Laney complained, squinting hard at him. She looked genuinely put out.

He broadened the grin, waggled a finger suggesting she get on with it, and said, 'I think you'll find I can. Good luck, Barry.'

SIXTEEN

With just under a thousand students, many of whom were boarders, Marlborough was one of the most famous private colleges in the country. With alumni ranging from the likes of John Betjeman and William Morris to Jack Whitehall and Chris DeBurgh, attendance was an impressive educational detail on anybody's CV.

Chase was never less than intimidated by the campus sprawl alongside the town centre. Its history was there to see in its grounds and buildings, from the neolithic mound second only to Silbury Hill in terms of size in the whole of Europe, to the eighteenth-century noble house that had replaced a Norman castle. The college had emerged from a previously chronicled refined past, opening its doors in 1843 to just shy of 200 boys. Marlborough had seen the back of many a Master since, the current one of which, Anthea Wright-Burrows, was not available when they arrived. Her second in command greeted them in her place, apologising profusely for her tardy arrival ten minutes after their scheduled appointment.

Marie Hodgson was small and plump and bubbly, all rosy cheeks and enormous blinking eyes behind oval-framed spectacles. She welcomed Chase and Alison May to the college, offering them both refreshments, which they refused. Having ushered them into a large office whose walls groaned with the weight of ornately framed photographs and oil paintings, Hodgson took a seat at her solid-looking walnut desk and waited for her visitors to sit, too, before asking them to explain the specific purpose of their visit.

'We're looking to identify two young people we suspect are either current or recent students here at Marlborough,' Chase began. 'Don't worry, neither of them is in trouble. Ours is purely a fact-finding mission. To that end, I was wondering if I might show you a photo, Mrs Hodgson.'

'Of course. By all means.'

Chase brought an image cropped from the original up on his phone and slid it across the desk. 'The two people in question are the young man with the Marlburian scarf around his neck, and the girl standing next to him wearing a college beanie.'

The Second Master picked up the phone and used two fingers to first select the image and then widen it, effectively zooming in. A moment later, she nodded and handed the device back to Chase. 'Yes, Sergeant, I am able to confirm that they are both current college students.'

'That's good to hear. We'd like to have a word with them, please.'

Hodgson cleared her throat and clasped both hands on the polished desk which, for all its obvious age, bore not a scar or scuff on it that Chase could see. 'As I'm sure the police appreciate more than most, the safety and security of our students is paramount. I can't simply drag them away from whatever it is they're doing to allow you to interview them. Not without prior arrangement.'

Prickling for the first time since entering the college, Chase asked, 'Arrangement with whom?'

'With the students themselves to begin with. Their families or legal guardians, too, of course.'

'I see. I take it they're both under the age of eighteen?'

'They are.'

Chase paused, breathing through his nostrils while he waited for his mental filter to slip into place. Finally, he nodded and said, 'I get what you're saying, but all we need is an appropriate adult to sit in with us while we're asking questions. I'm sure you can rustle one up.'

'I'm sure I can… under the proper circumstances. May I ask what it is you want with them, Sergeant?' Hodgson asked.

He smiled his most sincere smile. 'All we want to do is ask a few questions about the other people in that photograph.' He omitted the necessity to discuss the night they went camping, hoping to reach an agreement in principle before going into greater detail.

A relaxing of the shoulders suggested the woman was relieved. Unfortunately, her attitude to his request did not alter in the slightest. 'I'm pleased to hear that, Sergeant. However, we can take this no further at present. I remain conscious of our duty to our students in keeping their personal information secure. That said, I'm certain we can find an agreeable compromise.'

'Such as?' Chase asked.

'To begin with, I can arrange for calls to be made to the parents or legal guardians early next week. This will also allow us time to have words with both students. If everybody is in agreement, I'm sure we could squeeze something in towards the end of the week, or the following week at the latest.'

'That simply won't do,' Chase said heatedly, tension tightening his jaw. 'Mrs Hodgson, without being able to provide you with further details at this point, I must insist on speaking to these two young people as soon as possible. Today, if they are available. It is a matter of great urgency, I can assure you.'

Unmoved, her answer was equally forthright. 'Urgent or not, we have protocols I must follow.'

Realising he'd spoken hastily, Chase first apologised, then sought to offer a solution of his own. 'How about this?' he suggested. 'Contact the parents if you must, but do so immediately. Explain to them that all we want to do is ask their children about the photograph and those who appear in it with them. If they consent, then you ask the students themselves. The college can provide an appropriate adult to be present when we talk to the pair of them. It's pretty much what you already proposed, only speeded up. How does that sound?'

'If I'm being perfectly honest, it sounds rushed. And what if their parents insist on their children being legally represented?'

'That would be disappointing, and also completely unnecessary.' He shrugged and turned to May for support. 'I do hope you will make that clear to them. They're not in any kind of trouble, and we're not looking to trip them up. They won't even be under caution. We want their help, Mrs Hodgson. That's all.'

'It's entirely voluntary,' May emphasised with a firm nod. 'We need help in pursuing our investigation, and we believe this couple can provide it. To be honest, I'm surprised by your reluctance. I'm sure carrying out their civic duty by co-operating with the police is the kind of thing you'd want and expect of all Marlborough students. Doing the right thing can never be wrong, surely?'

Chase held back a smile. Anything that reflected positively on the college would be encouraged. Equally, what had gone unsaid was how it might play out if two Marlborough students failed to help the police with their enquiries.

It took only a couple of heartbeats for the Second Master to arrive at a decision. 'Very well. I'll see what I can do. If you'd care to wait here, I'll need a few moments to obtain some advice.'

The moment Hodgson left the room, Chase turned to his colleague and said, 'Well played, Alison. Did you see the change in her demeanour when you mentioned how things might look for the college?'

May bit her lip and wriggled in her seat. 'I'd like to take all the credit and say it was a well-reasoned gambit on my part, but the fact is, I just said what popped into my head.'

Chase winked. 'Better still. That suggests it was instinct, in which case you already have so much going for you.'

'Thanks. Will it get us any further, though?'

He gave that some consideration. 'I'm not sure. Our Mrs Hodgson played her cards close to her chest, but at the moment her mind will be in turmoil over how this could be reported in a Sunday newspaper. Thanks to your inspired thinking, I reckon that might just be the spur she needed.'

SEVENTEEN

They had to wait longer than Chase had anticipated they might, and he was not best pleased. But forty-five minutes later, he and Alison May were sitting inside a two-storey stone Victorian building allocated to the Preshute mixed boarding house on the south-west corner of the Marlborough campus. The Housemaster, Professor Jeffrey Lennon, had greeted the detectives with obvious wariness and displeasure, perhaps at having his day disturbed. Both students waiting for them in what looked like a common room appeared unfazed, albeit curious.

Lennon made the introductions. Chase instantly recognised Isaac Levy and Monica Cilliers as the two young college students in the photograph, which he showed to them both before explaining the reason for the meeting.

'The purpose of this discussion is for us to learn more about the other people in this photo,' he told them. Once again, he neglected to mention the night spent camping on Cherhill Down, believing the pair were more likely to be initially forthcoming if they believed identifying their companions that evening was the sole reason for their presence. 'What can you tell us about them? Monica, why don't you go first?'

The girl, lean and pretty with strong bones and shoulder-length reddish hair, glanced anxiously at her fellow student before replying.

'Not a great deal, if I'm being honest. We met in the Black Horse pub at Cherhill one night a while back. That was it, really.'

Chase nodded encouragingly. 'When you say you met, are you telling us you didn't know any of these other people prior to that particular evening?'

A shake of the head. 'No. It was the first time.'

'You do all look rather pally together, if I might say so.'

A faltering smile. 'By the time this was taken we were all pretty…' she stopped, looking across at Lennon.

He gave a solemn nod. 'It's okay, Monica. You can say it.'

'We were a bit smashed. Alcohol only, I can assure you. But we'd put away a fair few drinks that night.'

'That's what pubs are for,' Chase said with an affable grin. 'Okay, so you didn't know them going in. Tell me what you found out about them that night. Let's begin with their names.'

Cilliers puffed out her lips. 'It was a couple of months back. Like I said, we'd only just met, and we were pretty much out of it.'

'Mid-January,' he reminded her. 'Six weeks ago. I'm sure you can remember if you put your mind to it. Let me help you along, see if I can jog your memory. The five lads were together as a group, while the other girl was on her own.'

'Now, her I do recall more. Possibly because she was travelling alone. Grace. Not sure if she ever mentioned her full name, but definitely Grace.'

'And her story…?'

'Oh. Yes. She was on a walking trail. If I'm remembering correctly, she had completed one half and was about to begin the second. I don't know if it was the same route the boys were taking. Sorry, but that's pretty much all she spoke about. Does that help at all?'

'It may. Thank you, Monica. And the five lads?' He held up the phone, showing the photograph once more as a reminder.

She grimaced, as if to emphasise the struggle to remember. After a moment or two, she said, 'I can't really recall who was who. But there was a Gary and a Neville. That sticks in my mind because there's an old footballer by that name who works as a pundit these days. Then… oh, yes. They kept referring to two of them as Harpo and Groucho because they were both called Mark. You know… the Marx brothers? I had no idea who they meant, but they filled me in. I'm stuck on the final name, I'm afraid.'

'It was Ashley,' Isaac Levy said quickly.

Chase nodded at him. 'Thank you. And Monica, what can you tell me about them? Were they a decent bunch? A bit rough around the edges? What was your overall impression of them?'

'I thought they were good fun,' Cilliers said with a reflective smile. 'Enjoyed a laugh, you know? A bit too loud for Isaac's liking, though.'

'Is that right?' Chase said, switching his attention back to the young man.

'They were… boisterous,' he said tentatively. 'You know the way a group of young men can be when they're out together. I suppose others probably think that of me and my friends when we're enjoying ourselves.'

'I understand.' Chase smiled and nodded. 'You get some booze down your neck and lose your inhibitions.'

'Exactly that. I do remember one of them… one of the Marks, actually, trying to get a bit too friendly with Monica at one point.'

The girl's eyes widened. The look she gave him was one of betrayal. Perhaps she hoped to have kept that between them. When her gaze returned to Chase, she nodded. 'That's true, but it was nothing, really. He was just trying it on. As soon as I told him Isaac and I were an item, he let it go.'

Her boyfriend's cheeks reddened. 'That's fair. I probably made too much of it. He wasn't a problem. None of them were. Like I said, just a bit too rowdy for my liking.'

'You described them as boisterous earlier. Which is it?'

'I think in this case you could use either to mean the same thing. They were no trouble, if that's what you're getting at. Anyway, when are you going to tell us why we're being asked all these questions?'

Chase had been wondering how long it would be before one of

them asked why they were being spoken to. 'That'll become obvious soon enough,' he replied. 'One more thing before we move on: who took the photograph?'

The two students looked at each other, both frowning. It was Isaac Levy who spoke next. 'I honestly don't know for certain.'

'Well, was it somebody you spent the evening with along with the others? A fellow reveller? One of the bar staff, perhaps?'

'Just a customer, as far as I can recall. He definitely wasn't drinking with us, and I don't think he was a member of staff. Is it important?'

'At this stage, everything and everybody is important,' Chase said.

'Including us?'

'Insofar as you were with these other people that evening, yes.'

The lad shrugged, looking down at his feet. 'Sorry. I definitely think it was just a fellow customer. He might have used a phone belonging to one of the lads.'

'Okay. No problem. We'll eventually get a name one way or another. As for the lone female hiker, was she already with the five lads when you arrived, or did she join in later?'

'She was drinking with them when we walked in,' Monica Cilliers said, confirming with a definite nod. 'In fact, we initially thought Grace was a part of their group, until we discovered otherwise a bit later on.'

Pausing to weigh up everything he had heard so far, Chase considered his next question carefully and opted to preface it with a broad outline. 'So you met this group of people – the five lads and the female hiker – in the pub and somehow ended up spending the evening drinking with them. To the point where you had your photo taken with them. Tell me, how did that come about?'

'I'm sorry,' Levy said. 'What do you mean by that?'

'How did you two come to spend the evening with six complete strangers? What drew you together?'

This time it was the boy who glanced at his girlfriend. A look of concern passed across his face. Was it the look of a young man who knew the tragedy that had befallen Grace Arnold later that same night or in the early hours of the following morning? Chase couldn't decide, but stored the question away to ponder later on.

'Isaac?' he prompted. 'Monica?'

'We are keen hikers, too,' Levy eventually explained. 'That's how we came to talk to them in the first place. The girl, Grace, was about to take on the Ridgeway. The boys were going in the opposite direction.'

'Oh, yes,' the Cilliers girl said, nodding. 'I'd forgotten, but since you mention it, they did tell us that.'

'So the boys were headed down to Dorset,' Chase said.

Levy looked up in surprise. 'Yes. How do you know that?'

'It's come up before. You say you're hikers, too. So, were you both walking a trail at the time?'

'Yes and no. We were really just looking to camp out for a few nights and take in some walks during the daylight. No formal trails, not like the others.'

'In the middle of a bad winter?' Chase rolled his eyes. 'Where's the joy in that?'

'Taking on the conditions is all part of the outdoor experience.'

Having suffered through a blizzard all too recently, Chase took a different view when it came to how much pleasure the freezing cold provided a person. He made no further comment on the subject because it was time to address the elephant in the room. He thought he knew what the response would be, but he couldn't leave it unsaid. Not after Levy had left the door open for him.

'That all leads me nicely to what happened after the pub. You say you were camping, Isaac. So, tell us where you spent that Friday night.'

Professor Lennon, who until this juncture had remained detached, reacted as if stuck with a cattle prod. 'Now just hold on a moment,' he said, easing himself up out of his chair. He leaned forwards, hands splayed on the table. 'I was told you wished to speak with Isaac and Monica about the photograph and the people in it. Those were the agreed parameters.'

'Precisely,' Chase acknowledged, frowning as if confused by the interruption. 'Which is what I'm doing. Everybody in this photo camped out that night after leaving the pub. We'd like to know how that went… from Isaac and Monica's perspective. Starting with where they were all night.'

Far from relaxing, the housemaster became even more intense. 'Just you wait a minute. Does this new line of questioning have anything to do with the body discovered on the downs earlier this week?'

Chase was angry at the man for interrupting. He'd hoped to catch the young couple out with a lie that he and his colleagues could use against them at a later date. 'I'm afraid I can't discuss an ongoing investigation with you, Professor. Not that it should matter either way. Isaac and Monica agreed to talk to us about these lads and the young woman, and I suspect there's a great deal more for us to learn.' He turned his head to nod at the young man. 'Go on, please. Tell us about that night.'

'No, no, no!' Lennon moved to stand in front of the two students, as if presenting a barrier offering physical protection. 'Isaac, don't say a word. This was not part of the original agreement.' He took out a mobile phone and said to Chase, 'I'm stepping out of the room to make a couple of phone calls. I'll be right outside the door, so no questions while I'm gone. If I hear any, this meeting is over.'

After the man had left the room, Chase regarded the two students with a friendly smile and gave a shrug. 'I understand he's protective of you, but I think he's over-reacting. This is a continuation of the conversation we were already having. I'm sure neither of you minded answering our questions.'

'Housemasters take their responsibilities extremely seriously,' Isaac Levy said, his eyes straying to the closed door. 'They're as protective of us while we're here as our parents would be. Not that he needed to be in this case. We may not be inner-city kids, but we do know the way things work when it comes to the police.'

'Oh, and how's that?' Chase asked.

'It's your job to trick us. Get us to say things we ought to keep quiet about.'

'If you've done nothing wrong, why would you keep quiet about anything?'

'Because it's our lives, our business.'

'We only want to know how things went after you all left the pub. I'm sure neither of you has anything to hide.'

'Is Jeffrey right about the body?' Cilliers asked, edging forward and lowering her voice. 'Is that why you're here? Is that why you're asking us about the boys in the photograph? Was she killed by one of them?'

Before Chase could reply, he noted Levy's hand shooting out to rest upon hers. The movement was not gentle. He was still deciding how to respond when the door opened, and Lennon stepped back inside. He wore a self-satisfied smirk, which told Chase their interview was over.

'We're done here,' the Professor said, confirming Chase's instinct. He suspected the man had picked up the phrase from watching television. 'I've spoken with both sets of parents. I told them I was uncomfortable with the direction in which the topic of the meeting was headed. I also said I thought you had been disingenuous in respect of the subject matter. They agreed and asked me to put a stop to it. I must, therefore, ask you two officers to leave.'

Chase rose slowly to his feet. His eyes never left those of the Housemaster. 'You look particularly pleased with yourself,' he said, skewering his annoyance. 'Puffed up with your own self-importance.'

Lennon appeared unmoved. 'I'm neither pleased nor otherwise, Sergeant. I simply have a duty of care and carried out that duty.'

'Is that what you think?' He allowed his gaze to wander across to Levy and Cilliers. 'The fact is, you've done both of your students a massive disservice.'

'How do you arrive at that conclusion? I've withdrawn them from what was fast becoming an interrogation.'

Chase glared. 'Oh, I can assure you it was anything but that. This time. The trouble is, you've not looked far enough ahead, Professor Lennon. I'm sure you're delighted with the brownie points you've earned from the Levys and the Cilliers. I'd make the most of it if I were you. See, the way we'd arranged things here, both of your students could have answered all questions to our satisfaction behind these closed doors and away from the full glare of publicity. Do you think we're going to give them a second opportunity to do that? I doubt their parents will be thanking you when we collect Isaac and Monica in full view of their fellow students the next time we wish to speak to them, nor the inevitable publicity that will surely follow. All that's happened here is we've swapped the easy way for the hard way. That's on you, Professor. Your interference has made an unpleasant situation so much worse. Tell me, is that what you teach your students here? To win minor skirmishes but lose the wars?'

He didn't hang around for an answer.

EIGHTEEN

Back at the little Soley office, Chase replayed the meeting in his head while he outlined the conversation to Claire Laney, silently asking himself throughout if he had played it right. The abrupt ending suggested otherwise, yet he suspected nothing significant would have been uncovered if he'd continued to plough the same furrow.

When he was done, his partner turned to May. 'What did you think of them, Alison?' she asked. 'The students, I mean, not the staff.'

May seemed surprised but happy to have been asked for her opinion. 'Levy was shifty throughout. Nervous mannerisms, like moistening his lips and being unable to keep his hands still. He wriggled in his chair a fair bit, too. I also noticed he kept his head down and really didn't look directly at Royston when being questioned.'

'And her? Monica Cilliers?'

'Completely different. I thought she was quite relaxed. Composed. I got the impression she would have answered further questions, whereas he was definitely relieved when the Prof put the kybosh on the interview.'

'I have to agree,' Chase said, nodding. 'I kept trying to get a read of young Isaac, but whenever I happened to catch his eye, he looked away sheepishly.'

'You think he knows more than he said?' Laney asked him.

'About Grace's murder? I'm not sure I'd go that far. I reckon he suspects something occurred that night, though. As for being aware of the murder itself… I'd have to question him further to get a handle on that.'

'So not our murderer, in your opinion?'

Chase took a moment to consider before saying, 'My instinct tells me he didn't kill her. But I've been wrong before, and I could be this time as well. I just didn't get the sense that I was talking to a young man who'd recently taken a life.'

Laney glanced across at May. 'How about you, Alison? Do you see the young man as our main suspect?'

'No.' Her shake of the head wasn't entirely convincing. 'But I agree with Royston. There's something there. Something he's anxious about, something he doesn't want us to discover.'

'So what's the plan now, cupcakes? How do we go at them again? *Can* we go at them again?'

'That's going to require a major rethink,' Chase admitted. 'If we manage to speak with them a second time, it's bound to be separately and in the presence of a brief. However, I'm not sure if we'll get that far without arresting them. Their parents firmly slammed the door on us today on the say-so of the Housemaster, and I can't think of any approach that might alter their stance if we go down the exact same road.'

'How about approaching them directly?' Laney suggested. She opened up a packet of chocolate peanuts and scoffed a handful of them before continuing. 'Instead of going at their little darlings, we speak with the parents instead. We tell them we have reason to believe their children may have been witnesses to a crime, that they have knowledge of what happened to Grace Arnold that night.'

'Royston did make it clear that if we came for them again, we'd not do so quietly,' May offered. 'Perhaps the thought of that might make the parents consider a request for a more formal interview either back at the college or in their own homes, rather than having to face the full horror of the media circus.'

Chase was keen, but having had time to digest the earlier reactions, he was having doubts. 'I like the idea,' he said. 'And I think under certain circumstances that threat would work. But these people, whoever they are and whatever they do for a living, obviously have some clout. If a brief worth their salt gets so much of a sniff that we suspect these kids of anything, they're going to advise them against agreeing to a voluntary interview. If we think we'd need to arrest them to get them in the room again, then so will they. They'll also know that's not going to happen. I'm betting they've already been so advised.'

'So, what's our next move, then?' Laney asked, before chomping on another helping retrieved from the bag.

'You going to offer them to either of us?' he asked, nodding at the peanuts sitting on the edge of the desk.

'Not for me, thanks,' May said, warding off the suggestion with a raised hand. 'I'm watching my waistline.'

'Waistline?' Laney scoffed. 'There's nothing of you, girl.'

'Oh, there's plenty, thank you. And I don't want to go to seed too early.'

'Like me, you mean?'

'I didn't say that. Nor did I mean it.'

'It's okay if you did. I have to replace my ciggies with something.'

'You use patches, don't you?' Chase said.

His DC regarded him through narrowed eyes. 'I do, but can't stand the taste.'

Ignoring the feeble joke, he said, 'Then try the gum.'

'Tried it, dismissed it. Look, I can only give up one vice at a time. Ciggies first, chocolate treats next. Okay, enough of me and my awful eating habits. What's our next move?'

'You're just trying to get out of sharing,' Chase complained.

In a blur of motion, Laney snatched up the packet and scattered the contents all over the desk. 'Here you go, my love,' she said, sweeping a cluster over the edge and onto his lap. 'If you're that desperate, fill your boots.'

When they'd finished laughing, he found a peanut caught in the fold of his shirt and popped it into his mouth with a smile of satisfaction. 'I think for the time being, our students are out of reach,' he eventually said. 'However, I do quite like the idea of speaking to their parents to ask for time to explain ourselves, let them know precisely what we're looking for. On reflection, a threat might make them dig their heels in, but a more circumspect manner with cap in hand…'

'Do you do cap in hand?' Laney asked him with a smirk.

He arched his eyebrows. 'I don't even own a cap. But I can do gentle and persuasive when I need to.'

'Of course you can, my love, until they make the first dickhead remark.'

Chase smiled. 'Then we have to hope they don't. If they're reasonable, then so can I be.'

'You want to do that, then? Get hold of the parents, see what they'll agree to?'

'It's worth a punt. I want to explore the possibilities more fully before I go back to DCI Knight.'

Laney gave a thoughtful nod and turned her attention back to TDC May. 'How was it for you, Alison? I don't imagine Royston provides too many teachable moments.'

May chuckled. 'It was good. I pretty much kept my trap shut. I think I probably focussed too much on Royston's performance. I was busy working out the approach, the order of questioning, the type of questions. I probably ought to have listened more to the answers. But it's all good experience while I'm training.'

'And how's that side of it going?' Chase asked her. The role was a major step up from PCSO, and although May was intelligent and driven, he felt the weight of a more academic entry to being an investigator was possibly more of a burden than gaining experience out on the streets in uniform. Not all detectives approved of the direct entry approach, though many grudgingly acknowledged the programme filled a gap, providing warm bodies on the ground.

'It's hard, but anything worthwhile is, right?' May replied. 'The study work for the National Investigators exam is time-consuming rather than taxing, but what I'm learning by working cases provides me with a solid base for my PPP and PIP2.'

Attaining the criteria required by the Professional Policing Practice and Professionalising Investigation Programme at Level 2 demanded a lot of the applicants, but the professional standards and training provided to them produced capable investigators, each of whom was entirely familiar with the available tools and resources. Chase had always believed you learned more by doing, which meant the real-world lessons provided at this stage would serve an ex-PCSO like Alison May well in the future.

'Hopefully, we'll strike the right balance for you,' he said. 'An op like this is far reaching, and you'll find yourself getting involved in all sorts at all levels. Interviews like the one we had today are few and far between, but already you can see how troublesome they can be. Some kids are lippy and hide behind snide remarks and bluster, while others rely on their parents' wealth and social standing to protect them. Occasionally you'll encounter one or two who are naïve and gullible, but they're going the way of the dodo.'

May smiled at him. 'It was interesting, and essential. Knowing how to deal with a wide variety of people is part and parcel of what's expected of me, so as well as learning how to approach an interview from you, I also learned to study those being questioned.'

'Which is why you spotted Master Levy's tics and quirks. His anxiety increased the longer the questions went on, whereas the young woman remained somewhat detached throughout.'

'Do you think we can get at her?' May asked him. 'If we can get past her parents, that is.'

'I reckon we can go further with her than with her boyfriend,' Chase replied. 'He's too nervous, which makes him less likely to let us in. My guess is he'd keep us at arm's length, afraid to show his hand in case he reveals too much. Not so with Monica. I see her answering whatever questions we put to her.'

'So, you'll presumably prefer to get her talking first?'

'Oddly enough, no.' He regarded May with a wry smile on his face. 'Just because she's more likely to be open doesn't mean she's going to give us anything worthwhile. Why? Because the reason she's so relaxed may well be because she has no insight to offer us. Isaac might be a tougher nut to crack, but my gut tells me he knows more and so is worth the extra effort.'

May frowned, but also nodded. 'I have much to learn. I'd've gone at her first because it was the easier of the two alternatives. I missed the wider picture.'

'Don't be too hard on yourself, cupcake,' Laney chipped in. 'There's no right or wrong answer here. There's just different levels of confidence and experience. I wasn't there, but from everything you've told me, I'd also be champing at the bit to get to grips with Isaac Levy. If he knows more than he's been prepared to say so far, then I want to be inside his head.'

'Even though Monica Cilliers is possibly more willing to talk.'

'In this specific instance, yes. You pointed out he was the more anxious of the two, which suggests he has something to hide. Royston's idea, I think, is that despite them being on that hill together, Levy may know more than she does about what took place.'

'Okay. I get that. So how do you go about having a crack at the parents?'

'With great care,' Chase told her. 'At first. We can start by finding intel on them. Depending on who they are and what they do, we can then agree on the best way to tackle them. As mentioned earlier, a simple explanation might be enough. Smooth a few of the rougher edges as we provide it. Persuade them we're looking at their kids as witnesses only, even if that's not strictly the case. Another way to go could be to contact them and ask for the details of their legal representation. That way we show respect for the process, and it may lull them.'

'Which leaves us with the when.'

'That's for another day, I'm afraid.' Chase's lips twisted as he considered their way forward. 'Too raw to go back at them today. I think they'd refuse on principle if we attempted it on a Sunday. So, I'm thinking Monday morning. Before we head off for the day, then, let's obtain the information we need on the parents, starting with the Levys. Home, work, phones, family connections if they're big league.'

May gave a mock salute. Laney chuckled and scooped up her laptop. Chase hoped he was right about Isaac Levy, otherwise they were wasting time getting nowhere fast. While Laney and May cracked on with their tasks, he made a call to DCI Knight to fill her in on their progress.

'Those names you managed to pry out of them are helpful,' she told him. 'Social media searches have given us a few possibilities, but looking at my notes and comparing them to your own, I think we are able to confirm the identities of the three remaining hikers. Ashley Robertson, Mark Swallow, and we believe the final one is probably Mark Viner. When we look at Insta, Twitter, and Facebook, there are definite links between them and both the Hutton and Elder lads, together with the whole hiking and camping community.'

'When will you try to sweep them up?' Chase asked. 'Monday morning?'

'If at all possible, yes. We'll aim for a co-ordinated effort, but only after liaising with local forces. How about you and the two students?'

'I think they're worth speaking to again, provided we can convince them to engage with us a second time. We might get lucky.'

'I think you're probably right. It's worth taking the chance.'

'We're going to have a second crack at Isaac Levy first of all. We'll reach out to the parents, hopefully persuade them to do the right thing. As I mentioned, we're up against it in terms of breaking down the legal barriers first. I'm sure we'll get there one way or another.'

Chase was nowhere near as confident as he sounded, but he didn't want to be second guessed at this stage.

'Before you even think of going down the under-caution route, run it by me first,' Knight said firmly. 'I understand your frustration, but at that stage we may have all the information we need without putting them or the situation under even more pressure. If, at that time, you still think it's important to question Levy and even his girlfriend about the murder, then I'll support you in applying the caution if it's required.'

'I'll do everything I can to avoid it, Nicole,' he assured her.

'Please do. Bring matters forward as far as you can, but speak to me before taking that final step.'

Chase agreed, killing the call and tapping the phone against his chin thoughtfully. He hoped not to have to do battle with legal representatives working for the Levy family. But he was prepared to do whatever it required to get the boy answering questions again.

NINETEEN

Chase was out with his wife and daughter doing the weekly grocery shop at Sainsbury's opposite the Gablecross nick when he got a call from DCI Knight. He apologised to Erin and excused himself, walking outside the supermarket before continuing the conversation. The sky was a dull shade of pewter and looked as if it might unleash more snow at any moment despite the forecasts of clear weather.

'Sorry to bother you on a day off, Royston,' Knight said. 'But I thought you would want to hear this. Reuben and Paige stayed on yesterday evening to continue scouring social media. They wanted us all to be as prepared as possible when it comes to interviews and took another shot at gathering information. Anyhow, what they came up with was more than a little worrying.'

Top marks to DCs Cooper and Bowen, Chase thought. That kind of commitment deserved to be rewarded. 'Okay, you have my interest,' he said. 'Go on.'

'It wasn't so much what they found, more what they didn't find.'

'Which was… or wasn't?'

'Nothing. A complete lack of activity. The last post or comment from Mark Viner came on Wednesday. With Ashley Robertson it was Thursday morning, and just after noon in Mark Swallow's case. All three went from an almost constant stream of activity to absolutely zero. Given the account you got from Mrs Hutton, and knowing what took place at Elder's flat, I think we have to see these as connected.'

'I'd say you were spot on,' Chase said, immediately disturbed at this turn of events. An alarming thought then occurred to him. 'I wonder what this means for our two Marlborough students. With Grace Arnold dead and the group of five hikers apparently off the map, I have to wonder if our young couple are in some kind of danger.'

'Or perhaps the reason why these other lads are missing.'

Chase took a moment to digest that. 'You're suggesting either or both might be responsible?'

'Why not? It's something we have to consider. Moreover, why wouldn't they have also been grabbed up if that's what's going on here?'

It was a good question, but Chase thought he had the right response. 'Because they're both on campus,' he said. 'Harder to reach, much harder to extract without being noticed. My point still stands: if they have nothing to do with these disappearances, then they may be next on the list.'

After a moment, Knight said, 'Yes, you're quite right. They remain of interest to our enquiry in my eyes, but equally they might both be the next intended victims. We have to alert the college and their parents.'

'Actually, this may work in our favour,' Chase said. With his free hand, he yanked up his jacket collar to present a buffer against the worst of the chilly wind. 'Knowing their children could be next could just make these parents more co-operative.'

'True. Equally, if they have the wherewithal, it may have the opposite effect. They might withdraw them from campus and isolate them safely at home behind a wall of additional security protection.'

'I think that's a chance we have to take, Nicole. As you pointed out, we can't *not* inform them. The question is, how much do we try to influence them at the same time? If we want access and information, we need to avoid both sets of parents doing as you just described. I'd be in favour of arranging a meeting during which we explain the situation, but without emphasis.'

'Their safety is paramount, Royston. We have no idea what has become of the five young men, and if there's even half a chance of this couple being targeted in the same way then we must err on the side of caution to ensure their well-being.'

'Of course,' Chase said, wondering if the DCI genuinely believed he intended to throw the students under the bus provided he got an interview with them. 'I'm just suggesting we go about it in a casual manner at first. Let's face it, they can be no safer than when they're in a room with us. Plus, as you rightly pointed out, we also must approach it with half an eye on their possible guilt.'

They ended the conversation in full agreement. To his surprise, Knight volunteered to contact the college, in addition to both sets of parents. She told him she was happy to inform them of the latest developments, leaving them to decide on their own reaction rather than trying to steer them one way or the other. She also took it upon herself to call relevant force areas to check on the status of the remaining male hikers. The DCI hoped to have further news at the Monday morning briefing.

By the time their shopping trip was over, the weather had turned bitter, so Chase spent the rest of the day at home watching movies on the Disney channel with Erin and Maisie. His daughter was a huge Pixar fan, and they binged the entire Toy Story catalogue. As much as he tried to relax and enjoy films he usually loved, his wife sensed he was both conflicted and troubled. She mentioned her concerns and asked him to open up after Maisie was fast asleep later that night. He found himself unable to find the exact words to fit his mood.

'I'm feeling a little adrift,' he admitted. 'Like I've slipped an anchor somehow. It's not often that I find myself uncertain as to my next move, but this one has me stumped. While I don't get the sense that these two students have anything to do with Grace Arnold's death or the disappearance of the five male hikers, the fact that they are still out there living their lives leaves their guilt or otherwise open to debate. At the same time, if they're innocent we'd like to protect them, yet for the same reasons we suspect this couple we also want to question them as witnesses. I'm finding it difficult to wrap my head around the whole sorry mess.'

'Why not have a quiet word with Claire? Use her experience and knowhow.'

Chase sighed. 'Because I know what she'd say. She'd be ruthless, mainly because she doesn't have to consider the consequences these days.'

'That's what's holding you back? The potential ramifications?' The surprise in Erin's voice was evident.

'Not in terms of an internal response or reaction,' he explained. 'I'm thinking more about the end result in respect of how it affects our couple. Say they're entirely innocent and my desire to gain information from them leaves them vulnerable and exposed and they go missing, too? That's not something I want on my conscience. But then I think about those missing lads, and I wonder if our students are the only people who can help us identify who might be responsible for their disappearance.'

Erin's eyes sought his own. 'Do you honestly believe that?'

'If they're not involved, then yes I think they might know something useful, even if they're unaware of it without being asked the right questions. It's a nightmare, Erin. Eight young people camped out on Cherhill Down that night in January. One never left. Of those who did, one has almost certainly been abducted, one is missing from home, his whereabouts unknown, while their remaining three friends have also gone off the grid. That leads me to conclude that the remaining two must be able to identify the connection. And we're never going to know if we don't question them again.'

His wife made no response for a few moments. She stroked his arm and nuzzled into his shoulder. Then she pulled back to look up at him. 'Royston, from the way you're speaking, I think you do know how to address your problem. It seems to me you just needed to say it out loud so that you could voice your concerns. The thing is, DCI Knight either has or soon will be informing the college and the parents. You have no influence over their response. Plan for whatever that might be, but don't stress yourself about something over which you have no control.'

'I'm stressed because we have no evidence against them. Not enough to make arrests. We suspect them of knowing more than they've revealed – especially in Isaac Levy's case – but they're not yet suspects in terms of Grace Arnold's murder. I want to be able to use escalation as a threat, to force them to tell us what happened that night as witnesses and not have us look harder at them individually. But the law works in their favour, not ours.'

'Which it has done for your entire career in the job. So why let it anger you now?'

'I'm not angry,' he said. 'I'm frustrated. We're losing traction on this, and I can't help but see these two kids as barriers preventing us from getting to the truth.'

'Then find another way. Or let it go. Reacting the way you are isn't doing you any favours.'

Erin was right. He needed to ask Levy and Cilliers further questions. If there was a different approach, then he had to find it. If not, then he had to be as ruthless as Claire Laney would be. He might not like his choices, and Knight could easily shoot him down in flames either way, but he would eventually have a decision to make which rested on the reactions of others. For the time being, it was out of his hands and his wife deserved his entire presence despite five young men being missing.

And one murdered young woman still in need of justice.

TWENTY

It was four days since he had been taken, and still Gary Elder was having difficulty adjusting to his bitterly cold, austere surroundings. He occupied what might be best described as a 4x3 metre cell, whose ageing brick walls had become darkened and fragile over the years from water leaking through the joints where they met a rough concrete ceiling. An uneven floor, littered with strips of rotting wood, powdery chunks of brick, small slivers of concrete, and mounds of dirt, made it hard on his feet.

A dim caged bulb on the wall above the door bathed him in a bleak glow that was never extinguished. To his amazement, the filthy toilet in the corner still flushed. The hours passed to the tune of a cast-iron radiator clanking and grumbling, though it was barely warm to the touch. He wore only the clothes he'd dressed in the day he'd discovered the masked man inside the flat, and despite the low winter temperatures he'd not been given a blanket to wrap himself in. A low concrete bench supported by four brick pillars provided both his seat and bed, and each night he lay awake shivering as he hugged himself, praying for somebody to end this nightmare.

A nightmare that had begun the moment he'd laid eyes on his girlfriend, swiftly followed by the masked man stepping out into view.

'Do you want her to live?' the man had asked, his voice a deep, low growl that sounded unnaturally forced. Given the level and immediacy of the threat, his mind absurdly imagined the Dark Knight uttering those immortal words: *'I'm Batman'*. Finding himself mute with fear, he gave an urgent nod. *Yes. Yes, of course I want her to live.*

'Do you want your parents to live?'

Another nod, more fervent than the last.

'And your sister?'

Elder found his voice at last. 'Yes. Please, yes. Whatever this is about we can sort it. I want them all to live. Just tell me what you want from me.'

'That's simple enough. Follow every instruction I give you. Say nothing else, do nothing else. Only what I tell you to do.'

'Anything!' Elder said, injecting a pleading edge.

He complied with every subsequent command without further comment.

Shortly after leaving the flat with the man, he clambered into the back of a small van as ordered. He was then handed a rough cloth hood, which he was told to pull over his head. He lay silently on the steel floor panel while it rocked and swayed until, after what felt like hours, the man stopped driving, jumped out of the vehicle and moments later yanked the back doors open.

Stiff and sore from the journey, Elder climbed out and allowed himself to be led a short distance away. The warning reminder was unnecessary, but he grunted and nodded anyway. The ground beneath his feet was irregular, and twice he stumbled blindly. At first, he thought it must be a field, yet every so often he felt something solid but flexible brush against his hands, which he guessed might be branches or shrubbery. He strained to listen, to gain a sense of his surroundings. The breeze upon his exposed flesh ebbed and flowed, as if its passage was being intermittently blocked. The journey was brief, but he knew they were off the beaten track.

They paused briefly, and Elder waited as instructed while the man seemed to busy himself clearing something out of their way. 'Steps going down,' the man said eventually. 'Careful. If you fall, I might just leave you where you lie.'

Twelve treads in all. Solid underfoot. He felt the change wrapping itself around them as they descended; darker, colder, dampness all around, dripping water, the breeze becoming a draught before disappearing altogether. Their footfalls before had been soft and yielding, whereas now they were heavy and echoed back at him through the thick cloth draped across his ears. He heard the heavy groan of rusty hinges unattended for many years. Then a hand was pressed against his back and the man shoved him forward a couple of paces.

'When you hear the door close behind you, you can remove the hood,' the man said.

Elder felt the door move before he heard it.

He'd been allowed to keep his watch, which is how he knew how much time had passed. As for why he'd been brought to this dreadful place, he was none the wiser after four days. His captor came and went daily, bringing sustenance in the form of sandwiches, crisps, and bottled water. The last time, Elder gave in to his baser instincts.

'Why am I here?' he asked, knowing he was begging and not caring about it in the slightest. 'What do you want with me?'

The dark-clad figure paused as he stepped out of the room. He turned, eyes narrowing. 'What did I tell you?'

'I know, I know. I'm sorry. But I don't understand. I...'

The man held up a gloved hand, his index finger raised. 'That's your one chance. Ask me something again without my permission and there will be consequences.'

Elder closed his eyes. Tears squeezed out from between the lids.

Several hours later, and here he was still churning it over. Who on earth would want to punish him this way? What had he ever done to them that was deserving of such harsh treatment? No answers, only questions.

Every so often, he thought he caught hold of a distant sound. One time it was a solid thumping or crashing noise. On a couple of other occasions, it sounded like voices crying out. He'd heard that silence tricked the mind, filled the void by creating sound where none existed. He was certain that was all he was experiencing. He was alone here. Locked up in a brick cell with its steel door and concrete ceiling and rubble floor. Once, he was unable to resist the temptation fuelled by imagination, and had called out, certain that no reply would ever come. None did. There were moments when he questioned his sanity. This kind of thing didn't happen outside of movies, TV, or books. At least, if it did, it happened to other people. People who deserved it, perhaps.

Or people like him, who'd just got unlucky.

It had to be bad luck. That or mistaken identity. Had to be. Nothing he'd ever done in his short life justified this.

Nothing.

TWENTY-ONE

Chase was neither the first nor last to arrive for morning briefing. DCI Knight was standing by a window speaking on her mobile phone. She gave a nod of greeting as he came through the door into the major incident room. He made small talk with a couple of the other team members, but quickly made his way over to the information boards and settled in a nearby chair, both hands wrapped around a mug of hot tea. He zoned out, concentrating on how he wanted the meeting to go. When everybody was in place, Knight excused herself to whoever she'd been chatting to and moved centre stage to address the team.

'Good morning. Many of you here will not be fully up to speed, so let me briefly cover those gaps. Late on Saturday evening we learned that Neville Hutton and Gary Elder might not be the only members of their hiking group to have gone missing last week. Mark Swallow, Mark Viner, and Ashley Robertson ceased all social media communications and have not been contactable since.'

'That's telling,' DC Bowen said over the rim of her coffee cup.

'Indeed, it is. Yesterday I made a few calls, and I just confirmed with relevant force areas that all three are unaccounted for as of last night. I spoke with Foxy and Royston, and we agree that this leaves our two Marlborough students as not only witnesses but also either viable suspects or future victims. As a result, I decided to inform their parents and the college. For obvious reasons, I neglected to mention them being in the frame as potential suspects, but raising the spectre of both possibly living in the crosshairs of a killer did the trick.'

'They agreed?' Efe Salisu said, evident shock etched into her face. 'That does surprise me.'

Knight nodded. 'Me too. Consequently, Mr Levy is travelling to Marlborough today, arriving at around noon. Mr and Mrs Cilliers are abroad but have arranged for a barrister friend of the family to also travel to the college today. I've therefore scheduled two interviews. At twelve-thirty, Royston and DC Laney will meet with Isaac Levy in the presence of his father and, possibly, their solicitor. At two-thirty, they will interview Monica Cilliers and the barrister in the staff meeting room at the college. I determined it was better for DS Chase to be involved with both, considering he has the advantage of having met the two students concerned. It's for us to discuss at this meeting whether these interviews are under caution or not. Thoughts?'

All eyes turned to Chase, who though delighted by the news reacted without emotion. Remaining in his seat, he gave the question some thought before responding. 'I think we have to go into both interviews without formal caution.'

'Good,' Knight said. 'I happen to agree. Explain your own reasoning, please.'

'I think the disadvantages of making it an interview under caution outweigh the advantages. Having met the couple in question, I think it's highly unlikely that either of them is going to trip up if they have something to hide. If I'm right, that negates the issue of not being able to use anything they say against them at a later stage. But the main reason I'm against it is that their parents and representatives, possibly even the students themselves, will immediately realise we suspect them of something. We need to speak to them first and foremost as witnesses, hopefully getting them on the back foot if they refuse to play ball by reminding them they are also likely to be potential victims. I want to keep the advantage on our side for as long as possible.'

'Do you intend to mention your suspicions at all?' DS Jude Armstrong, the case officer, asked. He looked pensive, as if disapproving of the decision.

'Yes, and no. Firstly, it rather depends on what we learn throughout the interview. If it becomes obvious during that phase that neither of them had anything to do with the murder or the recent disappearances, then I can steer clear altogether. But even if what we discover doesn't entirely clear them of all suspicion, I won't be openly challenging them as if they are suspects unless we hit a complete brick wall. I will, however, prod and poke – as far as I can go without reprimand.'

'And if your suspicions go the other way?' DI Fox asked. 'If what they have to say puts them more in the frame in your opinion.'

Chase turned to look at DCI Knight. 'That's something for you to decide, Nicole. You all looked to me earlier wondering which way I was leaning, but the truth is it's not down to me. I'll need to know going in whether I have the authority to apply the caution under those circumstances, because the chances are good that if I do, we'll lose them.'

Knight gave an uneasy smile. 'I had an idea you'd say that, Royston. I think it's best if you and I have a word with Superintendent Waddington. Given who we're dealing with here, it's right that such a decision falls on his shoulders, not ours.'

Chase concurred, adding, 'I'll be as subtle as I can be making the shift from witness to victim to someone under suspicion, but any kind of decent legal representation in the room will spot the ploy and shut it down. I anticipate reaching that stage only if we can't rule this pair out during the initial phase of the interview.'

'Turning the tables on either of these kids by suddenly suspecting them of murder rather than being a witness isn't going to sit well,' Fox observed. 'Not with them or their parents.'

Chase nodded. 'Quite. Don't worry, I won't go there without approval. I might even decide to pull back altogether. Leave it for another day. If they put themselves in the frame, I'm not going to react without having something on them. I'm disappointed by that, but those are the rules, and we have to comply with them.'

'Both of you,' Knight said pointedly. Chase knew she was referring to DC Laney.

'Claire will follow my lead. Listen, none of you know her like I do. Her reputation goes before her. Yes, she can be stroppy and outspoken to the point of being downright rude, but unlike me she does have perfect control of her filter. When she chooses to be obnoxious, then stand back. But when she's working cases, she behaves herself. Believe me, she'll do fine.'

'As you brought it up,' Knight said, 'how do you feel about that filter of yours at the moment?'

'In terms of the interviews?'

The DCI nodded. 'Things could get awkward between you and these students, especially if they fail to respond well to your questioning.'

'I'm fine,' he said dismissively. 'When in doubt, count to ten.'

'Can you be certain of reeling it in when you need to?'

Chase gave a thin smile. 'I'm doing so now, aren't I?'

*

'Everything okay with you, cupcake?' Laney asked him as they headed towards Marlborough. 'Only you seem preoccupied.'

Chase had taken the more circuitous route from town, collecting his DC from Little Soley along the way. After updating her on progress, he'd fallen silent, which he knew could come across as brooding. In truth, he was a little put out after Knight had questioned his ability to function adequately. He understood why colleagues had their reservations about him, especially those whose command he worked under. He nevertheless found it tiresome. But that was his problem, and Laney had her own.

'I'm fine,' he told her. 'Tired, maybe. I had a restless night.'

'How was the rest of your weekend? Family all good?'

'Yes, thanks. Such as it was. You know how it goes, Claire. It's hard to keep our two worlds entirely separate, especially when you're either getting called in to work or the phone is interrupting your home life. How does your husband handle it?'

'Better now the kids are grown and off living their own lives. Having to dump them on him so often when they were younger didn't do us any favours.'

'Tell me about it. On the other hand, he's put up with you all these years, so he must have the patience and fortitude of a saint.'

Laney threw him a withering sidelong glance. 'Thanks for that. You're too kind.'

Laughing, Chase said, 'You are bloody hard work, Claire. Even you admit that. Anyhow, did you two get up to much yesterday?'

'A lazy morning, followed by lunch out, and then a lazier afternoon and evening. We're such a rock 'n roll couple.'

He gave a knowing nod. 'Yeah, us, too. To be honest, if it weren't for Maisie I'd probably have ended up sleeping the day away. As it was, we did a bit of shopping, then pretty much zonked out on the couch. Even had a takeaway for dinner.'

'Is there no end to our revelry and debauchery?' she asked.

'Face it,' he said, 'we party people live high on the hog, and work is our penance.'

Laney's expression turned sour. 'From what you've said, spending more time in the company of that bellend of a professor certainly is.'

Chase nodded. 'The man is a bit up himself.'

The downward turn of his partner's lips became a wicked smile. 'I think we should make the best of a bad hand,' she said. 'When in doubt, go for the throat.'

He made no reply. He was too busy imagining her doing so literally.

TWENTY-TWO

'Ah,' DC Laney said breezily as they entered the grand meeting room in the main Marlborough College building. 'I see we have the law firm of Dewey, Cheetham, and Howe with us today.'

If thunder had a face, it revealed itself on one of the three men currently grouped around Isaac Levy at the pale oak table that functioned as the centrepiece. Laney laughed and said, 'Oh, come on, Mister Lennon,' she said, recognising him from her partner's description. 'A little levity to ease the tension doesn't hurt, does it? You can't fail to break the ice with some Marx brothers' stuff.'

'That's *Professor* Lennon,' the Housemaster said by way of a rebuke, breaking away from the huddle and taking a seat at the table. 'And to be frank, I'm not sure what there is to find humour in.'

Chase waited for everyone to be seated before looking at the man. 'Professor,' he said to gain his attention. 'You're no longer needed as an appropriate adult and are here representing the college as a courtesy we agreed to. So as not to confuse the issue, please move and take a seat at the far end of the table. Oh, and please also remember you're here to observe, not to take part.'

They were not off to a good start. Laney had mildly irked him by kicking off proceedings by going on the charmless offensive, but Lennon's supercilious response riled him more. The frosty glare as the Housemaster changed seats was expected, though Chase ignored it.

'Now that we've settled our seating arrangements, please let me introduce ourselves. I'm Detective Sergeant Royston Chase, and this is my colleague Detective Constable Claire Laney.' He paused, peering at the two men sitting either side of Isaac Levy. 'And you are?'

The man who got to his feet first was tanned and solid-looking, with short brown hair and a square chin. He wore a suit Chase knew was worth more than his own monthly salary, and a silk tie bearing the famous Gucci bee motif. He offered a hand, his grip surprisingly strong. 'Adam Levy, Isaac's father.' He gestured towards the other unknown face in the room. 'We're here today with my solicitor, Gordon Bevel.'

Chase made no mention of Levy having brought legal representation with him. It was what you did when you had money to burn and a family name to protect. The brief looked every bit as well-fed, well-heeled, and well-bred as Levy himself. Bevel stood to shake hands, speaking only after dropping back down into his chair.

'Good afternoon, detectives.' He nodded at both Chase and Laney. 'My client and his son have agreed to this interview in good faith. I'm here to ensure that same probity is extended reciprocally to Isaac.'

With a nod, Chase said, 'Naturally. So let me begin by saying Isaac's integrity was never in doubt. It was Professor Lennon who insisted we bring our previous chat to an abrupt ending, not your son.'

'I did so because you were stepping beyond the limits of our original agreement, Constable,' Lennon said defensively.

'That's *Sergeant*,' Chase said, fixing the Housemaster with his own chilly stare. 'And please, let that be your last interruption. Observe and not speak, remember. Those were our conditions.'

Having reasserted his own authority, Chase took a breath. 'Let's take some pressure out of the room,' he then said. 'Mr Levy, Mr Bevel, I can assure you that our questions are intended to be benign. For the sake of one murdered young woman and five young men whose current whereabouts are unknown, our intention is to get to the bottom of this mystery. Now, when we last spoke with Isaac, we established that both he and his girlfriend, Monica Cilliers, had spent the evening drinking in the Black Horse pub at Cherhill with the group of people I've just mentioned. All we want from this interview is to explore that more fully. It's not new ground at all, as the Professor implied when he spoke to you on Saturday. It's merely a continuation of our original line of questioning.'

Mr Levy glanced across at his solicitor, who shrugged and gave a single nod. Levy then nodded himself. 'Please,' he said. 'Ask away.'

Chase thanked him and turned his attention to the boy. 'Good to see you again, Isaac,' he said. 'I imagine you've had plenty of time to consider this, so hopefully you have some answers for us today. I want to start with the transition between the pub and Cherhill Down. That is where you and Monica spent the night, yes?'

His change of tack owed much to the people in the room. Catching Levy out in a lie might have worked two days ago, but if he sought to do so at this stage the solicitor might start to get the impression that this meeting was designed to obtain more than a mere witness statement.

The lad took a few seconds, but eventually nodded.

Chase smiled and continued. 'There were eight of you that night: a young female solitary hiker by the name of Grace Arnold, you and Monica, plus five other males in their late teens or early twenties. Which of you suggested you all camp for the night on the Downs?'

Levy cleared his throat. 'I… I honestly can't recall. We'd been drinking, having a laugh together. We had a similar interest in hiking and camping, so we were getting along well. I don't know… I suppose opting to camp together was just a natural extension of the evening.'

'Why Cherhill Down, Isaac? Why that particular location?'

'I'm not sure. It was close by. And I think either Grace or perhaps the guys were already camped up there, so the rest of us decided to join them.'

'I see. And what time did you leave the pub that night?'

'Around closing time.'

'So elevenish, there or thereabouts?'

'Something like that, yes.'

Chase frowned. 'In your experience, Isaac, is it unusual for hikers to set up camp so late in the day when it's pitch-black out?'

'Hold on a moment,' Gordon Bevel, the solicitor, said. 'You're asking Isaac to speak for other people rather than relying on his own account.'

'Actually, I'm not.' Chase met the man's gaze. 'First, I asked him to tell me about his experience. Second, this *was* actually Isaac's experience that very night.'

'How have you reached that conclusion?' Bevel asked.

'Because if Isaac and Monica were already camped on the Downs, Isaac would surely have mentioned it when he had the opportunity. In fact, he clearly stated that it must have been either Grace Arnold or the group of lads who were already located on that hillside. Personally, it makes more sense to me that you would set up camp before going for food and drink so as not to have to lug your tent and gear around with you. Also to avoid setting everything up in the dark while under the influence of alcohol.'

The solicitor gave it a moment, before turning to both Adam and Isaac Levy and nodding.

'Thank you,' Chase said, his attention returning to the boy. 'Isaac?'

He left it there. No need to push or ask the question again. Let the lad think about it. Let him sweat over it if he had good reason to.

'I remember now,' Isaac said, rolling his eyes as if chastising himself for his poor memory. 'It was Grace who was already camped on the hillside. The lads had also made camp somewhere not far away, while Monica and I hadn't made up our minds about what to do that night. We had considered trying to get a room as it looked like it might snow.'

Chase nodded as if the explanation made sense. 'So, what happened? How did you all wind up sleeping in the same location?'

'There was some talk about carrying on with a few more beers and perhaps something stronger. I think the lads also had a bottle of JD. A party sounded like fun, so Monica and I tagged along.'

'You're saying the lads offered to share their beer and Jack Daniels with you, then struck their camp and moved it all up onto the Downs? Is that about right, Isaac?'

'Yes. Yes, that's how I remember it. I'm sorry, it's all still a little sketchy.'

'Okay. So, you're all up there together, the eight of you, you have a party, get a few more drinks inside you, and then what?'

'We crashed out. We went our separate ways, crept into our tents, and that was it for the rest of the night.'

'How separate?' Laney asked. She was taking notes, but at this she looked up. 'By that I mean, how far apart were your tents?'

It was an insightful question, Chase thought. The distance between the individuals could play a prominent role in what they saw or overheard.

Levy shook his head. 'I'm not really sure. All of us pitched our tents inside the thicket, that I do remember. It was bitterly cold that night, the wind was getting up, and we all thought it was going to snow. Even the bare trees offered some form of shelter from the worst of it.'

'That sounds sensible. But presumably you were close enough to each other that you would have noticed, or at least heard something if there had been a disturbance.'

'I… I guess so. But we were all pretty wrecked by then.'

'Are you saying you neither saw nor heard a commotion of any kind?'

'No. Nothing comes to mind.'

'And in the morning?' Chase asked.

'What about it?'

'How was everybody the following morning? Despite being hungover, of course.' He smiled, but kept his keen focus on the boy's facial expressions and eyes.

'I have no idea. Monica and I were the first to wake up and emerge from inside our tent. We made ourselves some tea, and by the time we'd finished and washed up nobody else had stirred. We decided to leave them to it and go on our way. As predicted, the snow had come during the early hours, and the entire hillside was white.'

Chase nodded. 'I see. So, after spending the whole evening with these people, and enjoying their company enough to extend your time together and have a party, you didn't hang around to say goodbye?'

'Like I said, they weren't even stirring, and we wanted to be on our way.'

'Where to?'

'Sorry?'

'I mean, where did you head next? Why did you feel you needed to head off there and then?'

'Oh, I see what you mean. We had no actual destination in mind. Monica and I didn't walk trails as such. We dipped in and out occasionally, but mostly made our own way depending on how we felt on the day.'

'So, where did you go? Where did you stay the following night?'

In his peripheral vision, Chase noticed the solicitor tense and lean forward. Before any objection could be voiced, he raised a hand and said, 'Forget that, Isaac. It's not relevant to what happened on the night in question. Instead, let me ask this: did you exchange contact details with anybody that night? Swap phone numbers, email addresses, social media information?'

'I think we'd planned to do all that the following morning, but it never happened.'

'I see.' The boy continued to look skittish, his eyes darting everywhere but directly at Chase. It felt like more than nerves from being questioned by the police. Isaac Levy was hiding something. 'Thank you for being so honest with us. A couple of final points, Isaac. First, before leaving that morning, did you notice anything at all suspicious? Was anything out of place? Disturbed? Any sign of something significant having happened there while you were asleep?'

'No. Not that I can recall.'

It was the answer he'd expected. Unequivocal, followed immediately by an equivocal. They'd definitely not noticed anything untoward… at least as far as he was able to remember.

'Fair enough. Final question, then: you and Monica are Marlborough students, presumably frequenting the local pubs and restaurants and coffee bars. Towards the end of January, police officers asked questions locally, distributed flyers showing Grace Arnold's photograph, concerned for her welfare having gone missing. You weren't aware of this? Monica never mentioned it to you?'

Without hesitation, Levy said, 'Of course not. Either of us would have recognised Grace and come forward immediately.'

'That's good to know,' Laney jumped in. 'It's what we'd expect from a decent person and upright citizen, but you'd be surprised at how often people don't do the right thing.'

'My son was raised to do just that,' Adam Levy said. He turned to the boy. 'Isaac, if there's anything else you can think of, please tell these two detectives. For the sake of your studies, this needs to be put to bed.'

'There is nothing else, Dad.' He spread his hands. 'Honestly.'

Not true, Chase thought. The boy's eyes and body language told him Isaac was lying to his father. And to them. But lying to cover up a murder he had committed, or something he had either seen or knew about? He let a few beats drift by, contemplating. His every instinct told him to go harder at the boy, but although his anxiety showed through, Isaac Levy was not on the verge of breaking. Taking matters further at this stage would serve no purpose, other than to warn Mr Levy and their solicitor that the police suspected the boy of being more than a mere witness to the events of that night. With some reluctance, he called a halt to proceedings and thanked everybody for attending.

TWENTY-THREE

They had half an hour to wait between interviews and spent it discussing strategy. Laney thought she had an angle on how they might approach the next encounter.

'The pair of them have had two days to get their stories straight,' she pointed out. 'I think it's safe to say that a well-drilled response is going to come across as... rehearsed. Isaac had to *recall* a couple of things differently in response to our questions, which means Monica will probably give us the same initial responses he did. If that's the way it pans out, we can go at her with both the inconsistencies and the similarities. The first for being exactly the same kind of incorrect as him, but also for being too precisely the same.'

Chase nodded in appreciation of his partner's suggestion. 'Sounds like a shrewd tactic. We slam through the questions, then pick apart her answers one by one. Before we do battle once more, what was your general impression of Isaac Levy?'

Laney had no need to hesitate. 'The poor little diddums is scared. A decent bluffer in terms of being able to think on his feet, but too evasive in the way he physically backs off from the questioner. Shifty too, glancing away all the time.'

'Yes. The physical confrontation is too much for him. His brain ticks along just fine, but he's intimidated. Seeing him again, I'm convinced he knows more than he's told us.'

'I agree. Perhaps Monica can help us out with that.'

Professor Lennon sat in once more, choosing to completely ignore the two police officers when he stepped back into the room. Monica Cilliers' legal representative introduced himself as Julian Millner, a London-based barrister and close friend of the family. He spent a few minutes going over the scope of the interview, intent on letting the detectives know he was on the ball and would step in if either of them transgressed. Once again, Chase was left to ponder how far to push the envelope. He wanted nothing left unasked, but neither did he want the girl to know she was even remotely suspected of wrongdoing.

The first phase went the way Chase and Laney had imagined. Cilliers gave the same answers to the same questions, falling down in the same areas and having to scramble for solutions. As with Levy, any lapses mostly came down to memory.

'That's all very interesting,' Chase said when they were done. 'But how about telling us again, only this time in your own words.'

'I don't know what you mean,' the girl said without a flicker of emotion.

'I think you do, Monica. You see, in our experience when responses sound overly rehearsed, we have to ask ourselves why. Your replies pretty much replicate those we got from Isaac.'

'What else would you expect?' Lennon snapped. 'They experienced precisely the same events, so surely it makes absolute sense if they have the same recollections.'

Chase turned his head, scowling. 'That's your final warning, Professor. One more interruption and you're out of here.'

The man reacted, his cheeks reddening. 'I beg your pardon! I'd remind you that you are asking questions of a Marlborough College student inside the Marlborough College staff meeting room. This is my domain, Sergeant, not yours.'

Chase stared the man down. 'And I'd remind you that the interview itself is our domain, not yours. I didn't want you in the room at all, so you're here under sufferance. My DCI persuaded me to let you to sit in on behalf of your college, but don't outstay your welcome by butting in. You have no voice here, Professor Lennon.'

Beside him, DC Laney ran her thumb and forefinger across her lips to suggest the Housemaster keep his mouth zipped. Chase forced back a laugh and contented himself with a smile only.

'Look,' he said. 'There's no need for this nonsense. Professor, you're doing your duty by being present and monitoring what we say. You are fully aware that you have no right to interject, and I would ask that you comply.'

'I will,' Lennon said, sullenly. 'Grudgingly. But you must also stick to your part of the agreement as well.'

'I'm sure Mr Millner would have spoken up if he thought we were out of line. That's his role here today, not yours.'

Chase waited for everybody to settle back down before continuing with his questions. 'As I was about to say, Monica, telling the truth requires no rehearsal. I'm not suggesting you lied to us, nor that you and your boyfriend conspired in any way, but it's possible that in going over everything that happened with Isaac your individual recollections became a single response. I want to go back over a couple of things, and this time I want you to think hard about your own personal experiences that night. Okay?'

The girl nodded. She seemed mentally composed and physically relaxed, though her lips were firmly pressed together.

'Once more, then. Our understanding is that Grace Arnold was the only one of your group to actually have made camp on Cherhill Down by the time you all met up in the pub. Is that correct?'

'As far as I can recall, yes.'

The brief statement had a familiar ring to it. 'As far as you can recall. Okay. In which case, I'll ask again, how did you all come to end up camping in the same location? Who suggested it?'

Cilliers shook her head this time. 'I genuinely don't know. That is, I can't remember. One moment we were knocking back our drinks prior to the pub closing, and the next we were joining everyone on the Downs. It just sort of happened.'

'Hmm. You see, that's what Isaac told us. He used pretty much those exact same words, in fact. I find it odd that neither of you can recall who decided to spend the night camped out on a freezing cold night in January with heavy snow about to fall.'

'It happens. When there's a whole bunch of you, sometimes you just get swept up in groupthink. We're not great organisers, we just go along with things.'

Chase wasn't buying it, but he moved on. 'All right, let me take you back to later that same night and then the following morning. You neither saw nor heard anything untoward? Nothing that troubled you? No yells or cries of alarm? No sound of disturbance, a quarrel, a fight of some kind?'

'No,' she said emphatically. 'We zonked out as soon as we settled inside our tent. I think it would have taken an earthquake to wake us. But we were the first ones up and about, and after making tea, Isaac suggested we slip away. He said he couldn't remember much and wanted to go in case we'd said or done anything embarrassing. Like you do when you're piss… sorry, drunk.'

'And nobody came out of their tents while you had your tea, nor while you were packing up your gear?'

'No. Nobody emerged, nobody stirred. You have to remember, we didn't jam our tents close together. Grace was on one side of the copse, we were pretty much on the other side, and the boys were spread out across the middle. Some of them we couldn't even see.'

Chase wondered if that was a line rehearsed but forgotten by Levy, or a genuine recollection that had just occurred to Monica Cilliers. Either way, it was something new. If the girl was telling the truth, their view of Grace Arnold's tent would have been obscured by trees and undergrowth, no matter how skeletal at that time of year. It led him to pose a new question.

'Tell me, Monica, you say the lads were camped between yourselves and Grace. Do you happen to remember whose tent was closest to hers?'

A shake of the head. 'No. Sorry. We really didn't take any notice.'

Chase glanced to his left. Laney caught it and nodded. She was happy enough with how things had gone and had no questions of her own to ask. It seemed to him that they had covered everything. Both Levy and Cilliers agreed on all the salient points, and while he suspected that was mainly due to them having gone over the story to resolve any discrepancies, there were no glaring lies or omissions. Their version of events had them joining together with fellow hiking enthusiasts for the night and leaving them to their own devices the following morning. He saw no gaps to prise open with additional questioning in reference to the night they believed Grace Arnold was murdered. That left recent events, something he'd raised but not pushed with Isaac Levy.

'Finally, then, Monica,' he said. 'Let's talk about afterwards. You spent an entire evening in the pub with a group of people, then partied with them into the early hours of the morning. You must have exchanged information with some of them. Their phone numbers, perhaps email addresses. Something, surely?'

Cilliers shook her head, curls bobbing. 'It wasn't like that. More like ships in the night. We had a few drinks and a few laughs. I suppose if we'd seen any of them the following morning, we might have done as you suggested when we said goodbye, but that's not what happened.'

'And during that entire time together, neither you nor Isaac took a selfie? I find that especially unusual.'

The girl gave a haughty sniff. 'Not for us. We're not exactly selfie people. Have a look at our social media accounts, Sergeant Chase. That's just not who we are.'

Unlike her boyfriend, the girl had taken the interview in her stride. But the young couple had used similar phrases when describing the events, which bothered him. He realised he might be seeing things that weren't there. Perhaps it was perfectly natural for two young people to get their stories straight ahead of an interview, even if only as witnesses. Cilliers came across well, and taking everything at face value he had to admit that this particular reservoir of information was probably now dry.

TWENTY-FOUR

Chase opted not to drive all the way out to Gablecross on the other side of Swindon. Before reporting back on their findings, he wanted time to mull over his impressions and discuss them with Laney. He was therefore disappointed to discover both DCI Knight and Superintendent Waddington waiting for them in his office at the Little Soley police station. Waddington immediately dismissed Claire, apologising to her and citing the need for an urgent senior management meeting. The DC showed her indifference with a mute shrug as she turned and walked away to join Alison May in the reception area.

'I thought you were going to control her,' Waddington said brusquely, turning to Chase when it was just the three of them shut away in the office.

'What do you mean?' Chase asked, genuinely puzzled.

'I think you know very well what I mean, Sergeant. The way I hear it, your partner openly mocked those waiting for you in the room upon arrival.'

'Oh, that? It was nothing. It's not her fault they'd made a pact with the Devil to trade their sense of humour along with their souls. She made a joke to lighten the mood. The fact that any of them complained about it says more about them than it does Claire.'

'You would say that. I hear you also got under the Housemaster's skin.'

Chase realised that Lennon must have called in a complaint during the interview break. He huffed out a deep sigh of annoyance. 'The man couldn't stop interrupting. We agreed he could observe, not take part. I was polite but firm the first time I had to speak to him about interfering. Admittedly, I wasn't quite so respectful the second time. If you ask me, the whining little shit needs to get over himself.'

'Okay, okay,' DCI Knight said, adding some edge to her voice. 'What's done is done. The purpose of this meeting is to exchange updates and strategise. I suggest we move on.'

Without waiting for confirmation from the DSI, Chase said, 'In truth, we didn't get a great deal further. The pair of them had clearly agreed on a story and a strategy, and for the most part it worked for them. Even so, we were able to confirm that both camped on the hillside on the night of Friday the thirteenth of January. That's crucial to establish because it's the night we believe Grace Arnold was murdered.'

'I'm not aware of pathology confirming that,' Waddington said, looking nonplussed.

Chase shook his head. 'They haven't, and they won't. Speaking to Ray Petchey, he's unable to narrow the window to a precise date or time. Other evidence points to that Friday night as being the most likely, but there will be no confirmation from Ray. On the other hand, those we question won't be aware of that.'

Nicole Knight betrayed her disappointment with a soft groan. 'Lacking a verified time of death is something we're going to have to address at a later date. For the time being, we work with what we do have and hope the rest of the pieces fall into line. But our existing information at least tells us this group of eight people spent that one specific night together.'

'They also confessed to having a boozy party up there after closing time at the pub,' Chase said.

'But neither admitted to knowing what happened to Arnold?'

'No. My impression of them remains the same: Monica Cilliers appears not to know anything about what happened that night. And while Isaac Levy demonstrates specific tics associated with anxiety and fear, I didn't see enough to suggest the boy was a killer. I still believe he knows something. I'm just not sure what that might be.'

'So, are we ruling them out?' Waddington asked.

'Not entirely, sir.'

'How about as potential victims?'

Chase nodded. 'At the conclusion of both interviews, I spoke more generally. I told them that we'd been unable to contact the five young lads, with one reported missing and another apparently abducted from his home in the days since the discovery of Grace Arnold's body. I let them draw their own conclusions.'

'The result of which was?'

'For the time being, both students will continue to live on campus. Staff have agreed to increase vigilance when it comes to visitors, and both Isaac and Monica are content to dig in at Preshute House so that they can remain together.'

'And your overall conclusions?' Waddington asked him.

'I've thought of little else since we left the college. A couple of things bother me. In this technological age, the lack of photos, social media updates, and exchange of information pertaining to that night doesn't sit right. Cilliers provided a perfectly acceptable explanation, but it's still unusual where people of their age are concerned. Also, it seems odd to me that with the others set to take on the next stage of their hike, it was the two with no real plans who set off first and without a word to those they left behind.'

'What do you think happened, Royston?'

Chase shrugged, annoyed with himself that they were still running to stand still. 'I don't know. If they're guilty of something or witnessed something, it's more likely that they rose early and crept away having decided not to encounter anyone else that morning. It's just a minor detail that feels a bit off. Nothing I can go back at them with, that's for sure. That line of questioning is now exhausted. But we know where to find them.'

'It sounds to me as if our focus ought to be elsewhere from this point on,' Waddington said. He looked at DCI Knight. 'Nicole?'

DCI Knight looked up from the policy notes she had been compiling. 'Thank you, sir. While you and Claire were interviewing the students, Royston, we put in some time on the phones and online. Regards persons of interest, we've spoken to local police in Devon, who will begin looking more closely at Grace Arnold's brother and her boyfriend. The revenge motive factor in respect of the missing group of lads is evident, so the starting point will be to identify their whereabouts last week. Once they've been located, they'll be questioned about Grace, their relationships, and what they knew about the hikes. We have our suspicions, but neither are obvious suspects at this moment. We hope to have phone data later today or tomorrow.'

'It would make sense for it to be one of them in terms of motive,' Chase allowed. 'But the biggest issue against that is how either of them could possibly have known about the five hikers, let alone manage to identify and locate them. We know Grace couldn't have told them.'

'But do we?' Knight asked, looking between the two men. 'Grace Arnold wasn't seen alive after that Friday night in mid-January, but that doesn't prove conclusively that she was dead.'

'We had to narrow down the timeline,' Chase argued. 'I realise the PM was of little help, with a window of at least seventy-two hours, but I'm confident Grace never left that hillside.'

'I understand that. But what if she did, albeit briefly? What if Grace used a public phone to call her brother or her boyfriend to tell them about the evening in the pub, or the party afterwards? Perhaps something happened later on that she felt she had to confess to or talk about. She could have mentioned the five lads then. For all we know, Grace knew more about the lads than Isaac or Monica claim to.'

Chase found himself nodding. 'I suppose it's possible that one of them tried it on with her. She then got scared, needed to confide in somebody. I follow the logic, Nicole, and I'm not saying it's impossible. Just unlikely if we go by the fact that we have zero sightings of her afterwards. However, we can't ignore it. It is the most realistic way for either the brother or the boyfriend to have known about the group of lads. And while we can't ask Grace herself, what we can do is find the closest public phones and see if anybody made a call on Saturday, and to whom.'

'Gathering in all the mobile data will be useful, too,' Waddington suggested. 'Grace Arnold didn't have her own phone with her, but who's to say she didn't borrow one that night to make a call?'

'We'll get on it,' Knight agreed with a firm nod. 'Outside of those who were on the hill that night, Grace's brother and boyfriend are definitely in the frame. Any other alternatives at this stage?'

'Something did just occur to me,' Chase said, still thinking it through. 'Gary Elder's confrontation with a masked individual led to a likely abduction. We can't locate the other four. So far, we've thought of them all as victims, possibly out of revenge for Grace's murder. But what if they're not? Not all of them, at least? It's possible that one or more of them hurt or murdered Grace Arnold, and that whoever did so is making sure nobody talks to us about it.'

Waddington turned to Chase. 'You mean one of those lads may not be missing because he was abducted like Gary Elder. He's missing because he's the one doing the abducting?'

Chase nodded, breathing heavily with renewed excitement. 'Yes, sir. That's precisely what I mean.'

TWENTY-FIVE

It had been the man's usual practice to come and go in silence, dropping off food and water and moving on as quickly as he had come. Unwilling to engage in conversation, and threatening punishment if you tried. Clearly, he wanted something, but worked to his own schedule.

This time began in the customary way: a heavy bolt being thrown back followed by the shriek of unoiled hinges. Elder looked up fearfully as the door opened all the way and the man entered the cell. In the dim light, it looked as if there were no eye holes in the heavy woollen balaclava concealing the figure's face, but he caught a vibrant glimmer shining out as if about to pierce his very soul. As before, the man set down a wrapped sandwich, a packet of crisps, and a bottle of still water. But unlike his previous visits, he did not immediately withdraw from the room.

Instead he remained standing, staring down at Elder who sat on the hard bench.

'What do you know about Grace Arnold?' the man asked him.

Arnold? Grace Arnold?

'I… I don't know who that is,' Elder said truthfully.

'That's not an acceptable answer.'

'Wait, what? Seriously, I don't know any Grace Arnold. You've got the wrong person.'

Hope shone a dim blush over his plight. If this man had taken him by mistake, then maybe there was a way out of this. Whatever *this* was.

After a moment of uneasy silence, the man spoke again.

'You're telling me the name Grace Arnold means nothing to you?'

'No. Look, you have to believe me. I don't know her.'

'In that case, think back. And think harder. You and your friends camped overnight on Cherhill Down. With you was a frail young blonde, hiking on her own, spending the night up there with you all.'

Elder swallowed. The faint spark of reprieve swiftly became smothered by darkness, before being snuffed out entirely as if by two moist fingers on the flickering flame of a candle. His mind hummed, churning tumultuously as he reflected on that night and how each subsequent event had somehow led to his incarceration. His captor had already demonstrated a willingness to act with conviction and was clearly capable of much more. Antagonising the man further could only lead to additional misery, but Elder knew he had to play this just right. If he did… he might yet emerge from his ordeal in one piece.

'Yes,' he admitted. 'Okay, yes. I'd forgotten her name. You have to believe me. I remember now that she was called Grace, but out of context the name meant nothing to me when you mentioned it. But I do remember her. And I remember that night.'

'Good. Tell me about it.'

Elder gave a wistful sigh. 'What is there to tell? We met her in the pub, we later joined her on the hillside. We had a few drinks together and a laugh and that was it.'

'And then what?'

'And then… nothing. We left the following morning.'

'Is that right? And nothing else happened? Nothing at all? Nothing… memorable?'

'No. Like I say, we had a few laughs, got a bit drunk, conked out, and that was it.'

'That's all you have to say for yourself? That's everything?'

'Yes. Absolutely. Why are you even asking me about that night? About her?'

The man edged a step closer, looming over him. 'Are you asking the questions now, Gary? You think you're in any position to be asking *me* questions?'

'No, no. Sorry. I just…'

'You just what?'

'I just don't know what any of this is about and you're intimidating me for no reason.'

'We'll see about that. But I have to wonder why you haven't mentioned the college students who also joined you that night.'

'Those two? Because you never asked. Yes, me and my friends, the two students, and this Grace girl, all camped out for the night beneath the trees on Cherhill Down. It was snowing, it was bloody freezing, but we had a good time and got tanked up. That's it. Honestly, that's all that happened. Look, is somebody saying otherwise? Is that what all this is about?'

The man took another step closer, bunching his hand into a fist. 'Was that another question for me, Gary? I do hope not.'

'I'm sorry. Okay, I'm really sorry. I'm just frightened and confused by all that's happened, and I don't know what any of it is about.'

'What it's about, Gary,' the man said, his voice deeper and more considered this time, 'is that I know what happened that night. And right now I need to know precisely what you know. But you're not telling me everything, which means I have to come at this in a very different way. I'm leaving for the time being. But I'll be back. I suggest you think on while I'm gone, because next time I ask you the same question you'd better have a different answer for me. Believe me, you'll regret it if you don't, because I can be persuasive when I have to be.'

TWENTY-SIX

THE WAITING GAME WAS the one aspect of every investigation that Chase hated most of all. It wasn't about inertia; they always had something to follow up on, somebody new to talk to, calls to make, discussions to have, online searches to navigate through. No, it was the time he had no control over, whether that was waiting for forensics, telephone data, CCTV footage, or people to trace. When one or more of those overlapped, it could feel like an eternity between breaks in the case.

It was Tuesday morning. He, Laney, and May worked tirelessly on their own actions, but the calls they were waiting for became the most powerful presence in the room, clouding the atmosphere and putting each of them on edge.

The previous afternoon, the emergency senior management meeting had ended in accord. DCI Knight and her team were to continue focussing on the group of five lads, while the Little Soley contingent pursued leads relating to Grace Arnold. They expected an intersect between the two lines of investigation at some stage, and each knew how to react and what procedure to follow when it did.

When, at shortly after 10.00am, Chase's mobile rang, he felt the weight of four eyes fixed upon him from the time he slid the green receive icon up on his screen.

'Detective Sergeant Chase,' he said, using his full rank to buy time to gather himself before listening to what he hoped might be good news. It was DC Bowen, and to his chagrin she sounded glum.

'Hi there, Royston. Rather than waiting for everything to come in, I thought I'd put you out of your misery on what we've learned so far. To begin with, the search on public phones close to Cherhill came up blank. Literally, in this instance, as there are no longer any working public phones in the area. There are a couple in the centre of Calne which are in service on and off, but no calls were made from either box.'

'Makes sense,' Chase said, though he'd been desperate for a lead. 'People barely even use their landlines anymore. Most phone boxes I've seen around are either wrecked or have been put to good use as mini libraries.'

'Precisely. It's a shame, but it was always a stretch. Anyhow, we also have mobile phone data back. Now, you asked about any link between the five missing lads and Grace Arnold's brother or boyfriend, and I'm sorry to say we drew a blank there as well.'

'Damn!' That one stung. To him it suggested there was no way anyone associated with Grace Arnold could have known about the group of boys, much less locate them in order to plan a series of abductions. 'That all sucks, if I may say so. I do hope you have something positive for me, Paige.'

'Well, I certainly have something for you. Just not quite sure what it means. We ran the data, and I can confirm that their phones all went dead at or around the times they dropped off the social media grid. However, there's something interesting in Ashley Robertson's records. On Thursday morning, he sent a text to both Marks. I'll ping it all over to you, obviously, but this is what his message said: *Meet me in the Red Lion car park. Get there now. You know what it's about.*'

'That was it? Just the name of the pub, not where?'

'That was the message, verbatim. However, corresponding GPS coordinates for both Marks and Robertson's phones forty-five minutes later has all three in a place called Milton Bryan, which happens to have a pub called the Red Lion.'

This was better. The development excited Chase, and he felt a familiar rush. 'Oh, good work, Paige. You played a blinder there. It must be a haunt they all know, and maybe have even met at before. What does GPS have to tell us about their movements afterwards?'

'Nothing. That's why I'm not exactly doing a jig. That same spot is the last GPS locator for all three of them.'

'Did all three have driving licences and own motors?'

'They certainly did. And I'm way ahead of you there, Royston. We had a local traffic vehicle stop off at the coordinates we provided them with. They discovered all three vehicles parked up on a road not far from the pub. I'm guessing the lads realised abandoning vehicles in its car park would attract attention, if only from the owner or landlord.'

Chase closed his eyes, trying to determine what this news meant for their case. Paige Bowen sneaked into the void of silence he'd created. 'Listen, Royston, I realise that's not what we were hoping for. But we'll scrutinise the data between all five lads and see what picture emerges. If we spot anything at all that helps you, or us for that matter, I'll send it across to you in a mail. Five phones leaves us a lot to work with, so it's going to take time to establish their movements and behaviour patterns. It'll require patience on our part, but the trawl might jog something loose.'

'Okay. You can run this by DCI Knight if you need to, but I'm in favour of vehicle forensics taking a look at those motors and putting lumps on them.'

'You want tracking devices fitted?' Bowen sounded surprised.

'I do. In case any of the lads return but don't have their usual phones on for GPS monitoring to tell us. I think it's worth the risk.'

He thanked her, ended the conversation before she could argue, and then turned to his two immediate colleagues. After walking them through each element of his exchange, Laney was the first to react by making a suggestion. 'You previously raised the question about whether one of those five lads was responsible for abducting the others. This text message and the subsequent meeting points a big finger of suspicion at Ashley Robertson, wouldn't you say? He lured Mark Swallow and Mark Viner to that pub, and nobody has seen or heard of them since.'

'I admit it looks bad for him,' Chase admitted. He sucked air between his teeth. 'On the other hand, all we know at this stage is that Robertson's phone was used. We don't know it was him who sent the message. Nor do we know if all three of them simply chose to go on the run together.'

'But what Claire suggested makes sense,' Alison May said, a worried frown on her face. 'Especially given his car was found along with theirs.'

'Sure. But just as we can't know for certain that he used his own phone to lure them, neither can we know for certain that it was him who drove to the pub.'

'CCTV,' Laney said urgently. She held up both hands, palms up. 'If the Red Lion has surveillance in the car park, it might give us something.'

'But they found the cars nearby, not in the pub,' May argued.

'I know. But that doesn't mean that's where they met. Remember, Ashley's message told them to meet him in the car park, so they would initially have driven into it. If he did as well, before they all moved their motors afterwards, then we may catch sight of him.' She turned to face Chase. 'What do you think, Royston?'

He gave her question a moment of thought. 'I think there are numerous possibilities. But before we consider the alternatives, let's work on the basis that this was Ashley and that he did draw them into that car park. I know I was the one who raised the awkward possibility of it not being him, but we can't simply presume it's somebody else posing as Ashley to manoeuvre the two Marks into a single location, and we can't assume they never went into the car park. We do the necessary grunt work and hope that gives us the answers we're looking for.'

TWENTY-SEVEN

NINETEEN-YEAR-OLD ASHLEY ROBERTSON LIVED with his parents in West Dunstable, a short walk from the town cricket club. Chase decided to deepen TDC May's experience, so the three Little Soley detectives drove up together. He spent much of the journey contemplating how to approach the conversation ahead. If the boy was not Grace Arnold's killer, he was at the very least a likely witness to her murder. The confused status made the interview more unpredictable than Chase preferred, which set him on edge.

The family home was one of fourteen semi-detached properties in a row surrounded by vast fields, with the cricket pitches directly opposite. It was a long drive, and because they were not interviewing a suspect, Chase had called before setting off to arrange an appointment. He pulled into the driveway ten minutes ahead of schedule, having made good time by avoiding the clogged motorways. The boy's mother, Cheryl, greeted them warmly and immediately set about making hot drinks. She also brought in a plate of warm, homemade chocolate brownies, which made Chase feel like a fraud. He'd led the woman to believe the police were there solely to help find her son, and he felt a pang of guilt because that was not the case.

Following a brief exchange of introductions and pleasantries, he explained in more detail the reason for their visit. 'I apologise for any misunderstanding, Mrs Robertson,' he said. 'Your son's continued absence is still being investigated by local police. We are in contact with them, and I can assure you we are offering our full assistance. However, we three are focussing our specific interests on events leading up to Ashley's disappearance.'

Perching on the very edge of her chair, the woman's expression immediately became crestfallen. 'So, you're not actively involved in looking for my son?'

'Yes, we are. But he's just one of several people we'd like to talk to in connection with our own ongoing investigation. Hopefully, all will become much clearer as we proceed. If not, please feel free to ask any questions you might have.'

Chase handed over to Claire Laney to begin the meeting more formally. 'First of all, thank you for agreeing to meet with us, Mrs Robertson,' she said, biting into one of the brownies. 'Mmm. These are delicious, by the way. Look, I realise you will have already spoken to local police about Ashley, but we're here to broaden the scope a little. Please, tell me, has anybody notified you about the discovery of your son's car in Milton Bryan earlier today?'

'Yes, I got a call not long after I spoke with Sergeant Chase to arrange this meeting.'

'Good. If it's any consolation, they do seem to be on the ball. Is the Red Lion one of your lad's regular drinking holes?'

A short and slight woman with a haggard appearance and sorrowful expression, Cheryl Robertson shook her head. 'Not at all. Not that I'm aware. It's a good twenty-minute drive, so not much use if you want to have more than a pint. We have been there for Sunday lunch on a couple of occasions, but I don't think Ash drinks there often.'

'Not to worry. Do the names Mark Swallow or Mark Viner mean anything to you?' Laney asked, changing course.

'Oh, yes. Both. I wouldn't describe them as friends, mind, but I'm pretty sure those are two of Ash's hiking buddies. Why are you asking about them?'

'Police found their vehicles parked next to your son's. Can you think of any reason why Ashley might have wanted to meet with them last week?'

'I don't think so. Not unless they were planning another hike.'

'But he didn't mention having arranged to meet with them before he went out that day?'

'No. That's not to say he hadn't made the arrangement. I don't know if you have teenagers of your own, but they don't always think to include their parents in their plans. We're always pretty much the last people to find out what he was getting up to.'

Laney allowed a thin smile. 'Forgive me if I'm going over old ground, my love. I'm sure the locals will have already asked you this, but was Ashley attending college or university, or did he work?'

The woman with skin so pale it was almost translucent gave a feeble shrug. 'None of the above, I'm afraid. He's been looking for a job but has struggled to find anything suitable. He's had a few interviews, but a lack of decent qualifications lets him down. If I'm being brutally honest, I also think Ash expects too much money for doing too little work.'

Chase nodded along with the conversation. The answer to Laney's question gave them some respite, as it meant they had no fellow students or co-workers to speak with in pursuit of additional information. He hoped Claire would move on and smiled when she did precisely that.

'It's our understanding that Ashley last went on a hike at the start of the year. Is that right, my love?' she asked the boy's mother.

'Yes. Bloody stupid idea, if you ask me. Traipsing around in fields in the middle of an ugly winter is not my idea of fun. But in truth, Ash doesn't have a lot going for him these days, so spending time in the outdoors with like-minded people gives him something to look forward to.'

'And the hike itself went okay? Your son didn't mention any problems? He seemed perfectly fine when he returned home?'

Mothers have a warning system their male counterparts simply cannot fathom. Something about Laney's question prompted a reaction. Chase saw it in Mrs Robertson's eyes when they flickered in alarm. Her body became instantly taut. She looked from Laney, to May, and finally at Chase.

'What's this all about, Sergeant? Why is your colleague asking about Ash's last hike? What does that have to do with my son's disappearance?'

'It's relevant to our investigation, Mrs Robertson,' Chase assured her, stepping in and moving on swiftly. 'Tell me, were you aware that Ash and his buddies spent a night camping with three other people while he was away in January?'

'I don't think so, no. I don't remember Ash mentioning it. What has that got to do with anything?' This time, her voice gained a hard edge.

Chase fired back in kind. 'Well, there were eight of them camping out together that night. One of them didn't survive, and now five, including your son, are missing.'

'What?! One didn't survive. What are you talking about?'

'Mrs Robertson, we're investigating the murder of a young woman by the name of Grace Arnold. Did Ash ever mention her name?'

'No. I've never heard that name before. What are you suggesting? Why are you telling me this and asking these questions?' she asked defensively.

Chase decided to back off. 'Please, calm yourself. I'm not for one moment implying your son had anything to do with Grace's murder. But he was with her on or around the night she was killed, as were his friends. We desperately need to question them all, because one or more of them might have seen or heard something that night.'

'My son is not the kind of boy to witness a murder but not tell the police afterwards,' she said with a sneer. 'In fact, he would have done everything in his power to prevent it from happening. If he saw something, the police would know about it. I'd know about it.'

'We think he – and his friends, for that matter – may not have been aware of it at the time but in retrospect he might recall seeing or hearing something that now makes more sense. We can't know unless we ask. But we also have to wonder why Ash and his friends are nowhere to be found.'

'Are you saying you think they have something to hide and have… what, gone to ground, run away…?'

With a firm shake of the head, Chase said, 'No, not at all. The fact is, we don't know what's become of them, but we do believe their sudden disappearance may be connected to our case somehow.'

'You said there were eight of them camping together. Who are the other two?' Clearly, she had gathered herself enough to think it through.

'A couple of students.'

'And you've questioned them as well, I hope?'

'We have.'

'And what did they have to say for themselves?'

'I'm afraid I can't discuss the witness testimony of others, Mrs Robertson.' Chase sensed he was losing her and wanted to keep the woman talking. 'Look, you seem to have misinterpreted my line of questioning, and I apologise for that. It's only natural for you to be suspicious of our motives, but we only want to ask Ash what he can remember about that night. That's all. We want Ash found safe and well for his sake and yours, but we'd also dearly love to speak with him as soon as possible. He's not in any trouble if he's not done anything wrong. I completely understand why you are beside yourself with worry over his absence, and I'm not suggesting he and his friends are on the run because they have anything to fear from us. As far as we are concerned, they're witnesses. That's all.'

Chase didn't want to frighten her more than she already was. The penny seemed not to have dropped that her son might be in danger from whoever murdered Grace Arnold, and he wasn't about to put that thought inside her head. Instead, he thought about what else they might achieve from this visit and began steering in that direction.

'Have the local police visited you since you reported Ash missing?' he asked after taking a gulp of his now lukewarm tea.

Mrs Robertson shook her head. 'I got the impression they regarded it as a low priority, especially given his age. They said they would call round if they found any indication that he might be in some kind of trouble.'

'In that case, would it be okay if we took a look at his room? I'd like to search it for any clues as to where he might have gone that day with his two friends. If he has any electronic devices, I'd like to take them away with us to have one of our tech experts give them the once over. There may be clues in his online search history or downloads.'

'Won't the local police want them at some point?'

'They might, and they can always obtain them from us. But we can save them some time and speed things up a little. They haven't collected them over the past five days, whereas we can get to work on them by tomorrow morning.'

His words did the trick. Having given her permission, Cheryl Robertson showed the three detectives to her son's room and left them to it. Chase asked May to bag any devices she found while he and DC Laney carried out a more thorough search. They discovered little in the way of written material; unsurprising in today's technological age. Nothing else looked out of place, but after rummaging through the single wardrobe, Chase left briefly to question the boy's mother about luggage. She confirmed his suitcase and backpack were stored in the garage, and that she'd already informed the local police that his other personal items and toiletries were all in their usual places.

Thanking her, Chase headed back to the others. The picture emerging did not look good for either the boy or his mother, because Ashley had clearly left home with the intention of returning. May had secured a laptop and a tablet by the time he returned to the boy's room. He nodded at a set of wooden shelves beneath the window. 'Don't forget his X-Box,' he said.

May frowned. 'Really? You want his game player?'

'I want it for his message boards,' Chase explained. 'A lot of kids are savvy enough to keep dodgy stuff off their more mobile devices these days.'

May nodded and hiked up her skirt a little to squat and retrieve the box. While unplugging and removing cables, she dislodged a section of what looked like shelving. As she pulled the device from the unit and stood upright, Chase knelt to replace the strip of wood. Pushing himself lower, he realised it was in fact a cover for a hidden compartment. His pulse started to race when he squinted and noticed a scrap of what appeared to be cloth that had previously been hidden from view.

'One of you give me a pen, please,' he said, having already removed and discarded his nitrile gloves. Laney took one from her pocket and passed it to him. He reached inside the cavity and when he withdrew his hand, a pair of red knickers dangled precariously on the end of the pen.

'Hand me a forensic bag, will you?' he said to May, feeling a surge of excitement bursting inside his chest. He got to his feet and dropped the item into the bag she gave him. As he sealed it up and wrote the date, time, and his name on the adhesive label, he looked at his colleagues and said, 'I'm not jumping to conclusions, because these could belong to anybody. But when Grace Arnold's body was found, she was wearing no underwear. I think we might just have uncovered the breakthrough we've been waiting for.'

TWENTY-EIGHT

Royston Chase spent the first day of March either in meetings or travelling back and forth between the Gablecross city HQ and Little Soley. It was tough waiting for DNA testing to be carried out, and harder still when you were hoping the results were going to blow your case wide open. There was only one way to overcome the frustration swelling in his blood, and that was to keep busy.

The morning briefing in Swindon essentially covered his find behind the X-box the day before, plus updates from the rest of the team. When it was her turn on centre stage, DC Paige Bowen walked them through everything she had learned from scouring mobile phone data issued by a variety of providers. The first thing she did was to confirm GPS plotting for the group of boys on the night of Friday the thirteenth of January, which put all five of them on Cherhill Down as expected. For emphasis, she displayed a graphic on the eboard screen that showed five overlapping circles of different colours.

'So, we know they were there just as our two Marlborough students told us,' she said. 'I think we all believed their story, but it's nice to have confirmation. What interests me in respect of the data, however, is the difference in terms of both tone and frequency in their text message exchanges before and after that night. What's more, there was a significant change of plan in the following days.'

'Sounds intriguing,' DCI Knight said.

Bowen nodded. 'I think it is. Let me explain. In the build-up to the hike, there was eagerness and anticipation, with communication between the boys via text, mail, and WhatsApp. There were also a lot of photos taken during the first stage of their trail. That all changed from Saturday the fourteenth of January onwards. First came the change of plan. Now, we know from Neville Hutton's mother, Beth, that the boys were hiking the Ridgeway National followed by the Wessex Ridgeway trails – in the opposite direction to the one Grace Arnold was taking.' She paused to change the on-screen graphic. Overlapping circles again, this time in a different area. 'But GPS indicates they didn't walk that second stage to Lyme Regis. In fact, their mobile data shows us they moved on to Salisbury Plain instead and were there for six days.'

'They might simply have changed their minds, especially given the atrocious weather conditions,' DI Fox suggested.

'It's possible. But here's the thing: there are no photos of their subsequent hike or their stay, in complete contrast to the first stage. Also, in the weeks since, messages between the boys fall away dramatically to the point where they seldom contacted each other; another significant difference to their behavioural pattern prior to the hike. Put it all together and it strongly suggests that something meaningful happened on the night of Friday the thirteenth of January. Something that affected them all deeply.'

'What about our students?' Chase asked, liking where this was taking them. 'Any comparable change in their habits?'

'No,' DC Bowen said. 'Good question, but then I wouldn't necessarily expect to find any. They limited their use of social media platforms both before and after, and neither had many photos on their phones to begin with. Text messages are as you might imagine from a couple of kids dating each other, but again I'm seeing no difference between before and after. Given they share a house at college and see each other every day, this comes as no surprise.'

Knight thanked Bowen as she retook her seat, then asked DC

Reuben Cooper to stand and tell the group what, if anything, he had unearthed searching through relevant CCTV footage.

'I have no further sightings of Grace Arnold after the night we believe she was murdered. That may be as close to confirmation as we're ever likely to get. I picked up Isaac Levy and Monica Cilliers on a couple of occasions over the next two days, culminating in their return to campus. They seem to have done precisely what they told us they had – hiked around the local area and camped out a few more nights ahead of returning for the new college term. I have nothing on the boys at all, I'm afraid. Clearly, they avoided larger towns and main roads. If you think it's necessary, I can look at routes from Cherhill to Salisbury, but I'm not quite sure what that would achieve.'

'No, I agree,' Knight told him. 'For whatever reason, they changed their plans. We know where they ended up, so that ought to be enough.'

'We know where their phones ended up,' Chase corrected her without thinking. He shrugged when he realised he'd spoken. 'Sorry, but it's a bit of a bugbear of mine. Phone tower records and satellite coverage tell us where their devices were, not necessarily the boys themselves. Did all five of them end up in the same place, or did one simply have all five phones with them?'

'I stand corrected,' Knight said, holding her hands up, 'but what do you imagine might have happened instead?'

'Oh, nothing at all. Like you, I suspect they all remained together and spent their time in Salisbury. I'm not suggesting otherwise, just reminding everyone that GPS data alone isn't evidence of where people are at any given time. It's a helpful tool when questioning them – if we question them – but let's not lose sight of just how unreliable such data can be in pinpointing individuals.'

'So, are you saying I should check CCTV after all?' Cooper asked, looking between him and Knight.

Chase waved a hand dismissively. 'No, not at all. Forget it – it's not important.'

'Okay. I'll put that on pause for the time being. Which leaves the

Red Lion car park in Milton Bryan. We drew a blank there, I'm afraid. They record to DVD, which is overwritten every two or three days.'

Knight held his gaze for a moment before nodding and turning her attention to case officer, DS Armstrong. 'Superintendent Waddington asked me if I was happy with our case strategy. He was concerned about tunnel vision, our focus fixated solely on those who were with Grace Arnold at Cherhill that night. I assured him we had no other leads. Was I right to do so, Jude?'

Armstrong gave a hesitant nod. 'I think you were, yes. Before we became aware of the group of lads and the students, we were working on the theory that Grace had been unlucky enough to have had somebody stalk her or find her alone up on that hill. We did consider a fellow hiker, but equally we knew it could just as easily have been a local having spotted her. We know she wasn't alone at the time, so nobody can argue that we've not utilised our attention and resources in the right area. I'm confident of that.'

'I agree,' Chase said without being asked for his opinion. 'If my small team had been running this on our own, our strategy would've been exactly the same.'

Knight ran a hand through her hair. She looked exhausted, as if sleep had been elusive in recent days and fitful when it eventually came. She managed a thin smile. 'Thanks, Royston. But where are we at present when it comes to Operation Silverback? Our working hypothesis is that one of the seven young people who spent the night with our victim also murdered her. Is there any room to argue that when they left her on Saturday morning, she was alive and well, and that somebody else then came upon her and killed her?'

'Of course. If we're being open-minded, then we're still considering all possibilities.'

'But if it was somebody else, how do we explain these five young men who seem to have vanished off the face of the earth?'

Chase had been asking himself the same thing. 'If that *is* the case, I suspect whoever has taken them wants to ask them the same questions we do.'

'That makes some kind of sense. But our theory remains the most likely. We must consider everyone who was on that hillside camping alongside Grace to be in the mix, yet the two we've managed to speak to so far have given us little. The disappearance of the five lads has to be significant. We just don't yet know how or why.'

'That's a fair summary,' Chase said. 'Everything points to that group of boys, and Ashley Robertson in particular. In my opinion, it's good work all round, and if DNA tells us the underwear we found belongs to Grace, then I think we can safely identify our chief suspect. How we locate him is another matter entirely.'

The room was momentarily quiet. Eventually, Knight gave a solemn nod. 'We must consider broadening the scope of this entire investigation. When it began, it was not a crime in action. But it changes everything if some or all or even just one of these lads has been abducted. Their safety becomes a priority, irrespective of their status as part of Silverback. As SIO, I'm ready to take this to a higher level and suggest a Gold Command Group taking over, with an entirely different focus.'

Chase exhaled in a single huff of disappointment. He knew the DCI was right, her response both predictable and professionally sound. But escalating to Gold command came with the kind of policing politics he wanted no part of. Worse still, the investigation extended beyond their own force area, which only ever added multiple complicated strands to an already tangled web.

'If the primary focus shifts to the missing lads, we could lose the entire case,' he said. 'After all, none of them live in Wiltshire, so why would the relevant locals allow us to carry on running it?'

With a shrug, Knight said, 'For that matter, why would our Chief Constable and PCC want to accept the costs associated with such an op when none of the five live here? We may need their help with our own enquiries, but none of them is our responsibility.'

'Whatever happens, we keep Silverback.' Chase set his jaw, his eyes piercing hers. 'I mean it. You have to fight for it, Nicole. It's our job to deliver Grace's killer, nobody else's.'

'I'm aware of your feelings, believe me. I share them.'

'Then do something about it. These other forces are already running their own misper investigations. As much as we want to talk to these lads, we can't waste time fighting other areas over them. It's a distraction, and in my view it's also unnecessary. We regard the murder of Grace Arnold as our job, which it is. They treat the missing friends as theirs. Which it is. Let them do the work for us.'

'And how do you suggest we go about that?' Knight asked.

Realising he'd allowed his voice to raise and his tone to border on unprofessional, Chase released his pent-up emotions in a single long exhalation. 'Bollock me later for my manner,' he said. 'I deserve it. But to me, it's time to back off from the mispers. Yes, I was all over it myself yesterday, but given what we learned and found, given everything we've been told here this morning, the most we should be aiming to do is liaise closely with relevant forces. We feed them everything we have and hope they reciprocate. Set up a liaison team to keep in contact with them. But our buy-in requires us to have first crack at these lads once they are found. We don't need to be the ones who track them down, we only need to speak to them afterwards.'

DCI Knight gave it only a second of thought before nodding. 'I'll bank that bollocking, Royston,' she said. 'I have a feeling I might need to cash it in very soon.'

TWENTY-NINE

Claire Laney and Alison May were eager for an update from the moment he arrived at Little Soley. Several media crews had strayed back to the village, but having gruffly dismissed them as he hurried by, they retreated without too much complaint. Besides, they were probably sick and tired of being harangued by locals for getting in the way of pedestrians trying to go about their business, while their large vehicles parked on the street made life difficult for road users.

The thought provoked a smile from Chase as he entered the station. The village was so small that a single stray sheep was liable to cause chaos, but the villagers were protective of their way of life and the media were unwanted intruders. In the aftermath of the investigation into Sir Kenneth Webster's abhorrent behaviour, news crews from around the world besieged Little Soley. The residents' close association with the Webster family and the estate had been tested to breaking point as each new atrocity was revealed. The building occupied by Chase, Laney and May had ostensibly functioned as a police station because of Sir Kenneth's previous position as Chief Constable. With him dead, the family name ruined beyond redemption and the estate and manor put up for sale, the future of the station was in the balance. A meeting of minds between Wiltshire police and the village inhabitants kept the doors open for the time being, its prospects to be discussed on an annual basis. Without the funding donations from the Webster family, the police commissioner had taken it upon himself to source alternative means to keep the station open, but privately, Chase believed the chances were bleak.

Once he'd settled behind his desk, he relayed the more salient briefing bullet points and the resulting discussions while sipping from a mug of hot chocolate. It was from May's personal stash, but she was in a generous mood.

'So, if DCI Knight gets knocked back, what will this Gold Group mean for us?' she asked.

'Impossible to tell,' he replied irritably. 'When the circumstances change as they have with Silverback, and we see a crime in action developing, the responsible thing to do is move it on up the chain of command. In this case, the first thing they're likely to do is contact the relevant force areas to see if a command structure has already been set up. Given their proximity and the context, they could put together a joint task force. Which is fine, except that I suspect they might attempt to include us.'

May cocked her head. 'I'm sensing we don't want this to happen.'

'No, we don't. And in fact, as I pointed out to Nicole, it's not necessary. They have their investigations, we have ours. We believe they are linked, but we have no conclusive evidence to prove our theory. Provided we maintain communications between relevant forces, there's no need for any amalgamation to include us.'

'Even though we need to speak to the missing lads as a matter of urgency?' May persisted.

'Even though. Alison, it's too easy to take your eyes off the prize when something like this happens. We can all help each other, but in the absence of the lads our focus must be on finding another way to identify Grace's killer. Let others move forward with the hunt while we tend to our own op. Speaking of which, any thoughts as to how we spend our time while we wait for the DNA results to come in?'

Laney, who'd been listening keenly while sitting with her feet up on his desk, surprised him with an immediate response. 'I can think of two things to chase up. We know the precise moment Gary

Elder was taken, so let's find out where Levy and Cilliers were at the time. If they were on campus that afternoon, we can rule them out. If not, we take another look at them. As far as I'm concerned, cupcake, that's a positive step forward. I'm also keen to follow up on Grace's brother and boyfriend.'

'What have you two been doing while I was at Gablecross?' Chase asked.

'We've not been plucking each other's eyebrows or getting Brazilians. Alison spoke to local police earlier this morning, but they weren't able to rule either of them out. The brother hasn't been to visit his parents since he spent time with them immediately after we'd confirmed Grace's identity. They've spoken with him on several occasions, so he's not off the grid. However, nobody can verify his whereabouts and police haven't managed to talk to him.'

'And the boyfriend?'

'Closer to being ruled out, but not quite there yet. His alibis are being checked, but other than in Elder's case we have wide windows of opportunity. We're told to expect him to be cleared today.'

Chase nodded thoughtfully. 'Grace's brother is the more likely candidate. He's family, so he's going to have the more emotional reaction.'

'We still have the issue of how he could have known about the hikers and how to reach them,' May reminded them. 'That makes no sense to me.'

'Which doesn't rule him out, Alison. It just means we don't have all the answers. If we look at our most viable options when it comes to these missing boys, it's either him or one of the lads has turned on the others.'

'But why?' Laney asked. 'To save his own neck? We're saying one of them killed Grace and then he and the others covered it up, but now our killer doesn't trust them to keep schtum?'

'It's not impossible. In fact, in many ways, it makes the most sense. But you're right, Claire, we could do with taking a look at the brother. Let's start by asking the locals for their notes and observations. We can then examine in closer detail what they've done and what we might be able to do that they haven't thought of.'

'You still don't sound convinced, Royston,' May told him.

Chase scratched the back of his neck. He gave a weary sigh. 'That's because I'm not. We're chasing shadows and have been for days. Other than Gary Elder, any one of the remaining four lads could be our killer. Ashley Robertson is top of that very small list, and I think DNA is going to point in his direction. If he murdered Grace, then I want the little bastard. But he may well have four other victims on his hands, so we have to do this right.'

THIRTY

He couldn't tell how many hours had passed since the masked man had last visited him, but the moment he heard the bolts being snapped back, Gary Elder began to sob. He was still weeping and wailing when the figure stood before him, looking down and shaking his head as if ashamed on behalf of the rest of the human race.

'Got yourself into a bit of a lather, haven't you, Gary?' the man said. He tutted and huffed his contempt in a cloud of frosty breath. 'Is that because you weren't telling me the truth the last time we spoke?'

Elder had thought of little else since their previous conversation. He'd held back, believing only a handful of people could know for sure what happened that night. It had come as a massive shock when his captor spoke about knowing the truth, yet a part of him doubted the man's words. Was it all a bluff? Could he possibly know for certain? And if so, why did it matter so much to him? Why the abduction? The threats? And as for Grace…

This time he made no reply. The man stared at him for a while, leaned forward until their faces were close together, and said, 'What happened that night, Gary? Tell me everything you know. And this time remember… if you lie or leave anything out, I'm going to punish you. I won't tell you precisely how, nor for how long, but you don't have to suffer needlessly. All I'm after is the truth. You give me that, and you and I will be okay again.'

'Am I allowed to ask a question first?'

A snorted, stifled laugh. 'You just did.'

'I… I don't want to be punished for asking, that's all.'

The figure nodded. 'Go ahead.'

'What do you want to know?' Elder asked. 'Specifically.'

'This is not about what I want to know. I want you to tell me what happened to Grace Arnold that night while you were up on that hillside. I have to know, and if you won't tell me, then you're of no use to me.'

Elder released a soft moan and began to weep gently once more. The longer he thought about it, the less holding on to the secret seemed to matter. Why not spill his guts? After all, this man acted as if he knew everything anyway. And if he wasn't bluffing…

'While we were drinking and partying,' he said through his sniffling, 'Grace lost all her inhibitions. She began flirting with me first. We danced together, and she was grinding herself up against me the whole time. When I got a hard-on, she pulled her head back and smiled, licking her lips as if to say I'd like to be enjoying that. I rubbed myself up against her, squeezed the cheeks of her arse, and then she put a hand on me over my clothes and started stroking me. I thought I was going to get something more right there and then, but when the next song came on, she did the same thing with Nev, and then Ash, and… then the others. While it was happening, we were all looking around at each other not knowing what the fuck was going on. Yet at the same time we were all enjoying the moment. It wasn't long after that when Isaac and Monica slipped away to their tent, and about half an hour later Grace ended up in the middle of the five of us and we had our hands all over her. She was lapping it up, and so were we. Then in the silence between songs, she said something about feeling woozy and was going to bed. As she turned away and started walking towards her tent, she said… she asked which of us was going to join her first.'

'And you took that to mean go back to her tent with her?'

'Yes.'

'To have sex with her?'

'Yes.'

'And which of you did?'

'I'm pretty sure it was Nev, though it might have been Ash. But look, we didn't do anything wrong. It was probably tasteless, even a little squalid, but Grace was old enough and you could tell she wanted it. You have to believe me… she was more than willing.'

'Okay. For the moment, let's say I believe you. That was it as far as you're concerned? You all had your way with her, then went off separately to your own tents.'

'Yes,' Elder said with conviction. 'I mean, we were pissed and buzzing with everything that had happened, but that's how I remember it. Honestly!'

For a moment or two, neither of them spoke. Then the man in the balaclava said, 'You never thought to question why this young girl might have behaved in such a way? You never asked yourself if she was too drunk to truly agree to having sex with each of you?'

Elder shook his head, desperate for this man to understand. 'No, no, it wasn't just that she agreed. It wasn't like that at all. She put it out there. Offered it up on a plate. The girl was all over us, and she was gagging for it.'

'And it never occurred to you that one of your friends might have drugged her? That her sudden lack of inhibitions might be chemically induced?'

'No. They're not like that. None of them. Besides, she was as drunk as we were.'

'That's the litmus test, is it? If they're drunk enough, they're good enough.'

'No.' Elder gave a sullen shake of the head. 'Look, you weren't there. You can't know if you weren't there.'

His captor laughed at that, which puzzled him.

'Would you have even cared?' the man asked. 'Or was the thought of having sex with Grace enough for you to overlook the circumstances?'

'I already told you… she was drunk but she wasn't drugged.'

'Though you admit she told you she felt woozy.'

'I keep telling you she'd had a few drinks. But that was it.'

'Don't raise your voice to me, Gary.' His voice was cold, but uncomfortably calm.

'All right. I'm sorry. I'm doing my best.'

'Perhaps. So, according to you, Grace was alive when you all turned in afterwards? Is that what you're saying?'

'Yes. Yes, she was fine.'

'We'll see.' He took a step backwards and turned towards the door. 'If I hear anything different, Gary, I will be back. Next time there will be no more questions. Think about that. Now, do you have anything else you wish to say to me? Anything to add, any part of that story you might want to change?'

'No.' Elder curled up into a ball then turned to face the wall. 'This time I told you everything I know.'

'I doubt that,' the man said. He paused on the threshold. 'But for your sake, I hope you're telling me the truth.'

THIRTY-ONE

It was difficult not to allow his impatience with the case to spill over into his family life, but Chase throttled it back, if not quite all the way off. They were close. He could smell it. They'd made excellent progress, given how little they'd had to go on to begin with. Grace Arnold was never going home to her parents, but at least he and the team would hopefully provide the poor girl's family with answers why.

He got home early enough to take Maisie to her gym class. It was hardly Olympic standard, but his daughter enjoyed herself immensely. She took part in several sporting pursuits and had hinted at taking up karate. By no means a tomboy – if you were even allowed to use the harmless term anymore – his little girl was more interested in physical pastimes than playing electronic games, which pleased him and Erin enormously.

On the way back, he treated his daughter to a fishfinger Happy Meal and got himself a chicken sandwich with fries. Erin wasn't a fan of fast food and had insisted on making do with a bowl of her own homemade vegetable soup. 'It was lovely,' she told him, smacking her lips. 'I added frozen spinach cubes, which were delicious.'

'Spinach, eh? Nice.'

'I yam what I yam, Olive.'

He laughed. 'Yeah, come back to me as Popeye when those scrawny forearms of yours are big enough for anchor tattoos.'

Erin punched his arm and then set a pose, flexing her biceps. 'Spinach is better than the crap you shovelled down your neck tonight.'

'Not so. Chicken is full of protein, and chips are essentially vegetables,' he argued.

Now both hands were resting on her hips. 'Hey, if I'm the Popeye in this relationship, I reckon that makes you Wimpy. In more ways than one.'

Chase patted his stomach. 'Very little fat here, I'll have you know. Plus, I can be rather butch when I want to be. Besides, that was a rubbish cartoon.'

That was something they could agree on.

As the evening wore on, Chase managed to switch off, yet he knew the image of Grace Arnold's blackened, frozen face was waiting for him in his dreams. Five young men were missing, but for him this was still all about that one young woman whose life had been so grotesquely cut short.

Erin spent the night with her nose in a book. A fan of Stephen King, she was working her way through her collection of his novels for about the fourth time and had recently opened up *Firestarter*. Chase watched some TV before settling in with headphones on to watch YouTube clips. He tried to lose himself in the banality of what passed for entertainment these days, but wandered into dangerous territory with some content that seemed determined to skew its position on fundamental topics. He quickly lost interest and found his mind drifting.

Later on in bed, he took one last look through the case file, observing DCI Knight's final updates to the policy book. Doing so gave him a greater appreciation of Superintendent Waddington's perspective. Without context, the investigation might easily appear blinkered, leaving no room for different interpretations of the same information. When you worked the case your instincts and experiences took over, and while the DSI had earned his climb through the ranks by doing the job, and knew all there was to know about the various roles and responsibilities, he was detached from the front line these days and had only infrequent discussions and electronic files to guide him.

'You're distracted again,' Erin said, startling him as she touched his arm.

Chase recovered quickly. 'I know. Sorry. It's just that you get used to playing your part in these ops and you forget about all the other moving parts that come into play. The checks and balances are there for a reason, and it doesn't hurt to have that pointed out to you every now and then.'

'This your new DCI or Russell Waddington again?'

He smiled. 'The latter. I got a bit narked when he suggested we might have tunnel vision, but he was right to make the point.'

'You think you have?'

'In this case, no. But I can see how it might look that way if you're not in the trenches alongside us. No, I think we're all agreed when it comes to our focus.'

'So why so preoccupied? I read doubt in your face, Royston. That's unlike you.'

Chase stretched out his arms and yawned. 'It's just the way things are stacking up against us. We're waiting for answers on some crucial DNA testing, but even if that comes in with the expected result, I'm not sure how much additional progress we can make. This is a bugger of a case, and our options are thin on the ground.'

'Something will break for you. It always does.'

He turned to his wife, narrowing his gaze. 'I wish that were true, Erin. We're not the Canadian Mounties – we don't always get our man. The sad truth is that some ops don't go the way we'd like. I can feel this one slipping through our fingers.'

'And that bothers you most of all because of what happened to your victim?'

Nodding, he said, 'Have I ever told you how insightful you are?'

'Never.'

'Well, it's true. You're actually much brighter than you look.'

Erin swatted his arm with the back of her hand. 'And you're every bit the arsehole *you* look, matey boy.'

Chuckling, Chase gave a sigh and said, 'I'm so glad I have this. You to come home to. You to talk things through with. Maisie to distract me by just being Maisie. You both help keep the darkness at bay, even if only for a few hours. Not everyone is as fortunate as I am when it comes to home life and family.'

'You mean you're not a cliché cop, all burned out and soaking in alcohol?'

'No. But remember, it's a cliché for a reason. It happens more often than we'd like to admit. Not the boozing part necessarily. I don't think an alcoholic cop could function properly doing the job we do. Not these days. But the hours, the things we see, things we have to do… they can wear a person down. That often leads to them in turn wearing down their relationships. You do your very best to be empathetic, but only another copper really understands. Except that you listen, and what you do grasp and never complain about is the time I spend either working or thinking about work. That goes a long way, Erin.'

His wife gave him a hug, grinning. 'And all because I'm brighter than I look, right?'

Chase hugged her back. 'Right,' he whispered in her ear. 'And to be honest, you'd really have to be.'

This time, his quip earned him a light punch. He laughed it off and sent his thoughts in another direction. 'Maisie really enjoys herself doing gym, doesn't she? At first I thought it was another fad or a phase she was going through, but she puts her all into it.'

Erin's smile was wide. 'I know. And how cute does she look in that little pink leotard?'

'Have you seen her going up on tip-toes just before she runs, tucks, and rolls? She must have seen that on the telly while the gymnastics was on. I wonder if she might want to do more of this rather than take on karate.'

'Knowing our little duckling, she'll want to swim in as many lakes as possible.'

He grinned at that, nodding. 'I was much the same way. Tried my hand at most things.'

'Now that I think about it, so was I. Not such a bad instinct for our girl to inherit. I love seeing her experience life.'

'Me, too. I only wish I could involve myself more.'

'Don't be daft. You do what you can, and more than many other fathers. Maisie understands you can't be there for her every single time. She knows you have an important job to do. Don't you worry about her, Royston. Your little girl is happy and appreciates everything you do to be around when it counts most of all.'

Chase had his doubts. 'You're making her sound extremely mature for her tender age, Erin. I'm sure she has cause to wonder sometimes. Tonight was only the second time I've taken her to gym, and if this case rumbles on, I'm not sure when the next time will be.'

His wife shook her head, switched off the bedside lamp, and slipped her hand into his. 'Why don't you concentrate on solving it more quickly then? But either way, Maisie will be just fine. She's our little duckling, and are we not pillars of strength?'

Relenting, he gave Erin's hand a squeeze. 'We are,' he agreed. 'And we must never forget that.'

THIRTY-TWO

It was just before noon the following day when they received the call they had been waiting for. DNA samples tested from the underwear came back with the two positive results the team had expected to find; traces from both Grace Arnold and Ashley Robertson. The presence of a third came as a complete shock.

'Gary Elder?' DC Laney said, almost in disbelief when Chase revealed the findings to her and Alison May. Recovering quickly, she asked, 'What type of trace did he leave behind?'

'Three in all,' Chase replied. 'Semen and skin cells, plus hairs of the short and curly kind.'

'What the actual fuck?!'

'I know, I know. Small deposits, evidently, but enough to tag him, probably following a single encounter. Robertson's were more copious and recent. He's clearly been jerking off into the knickers. Elder's trace is older and more in line with the time we believe Grace was murdered.'

'We're thinking they both sexually assaulted her?' May stated and queried at the same time.

'Let's call a spade a spade here,' Laney said, her face rigid and starting to flush. 'The gutless little shites raped that poor girl. Sexual assault or sexual abuse be buggered. It's called rape. No more, no less.'

'With all due respect and apologies to the movement, ladies,'

Chase said heavily, 'we have no evidence to back that up. I don't doubt that it's true. Except neither the postmortem nor the forensic examination has proven that Grace even had sex that night, let alone whether that sex was consensual.'

Laney turned a wrathful face on him, her features twisted. 'So, what, you're suggesting our victim willingly put out for both these lads? That she's some kind of slut looking to screw the first blokes she comes into contact with after a drink or two?'

'I'm not *suggesting* anything of the kind, but is it really so far-fetched? So inconceivable that we should dismiss it from our thoughts?'

'I can't believe you just said that, Royston. I never had you down as a victim-blamer.'

Chase rolled his eyes and groaned. 'Oh, for fuck's sake, Claire, grow up. You know damned well that's not what I'm doing. Nor would I. What I'm telling you is that we have no way of knowing for sure, and therefore it's our duty to consider all possibilities.'

Neither Laney nor May responded this time. Chase understood their unwillingness to think along those lines, but he also knew he was right. Unmoved, he drove the conversation on. 'Look, irrespective of what may or may not have happened, we're confronted by what this new evidence means. What I believe is this: both Ashley Robertson and Gary Elder had sex with Grace Arnold on the thirteenth of January. At some point, Robertson stole Grace's underwear, hid them away in his bedroom, but continued to remind himself of that night every time he masturbated by using them to help pleasure himself. If that's all we can prove – and at this stage, we can't even do that – then there's no wrongdoing whatsoever. The DNA results give us a strong and definite link between these three young people, but a good brief will argue that even if sex occurred, all three were willing participants and Grace subsequently gave her underwear to Ashley as some kind of memento.'

'You're kidding me, right?' Laney snarled. 'Please tell me you're kidding me, Royston.'

He felt something pulse in his cheek. 'Cut it out, Claire,' he said with venom. 'And I mean right this second. If you can't wrap your head around this case logically and professionally, if you're going to allow your emotions to spill over, then perhaps you ought to take a back seat. If you want to stay on it and work the puzzle with us, then stop shooting the messenger. Is that understood?'

Laney responded with a sullen nod. The gesture didn't satisfy him, but he let it go. 'Now, once and for all, please understand what I'm saying here. I don't think that's what happened. I'm telling you what a defence solicitor will see in this evidence. Sex or no sex, rape or no rape, the one thing we can be certain of is that this offers no definitive proof that either of those lads murdered Grace.'

It was just as he had feared. Having forensic evidence to prove a link between their victim and not one but two of the lads who spent the night on the hillside with her was a step in the right direction, but that's all it was. It got them no closer to finding any of the young men, nor to proving which of them – if any – had murdered her.

Chase had all but dismissed Grace Arnold's boyfriend as a viable suspect. Her absent brother remained a genuine person of interest, as were the six male hikers who camped on Cherhill Down alongside her. If Grace had engaged in sexual activity shortly before her death, the underwear and DNA evidence opened up a range of questions police had for both Ashley Robertson and Gary Elder. Yet to take the investigation further they required more. They were going to need either a confession or somebody to talk, because what they had would not hold up in court.

Before that could happen, they had to find the missing lads or seek other avenues to pursue.

'I'm open to suggestions,' he said. 'We could really do with finding these boys, because without them to interview, I'm all out of inspiration.'

'Not to piss all over your chips, Royston,' Laney said without rancour, 'but I'd remind you that finding the boys is no longer part of our remit. At your suggestion, I would add.'

Chase acknowledged this with a nod. 'True. But we've done our specific job and got nowhere so far. Unless you think the truth lies with Grace's brother or our Marlborough College couple, we're all out of plays here. DCI Knight and the Gablecross team are beavering away, as are local forces where these lads live. If we've got nothing to offer, then so be it. But I had to ask the question.'

If you stripped away every other consideration, what they were dealing with was missing persons believed to have been abducted. The usual approach was to examine electronic equipment that might help police discover where they were, or at the very least where they had been. Chase considered that aspect and asked if there was any point in following the path further.

'What do we know or think we know so far?' May asked, looking between them. 'Gary Elder went to work, came home, and was then persuaded to leave his home shortly afterwards with a masked man. Ashley Robertson insisted the two Marks join him, which they did. Or at least, we believe that's what happened. Ashley could well have been the masked man who took Elder and was equally persuasive with the Marks after meeting them at or close to the village pub. If it is him, can we place him with Neville Hutton prior to *his* disappearance?'

'That's good thinking, Alison,' Chase told her. 'See if you can rule that in or out.'

May held a hand to her chest. 'What? You want me to contact Mrs Hutton?'

'I do. And why not? It was your idea. Run with it.'

'I thought we were leaving it to the locals.'

'We are. But some overlap is inevitable. Go on, you'll do fine.'

As May dashed from the room to make a call, Chase followed her with his eyes and then smiled at DC Laney. 'She'll do,' he said with some satisfaction.

'Careful,' Laney warned him with a wink. 'Saying that about a sweet and innocent looker like Alison could be misinterpreted.'

He laughed. 'Yeah, only by somebody with a mind like a cesspit.'

'Hello? Have we met?' Her face softened. 'I'm sorry for my outburst earlier, my love. I know you're not that kind of copper. You were simply asking us to look at how it might be perceived by others, especially when forming some kind of defence. I let it get to me, and that was terribly unprofessional.'

Chase waved away her apology. 'It just shows your human side. Which, I have to say, came as a surprise. I had no clue you were capable of being human.'

'I have my moments, cupcake. That, alas, was not one of my finest.'

'It's who you are, Claire. If we want the smooth, we have to accept the rough.'

'And they don't come much rougher than me, right?'

'So, what do you think?' he asked, this time on the back of a throaty chuckle. 'I'm still looking hard at Ashley Robertson. You?'

'My hard-earned sheckles would be on him, yes. Not quite sure what to make of the boy Elder's jizz being on Grace's knickers, though.'

'Forensics suggest the volume and pattern implies post-ejaculate spatter rather than full loads like we're seeing with Ash.'

Laney's lips puckered in disgust. 'Which to me suggests that either the gusset of her knickers was pushed to one side while he humped her and his jizz dribbled onto them as he pulled out, or his dick brushed against them after he'd emptied his nutsack.'

'I doubt those will be the words used in the official report,' Chase said. 'But that's the gist, yes.'

'Which leaves us with what you were trying to say before I threw a wobbly: either Grace allowed them to double up on her, or they took it in turns to rape the poor kid.'

Chase shrugged. 'Does it matter? And before you jump down my throat again, of course I am horribly aware that it would have mattered a great deal to Grace. What I mean is, in terms of our investigation. Neither of those two scenarios tells us why she was murdered. Half-strangled and then some kind of cleaver slammed into her head is overkill by any stretch of the definition. Why would either of those boys go so far?'

'I see what you mean. And to be brutally honest, you wouldn't want or need to do either if she'd allowed you to slip her one, would you? Both are the acts of somebody who realises they've done wrong, somebody feeling the need to silence her afterwards.'

'I agree. Which makes rape the more likely. But it's still a puzzle. I mean, why take such extreme measures? Don't you just wait to see if she screams rape the next day and when we turn up at your door you claim consensual sex?'

'Unless you panic.'

He nodded. 'Yes. Unless you panic.'

May returned to the room lost in thought, tapping her mobile against her chin. She looked up when Chase asked if she'd had any luck.

'I think so,' she replied. 'I'm just trying to piece it all together. Mrs Hutton says she remembers her son mentioning Ashley Robertson the day before Neville went missing.'

'That would have been last Tuesday,' Claire Laney said. 'The day Grace's body was discovered. But we weren't able to identify her the same day. Not formally.'

'True,' Chase said. 'But if either or both of them were responsible, they would have known who it was.'

'Of course.' Laney nodded and turned to May. 'Sorry for interrupting, Alison. You were saying…?'

'Yes. According to his mum, Neville Hutton was surprised to hear from Ash, because they had no immediate plans for another hike.'

'Any additional context or content relating to that conversation?'

'No. Neither did he mention seeing Robertson again, but that doesn't mean a meeting wasn't arranged at the time. Nor that it wasn't arranged the following morning.'

Chase raised a finger. He took out his phone and placed a call. 'Hi, DC Paige Bowen, please,' he said without preamble. A moment later, he hissed through his teeth and said, 'In that case, I'd like to speak with either DI Fox or DS Armstrong, please. This is Detective Sergeant Chase from Little Soley.'

He ignored the stares coming from the other side of his desk. A couple of seconds passed before he was put through. 'Jude,' he said with a smile Armstrong could not see. 'Listen, we have fresh information telling us Ash Robertson contacted Neville Hutton the day before Hutton went missing. It would have been last week on Tuesday. Yes, the twenty-first. Can you check that against their relevant mobile data and tell me if you have any record of a call taking place between the two of them. It's thought the call originated from Ashley Robertson to Neville Hutton. If not, let me know when their last contact was, please. If so, the time and duration would be good. Oh, and while you're at it, any text exchanges would also be useful. Cheers.'

He muted the call and turned to his colleagues in the office. 'Let's see if the data confirms Mrs Hutton's account. I'm not suggesting she made it up, but she could have been out by a day.'

Chase unmuted when DC Armstrong came back to him. He listened and nodded and thanked their Swindon colleague before ending the call and setting his phone down on the desk. 'Interesting,' he muttered. 'There's no record of the two communicating with each other since last month. But the Hutton boy did receive two calls the day before he went missing. One was from another friend, unrelated to our enquiries. The other was from an unregistered number.'

'A burner?' Laney said, leaning closer.

'Looks like it. Duration of the call suggests a lengthy conversation.'

'Does that make sense to either of you?' May asked. 'Ashley Robertson called the two Marks on his own mobile. That would have been after this call to Hutton. So, if the call to Robertson was him, why revert to his own phone when he called the Marks?'

'Perhaps it was important to him that the Marks recognised his number,' Chase suggested.

'But not Neville Hutton?'

Chase expelled a long breath. He shook his head. 'No, you're right. It doesn't make sense. That could be because we don't know the circumstances, but I see where you're headed. The call from the burner might have been from someone other than Ashley Robertson.'

'Doesn't rule it out, either,' Laney said dourly. 'I'm keeping an open mind on that score. Thing is, Mrs Hutton swears her son spoke to Ash the day before he went missing, and that's the only call he received that we can't account for.'

Chase pushed himself back from the desk. 'I think it's more likely than not. If I had to guess, I'd say that was Ashley calling him. That boy is right at the centre of things, and my every instinct tells me he's our man.'

THIRTY-THREE

The police building on London Road, Devizes, had been the county headquarters for almost sixty years. Three storeys of sand-coloured brick gave the structure a grand appearance, if somewhat lacking in architectural flourishes. DS Chase preferred its formal presence to the more modern and corporate-looking Gablecross station and was glad to have a chance to visit.

The reason he and Laney had travelled there that afternoon sat in a witness interview room on the ground floor, just off the central reception area. Based on photographic comparison alone, Jamie Arnold looked nothing like his sister. While Grace had been physically diminutive and strikingly attractive, her brother was tall and wide, with a hard and flat slab of a face. A roofer by trade, he had the rangy, muscular build of somebody whose physique had been honed naturally rather than in the gym.

Chase weighed the man up as he and Laney took their seats on the other side of a square table wedged against the wall alongside a tall sash window. Arnold appeared perfectly relaxed, his breathing calm and steady. Following the introductions, Chase asked the man to explain why he had walked into the area HQ an hour earlier.

'I heard you were looking for me,' Jamie Arnold said, his voice pitched higher than Chase had expected.

'Where did you hear that?' he asked.

'I called my parents last night. Told them where I was, what I was doing. They said you lot wanted to speak to me. So… here I am.'

Nodding slowly, Chase said, 'And what is it that you're doing in this area, Mr Arnold?'

'Same as you. Looking for the bastard who murdered my sister.'

'And how exactly are you doing that?'

'Asking questions. I visited Cherhill, spoke to people in the Black Horse pub. I traipsed around Marlborough. Dad told me Grace had stayed overnight at a B&B, so I eventually found the right one and had words with the people there, too.'

Chase stroked his chin before asking, 'Sir, have you been following the case in the media? Have you obtained all the current updates and details from your parents?'

'Yes. To both.'

'Then what makes you think you're going to discover something we've not yet learned?'

Arnold shrugged. 'I don't. I mean, you never can tell, but I'm not expecting to. I… I just want to be doing something. Anything. I want to be here, where I can feel close to my sister. I want to be here in case you identify her killer.'

'With what intention?'

Another rise and dip of the shoulders. 'I'm not sure. But I'd really like ten minutes alone with the prick.'

Chase understood Arnold's thirst for extracting some kind of revenge, the desire to punish Grace's murderer. But the lad was misguided and had to be set straight. Before that, though, he needed to be questioned about the missing hikers.

'Jamie, I feel for you,' he said with genuine empathy. 'I really do. I can't honestly say I wouldn't be doing something similar if I were in your shoes. But there are two main avenues we are currently exploring, so let's wind back and begin there. First of all, do you know anybody who would want to hurt Grace?'

'No. Of course not.' Arnold looked appalled by the very idea.

'Nobody's name or face flitted across your mind when your sister first went missing, or was later found dead?'

'No. Why? Are you saying you think it was somebody she knew?'

Holding up both hands, Chase said, 'No, Sir. Not at all. It's just procedure. How about Marcus Holland? What was your impression of him?'

The young man's lips puckered at the mention of Grace's boyfriend. Chase noticed and pounced. 'So, not a fan, then, Jamie?'

The young man collected himself before replying. 'Not so's you'd notice. I don't like him as a person, because he's work-shy and a bit of a ponce. But I know he thought a lot of my sister, which goes a long way.'

'Enough for him to do something similar to what you're doing right now?'

'I doubt it. But then, Grace wasn't his flesh and blood. They hadn't been with each other long.'

Chase nodded. Holland wasn't in the frame, and he was starting to get the same impression about Grace's brother. It was time to move on. 'Fine. Thank you. As I said before, Jamie, there's another aspect to this case. One which concerns me all the more now that I know you're here in the area. I don't like to assume anything, but I take it you are aware that your sister spent possibly her last night camping on that hillside with *seven* other people?'

'Yes. I know all about that. Not their details, mind. You lot haven't released names or anything.'

'Quite. So, then you're also probably aware that five of those seven fellow campers went missing within days of Grace's body being discovered.'

When Arnold nodded, Chase continued. 'Jamie, because our investigation includes those other campers as potential witnesses, we're also involved in the enquiry into their disappearance. Our line of thinking includes revenge as a possible motive. Therefore, we have to look closely at whoever is most likely to seek retribution for what happened to Grace. I'm sure you understand that means one of the people we're interested in is you. What do you have to say about that?'

The young man's expression didn't falter. Every bit as composed as he was when the questioning began, he gave an expansive shrug and said, 'Nothing. You say these blokes went missing within a couple of days of Grace being found, but the first my parents heard about them was long after that. And even now we don't know exactly who they are, only that they exist. How could I be involved in whatever happened to them if I didn't and still don't know their names or where they live?'

It was the critical question, and one Chase had pondered on several occasions. The investigation had so far not discovered any communication between Grace and her brother since she'd left home on the first day of the new year. Jamie Arnold seemed sincere, but appearances were often deceptive.

'While everything you said is true, there are enough rumours around at the moment to suggest who these five young men are. They're missing from their homes, and news of this has appeared on TV, in newspapers, and online. However, I accept that these reports are recent and that you couldn't have heard about them a week ago.'

Arnold gestured with his hands. 'There you go, then.'

Chase paused, easing into his next move. 'We know Grace contacted you, Jamie,' he said, taking a punt. 'Late on Friday the thirteenth of January or early the following morning. Telling us how and what you two discussed will go a long way to putting you in the clear.'

Arnold leaned back in his chair, eyeing Chase shrewdly. A few moments later, he pulled a tight, humourless smile and shook his head. 'No, no, no. You don't know anything of the sort.'

'You can't be sure what we do or do not know,' Chase retorted.

'I can on that score, Sergeant. I can be absolutely bloody certain that you don't know my sister contacted me. For the very good reason that she didn't. I last spoke to Grace in the early hours of New Year's Day. I called to wish her a happy new year and to warn her one last time about travelling without her mobile. We had no contact after that. So please, if you're going to bluff me, you have to do better than that.'

Chase gave up gracefully. He allowed a momentary smile of mea culpa. 'Fair enough. I had to give it a go. You're quite certain none of the people she camped with that night were known to Grace prior to her hike, or known to you in some way?'

'I can't know for certain if Grace had met any of them before. They all seem to enjoy hiking, so it's possible, I suppose. But this was the first time she'd walked this trail. She'd never tackled anything like it. This was her first big challenge.'

Chase switched tack once more. 'How about these college students, Jamie? You've admitted to trying to find the five friends, so I have to assume the two students are also of interest to you. What have you done and found out about them?'

'I've done nothing. I mean, now that I know who and what they are, I also know where to find them, right? Look, I'm working on scraps, and it seems to me that one of those blokes in the group is more likely to have been involved. I haven't finished with them yet. I figured I'd eventually get around to the students.'

Chase cleared his throat. He raised an extended forefinger. 'That's where you're wrong, Jamie. On both counts. You are done with those five lads, and you won't be going anywhere near those two students.'

'Says who?'

'Says me. Go home, Jamie. Go home and be with your parents. They're a lovely couple who are suffering greatly. They need you more than Grace does.'

The lad scoffed, shaking his head bitterly. 'You think you know my parents? You think you've even met them? That's not my mum and dad sitting in that house. Two months it's taken to turn them into the wreckage they've already become. Imagine how worn down they'll be in another two, or six, or a year…' He flapped a hand as if to say neither detective could possibly understand.

'You're right,' Chase admitted. 'I don't know them. But believe me, I know what they are going through because I've been doing this job for a long time. I may not understand at their level or yours. But I try my best to be empathetic. And when I say you're of no use here, no use to your sister, but that you would be an immense source of comfort to your parents if only you were with them, I mean it. Now, please, go home, Jamie. Leave us to do our jobs.'

Arnold sneered at him. Surly, but not fully committed to it. 'You have no right to tell me what to do. I'm breaking no laws by being here. And I'll tell you something else: I came to this nick voluntarily, and now I'm going to leave. I'm done with you and your silent partner here.'

As he rose, shoving the chair back with his legs, Chase also got to his feet. He met the young man's firm gaze with equal flint. 'Jamie, I can't insist you go home. I'm simply letting you know it's the right thing to do in the circumstances. Your mother and father are grieving, and they need the comfort of their now only child. But what I can and will do is prevent you from carrying on with your plans to track down the other men and young woman who spent the night camping with your sister. You're interfering with an ongoing investigation, and if I have to, I will have you arrested and charged.'

The young man stood there seething, his mouth curling. 'You can't do that. What about my rights?'

'Jamie, please see reason. Let's not allow it to get that far. I don't want to see you in the nick facing charges, but I can't have you running across our path while we investigate. I just can't. We're trying to find your sister's killer, and you're hampering our efforts.'

'How? You weren't even aware I was doing it until I came in here and told you.'

Aware that Arnold's rage was building as his voice grew louder and more strident, Chase softened his own stance and took a small step backwards. 'Listen to me. Just having you walking around asking questions might in some way interfere. As for the students, well, having you track them down and going at them blindly could undo whatever trust we've built up with them. If you put them on the defensive, we might learn nothing further from either of them. And what if you actually speak with Grace's killer, or an accomplice, without even being aware of it? What if whatever you say causes them to make a run for it? Please, take my advice and go home where you can do some good. Only harm can come from you trying to run your own investigation here.'

Following a moment of final resistance, the young man's shoulders sagged, and he hung his head. Chase knew he'd won this battle, though he couldn't be sure that Arnold would go home and leave them to it entirely. The pair shook hands before parting with no further words spoken.

When they were alone, Chase turned his attention to his colleague. 'That young lad was right about something,' he said.

'Oh, yeah? And what might that be?' Laney asked.

'About you being the silent partner. You didn't utter a single word. Not even a huff of frustration or annoyance. What's that all about?'

She shrugged. 'Occasionally, very occasionally, I see no value in adding my words of wisdom. You handled that so well, I didn't think I could improve upon it.'

'My, my. High praise indeed.'

'Ah, maybe I'm on the blob and not feeling myself.'

Chase wrinkled his nose. 'I don't need to know that, thank you.'

She reached up to pat his cheek and give it a tweak. 'Aw, is my little cupcake embarrassed by women's problems? Does he go all queasy at the thought of me having the painters in? When I'm having a visit from aunty Flo? When I'm on the rag?'

Shaking his head, Chase said, 'Enough, please. You call it whatever you want to call it, but I don't have to hear about it.'

'No, you just don't want to have to think about it, more like.'

'You may be right. So why not just let it go?'

Laney gave a huge broad grin. 'Because then I wouldn't get to fuck with you, Royston. And where would be the fun in that? But getting back to the job in hand, while you and Jamie were gabbing, I had a missed call from DI Fox.'

'Call him back, would you? We could do with some good news.'

Laney did as he asked. She'd barely started speaking when her body went stiff, and her eyes found Chase's. He instantly knew something was wrong, and when she ended the call, he said, 'Just tell me. No sugar-coating.'

Laney swallowed once. 'Gablecross received a call from Marlborough College. Isaac Levy left the campus at lunchtime but has not returned for his afternoon classes.'

THIRTY-FOUR

Marie Hodgson was not pleased to see them. Sitting alongside her in the Second Master's well-appointed office, Professor Jeffrey Lennon was tight-lipped and clearly enraged about something. DS Chase thought he understood their unease – after all, they had somehow managed to lose a student under their protection and were bound to be both embarrassed and defensive. Perhaps that also explained the Housemaster's anger, though it looked as if both college staff members were avoiding the sidelong glances of the other. Chase wondered if words had been exchanged prior to his arrival.

'Where to begin with this one?' he said as he and Laney took their seats. 'It's a bit of a mess, wouldn't you agree?'

'It ought not to have happened,' Hodgson said with obvious reluctance. 'I regret to say that in this instance we have failed the Levys.' As she spoke, she turned her head to glare at Lennon, making it clear to the two detectives where she was apportioning blame.

'It really couldn't have been helped,' the professor snapped, hooking one leg over the other and turning his gaze upon the tall central window overlooking the quad. 'I cannot be expected to keep my eyes on both of them if they choose to go their separate ways.'

'How about we save the recriminations and get on with why we're here,' Laney suggested curtly. 'You're a man and a woman so you can't compare the size of your todgers – though please do accept my apologies if I've misgendered either of you. Without the pissing contest, then, would one of you please explain what happened and how you managed to screw up?'

Hodgson's tight focus on her colleague narrowed all the more. He must have felt its weight, because after a few moments of silence he shifted his attention back to the two police officers.

'First, let me make it crystal clear that we are not their keepers.'

'I thought that's precisely what you were, Professor,' Laney said sharply. 'And all the more so given the current situation both Isaac and Monica find themselves in.'

'Not their keepers, no,' Lennon argued. 'Their de facto guardians, perhaps. But I would remind you that Isaac Levy chose to remain at college, chose to remain under our watchful eye. What's more, his parents agreed to it. They did not attach additional security to their son, which they could easily have afforded to do. In effect, they were happy to allow us to do our duty in safeguarding the boy.'

'And how's that going for you?'

'Your sarcasm is noted, *Constable*. But the fact is, myself and others were keeping close tabs on both Isaac and Monica. It was Isaac who chose to leave the grounds and meet friends for lunch in town. I asked him if that was wise under the circumstances, but as he rightly pointed out, he'd be in the presence of others throughout and we were not his jailers.'

Chase took up the conversation. 'Okay. Presumably you have a list of names of those he was due to meet with. Have you checked with them to ask if he arrived, and if so, what time he left and with whom?'

The Housemaster's cheeks reddened, and he started to blink rapidly. His hands found itches to scratch. 'I… I neglected to ask Isaac who he was meeting for lunch. He said friends, I assumed they were from college and that they would walk into town with him and escort him back again.'

'You assumed rather than clarified?' Chase asked, appalled.

'I just said so, didn't I?' Lennon's voce dripped with arrogant contempt.

'So you did. Precisely how bright do you have to be to work here as a Professor?'

'More so than a detective, I assure you.'

'And yet this detective would have clarified. But let's put that to one side for the time being. You have no idea who he was having lunch with, but do you know where he was going?'

'No.'

'You didn't ask, or he didn't say?'

'I didn't ask.'

'Hmm. I don't suppose Mensa will be calling any day soon. Have you since spoken to Isaac's known friends in college?'

'Yes. Of course I have. None of them had arranged to have lunch with him, but one of them did spot Isaac carrying his backpack as he left the grounds.'

'We'll need to speak to them. How about at the gate – do students just come and go? Do you have surveillance cameras at the gates?'

'Our younger students must sign in and out and have valid reasons for doing so,' Mrs Hodgson interrupted. 'But our older students are adults and we naturally respect their greater freedom.'

'Have your staff manning the gates been spoken to about Isaac?'

'Yes. I did that myself. Neither of them noticed him, I'm afraid. The flow of foot traffic at that time, even with staggered lunch breaks, is considerable.'

Purely out of interest and to poke the bear one more time, Chase found himself asking, 'In that case, how can you be certain your younger students always sign in and out?'

'Because we instruct them to, DS Chase.'

'And being Marlborough students, they, of course, always do as they are instructed. What time did Isaac's friend see him leave the campus?'

Ignoring the rebuke, Hodgson said, 'A little after twelve-thirty.'

Chase checked his watch. Allowing an hour at most for lunch, the boy was more than two hours late. He was not immediately concerned about Isaac Levy's welfare. The backpack made all the difference, suggesting his absence was by choice. He'd simply made up the story about meeting pals for lunch and had instead made a bolt for it with his gear. Which begged the question…

'Professor Lennon, have you checked Isaac's possessions? Is his camping equipment missing along with the backpack?'

'Actually, Monica did so, and she confirmed he must have taken it with him.'

'In that case, I'm sure Mr Levy will have his own questions for you about how this was allowed to happen. I'm more interested in speaking with Monica Cilliers.'

Lennon started to speak when he was abruptly cut off by the Second Master coughing and raising a hand. 'No protests, please, Professor,' she said. 'We are way beyond that kind of petty behaviour. I've already cleared it with Monica's parents.'

The man sprang from his chair as if hastily ejected from it. He stood glaring down at Hodgson, his hands balled. 'This is an outrageous abuse of authority,' he snapped. 'And you really ought to know better, Second Master. Just because these people snap their fingers doesn't mean you have to jump.'

Hodgson met his gaze for a couple of seconds, then calmly said, 'Professor Lennon, I have made allowances for your recent personal circumstances. But enough is enough. Either retake your seat and be quiet unless you are asked a question, or leave the room. Frankly, I don't care much either way. I refuse to be patronised, and these officers deserve some respect.'

Lennon's mouth quivered in concert with his chin, and for a moment, Chase thought he might actually cry. But then the man took a deep breath and folded himself meekly back into his chair. Chase thanked Hodgson for her co-operation and asked if it would be all right to speak with Cilliers immediately. More than anything, he wanted to take the girl back to the nick, to force her out of her comfort zone, but it wasn't a hill he was willing to die on.

*

When they'd met the girl previously, she had come across as unflustered and level-headed, but when she entered the room on this more strained occasion, Monica Cilliers was clearly distraught. Her face was drawn, eyes red-rimmed. She sniffled with every step, and the moment she sat down she began to shift uneasily in her seat.

Unable to help himself, Professor Lennon filled the initial silence. 'For the record, I want to make my concerns clear one last time. I am against the police questioning Monica in this or any other matter at this time. It's unacceptable for our college to allow it.'

'Then you are excused, Professor,' Hodgson said, a hard edge to her voice. 'Please, leave us.'

At this, Cilliers looked up, startled and blinking. 'No, please, let Jeff… the Prof stay,' she pleaded. 'He is my Housemaster, after all, and I feel I need somebody sympathetic in the room with me.'

'What on earth makes you say something like that?' Hodgson asked her. 'You have the full support of the college, Monica. And myself. Please, don't be misled into thinking these police officers wish you any harm or ill-will. They are here to talk to you about Isaac, nothing else.'

'I'd still prefer it if the Professor remained in the room.'

Hodgson glanced at Chase, who nodded. 'Provided Professor Lennon doesn't make any further outbursts, I have no problem with that,' he said. 'But given his previous form, I wouldn't count on his restraint.'

The Second Master turned to her member of staff. She held up a hand with a single finger raised. 'You have one final chance,' she told him. 'Another interruption and I will have you escorted from the building pending disciplinary action.'

The energy crackling with tension, DC Laney looked over at Lennon and said, 'Don't make this any more difficult than you already have, cupcake. Believe me, if you need ejecting from the room, I'm more than happy to do it myself. And with one arm tied behind my back. To be honest, I'd like to hear you squeal like a little girl.'

'Let's move on, shall we?' Chase said after clearing his throat. His eyes settled on Cilliers, whose features were all taut lines and sharp angles. 'Monica, in your own words, please tell us what you know about Isaac's absence.'

After two false starts, her lips trembling, the girl leaned forward, hands wringing when she replied. 'I have no idea where he is. You must believe me. This has come as a complete shock to me.'

'So as far as you were aware, Isaac was simply meeting some friends for lunch.'

She nodded, her eyes glassy. 'That's what he told me, yes.'

'Did he also tell you who and where?'

'No. I asked him, but he… I suppose he shrugged it off.'

'You didn't see him leave?' Laney asked her.

'No. We weren't in the same lessons together before lunch, so I hadn't seen him since breakfast.'

'I believe you checked to see if his camping gear was missing, correct?'

'Yes, that's right. We cleaned our kit together after our last hike in January, and I helped him pack everything and stow it away. He did the same for me.'

Chase nodded, but he sensed something wasn't quite right. Cilliers seemed to be more than concerned for her boyfriend. There was fear in her voice, anxiety bordering on despair. Her body shook as she hugged herself, her reaction more than that of a girl worried about her close friend.

'What is it, Monica?' he asked softly. 'What is it you're not telling us?'

She shook her head. 'Nothing. There's nothing wrong.'

'I didn't say there was something wrong. I wondered what you were leaving out, but I'm also concerned about what you're going through. What could be wrong, Monica? Please tell us… we're here to help.'

Gradually, as if in slow motion, Monica Cilliers fell apart. Dissolved right in front of their eyes. She put her head in her hands and began to weep, moaning and snuffling as she angrily brushed tears from her cheeks. Chase noticed Lennon start to leave his chair, but he was beaten to it by the Second Master, who crouched down by the girl and wrapped both arms around her.

'There, there,' she whispered soothingly. 'It can't be that bad, my dear girl. Things never are in the cold light of day. Please, tell us what's wrong. None of us can help you if we don't know how.'

When she looked up, Cilliers was a picture of misery. 'He told me not to tell. Not to say anything to anybody.'

'Who told you not to say anything?' Chase asked. 'You mean Isaac?'

When the girl nodded through her tortured sobs, he prodded further. 'Monica, what are you not supposed to tell us? I can see it's disturbing you enormously to hold onto it, so just tell us and we'll do everything we can to help.'

Weeping uncontrollably, she shook her head. Hodgson, still clinging to the girl, turned to look over her shoulder at the two detectives. 'I think we have to stop this,' she said. 'The poor thing is close to hyperventilating.'

She was right. They ought to step back, allow the girl to settle. But Chase had the overwhelming impression that this was their one chance to learn whatever Cilliers was keeping from them.

'Monica,' he said in a flat and even tone. 'The only way you're going to overcome this is by telling us everything you know. Is it Isaac's location? Do you know where we can find him? Do you know why he ran?'

This time, Cilliers put her head back and shrieked, a cry of utter misery. When she was spent, she turned to him, shaking her head but somewhat calmed by venting. 'This isn't about him leaving. You think I'd be that upset about something so… He told me he'd slit my throat if I said anything. Said he'd do the same to every member of my family, too, if I didn't keep quiet.'

Chase felt his heartbeat quicken. 'What do you mean, Monica? What aren't you telling us?'

Her face became a mask, eyes widening and cheeks hollowed out. 'How don't you already know!?' she screamed at him. 'Why do you think he's running? You think he's frightened of one of those boys? Why would he be? *They're* not the problem.'

'Then what is?' Laney demanded. 'Or *who* is?'

'*He* is. Isaac. Isaac killed her.' The girl's words seemed to freeze time for a moment. Before the echo of her voice fell away, she added on a faltering sigh, 'Isaac murdered that girl on the hill.'

THIRTY-FIVE

'Walk us through everything she said to you,' Knight told Chase. The DCI sat in her usual spot, one leg crossed over the other, her foot bobbing.

He and Laney had collected Alison May on the way over to Gablecross for an urgent briefing. Before leaving Marlborough, they had the college nurse check out Monica Cilliers to ensure she was fit to continue. Laney then requested a uniform presence to remain with her until such time as she was able to provide a formal statement. The hastily arranged meeting back at GC was well attended, and Chase referred to the notes he had taken.

'According to Monica, on that Friday night when the hikers first got together inside the Black Horse, it was the usual revelry you might expect from a bunch of like-minded people coming together. They shared an interest and fed off that. But the more drink they put away, the more Grace Arnold amped up the flirting. Both Monica and Isaac noticed what was going on, and when they found out that the boys had decided to decamp from the field they were in to join Grace on the hillside, the pair went along with them as they were concerned for the girl's safety.'

'Christ!' DI Fox said. 'There's bloody irony for you.'

Chase nodded. 'Yeah. Anyhow, the drinking continued and when one of the lads used his phone to play some music, Grace started smooching with each of them in turn. Evidently, it got pretty steamy, and our students went from feeling protective towards the girl to realising she was well up for it. They came to realise that if anything happened of a sexual nature, she'd be a keen participant. Seeing the way things were going, Monica and Isaac turned in for the night and left the others to it.'

'They weren't bothered that Grace might well have lost her inhibitions to booze or drugs rather than just fancying these lads?' Knight asked.

'Apparently not. Monica told us Grace was the instigator even before she got drunk.'

'And she ended up going with one or more of the lads that night.'

'It certainly looks that way. Neither Isaac nor Monica actually saw what took place, but they heard it. To them it sounded as if she might have taken them one after the other. So, yes, Grace definitely had sex with more than one of them, and most likely all five.'

DS Jude Armstrong blew out his cheeks. 'Shit! That's one part of this whole sorry mess I do not want to have to relate to her poor parents.'

'I know what you mean,' Chase muttered. 'And I hope to find a way to avoid having to. Thing is, Monica told us that while it was going on, Isaac got excited by the sounds drifting across to them. He wanted to have sex with her while it was all happening, but she refused. She says the very idea disgusted her and she couldn't wait to leave the following morning. In fact, if it hadn't been for the awful weather she'd've insisted on going there and then.'

'Can't say I blame her.'

'Me neither. After a while she fell asleep, but something woke her, and she realised Isaac was no longer with her in the tent. Her mind immediately drifted to Grace putting it about earlier and Isaac being annoyed when Monica refused him, and she wondered if he'd crept over to the girl's tent. As you might expect, Monica pulled on a jacket and her boots and went to see for herself. But when she got there, she walked into a completely different scene altogether. She says she found Isaac standing over Grace's body, and that he was breathing heavily and holding an axe that she hadn't noticed was missing from her camping equipment. Isaac turned and wrapped a hand over his girlfriend's mouth to stop her from screaming. When he thought she had calmed down, he let her go, returned to Grace, and started covering her body over with snow. When he was done, he calmly took Monica by the hand and led her back to their tent. Neither of them said a word.'

Chase paused to take a deep breath before continuing. 'Based on a conversation Monica says the two of them had afterwards, Isaac's version of events is that a mixture of booze, lust, and curiosity got the better of him. He decided to sneak across to the other side of the copse to see if he could spy on Grace and whoever might be with her at the time. He admitted he intended to gratify himself. Instead, he virtually stumbled into Grace who was wandering around outside in the snow, still buzzing, and apparently still horny. She embraced him, put her hands all over him, and against his will tried to have her way with him. He reckons he panicked, tried to fend her off because by this time he was flaccid, but in doing so, he somehow managed to choke her. With Grace gasping for air and threatening to tell the police the following day, the boy's panic dug deeper and instead of trying to help her, he went back to the tent, fetched his axe, and swung it at her a couple of times.'

'Jesus!' Knight breathed. 'The very thought chills me to the bone.'

'Yeah, I know. Monica was far from convinced by his bullshit story. She thinks he went there looking for sex, tried it on with Grace, who was having none of it, that Isaac raped her or at the very least tried to, and then murdered the girl. Monica revealed that their own relationship could be fairly turbulent at times, and that he had fake choked her on a couple of occasions during sex. She told us she doesn't believe he would have done anything had he not been both drunk and frustrated, and that it all just went so badly wrong in that one fateful moment. Essentially, Isaac killed Grace because he couldn't face living with what he'd done.'

The air was electric inside the incident room. It was the breakthrough they had striven for, yet it left them with as many questions as it had answered.

'All of which means Monica covered for her boyfriend, despite him wanting to have sex with the girl he ultimately murdered,' DC Efe Salisu said, seemingly nonplussed.

'Not because she wanted to,' Laney replied. 'According to her, anyway. The way she tells it, he bullied and coerced and literally terrorised her into it. She told us the threats he made against her and her family were awful, and after seeing what he'd done to Grace, Monica had no doubt that he was capable of carrying them out.'

'Even so,' Fox chipped in, 'that's a massive lie to live with.'

'And she did it astonishingly well to begin with,' Chase observed. 'She was extremely convincing when interviewed.'

'One of which she did without Levy present,' Knight pointed out. 'Surely if she was going to break, she had every opportunity to do so then.'

'I mentioned that to her. Monica said she couldn't really explain it, except to say that Isaac had repeated his threat shortly beforehand. He told her how much her family would suffer, and that seems to have done the trick. What we thought was composure was, in reality, terror. I failed to read it.'

'Me, too,' Laney said. 'She had me fooled as well.'

'Sounds to me as if she needed to do precisely that,' said DS Armstrong. 'A case of saying whatever he told her to and behaving precisely as she had to in order to keep herself and her family safe.'

'The details are convincing enough,' Chase said, eyeing the entire group. 'The only people other than us who knew exactly how Grace was murdered were her close family. Even then, we neglected to mention the sexual abuse. I suppose it's possible that one of them might have leaked some details, but they weren't privy to what we held back.'

'The fact that Grace's body was found yards away from her tent for a start,' DCI Knight finished for him.

Nodding, Chase said, 'That could only have come from somebody who was there and who either witnessed what took place or saw the aftermath.'

'That's not quite true, Royston,' said a weak voice. All eyes drifted across to TDC May. She bit her lip, but then sat up straight and gathered herself. 'Sorry, but I think you're overlooking the man who discovered her body.'

Chase winced. 'Ouch! You're absolutely right, Alison. Thank you for picking me up on that. We obviously asked him to keep the details of the crime scene to himself, and I've not seen anything in the media accredited to him, but he saw enough to have let something critical slip.'

'Even so, the fact that Monica Cilliers knew it counts for a lot,' Laney said. 'That and the sexual activity, the two blows to the head…'

'I agree. I don't think she heard it from anybody else. She was there, she saw it all. Plus, why lie about it? She's already admitted to covering for Isaac. Alison makes a valid point, but I think Monica spoke from first-hand knowledge.'

'In that case,' Knight said, 'we have a genuine suspect and will pour all our resources into locating him. However, it still begs one question: what happened to those five young lads? If our previous suspect, Ashley Robertson, isn't the killer and didn't take or lure his friends somewhere, who else has them? And why?'

THIRTY-SIX

He knows it must be dark outside, the temperature plummeting. In all likelihood, frost was already forming, gradually overtaking the land like some icy virus freezing everything it came into contact with. The world would soon become stark and brittle, a fragile environment into which few would willingly stumble.

On the first day of captivity he had consumed an entire bottle of water in several greedy gulps, not considering conservation. Later, he had taken a drink from the cold-water tap hanging over the tiny porcelain basin. It tasted metallic and oily, and no matter how long he allowed the water to run, its stream retained a cloudy brown colour.

It's only dirt. Mud. It's not shit, man. It's really not.

He could drink it if he had to. The man in the balaclava was running late, and if for some reason he had stopped coming altogether, then there really was no alternative. A person simply couldn't function for long without water, no matter how bad it tasted, no matter what level of faecal matter it contained.

When it came to a lack of food, his body would quickly start to break down its own fatty deposits to help sustain him. Without water, he wouldn't last much longer than three days. With water intake but no food, he maybe had a month or two. But add the cold temperatures and damp into that equation, and he really didn't fancy his chances of living beyond four-to-six weeks.

So where are you? he asked himself.

An abandoned prison? Perhaps a juvenile detention facility? He recalled being led down a set of what felt like concrete steps, so given the damp and water leakage he must be being held in the basement of whatever type of building lay above. Perhaps situated on the site of an old unused armed forces base, this might even be the place where they sent the men and women who failed to live by the rules.

Does it matter?

Yes. It did. In that moment, it mattered more than anything else he could think of. Because his location determined how long he might remain locked away in the room without being discovered. Land was expensive. Not many people let it sit with derelict buildings serving no useful purpose for too long. They'd surely want to sell up, make a killing from the intended development of a new shopping centre or plot of houses. Even the armed forces needed an injection of cash, didn't they?

He tried to raise his spirits, clinging to the last vestiges of hope. But in the end, it was useless, and the stark reality of his situation held sway. It took a long time for places to become as run-down as this one, and although its utilities worked, the heating and water supply were on their last legs. All of which told him none of it had been used for its original purpose in many years.

What were the chances of them selling up any day soon? And even if they did, how long before the new developers explored the basement of whatever this building was? The answer was obvious. And terminally bleak.

Too long.

He realised that just because the man had not come so far today it didn't automatically follow that he wouldn't arrive later on, or turn up the next day, or the day after that. That unforgiving figure might simply breeze in at any given moment and begin his routine. Yet he sensed a dramatic shift had led to this change in routine. Something had altered, fundamental enough to explain why the man had not come to drop off the sandwich, bag of crisps, and bottle of water. Or to deliver a threat and ask his questions.

What do you know about Grace Arnold?

Not even her surname before the masked figure had first asked him.

What happened to her that night?

Now, that was the real question. And had been all along.

THIRTY-SEVEN

An hour later and Chase was sitting in Detective Chief Superintendent Crawley's office alongside Superintendent Waddington and DCI Knight. The DCS had listened without interruption to their breakdown of events. When they were finished, he spread his hands and said, 'In reality, despite everything we're doing and are about to do, locating Levy will most likely rely on information received from the public. That's just the way this works according to the stats, and I have no reason to doubt them or suspect this will be any different. It's a simple matter of numbers: there are more of them than there are of us.'

It was hard to disagree, but Chase remained silent. As did the others. After a moment, Crawley leaned back in his chair, laced his fingers together and cupped his neck in his hands. 'The capture of Isaac Levy may not result from our own efforts, but tell me what policing is in play here anyway.'

Waddington looked at Knight, who picked it up from there. 'Beginning at the college and working our way out, we're already obtaining all the CCTV we can, plus in-store security footage from all the shops in the area. We're talking to bus and cab companies in case Levy used transport to leave the town more swiftly and have also asked them for their own security feeds starting from the minute the lad left campus. Unless you have any objections, we'll be opening it up to the media on a limited basis, appealing for people to report any sightings of the boy. The college is asking students if they saw Levy off site, and if so, getting them to expand on that.'

With a grunt, the Chief Super turned to Chase. 'Royston, you're the only one here who has actually spoken with the boy. What are your thoughts?'

Chase had been considering this aspect since learning about Levy going missing. It cast him in a bad light, but he was nothing if not honest. 'It's clear that I misread him. I mean, he was jumpy, and I always thought he knew more than he was willing to tell us, but I didn't read him as a killer. As it turns out, my radar was well off, because I misjudged Monica Cilliers even more.'

'How so?'

'The girl admits to knowing her boyfriend murdered a young woman. She knew this on both the previous occasions that we spoke, yet I never saw it. Not even a little. She was – or at least seemed to be – perfectly relaxed on both occasions. Yet she had this and Levy's threats hanging over her, which must have been churning her up inside. And I completely missed it.'

'We've all been there, so don't be too hard on yourself. These were not formal interviews and at the time you weren't questioning either of them as suspects. Still, in retrospect, can you think of anything that might have tipped you off?'

Chase shook his head, his mood deteriorating rapidly. 'That's just it. I've got nothing. I saw something out of place with him, but nothing at all with her. Yet they were both hiding all this from me. I can't think what I missed, or how.'

'Maybe you didn't,' Knight offered with an understanding smile. She hooked one trouser leg over the other. 'Perhaps they were both just good enough to keep it from you.'

Wrinkling his nose in disgust, Chase said, 'Thanks, but I ought to have caught it. With one of them, at least.'

'Any idea at all where Levy might be, or where he's heading?'

'My best guess is he turned right out of the college and headed to the High Street. If he hasn't called a cab or jumped on a bus and his intention was to camp, he'd've needed some provisions. We've asked the Waitrose there for their footage as a matter of urgency and I would expect to see him inside if he didn't use transportation. Would he then risk coming back past the college and heading west? I doubt it. If he continued east, he could then turn either north or south on the A346. There's a lot of open land if you go north, whereas if he takes the A346 south he's got Savernake Forest to hide himself away in. You have the Postern Hill campsite there, but I'm quite sure he'll avoid that. If I'm him, I'm going for deep forestation over open land any day of the week, but all the more so when I'm on the run and we've got snowstorms headed our way.'

'I don't know the place well,' Waddington confessed, 'but a forest doesn't sound good for us.'

'It's not,' Chase said. 'It's four and a half thousand acres, and dense. If he's clever – and he is – he'll keep on the move and switch location on a regular basis. Our chances of finding him with a physical search alone are not good. I think we need an eye in the sky with night vision and thermal imaging.'

'I can have a word with NPAS,' Crawley offered. 'Emphasise the urgency if there's a bidding war for time. After all, we are hunting for a murderer who might be regarded as armed and dangerous if he still has that axe with him.'

Chase nodded. Since waving goodbye to their own chopper in 2014, Wiltshire Police had relied on air support from the centralised National Police Air Service, which covered over forty territories. With both base and aircraft numbers cut, it had become increasingly difficult to summon up air support, and even more challenging to keep them airborne for any length of time once you had secured them. Almondsbury and Benson were the two closest bases, though requests could be made elsewhere if the more local aircraft had already been deployed.

'Without one, I fear we're scuppered,' he told the DCS. 'What you said about the public is true, in the majority of cases. But if he's in that forest, then thermal and night vision cameras from a chopper are our best bet of finding him.'

'I'll do what I can.' The DCS turned to Waddington. 'If we get that eye in the sky this evening and tonight, Russell, make sure you have sufficient forces deployed to move in to whichever locations they pinpoint. If Levy is out there, he won't be the only one, so we're bound to have some false shouts. But if it's him, I want him in handcuffs.'

'Give me the nod on funding and I'll make it work.'

Crawley cleared his throat. 'It's already going to cost us for the airtime, so let's you and I work on the numbers at the conclusion of this meeting.'

'I'll put myself on call,' Chase insisted. 'I can be there to ensure correct identification if need be.'

'Thank you, Royston,' Knight said. 'I suggest we move on to discuss our approach if we happen to reel him in overnight.'

'Monica Cilliers identified him as a killer, so there's no question in my mind that we have enough to make the arrest and then bring him back here for questioning. However, I think we can afford to keep our powder dry on charging. With extensions we'll have him for a few days, and if we need every hour, I say we use them.'

'Sounds to me as if you think he's unlikely to confess,' Waddington said.

'I think he'll say nothing until he has a brief, and I'm reasonably sure he'll keep it zipped for most of the questioning. His solicitor will be good enough to understand which questions he'll need to provide an answer for in terms of relying on in court. It would be pointless and not in his best interest to make no comment when asked about being on the hillside, meeting Grace Arnold and the other lads. So, yes, I reckon it will be slippery at best.'

'And Monica Cilliers' statement?'

'Let's see the precise nature of that once we have a copy. In my opinion, she fed us enough details to put insightful questions to him without showing our hand.'

'And if he doesn't believe it when we eventually let it be known?'

'His brief will confirm the veracity of the statement once we offer it up. They won't be able to deny her accusations.'

'But will the boy respond to them?'

Chase took a breath. He thought about the meaning of the question before replying. 'There are particular dynamics in play here, sir. These two were once close, but if everything Monica tells us is true then she must feel betrayed by him, not to mention scared shitless. He will understand that probably means she'll testify against him in court. Under those circumstances, he could go either way.'

'But what's your gut telling you, Sergeant?'

'My gut failed me before, sir. My mind also keeps wondering how and why the five lads were taken, and by who. The explanation behind that continues to elude us. Those unanswered questions might be clouding my judgement, but my instinct is telling me there's still more to this story than we know.'

THIRTY-EIGHT

Chase arrived home late and in a foul mood. Erin heated up some lasagne and served it with warm garlic bread. He wolfed the food down without tasting it, for once unable to appreciate his wife's cooking. It was a minimum of a two-beer night, and he savoured them more than usual. As if sensing his anxiety, Maisie was unusually quiet and kept curling up beside him on the sofa whenever she had the opportunity. He held his daughter close, laughed appropriately at her silly jokes, her gurning faces and stupid voices, before reading to her as she lay in bed. This perfect example of what he regarded as his idyllic homelife made little impact, however, and his wife was in tune with it the moment he came back downstairs.

'You want to talk about it?' she asked.

He closed his eyes, took a long, deep breath. 'That's all you seem to be saying to me lately. I'm sorry. I'm bringing this one home with me too often.'

'Don't you dare,' Erin said sharply. 'Don't treat me as if I'm some fragile little thing unable to cope when all is not chocolates and roses. I don't need you to apologise. I don't want you to apologise. In fact, I'd much prefer it if you took it back.'

Her look was stern enough to make him comply. 'I'm not sure there's anything to discuss, really,' he went on. 'I think my lousy mood is all my fault, so we might have to wait until it goes away of its own accord.'

Erin's eyes narrowed as she rested her chin on one hand. 'If it's your fault, then surely that means there is something we can talk over. If you're adamant, I don't want to pressurise you, but if you're wavering at all then let me in.'

Chase nodded, biting into his bottom lip. 'I messed up, Erin. We have a young kid on the run, and his girlfriend is telling us he's a killer who threatened her life to keep her quiet. I interviewed them both, together and separately, and somehow missed it all. The boy was nervous – even Alison May could see that much about him. But if he displayed any mannerisms associated with a killer, then I didn't notice. Equally, the girl was calm and collected, and I saw no evidence of her being under duress. How could I have missed all that?'

'Because you're human.' She touched his cheek and ran a thumb over its curve. 'This is the two Marlborough students you told me about, yes?'

'Yep.'

'But didn't you speak to them before as potential witnesses?'

'I did, yes.'

'So, not formal interviews under caution with you questioning them as suspects.'

'No, because they weren't at the time.'

'Right. But to me that says you didn't miss anything; you just didn't switch on to the possibilities.'

'In the context of what's happened since, that's just as bad. Yes, we did regard them as witnesses, but there was always the remote possibility of their involvement in Grace Arnold's murder.'

'But not there and then. Not during those interviews.'

Chase smiled at his wife. 'I know what you're doing. I even agree with you in part. I wasn't in full attack mode when I spoke with them, and in fact on the second occasion we thought they might be potential victims. I understand that, and perhaps it's the only consolation. My get-out clause. But deep down, I have to ask myself how none of what I've since learned registered with me at the time. How did it escape my attention? They're kids, not experienced, hardened criminals.'

Erin sat back, gesturing with an open hand. 'There you go. You've said it yourself. No, they weren't the type of criminal you usually deal with, so you didn't see them as such. You first saw two kids who might have witnessed something brutal but were staying silent to keep well out of it. Then two kids who might actually be in danger themselves. You weren't anticipating interviewing a vicious killer, nor a frightened girl keeping quiet out of fear. If you need one, there's your reason for missing it, Royston.'

Chase finally felt the tension go from his shoulders. 'You're a miracle worker,' he told his wife. 'Only you can take my foulest of moods and spin them around like that.'

Erin shrugged. 'It's sometimes easier to see when you're on the outside looking in. So, is that why you volunteered to be on call tonight?'

He nodded. 'Yeah. We had a confirmed sighting of the lad in the High Street and in-store footage from Waitrose showing him buying groceries and miscellaneous items. We didn't give up on the possibility that he'd hopped on a bus or called for a cab, but the camping gear and the purchase of provisions suggests we were right to think he'd chosen to move on and pitch a tent later the same night. I thought Savernake Forest was the most likely location. We have search teams and a chopper out there looking for him. If they grab him up, I want to be there when he's questioned. I can also help confirm ID at the location prior to that if there's any doubt.'

She pecked his forehead with her lips. Rested her brow against his. 'You do what you need to do, sweetheart. But you apologise to me for coming home in a bad mood again tomorrow night and you'll see my bad side.'

Chase laughed as he brushed hair from her face and tucked it behind an ear. 'That'll be an experience to savour,' he said. 'You don't have a bad side.'

*

Chase was wide awake when the call came in shortly after twelve-thirty in the morning. He moved slowly so as not to disturb Erin, speaking softly until he was downstairs in his tiny office.

Having plopped himself down into the chair, he beamed as he listened. After three false starts, spotting and moving in only to find the individual picked up by the helicopter's cameras was not Isaac Levy, they finally had their man. A thermal image – perhaps spooked by the sound of the aircraft hovering above – had been highlighted as it hurried through the forest, heading south-east. The pilot followed, guided by his co-pilot, whose eyes never left the screen. The police cordon moved in with grim purpose, shifting their point of attack. The figure emerged out onto open land before entering Bedwyn Common, which was as heavily wooded as the forest. There he hunkered down, perhaps believing himself to be invisible provided no dazzling torchlight picked him out from above. But as he waited for the danger to pass, the net closed in around him until he was eventually surrounded, confronted, and captured without putting up a fight.

Isaac Levy went without so much as a struggle. Having been cuffed and arrested on suspicion of murder, he was driven in a liveried traffic vehicle to Gablecross police station. By the time Chase received the call, Levy had been assessed by the on-duty police surgeon, processed by the custody officer, and was already sitting in a holding cell. His parents had been notified, and they were arranging for a solicitor to attend.

Chase was beside himself with joy. At times like this, it didn't matter who missed what. All the *what ifs* and *if onlys* counted for nothing when you eventually bagged your suspect. Although this was generally accepted as the easy part, with the much tougher stages to come in the form of reaching the charging phase followed by piecing together everything required by the Crown Prosecution Services to proceed to court, it was one of the most fulfilling aspects of any criminal investigation. Perhaps second only to achieving a guilty verdict.

He had a quick wash, got dressed in silence, let himself out, and drove a few minutes down the road to the station. Arriving at the same time as DCs Reuben Cooper and Paige Bowen, who'd been tasked with interviewing Levy, Chase spent some time with them sipping hot drinks and going over their strategy.

The planning and preparation phase of the process allowed them to review all available evidence relating to the offence. In this case, they had the circumstantial, in respect of Levy fleeing college and going into hiding, plus running from the police. This, Chase suggested, would be a cinch for the solicitor to bat away after consulting with their client; Levy was not on bail, had not been previously identified as a suspect, and had every right to camp out if he chose to. His only misstep was in skipping college classes. As for his attempt to avoid the police, at the point that he had begun to escape, the officers had not identified themselves and Levy could easily claim he'd fled in fear of whoever might be approaching him in the dark forest.

DCI Knight, who'd joined them as they covered what they had on Levy, agreed with him. 'It's weak, and we should use it as pure window dressing. What we do have and will rely on is witness testimony. I'll grant you that's nowhere near as much as I'd like to have going in, but it's something to use against him as and when we need to. Drip feed little snippets, keeping him puzzled and on the back foot.'

'Once we've provided him and his brief with the reason for the interview,' DC Cooper said, 'we'll move swiftly on to asking him to provide a fresh account of events in his own words.'

Nodding, Bowen said, 'I suggest we begin at the Black Horse pub. To my mind, nothing prior to that is relevant. Where his story deviates from the one provided by Monica Cilliers we challenge and allow him to clarify and confirm. We can then take a break and discuss his version and decide on how to proceed from there.'

'When you give them the reason for the interview, I assume you'll hold back on the details?' Chase asked. 'Such as who named him and precisely what they told us.'

'Of course. We'll let them know an allegation has been made concerning his actions and behaviour on the night in question, and then ask him to explain himself. We won't go into detail unless we feel comfortable doing so, which won't be until we've taken the first break. That way, either he coughs, or he provides us with a story we can begin to pick apart.'

'I think we all know the likely outcome,' Cooper said, his expression resigned. 'Based on the arrest details we hand over to the brief, Levy will be advised to provide a written prepared statement about that night and refer to it as and when the solicitor feels the kid needs to offer clarification. A decent brief is going to want the meat of our case laid out on the table before advising Levy again.'

Chase sighed. It sounded about right. Interviews were mostly frustrating affairs. Duty solicitors were no mugs and had their own routines, but were generally affable and might try to meet the police halfway. Any highflyer brought in by Levy's parents was bound to present himself as a barricade in his representation of his client, especially considering the weakness of the case against the lad.

'The lack of forensic evidence will count against us,' he said dourly.

Paige Bowen nodded. 'Undoubtedly. Mitigation in our favour are the circumstances under which Grace was found and the time she had been frozen. But as I'm sure Levy's brief will point out, that's the prosecution's problem. All we have to offer is the girl's statement and allegation.'

'But it may not be all we can acquire,' Chase said, his mind slipping once again to the five missing hikers. 'If we can find those lads and speak to them, it's possible that one or more of them saw everything that happened. After all, we were under the impression that their subsequent movements and lack of communication came as a reaction to one of *them* murdering Grace. But it could be equally explained as a reaction to having witnessed it.'

Cooper was keen on the idea. 'We could need it if this goes further than detention at this stage,' he said. 'Without a confession, the allegation and statement made by Monica Cilliers is unlikely to be enough for us to charge him. Just her word against his, though we might argue what she has to gain by telling us all about it. We might have to bail him at some point and hope that these lads are found and know something useful.'

'He's not going to confess,' Chase said firmly. 'I read him wrong before, when his anxiety was obvious, but there's no way he's going to cough. Especially with a brief sitting alongside him this time.'

THIRTY-NINE

DS CHASE, DC LANEY, DCI Knight, and DI Fox crammed themselves into a tiny room designed to hold no more than two people. None of them wanted to miss the interview being played out on a small monitor hooked up to the room's recording system.

The process began as Chase had predicted: having heard the broad stroke reasons for the arrest, Isaac Levy's solicitor, Brendan Hyde, spent an hour locked away with his client. In the interview room afterwards, Hyde, the expert criminal defence lawyer who had replaced Mr Levy's personal solicitor, Bevel, produced a handwritten statement from which Levy read. In terms of content, it was pretty much everything the boy had previously admitted to. When it came to delivery, Chase saw a difference in Isaac Levy's eyes. He noted an undercurrent of fear behind a frown of concern, as if the boy was mystified by something his solicitor had told him during their consultation.

'He's worried,' Chase observed to nobody in particular.

'Of course he is, cupcake,' Laney said with a gentle chuckle, which quickly became a cough as her lungs fought to clean themselves. 'He's in the nick with two hard-faced detectives on the opposite side of the table giving him evils. If I was in his shoes, I'd be bricking it.'

'No, it's more than that. I can't quite put my finger on it, but there's something in his expression this time that tells me he's disturbed by what his brief told him.'

They looked on as DC Bowen followed up. 'Tell us, Mr Levy, if everything in your statement is the truth, why did you go on the run?'

Their suspect licked his lips. 'On the…? I did no such thing. I wanted a break from college, that's all.'

'Without asking permission from your Housemaster? Without even telling your own girlfriend?'

'I probably wasn't thinking straight. I felt stressed out. My mental health has been suffering, which is why I needed to get away for a few days.'

'And yet the moment the police encroached on your position, you made a break for it. You tried to avoid capture. Why would you do that?'

'I had no idea it was the police in that forest with me. I heard noises, the sound of more than one person coming my way. I was frightened – it could have been anybody out there. I didn't want to be found by whoever it was.'

The sidelong glance at his solicitor prior to answering was telling, Chase thought. Hyde hadn't had long with the boy, but he'd coached him well.

Bowen wrinkled her nose as if to suggest her disbelief before moving on. 'Mr Levy, on the night of the thirteenth of January this year while you were camped on Cherhill Down, did you witness any physical contact between the lone female hiker, Grace Arnold, and the five young men who came as a group?'

Levy turned to look at Brendan Hyde, who nodded. This told Chase that the two had discussed specific questions the police might pose and had chosen to answer some. This was one of them.

'I wasn't aware of any, no.'

'So, you didn't, for example, see the young girl embracing any of the men, or any of them embracing her?'

'Not that I recollect, no.'

'You didn't see them dancing, kissing, perhaps?'

'I suggest you move on,' Hyde said curtly. A man of average height, weight, and appearance, the solicitor from one of London's top law firms nonetheless made his presence felt. 'My client has already told you that he does not recall any contact between the victim and these five men.'

Chase shook his head. The strategy was clear, and their job had become more difficult as a result. Claiming a lack of awareness or a lack of recall was not the same as saying it never happened, only that Levy was unaware of it or could not remember if it did. It meant he could not be caught out in a lie. Having suspects who provided only vague responses, if at all, was standard fare, and clearly the lawyer had spoken about this approach with his client.

Bowen kept her eyes on the boy. 'How about after you and your girlfriend, Monica Cilliers, retired for the night to your tent… did you overhear anything that sounded like Grace Arnold was perhaps enjoying herself with one or more of the young men?'

'Not to my recollection.'

'How about sounds of distress?'

'Not to my recollection.'

'You don't appear to remember much about that night, Mr Levy. Is there a specific reason why your recollections are so hazy?'

'Yes. I'd had a fair bit to drink.'

'I'm sure there must be something lodged in there. You do, after all, recall your evening in the pub. Do you remember seeing Grace flirting with the male hikers, or any of them flirting with her?'

The young man hesitated before allowing himself a nod. 'She was a little bit flirty, I suppose.'

'But not with you?'

Here his head popped up, jaw thrust forward. 'I was with my girlfriend, so, no.'

'Did that bother you at all, Mr Levy?'

'No. Why should it?'

Hyde cleared his throat heavily, shaking his head having drawn the young man's attention. Chase smiled to himself. Levy had asked a question of his own, inviting a response. Hyde did not approve. But at least they had begun to get a mixture of responses.

'Envy?' Bowen suggested. 'Jealousy, even.'

Levy gave a withering glare and scoffed. 'That doesn't make any sense. I was with Monica. What did I have to be jealous about?'

The DC nodded, paused, then asked, 'You were with her all night, Mr Levy?'

'How much longer before you get to the meat of this?' Hyde demanded, throwing his hands in the air as if exasperated by the line of questioning. 'For the benefit of the recording, I would like to register my disapproval that you have not yet disclosed the full nature of the allegations against my client, nor the identity of the person who made them.'

'If one of those fucking hikers said it was me, then they're lying bastards,' Levy snapped, clearly encouraged by his legal representative's outburst. But Hyde glared at him, a silent rebuke that prompted the boy to almost physically shrivel in his seat.

DC Reuben Cooper, who until this point had asked no questions, leaned forward and said, 'We'll conduct the interview at our own pace, Mr Hyde. We're coming to it, believe me. As for you, Mr Levy, please calm yourself down and answer my colleague's question: were you with Monica Cilliers all night?'

Levy's expression had turned glacial. He crossed his arms and nodded.

'For the recording, please,' Cooper said.

Before the boy could answer, Hyde leaned across and said something to him from behind his hand, obscuring his own mouth. Levy took a breath and said, 'No comment.'

'Are you sure about that?' Paige Bowen asked, a deep frown conveying her bemusement. 'Surely it's a simple enough question: you either were or were not with your girlfriend for the entire night.'

'I have no comment to make,' Levy confirmed.

'Very well. Then I put it to you that the two of you were not together for the entire night after you'd both retired to your tent. I put it to you that at some point you left the tent in search of Grace Arnold, that having discovered her outside her tent you tried to persuade her to have sex with you as you were fully aware that she'd earlier had sex with one or more of the other hikers. I further put it to you that Grace rebuffed your advances, and when she did, you attempted to have sex with her against her wishes, and that at some point you lost your temper and began to strangle Grace with your bare hands. Finally, I put it to you, Mr Levy, that when you were unsuccessful, you struck Grace Arnold twice on the back of the head with a small camping axe. Please, tell us about that in your own words.'

Chase was watching the boy's eyes the whole time, and rather than gleaming in defiance against an outrageous allegation, they dimmed and became flat and lifeless. Levy momentarily retreated into himself, suddenly unsure and unsettled. Something about the specific nature of the allegation had struck home, and Chase felt he knew the reason for the change in his disposition.

'Mr Levy,' DC Cooper prompted. 'Please tell us what happened. You've heard the allegation, and it genuinely is in your best interests to respond.'

The lad swallowed thickly and, running both hands across his head and through his dishevelled hair mumbled, 'No comment.'

'Do you not wish to defend yourself against that allegation, Mr Levy?'

'No comment.'

'Sir, what has been alleged is quite obviously extremely serious. We're giving you the opportunity to tell us your version of events, to either deny or admit to what we've put to you here today. Providing no comment does not, despite what Mr Hyde may have told you, help you in this situation. If, when this comes to court, you attempt to explain yourself, a jury might wonder why you elected not to do so when interviewed. Whatever inferences they take from that are up to them, but I suggest they won't regard the matter favourably.'

'My client has no comment to make to these allegations as they stand,' Hyde insisted, furiously scribbling notes on his A4 lined pad. 'What's more, you're skating perilously close to harassment.'

'That's nonsense,' Bowen replied, shaking her head. 'We're trying to help your client. I suggest you do the same. Now, Mr Levy, I'm going to give you one last chance to offer some defence to what has been alleged.'

The solicitor was the first to respond. 'It might help if you revealed which of the five hikers made these allegations, and whether they are, in fact, supported by a formal statement and any tangible evidence.'

Bowen glanced at her colleague, who nodded. 'I want to hear Mr Levy's response one last time before we move any further,' she insisted. 'I want it on record.'

'I don't wish to comment at this time,' the lad said, for the first time possibly remembering the precise phrasing suggested by his lawyer. Even so, his body language betrayed the words he had uttered. Isaac Levy was broken. Emotionally wrung out.

'Okay. You had your chance, Mr Levy. Let's take it one stage further, shall we? In fact, we know that when you approached Grace Arnold seeking to have sex with her, you did not have the axe with you. We know that you returned to the tent to snatch up the axe, retraced your steps, found Grace kneeling on the floor several yards away from her tent trying to recover from you having choked her, at which point you delivered two blows to her head. Does that additional information encourage you to provide us with the true version of events in your own words?'

'How...?' The words stuck in the boy's throat. He looked at both detectives in turn. His eyes were wide and round, unbelieving yet at the same time acknowledging.

Chase jerked his upper body closer to the screen, intent on Levy's twisted features. There it was. The expression he'd been waiting for. The realisation, followed swiftly by the overwhelming, gut-wrenching betrayal. But because he still couldn't be absolutely certain, clinging as he was to the faintest of hopes, the young man forced himself to resist.

'Who told you that?' Levy asked, shifting the focus of the question he had been about to ask.

'Who do you think might have told us?' Bowen asked him. 'Who would have been in the position to tell us?'

'It had… I don't know how, but it had to be one of the hikers. One of them covering for what they did themselves.'

'But surely by this time they were all tucked up in their own tents like you told us earlier.'

'Not whoever killed her, clearly.' Despite the boy's resilience, his insistence was growing weaker.

'But that was you, Mr Levy. You killed Grace Arnold. We've already established that.'

'You've established no such thing,' Hyde interrupted vociferously.

Bowen reacted in kind. 'I'd suggest the allegation and subsequent witness statement says we have. To our satisfaction, at least. Now, Mr Levy, I'll ask you once again to provide us with your own version of events by way of a response to the allegations put to you. I can categorically tell you that a full confession will have a positive effect on any sentence passed down. Personally, I'm not a fan, but judges tend to look favourably on a confession and a guilty plea as it doesn't waste court time.'

For a moment the room was silent, but then Levy's chair squealed as he leaned back and said, 'Tell me who made the allegation and I'll tell you what you want to know.'

DC Paige Bowen took her time. She either read or pretended to read through some notes contained in a folder on the table in front of her. In the room close by, those gathered around the monitor were hushed. Eventually, the detective nodded to herself. 'I suspect you must already know the answer to your own question, Mr Levy. I think the precise details relating to the murder itself gave it away. It wasn't one of the hikers, as your solicitor seems to believe. It wasn't you, and it can't have been Grace. That really only leaves one witness on the hill from that night.'

'Monica,' Levy breathed.

Bowen nodded. 'Yes. Monica Cilliers.'

The boy's face crumpled like paper squeezed in a tight fist. Tears leaked from both closed eyes. He lowered his chin almost to his chest and sat there like a deflated life-size doll.

DC Cooper gave him a few seconds before prompting their suspect with a verbal nudge. 'Mr Levy. Do you have anything you wish to offer in your defence?'

This time the young student looked up with purpose, tears unchecked. 'Are you telling the truth? Did Monica really tell you all that?'

'Yes, she did.'

'You have this girl's statement to that effect?' Hyde demanded.

'We do. What's more, Ms Cilliers has agreed to provide testimony in court.'

Hyde made to speak with Levy privately, but the boy shooed him away with his hand. 'I'll tell you,' he said, looking at both detectives in turn. 'But it won't be my *version* of events like you asked. There is no *version* of what happened. There's just what happened. The truth. And I'll tell you everything, because believe me, you don't know the half of it.'

FORTY

I can't recall ever being as cold as I was that night. Or as excited... at one point, anyway. As it eventually turned out, that excitement didn't last long. Just... just long enough to matter, I suppose.

It was Monica who coaxed me into going camping in deep mid-winter. With the freezing temperatures, heavy snow, and predicted storms, I told her she was insane. But she insisted on testing ourselves in the bleakest conditions. Examine our endurance, our mental health, not to mention physical strength. And well, when Monica wants her own way, Monica usually gets her own way.

We did the lazy thing to begin with by taking a bus, having chosen to stop off at the Black Horse pub before making a final decision about where to stay the night. I was still harbouring hopes of changing her mind, especially once she saw the snow holding up and laying a fresh new layer over the terrain. I asked about a room at the pub, only to find out they didn't do B&B. We were stuck on our own. But then we ran into those other hikers, and everything changed.

It's rare that you find that kind of instant chemistry with a bunch of strangers, but we hit it off with them right away. Fellow hikers, I suppose. In the blood. It is all we talked about at first, sharing our love of hiking and camping, telling our stories, and discussing the great hikes. We all agreed we'd love to do the Pacific Crest Trail one day, but if you're going to complete that one you really need some good hiking experience behind you. It requires a monumental feat of physical and mental endurance. The PCT is over 2,500 miles long and takes several months to complete the whole thing. But there are detour trails you can take that include snow time, which is why we decided to brave it back in January.

At first, we assumed Grace was with the five lads, but when we found out she was on her own, we were pretty shocked. I mean, I'm not sure if either Monica or I would have walked that trail in such bad weather on our own, but she did and was completely off the grid, too. She was nice, and yes, she was gorgeous, so every time she and I spoke I felt Monica's eyes on me. I wouldn't have said she was the jealous type, but that was before that night.

It felt like the natural thing to do when they all asked us to join them on the hillside, and we were both up for it, especially when they said they had booze and music, and we could have a bit of a party up there around a campfire. I don't even remember if we discussed it first – we just went with them.

It was snowing hard by this time, so we made camp under the trees to keep it at bay as much as possible. They provided a decent protective canopy, depending on how harsh the wind got and in which direction it blew. It was a strange sensation, a bit like when a tube train rushes into the station while you're standing on the platform.

One of the lads got the fire going, put some music on and the drink started flowing. Like I said, Grace was a nice girl, but at one point something clicked inside her like a switch was thrown. She was friendly, funny, attentive, and very outgoing to begin with. But as the party went into its second hour she really began to loosen up. Believe me, this went way beyond flirting. She was making it abundantly clear to every single one of those guys that she was available, and she didn't seem to care in which order or how many at a time. She danced with them, clinging to them, rubbing her…

herself up against them. You could tell she was getting them going, even though we were all wearing heavy clothing.

Grace's personality changed so much that at one point I leaned across to Monica and asked her in a low voice if she thought one of the other hikers had slipped something into the girl's drink. Monica reckoned Grace was simply drunk, but I had a hunch it was worse than that. The change seemed too severe for the amount of booze she'd put away. But then, I suppose it could have been that she was just pissed out of her skull because she wasn't used to it.

To tell the truth, it started to get a bit embarrassing, and a couple of the lads looked our way as if wishing we were not there. Make no mistake, all eight of us knew what was going to happen. I remember Monica getting a bit snappy with me, asking me if I wanted to join them in teaming up on Grace. Of course, I told her I wanted no part of it, but the truth is Grace was attractive enough to make you at least think twice about what it might be like to fu… sleep with her. The way she gyrated her body and behaved, she was as horny as hell, and I admit I wanted her.

I knew nothing could happen, though. Yeah, it turned me on, but I had my own girl. And while I really wanted to see Grace in action, I didn't want to see her screwing those other hikers. I suggested to Mon that we called it a night and went to our tent, and although everybody asked us to stay up and enjoy the party with them, I knew they didn't mean it. They couldn't wait to see the back of us.

Turns out, it was like the last days of Rome up there. I honestly can't tell you if Grace had more than one of them at the same time, but she screwed them all as far as I could tell. We were on the other side of the copse, but we could still hear them. You know… sex sounds. Grunting and moaning, laughter, others cheering them on. I think that whatever she did, she did it out in the open by the fire, and if I had to guess I'd say she had a few of them teaming up on her at one point.

After a while it all settled back down. We heard them saying goodnight to each other – though nothing from Grace. While they were… doing whatever they were doing, I tried to get Monica interested in our own bit of fun. I managed to persuade her to start using her hand on me, but then after just a few seconds she accused me of thinking about Grace and not her while she was tugging me off. She wasn't wrong, but naturally I didn't admit it. Monica told me to do it myself if I wanted finishing off, but said she wouldn't touch me again that way until either we or Grace were off that hillside.

She went to sleep quite quickly afterwards, but I was still horny, and I started to wonder what it might be like with Grace. I thought if I got up and went for a walk, I might catch a glimpse of her, even take a peek inside her tent to see if she was naked. I found her dozing on top of her sleeping bag. She had pulled her clothes up, but you could see she'd done it hastily because there was still plenty of flesh showing. I knelt down and started touching her and myself at the same time. I felt her tits at first and then between her legs. Outside her clothing to begin with, but when she squirmed and let out a groan, I put my hands inside her thick leggings and she wasn't wearing any knickers. By then I couldn't resist, and I tried to… well, penetrate her. And why not? She'd just fucked five other blokes without complaint, so what was one more? Not rape, that's for sure.

Only… she did resist. She started struggling, and I'd barely managed to get myself inside her when she began to fight me off, swiping at me and trying to call out. I put one hand over her mouth and then suddenly realised I had the other clamped down around her throat, squeezing hard. At first, I couldn't stop myself, but when I heard her gargling and choking and felt something snap beneath my fingers, I pulled out and scrambled away. In a panic, I drew my knees up to my chest and sat there rocking, not quite believing what I'd done. I blame it on the drink, the circumstances, but I knew how close I'd come to properly raping her and then killing her, and I just shut down.

I sat like that even when Grace flipped herself over, levered herself up onto her knees, and started crawling out of the tent. Because of what I'd done to her throat, she couldn't force out a scream or raise her voice, and her call for help was pathetic really, like a hoarse whisper. I looked on like a dumb jerk, but I just couldn't move. Not to help, nor to finish her off.'

'Is that the moment when you went back to your tent to get the axe?' DC Cooper asked, breaking into the boy's soliloquy.

Levy shook his head, his eyes glassy. 'No. No, you don't understand. That's what I'm trying to tell you. Yeah, I had a go at Grace. Hurt her when she tried to fend me off. But I didn't go back to get the axe. I wouldn't have. No fucking way. But I didn't need to, as it turns out. Because Monica suddenly appeared from nowhere, rushing between the trees. She altered her approach and came up behind Grace, and as the poor thing tried to raise herself up off the ground, Monica called her a slut, swooped in and swung at her. And then a second time. Fierce blows, they were. But it was only after the horror of those sounds… sounds I will never forget, that Mon turned around to face me and I saw the axe in her hand, its blade dripping blood.'

I stared at her in silence. She stared back for a second or two. Then she pointed at Grace and said, 'Look at the state of that. You still want her? Well, do you, Isaac?'

*

Isaac Levy's solicitor had tried to stop him. He voiced his objections on several occasions, but his client wasn't having any of it. At one point, the boy also admitted he would never have grassed on Monica had she not thrown him to the wolves to save her own skin.

'I came so close to raping and strangling Grace, and having avoided both there's no way I'm going down for a murder I never committed.'

Chase was shocked. Levy apparently assumed that his own actions that night were somehow absolved because it was Monica Cilliers who had ended Grace Arnold's life by applying the final two blows. He didn't seem to realise he was still looking down the barrel of sexual abuse and attempted murder charges. Not to mention conspiracy after the fact.

'I think right from the off he half-suspected the allegation came from his girlfriend,' Chase said, his eyes still gripped on the monitor. 'When he first sat down, Levy looked as if he was chewing something over, something that tasted foul. Some detail Hyde had discussed with him that made him ask how any of the other five hikers could possibly have known about it. He knew where this was headed. He just refused to accept it.'

Laney looked up at him and nodded. 'I make you right, Royston. He wasn't as shocked as he ought to have been in learning what his girlfriend had told us.'

'I reckon that's probably *ex*-girlfriend as things stand,' DCI Knight said with a pensive smile. 'But we have a *he said-she said* on our hands, folks, so where the hell do we go from here? Do we even believe him?'

'I do,' Chase said, flatly, having come to a stark realisation. 'It's why Monica Cilliers was able to put one over on me. It's how she was initially able to remain so calm, only to come up later with that calculated but entirely plausible story blaming Levy and managing to sound so convincing. The girl's a psychopath. Plain and simple. She's our killer. No question in my mind.'

'And yet you also believed her version.'

'I did. Like I say, she was persuasive. She kept largely to the truth, only to then twist things around to make Isaac our killer. And I know that because I finally see her for what she is.'

'Something you don't see in him.'

Chase shook his head. 'Because it's not there.'

'We have to arrest Cilliers either way,' Fox said. 'But do we have anything else on her? Otherwise, we have her statement versus his, and to my knowledge no actual evidence as to which of them used that axe to strike the fatal blows.'

'We have to find that weapon,' Chase said. 'Test it for prints, DNA. If we get lucky, there will be only one matching set.'

'Let's ask Levy where it is,' Laney suggested. 'I mean, if they have two brain cells between them they'd've dumped it a long time ago, but perhaps they did so in a location we can search.'

Knight tore a sheet of paper from the pad on which she'd been writing copious notes. She scrawled something down before rushing out of the office, and moments later they saw her appear on the monitors inside the interview room. She handed the note to DC Bowen, who scanned it, looked up at her DCI and nodded.

Turning back to the Marlborough student, she said, 'Mr Levy, clearly what you've told us will have to be investigated. It would help your own defence, though, if you could tell us what Monica Cilliers did with the axe afterwards.'

The boy scowled. 'Now that I think about it,' he said, 'I'm guessing she played me right from the moment she killed that poor girl. Because the thing is, she didn't dispose of it at all. What she did, in fact, was to hand me the axe, told me to clean it and then get rid of it somewhere. Obviously she was making sure it was in my hands, possibly ending up with my prints on it, and me being the clueless idiot who threw it in the river or buried it somewhere.'

'So what did you do with it?'

Chase admired how calmly Bowen had asked the question, his own anxiety causing sweat to trickle down the back of his neck.

Isaac Levy looked from the detective to his solicitor, winked and turned back with the self-satisfied smirk of a man holding all the right cards. 'Not what she asked me to do, that's for sure. To tell the truth, I don't even know why, but I kept it. I didn't clean it, either. Just wrapped it up and hid it away.'

'You're telling us you still have the axe?' DC Cooper asked, unable to remain as collected as his colleague.

'Yep. And it'll still have that poor girl's blood all over it.'

After a moment's pause, Cooper said, 'That's good news, Mr Levy. Although the axe itself won't tell us who used it on her.'

'True.' The young man nodded, and his smile became broader still. 'But along with the axe, I also have the gloves and boots Monica was wearing when she used it. She told me to burn those, but I didn't. She never even asked if I had. She trusted me to do it because I was her lapdog. Again, I can't really think why I held on to them. I just did. Maybe some part of me thought I might need them for this very reason. I can't be sure. But I have them and you'll know they're hers. Mon has tiny hands and small feet. No way those gloves or boots would ever fit me. And like the axe, they are also covered in blood. If that isn't enough to convince you, I don't know what is.'

FORTY-ONE

After Levy had been led away to his holding cell, the six detectives moved to a different office where they discussed their strategy for making an arrest. Levy claimed to have hidden the items in his room at Preshute House. The question facing the detectives was whether it would be more beneficial to obtain the objects and have them forensically tested before bringing in Monica Cilliers. They all agreed that under normal circumstances and with no time pressures, gathering the evidence first would be ideal. The debate, however, concentrated on how practical doing so was due to the risk of also alerting the girl.

'Because we've made no statement to the media, nobody at Marlborough College is aware of Levy's arrest,' Chase reminded them. 'Provided it stays that way, there's nothing for Cilliers to react to. That said, she must be anticipating him being apprehended at some point and expecting the boy to defend himself whenever these allegations are put to him. And while she'll realise that means it's his word against hers, learning that we've caught him might spook her enough to run.'

'We ought to have a word with Levy's parents to make sure they don't contact the college,' DCI Knight said. 'We can keep a lid on it in respect of the media. But for the life of me, I can't think of a way to get our hands on the hidden items without tipping off the girl.'

'Is there any way one of us could sneak in and out of there unseen?' DC Cooper asked. 'Perhaps selecting a period during which lessons take place elsewhere around the college. PE, for instance?'

'That would necessitate contacting the college,' Chase said. 'First to identify when we could sneak in, but also because staff there are being extra vigilant at the moment and would need to be told to back off. I'm just not happy with that solution. Personally, I don't think we can pull it off.'

'Leaving us with making the arrest and collecting the evidence at the same time,' Laney said. 'Is that so bad? We can still question her, and with what we have we'll get the extensions we need. Monica Cilliers knew she had Grace Arnold's blood all over her axe, boots, and gloves, but she also believes they're out of the picture. The moment we tell her we have those items and have sent them off for forensic analysis, she'll know the results will be in while she's still under arrest and available for further questioning. In the old days, time might have been a factor, but even if those results take a full twenty-four hours, we'll be fine. Her brief will advise her accordingly, and we'll make sure she knows it from us as well.'

'Do we think she's likely to confess?' Knight asked, looking around the room.

Paige Bowen blew out her cheeks and shrugged. 'Your guess is as good as mine, boss. She's better under pressure than Levy, but then we've not yet charged her with murder, so she's not felt that kind of weight before.'

'Her brief will advise her not to co-operate,' Cooper said flatly. 'What we have on her is more than enough to get her in the room: Levy's statement, the axe, boots, and the gloves. The counter-allegation against her may be the weakest element, but we're able to back it up with physical evidence.'

'They'll contend the importance of the axe,' Chase argued. 'Even if forensics finds only Monica's prints on the weapon, big bloody deal. It's her camping axe, so what? Having Grace Arnold's blood and tissue matter on it doesn't prove Cilliers was the one who struck the fatal blows. No, for me it's the gloves and boots that are the most telling. There are bound to be DNA indicators from skin cells and sweat showing us she wore them, and with Grace's blood and DNA on them, too, that will stump even her brief.'

'Won't they simply suggest somebody else could have put them on before attacking Grace?' Fox said.

'I imagine so. But it's a weak argument, and our evidence is strong. If her hands and feet are as small as Levy claims, then who else could have worn them on the night?'

'One of the other male hikers, perhaps.'

Nodding, Chase said, 'I'm sure that will be suggested. But as and when those lads are found, we can check hand and feet size no matter what condition they're in. Plus, the forensics team is bound to find only her skin cells and her DNA inside all four items. You can put all of this to Cilliers if she and her brief try that argument. It might be enough to persuade them to cough. In consideration of a more lenient sentence for a guilty plea we can only hope they go for it.'

'And if they don't?' DCI Fox asked pointedly. 'Which I suspect they won't.'

'I'm with you. It's a faint hope at best. Given the premeditated nature of her actions, how much can she genuinely expect to trim off her sentence by pleading guilty? I'm sure her brief will push to argue charges in court.'

'But we do have enough to charge, irrespective of what she says, agreed?' DCI Knight pushed. 'Provided those gloves and boots of hers come back with the forensics we're hoping for.'

Nods all round. They were beginning with four elements of evidence, but that didn't mean it was all they would have by the time a trial came around. Chase was as certain as he could be that they'd have enough for the CPS, especially if they were able to confirm the items of clothing could not have been worn by anyone else that night.

But we still have to find those lads, he reminded himself. *If only for their sake.*

Knight got to her feet. 'I'm popping out for a moment to give the

DSI and DCS an update. I'll advise them of our decision and obtain their authority. Royston, you've been part of this since the off, so am I right in thinking you'd like to make the arrest?'

He nodded. 'Me and Claire, yes. I'd appreciate that. Perhaps have Alison and Efe attend to collect the evidence. Under the circumstances I'm sure the college will agree to any searches we request, but just to be on the safe side let's have a search and seizure warrant for our students' rooms plus any common areas, including cupboards and associated outbuildings in our back pockets should the Master decide to offer resistance. I'd also suggest Reuben and Paige join us, so that after making the arrest we can pop Monica into their motor and then all head over to Gablecross for the interview.'

'Can do,' Knight told him with a puzzled frown. 'Why do you want Reuben and Paige to drive her?'

'They'll be running the interviews afterwards. They can chat with her in the car, see what she has to say for herself beforehand. We may or may not be able to use it against her, but she might let something slip that they can take with them into the room. It's worth a punt.'

The DCI's face clouded over. 'I'm not so sure that's a good idea, Royston. We have PACE to think about, and I'm quite certain none of us wants to follow certain footsteps by wading in those murky waters. I certainly don't.'

The room fell silent. A dark cloud continued to hang over Gablecross police station more than a decade after a Detective Superintendent's adjudged breach of the Police And Criminal Evidence act made national headlines. The location, duration, and conditions of an interview following an arrest are thought to be inviolable, yet special circumstances allow for variances. And the now ex-detective had used his discretion to obtain a confession, hoping to save a life. Chase had known the man well and had fully supported his actions that day. For many serving officers, the internal rulings against the DSI had left them questioning the loyalty of those at the top of the pyramid. There were hills you were willing to die on, though. The Superintendent that day had chosen to place victims and their families ahead of his own career. For Royston Chase, this was not the same kind of moral dilemma, which allowed him to relent.

'I'm not suggesting they carry out an interview,' he said. 'Nor even ask questions of any kind. But they are allowed to make conversation. Trust them to know where the lines become blurry. No risk, Nicole. We'll probably not get a thing out of Cilliers, but if there's the chance of even a single slip then why not go for it?'

As reluctant as she was, Knight saw the legitimacy of Chase's suggestion and eventually agreed. As he and Laney headed back to Swindon, Chase placed a call to DS Jude Armstrong. He was certain that whichever of the two students was ultimately responsible for the murder of Grace Arnold, they were also working with a third party – the person who had snatched the remaining hikers; one of whom might well *be* that person. His head was swirling with questions, but it had also landed on an idea.

'Just a thought,' he explained to the case officer, 'but I reckon it might be worth going back over phone data. There are two timelines that I'm interested in: before and after the thirteenth of January, the day Grace was murdered, and before and after February twenty-first, the day her body was discovered.'

'Okay... what are you thinking, Royston?'

'It occurred to me that even if our killer changed their pattern of behaviour after either of those dates, there's nothing they can do about whatever preceded them. So, check data for both Levy and Cilliers. This time, look for a contact number that features regularly up to January the thirteenth and perhaps even a couple of days beyond, but which then suddenly drops off the list completely. If you find one, get everything you can on it. Also, look for a new number that appears within a day or so of that one disappearing. Do the same with the second date I gave you.'

'I get you,' Armstrong said. 'You're thinking that whoever their contact is they were most likely in touch regularly, but then the third party switched phones afterwards to offer themselves some protection.'

'I am. It's a defensive move many people would make, trying to distance themselves while staying in contact. And I'm sure they remained in contact over these five missing hikers.'

'But then would whoever it is risk their new phone being traced?'

'They almost certainly wouldn't regard it as a risk. If they thought about it at all. Because whoever this person is, they're unlikely to be a hardened villain. What they've done is criminal, but they are not – as a rule. As you and I well know, Jude, most people aren't steeped in criminal behaviour. So, while they might think about dumping their old phone, they probably wouldn't consider the possibility of us finding their new one so easily.'

'Okay. Leave it with me,' Armstrong said. 'I'm on it.'

'It's a chance,' Chase said to Laney when he was done with the call.

'A slim one, cupcake,' Laney replied. Then she shrugged. 'But it's better than no bloody chance at all.'

FORTY-TWO

The operation silverback incident room was a seething cauldron of activity by the time Chase and Laney got to the Swindon police station, where DS Armstrong was briefing Trainee Detective Constable May and DC Salisu. The warrant they'd requested had come through, but as the Detective Sergeant was explaining, the pair were directed to first attempt to obtain permission from the Master at the college upon arrival.

'It's not only better for our relations with Marlborough,' he told them, 'but if they do give their consent, then our search parameters increase. The warrant request gives us access to the areas we want to search, but if it becomes necessary to look elsewhere, then you can do so without having to wait for another warrant.'

'Why not start with one to cover the entire campus?' May asked.

'Because it's too far-reaching. We'd be requesting access to the private living quarters of staff and students uninvolved with this case, and the chances of it being granted are not good. We can always go back and ask for more, but at this stage it's better to request what you'd expect to be given.'

Chase observed as quietly and patiently as he was able, but found his attention snagged by a uniformed officer sitting at a nearby computer station. 'Sir, are you the detectives waiting for phone data?' she asked.

'That's us,' he said, swivelling fully to face her. 'I thought DS Armstrong was putting it together for us.'

'He was, but when the warrant came through, he asked me to finish off for him. I think I have what you asked for.'

'Then we're all ears, my dear,' Laney said, planting herself in a chair close by and resting both feet on the edge of a desk. Chase nodded but remained standing.

The uniform smiled. Her hair was pulled back into a ponytail, revealing a long neck. Her face was pleasant and shone with energy and vigour beneath a bank of ceiling lights. 'We have nothing suspicious on Isaac Levy's phone, but Monica Cilliers' data is more than promising. A particular number I managed to find was in regular contact with hers until the night of Tuesday the twenty-first of February. Prior to that date, there are plenty of exchanged texts, phone calls, and WhatsApp messages. But not a single thing afterwards. Yet the very next morning, a new number appears. It then follows a similar pattern to the one that dropped off. Specifically, the phone calls pretty much all take place late at night. During the day there are various messages, but they spoke often and for lengthy periods during those late-night calls.'

Chase felt a flush of excitement pass over him like a wave. Hairs rose on the back of his neck and on his hands. This was precisely the news he'd hoped for but hadn't dared to believe he would hear.

'And you've dug into both of those numbers?' he asked breathlessly.

'Digging, sir. I only just got there when you came through the door. I paused to update you.'

'That's great work… sorry, what's your name?'

'PC Mullins. Sarah.'

'If I knew you better, Sarah, I'd kiss you,' he said, offering his broadest smile. 'As it is, please do carry on.'

'You did well to avoid that,' Laney advised the constable. She gave a conspiratorial wink. 'He slobbers like a Saint Bernard. I can only imagine how traumatised his poor wife is.'

Chase ignored the laughter that followed. He was too wrapped up in the investigation possibilities to have a pop back at his tormenter.

'Any luck?' Armstrong asked him, wandering over having ended the evidence collection briefing.

'Still waiting, but it's looking positive. I haven't heard from DCI Knight about the arrest. You?'

'I gather the DCS was initially unavailable, but as we speak he is locked in discussion with Superintendent Waddington.'

Chase rolled his eyes. 'What the hell is there to discuss? You can bet your life that if it was some scrote from a council estate we'd've had the nod by now.'

'I know. Politics, eh? Just be grateful her old man is only an advisor and not actually employed by the South African Embassy, or we'd have no chance whatsoever.'

'Small mercies.'

DC Armstrong opened his mouth to reply, but snapped it closed again when PC Mullins gave them a shout. She looked up from the keyboard, beaming. 'We've got something here,' she said hurriedly, finger pointing at the screen. 'Does the name Jeffrey Lennon mean anything to you?'

'Professor Tosspot,' Laney said abruptly. 'What's that limp dick got to do with anything?'

The uniform stared blankly at her, uncertain how to proceed.

'He's our students' House Master at Marlborough,' Chase informed her, leaning closer to read the monitor. 'What about him, Sarah?'

'The first phone I mentioned is listed in his name,' Mullins told them.

Chase felt his flesh go cold and start to prickle. 'The phone making and receiving calls, texts, and WhatsApp messages?'

'That's the one.'

'Well, he is their professor and their House Master,' Armstrong said. 'Is that really so unexpected?'

'Perhaps not,' the constable acknowledged. 'You'd expect some level of contact between a professor and his students. But here's the thing: that phone never once contacted Isaac Levy's.'

'Also,' Laney interjected. 'While the occasional message might not be completely out of order, what's with the late-night phone calls? That screams more than teacher-student communication to me.'

PC Mullins raised her eyebrows. 'Hold on, we have two saved messages. I can access both. Let me play them.'

A couple of mouse movements and clicks later and they were listening to a voice that Chase immediately recognised as that of Professor Lennon. *'I can't get our conversation out of my head, Mon. I'm overcome. I never thought you could ever feel the same way I do. How long before we take it to the next level? I want you. I want you so much.'*

'Bloody hell,' Armstrong breathed.

'Jesus H Christ in a sidecar,' Laney followed up. 'I'd never have thought that prawn had it in him to be a perv.'

'Play the next one please, Sarah,' Chase said, his mouth dry. With a brief nod, she adjusted the mouse pointer and clicked.

'Sweetheart, whatever you've done, whatever it means, rest assured I'm here for you. Tell me what you want from me. I'll do anything. Anything at all. Just so long as we can be together.'

Chase's mind was reeling. Was Professor Lennon the third party, the man who had abducted the other hikers? Clearly, he was in some kind of personal relationship with Monica Cilliers. The message he'd left indicated he would do whatever it took for that relationship to continue, irrespective of what the girl had done. Did that mean the professor would go so far as to abduct five young men if Cilliers asked him to? Chase reflected on the urgency and passion in the man's voice and believed he would literally do anything to please her.

He swallowed a couple of times, wet his lips and said to the uniformed PC, 'Sarah, please get us everything you can on that other phone. And see if it has a working GPS. If it does, I want to know where it's been and its current location. It has to be him. Lennon is our man.'

FORTY-THREE

As was often the case at the back end of an operation, a huge amount of work occurred in a flurry of activity over a relatively short period of time.

First came the sanctioning of Monica Cilliers' arrest. She had fooled him, taken him in completely, but as much as he wanted to see the look in the girl's eyes when the cuffs were snapped over her wrists, Chase was more desperate to follow the lead he had created through the phone data. He called DCI Knight and asked if she and DI Fox would do the job instead. He explained his reasoning, and Knight accepted without argument.

Next, DC Salisu and TDC May left the station armed with their warrant, setting off for Marlborough College where they were due to liaise with the more senior detectives before speaking to the college Master and then conducting a search of Preshute House for evidence.

Finally, after a wait of no more than thirty minutes, DC Mullins had more news for them. 'I have his GPS coordinates,' she told them. 'I'm going to show my monitor on the main whiteboard so that you can get a clear view of what I'm seeing.'

A few seconds later, a split-screen image appeared for them all to follow. It was divided between a text-based data readout and a graphical version of the same information. Mullins switched to the latter, then used the mouse to move the pointer around the map displayed on the board.

'This large cluster of readings that I've highlighted for you here is the college,' she said. 'It's also the location at which we most often see the GPS turned off and back on again, presumably when he shuts down his phone, perhaps to charge it more quickly, maybe for meetings or lessons. That's not the only place where we lose the signal, however, but I'll come back to that in a moment. So, the next thing I want to show is this.' The mouse pointer moved across the map and jiggled in a rough circle. 'This spot is close to Neville Hutton's home on the morning of Wednesday the twenty-second of February. In the next one as I move the mouse over, we see the signal in Milton Keynes at the exact time that Gary Elder was taken. Then, the following day just outside Dunstable, not far from Ashley Robertson, and later here we are at Milton Bryan, which is where Robertson supposedly demanded to meet with Mark Swallow and Mark Viner.'

Chase gasped. 'So, we can geographically connect this phone to all five lads? No doubt whatsoever?'

'Looks that way,' Mullins said, before continuing. 'But this is the bit I think you'll be most interested in, sir.'

'I think we've become intimate enough to work on a first name basis,' Chase told the young constable. 'It's Royston, not sir.'

'If you say so… Royston,' she replied, looking flustered for the first time. 'Like I said, this is the really interesting part. After each of these individual visits, the GPS signal travels directly to the same location just north of Hungerford. The closest I can pinpoint location is on the edge of a place called Membury Camp, also known as Membury Fort, which is right by the M4. But you remember I told you there was a second place in which the GPS regularly drops off? It's here.'

Chase stroked his chin. 'At this camp or fort?'

'Yes. And the phone doesn't just travel there after visiting the locations relating to the missing hikers. There's also a daily trip between the college and this spot, and back again some time afterwards. That surely has to be where he's keeping them. But every time it reaches this precise position, the GPS vanishes. The time it spends offline varies. The shortest period is fifteen minutes, the longest just over an hour.'

'He's trying to cover his tracks by switching his phone off,' Armstrong suggested.

Chase had initially thought the same, but now disagreed. 'I don't think so, Jude. If he even suspected he needed to, he would have done so before leaving the College. That or just left it there while he was on the road. No, I think what's happening here is he's losing signal.'

He risked a sidelong glance at DC Laney, whose amused curl of the lips told him she knew he was thinking about the tiny signal jamming device in his jacket pocket.

'So, you're saying he enters a black spot?' Armstrong said.

'Yes. Perhaps in a deliberate act, but it may be a natural feature of the area.'

'I'm pretty sure the tower coverage there is fine,' Mullins said.

Chase thought about that for a moment. 'And yet from what I can tell, we're losing both – the phone's provider signal and the GPS.'

'Which again tells me he's deliberately switching his phone off,' Armstrong reiterated.

'I don't think that's the case. First of all, I see no reason why he would do so only at that specific location. Also, it's far too consistent in terms of where it goes off and when it reappears again. The exact same spot every single time. I don't see that happening by chance or by choice.'

'Are you saying you think he has those hikers shackled in some kind of… Faraday cage?' Armstrong asked.

'He may well have, yes. I'm not suggesting that part of it is a deliberate ploy. He most likely lucked out in terms of the structure. We must assume he has them in a building of some description, and if its materials include a lot of wire mesh, coils of wire, or metallic sheets, tubes, or bars, then it may create a natural Faraday-like effect. Lennon may not even be aware of it.'

In response, Mullins toggled to another open application, this time Google Maps. She brought the focus to the location in question and zoomed in as tight as the app would allow. 'Sir… sorry, Royston, although the hillfort area is pretty flat and open, it's surrounded by trees. As you can see, there are no constructions of any size or type at the precise point where the GPS signal dies. There is a nearby building, but the signal travels beyond that before it dies.'

It was a puzzle, and Chase felt frustrated because he thought he had the solution tucked away somewhere in the back of his mind. He often found the best way to unlock his memory was to keep his mind busy, so he turned his thoughts to Professor Lennon and the phone.

'We have a phone linking somebody at Marlborough College with the abduction of the boys. Sarah's intel suggests it belongs to Lennon. How do we prove he made those journeys, that he had that phone on him and not only abducted the lads, but clearly visited them on a daily basis afterwards as well?'

'We perhaps can't offer proof that it was that dickhead,' Laney said with regret. 'However, what we can do is contact the college to find out if it couldn't possibly have been him.'

Armstrong was nodding. 'Yes, of course. If he was teaching or otherwise provably engaged at the college surrounded by witnesses when any of these trips were made, then he's not our man.'

'Likewise, if he was absent during every one of those occasions then although we can't yet prove it was him who carried the phone, it does leave him wide open to the right kind of questioning.'

'Is this Professor likely to have been free enough from college duties to have done that amount of travelling in such a short space of time?' PC Mullins asked.

The DS checked the clock on the wall. 'That's the real question, isn't it? I can find out, but we have to wait until the others have arrived at Marlborough. Once we know the arrest and search are underway, I can then call and ask about Lennon's schedule and attendance.'

'It's him,' Chase said, looking at each of them in turn. 'Are any of you actually in any doubt? The calls, the messages, the voicemails. He clearly has something going on with Monica Cilliers, and she has him wrapped around her little finger. He did all this for her. For them.'

Armstrong gave it a moment's thought before placing a call to DCI Knight, who informed him that both the arrest and search were imminent, the college Master having agreed to their every request. 'It's on,' he said to his colleagues in the incident room. 'I'll give the college a bell.'

'Oh shit!' PC Mullins said suddenly. She had switched back to the GPS mapping. 'Royston, earlier you asked where that signal was, and the last time I checked it I picked it up at the college. But look at it now… it's on the move.'

'Of course,' Chase said in alarm. 'He's just learned about the arrest. He's running.'

'But in which direction?' Armstrong asked.

The uniformed constable zoomed out on the GPS map. 'Hard to tell for sure at this early stage, but so far it's taking the exact same route it uses when visiting Membury Fort.'

FORTY-FOUR

Chase took the M4 to avoid the worst of the snow, which blew in thick and strong. The world outside had become monochrome, with the exception of the virgin canvas washed in streaks of scarlet from pulsing brake lights. The heavy motorway traffic kept the road surface relatively clear, but the moment they turned off onto single track minor roads, the white stuff was virtually unscarred and he had to drop the speed to half the posted limit.

Slow progress toyed with his anxiety. Professor Lennon had a head start and not a significantly longer drive to make, so it was going to be a close-run thing. In addition to the other area forces involved, Laney had advised Knight of the development. The DCI had immediately arranged for a traffic car to drop by the college to collect Cilliers after her arrest and take her on to Gablecross, at which point the rest of the team would join Chase and Laney at Membury Fort. Other available traffic vehicles had also been summoned to assist, but Chase was worried as to who would arrive first.

Throughout the drive, he'd been relatively quiet. His thoughts were snagged up in the unidentified phone's GPS and the reason why its signal was being lost in the area. He didn't know the precise spot very well, and it was always possible that the hillfort was situated in a hollow and therefore interfered with signals from the closest towers. But the information he'd seen on the incident room board hadn't read that way to him. It might explain why a phone would lose its provider connection, but not satellite transmission. It was hard to conceive of a spot so close to a major town hub that would be incapable of picking up neither. Without phone towers to provide tracking at a cellular level a GPS signal might not be as quick or as accurate, but it would surely still work.

If there are no buildings and, therefore, no natural Faraday cage, what else are we dealing with here? he asked himself over and over.

Eventually, he felt a nudge on his arm. He glanced across at Laney, whose eyes widened as she said, 'Ground control to Major Berk. Come in Major Berk.'

He guessed she had been trying to capture his attention for some time. 'Sorry,' he said, squinting ahead as the road did its best to blend in with the white background. 'I'm a little distracted.'

'Well, I hate to say this cupcake, but you're in danger of distracting us into a ditch. Tell Auntie Claire what's on your mind.'

'This isn't making sense to me,' he admitted. 'We're looking at an isolated area of open land with a ring of trees around it. No buildings that we know of or can see. So where's he keeping these lads? And he must be keeping them, otherwise why revisit the same location every day since?'

'Perhaps there's some kind of shed, or barn, or even a cabin in there tucked away beneath the trees. That aerial map shows the spot at a time of year when the leaves were in full growth, so there could be something hidden away out of sight.'

Chase gave a reluctant shrug. 'I suppose so. But is a wooden construction going to stop a GPS signal?'

'I have no idea, cupcake,' Laney said on a sigh of exasperation. 'I'm not a buggering scientist. Look, you just concentrate on getting us there safely and we'll figure out the rest when we do.'

They continued along a narrow B road, traction both unreliable and hazardous. The SUV's wipers struggled to bat away the unrelenting torrent of snowflakes thrust by fierce gusts against the windscreen. The sound of the wind rushing over the vehicle was eerie, like a creature howling in the distance. Driving conditions had become perilous, but they were little more than five minutes from their destination.

'You think he's going there to kill them?' Chase asked his partner.

'Wouldn't you if you were him?'

'Why do you imagine he snatched them in the first place? Because of what they knew?'

'I'm not sure,' Laney said. 'My guess is they weren't at all certain about what these lads knew or didn't know. Whichever version of the story you believe, everybody had returned to their tents by the time Isaac paid a visit to Grace. It wasn't as if they had an audience. So, they couldn't possibly know for sure what one or more of the group heard, or perhaps even saw if the attempted rape happened to draw one of the boys back out into the cold night.'

'So they'd want to ask them in order to be absolutely certain.'

'Of course. Again, wouldn't you?'

Chase paused to reflect. 'So Lennon grabs them up, stashes them away somewhere, returns every day to keep them fed and watered, and then what… questions them? Tortures them for answers. A man like that?'

'It's possible, Royston. Monica Cilliers seems to have him well and truly under her spell. He'd probably never done anything like this in his entire life before and never intended to again.'

'But how did he do it?' Chase asked, puzzled by the technicalities. 'He's a fair size and looks in decent shape, but getting the drop on all five, two at a time when it comes to both Marks? How's that possible?'

Laney didn't have to consider her response. 'Coercion. Has to be. Threats made against others. That way, they go with him voluntarily.'

He nodded. 'I guess. It fits.'

'Shit!' said Laney, who'd been monitoring their progress on her phone. 'There's a small stretch of private road leading directly to Membury Fort. Even then it peters out and becomes nothing more than a rutted byway.'

They'd reached a sharp hairpin bend. Chase took added precautions, even though there was not another vehicle to be seen. He followed the road around and straightened before replying. 'I think we have to regard the private road as accessible. After all, Lennon has been popping back and forth for days.'

Moments later, the entrance came up on their left, set at an oblique angle. Chase made the turn and immediately they spotted a derelict manor house set back off the road. 'There's your reason why he's been able to come and go as he pleases,' he said, hooking a finger at it. 'Private road leading to private land, but nobody here to secure it or complain about trespassers.'

'We just passed a barred gate leaning open, so clearly this track has been used recently.'

As Laney spoke, Chase stood on the brakes a little too forcefully, causing even the fat Volvo tyres to lose their grip. After a second or two of slithering and sliding, they ended up at a forty-five-degree angle across the narrow road. His hands gripped the wheel so tight he thought he might need help to prise them off.

'What the hell, Royston?' Laney barked at him as he eventually wriggled his fingers free.

He pointed beyond her. 'Look along there,' he said. 'What don't you see?'

She turned her head to look out of the side window. The features of the single-track road were barely visible. Fresh snow lay there sparkling and crisp as more continued to fall, doing its best to obscure the view. It took her a couple of breaths, but then she nodded. 'No vehicle tracks.'

'No. Which means we beat him to it. We're the first ones here. Get on to Jude. Have him ask Sarah Mullins where Lennon's signal is and if it looks as if he's still headed this way.'

While Laney made the call, Chase carefully reversed back along the way they had come until they were parallel with the ramshackle house. He continued reversing, only this time up onto the driveway and around to the side before coming to a complete standstill behind a tall bramble. Effectively, he had concealed them from any other vehicle passing along the same lane.

'We're in luck,' Laney told him excitedly when she ended her call. 'Lennon got caught up in traffic trying to get out of Marlborough, then an accident on the A4 forced him to divert around it. But the side roads were like the one we came down and with the traffic all diverting the same way it was slow going for him.'

'Where's he now?'

'He's going to be with us at any moment.'

'Okay. Listen, call Knight and tell her and the cavalry to hold back until Lennon is on the plot. And when they do come, no blues and twos.'

'Will do. What's the plan?'

'First of all, we hope Lennon doesn't notice our own tyre tracks. He won't be looking for them and we only came a short way along, so I think by the time he straightens he'll be past any impressions we've made. Then we wait for him to continue on down to the hillfort and park up. Once he's into the trees, we trundle up there, pull up behind him and follow.'

Laney's face beamed at him. 'Of course. At any other time, we'd risk losing him in there. But today we'll have a nice new set of footprints in the snow to follow.'

Chase took a breath and forced out a grin. 'Fingers crossed,' he said softly as his partner got back on the phone. 'Fingers crossed.'

He sat back to wait for Lennon to arrive, but could tell from his DC's voice that something was amiss. When she ended the call, she puffed out a long breath before turning to him.

'Problem?' he asked.

Laney gave a solemn nod. 'Problem.'

FORTY-FIVE

Professor Jeffrey Lennon could not believe his rotten luck. It was bad enough getting stuck in the steaming pile of metal moving out of town at a snail's pace, but then came the complete standstill, followed by a foot-by-slippery-foot crawl, before finally having to take a major detour due to the carelessness of whichever terrible drivers had caused an accident currently blocking both lanes of the A4.

He calmed himself a little when he remembered he was in no hurry. Nobody knew about him. Nobody knew about the five hikers. Yet the mere thought of them ratcheted up his stress levels all the more.

What did I do?

And what am I expected to do now?

His reaction to learning of the police presence at the college and their intention to arrest Monica had been both instinctive and instantaneous. He had no idea what evidence they had, though he immediately suspected they must have caught Levy; the boy would have spilled his guts like the weak-minded dullard he was. What Lennon did know for sure was that the hikers provided a connection to himself and to Monica, and he needed to make sure none of those boys was ever able to tell their stories.

Later, when all this was behind them, some people might regard him as a gullible fool. But what he had with Monica was real. So far all they had to show for their burgeoning relationship were snatched moments, whispered words of courtship and promises of what would be when she left Marlborough and their love was no longer restricted by his responsibilities as both her teacher and house master. Six long months of sneaking around had only served to strengthen the depths of his feelings, which he knew were entirely reciprocated.

So beguiled was he by the thought that such a precious and enticing young woman as Monica could ever consider him as her suitor, that when she came begging for his help, he had no thought for himself. Only for her and what might become of her and their future together should the truth ever be revealed.

'Did you hear about what's going on over at Cherhill?' she'd whispered as they stole a few precious minutes alone together. Her fingers caressed a warm spot on his arm, which began to tingle all over.

He had heard. A large police presence, evidently. Rumours of a terrible crime uncovered.

'I think they've found a dead body, Jeff,' she'd said next, her lips forming a pout. 'A murdered young woman, to be precise.'

He squinted at her, an admiring half-smile thinning his lips. 'How could you possibly know that?'

Monica blinked once. A slow, feline movement. And again, her voice became hushed when she spoke. 'Because I was there when it happened. Isaac, too.'

His gaze narrowed further. 'When you and he… the camping trip?'

He hadn't approved of that. Hated the time the pair spent together. Monica frequently teased him, insisting it was all part of the cover, that nobody would ever guess about the two of them while she and Isaac so openly displayed their love for one another.

'I couldn't tell you before, but something bad happened up there, Jeff.' A single stray tear trickled down the side of her nose and fell upon lips he longed to smother in kisses. His heart fluttered, and in that moment of her apparent anguish, he was hers.

'What do you mean by that? Like what? You saw this girl being killed?' he asked, concern for Monica's well-being his overriding emotion.

She shook her head. 'No, no. Nothing like that. At least… at least, I don't think so. I… I don't know for sure. And that's the problem, Jeff.'

It all spilled out then in a breathless rush. She and Isaac had met up with a bunch of lads and a girl by the name of Grace. Alcohol flowed, first in the pub and then around a campfire on Cherhill Down.

'I think it was more than that, Jeff,' she told him, sobbing like a baby. 'I think somebody spiked our drinks. My memories are fractured. But I know that at one point I became frightened. Things happened. Bad things. *Sexual* things. And worst of all, I can't remember if it was imagination, hallucination, dream, or memory. All I know is that the night ended with Grace dead. And Jeff… I don't know how much I was involved.'

Monica's subsequent plan was both outrageous and simple. He had to track down the five young men who'd camped out with them that night. Find them, isolate them, and then discover the truth.

'Isolate them?' he'd asked, uncertain what she was asking of him.

More tears, great body-shuddering sobs and gasps for air. Each a dagger to his very soul.

'I have to know the truth, Jeff,' she finally managed to whisper. 'I have to know what they know. What they saw, heard, and did. But it's not that easy. I can't simply ask them and expect an honest reply. Do you think if they were responsible for spiking our drinks, for perhaps killing that poor girl, that they're just going to admit it?'

He shook his head, speechless and almost giddy with delirium.

'No. Quite right,' she insisted, her hand gripping his arm. 'I can't slip away from college, but you can. You have to find them and force them to tell you, Jeff.'

'But… but how?' he'd managed to ask.

'You make them see it's a matter of life or death. Theirs.' She paused, then looked up with an excited glimmer in her eyes. 'Others, too, for that matter. Those they love. Tell them you'll spare nobody if they lie, everybody if they tell the truth.'

She paused to let that sink in.

Before continuing with her plan.

To explain away his absences, he was to inform his line manager of a death in the family. Compassionate leave required. He'd then be able to come and go as he pleased, would be available for his evening house master duties, but for a few days his teaching responsibilities would require cover. This, she told him, allowed him the freedom he would need to do whatever was necessary.

'I need this, Jeff,' she'd insisted tenderly. 'I need you to be my hero.'

Finding the five boys was nowhere near as difficult as he had imagined it might be. After the photo was taken in the pub that night in mid-January, Monica had secretly exchanged details with the lad she knew as Nev. Which meant that although she had subsequently told the police otherwise, she had his email address. Following her conversation with Lennon, she sent the boy a mail asking if he would like to meet up with her. Naturally, he replied soon afterwards and told her he was thrilled to have heard from her again. They made arrangements and agreed upon a location.

Only it was Lennon who had been waiting in his vehicle for the kid.

He considered himself to be in fine shape, and he was a naturally large man. Imposing, even. And dressed in black, wearing a balaclava, he supposed he might even pass for intimidating. But he'd never been involved in an act of physical violence in his entire sheltered life, so this was the point at which he had balked.

'Don't worry about it,' Monica had told him, her soft touch electrifying as she smiled up at him. Her fingers were soft and warm, and those eyes…

His head slumped forward in supplication. 'How can I not do as you ask, my beautiful Mon? I know what you need of me, and

I've even thought of a place I can take them. I just don't know how to… force them to come with me.'

Stroke. Smile. Eyes.

'You won't need to use force if you do this right, Jeff. I realise you're out of your comfort zone, so dig deep and do what you do best: think. Use the weapon you do have, which is your intelligence. You're brighter than they are, Jeff. You know how to do this. You do. Because everything you need is already inside your head.'

Monica was right. She always was. If there was one thing he knew better than most other people, it was psychology. He'd learned from the best at university, and he taught others the way of the mind. He had the physique to back it up, he had the menacing clothing, which left him to add further elements to his armoury.

He had no access to a firearm of any description, but a large knife was equally terrifying when brandished with purpose. He would never – could never – use it, but its mere presence in his hand would cause most young men to suddenly find themselves struggling for breath as terror held them in its firm embrace. The threat alone was explicit, and perhaps all he would need. Yet there were two more ingredients to throw into the mix: the first of which was to raise the awful spectre of harm coming to others.

'I'm not just threatening *you*,' he told Neville Hutton with all the sincerity he could muster. 'Because if I don't believe I've got the truth from you, then nobody you love is safe from me. Not your parents, siblings if you have them, girlfriend, boyfriend, for that matter… they're all vulnerable and they are all my next targets if you lie to me.'

All of which left him with one final move.

Psychologically, if you put people in a position from which they fear escape is impossible and apply the pressure of threatened violence to them and others, there's always the possibility that they might react in precisely the wrong way. The fight-or-flight impulse is strong, and if a person is unable to flee and believes there is no way out but to fight, then fight is what many of them will do.

Which is where hope comes in.

Give them hope and you remove the most significant stressor of them all.

'Your life and the lives of so many others in exchange for straight answers to my questions,' he'd said to Hutton. 'You tell me everything I need to know and they survive untouched. You lie to me or plead ignorance and they suffer. It's not really even a choice, is it?'

It wasn't.

After which, they fell like dominoes.

Hutton gave him Gary Elder's address. Adding the vision of his girlfriend in real and present danger had made the boy instantly compliant. Elder gave him Ashley Robertson. Lennon then realised that travelling was taking up too much of his valuable time, so he used Robertson's phone to lure Mark Viner and Mark Swallow at the same time to the same location.

He approached each encounter with a sense of dread, fearing a volatile reaction, a natural primitive response to threats of violence and incarceration. But he'd gone ahead with Monica's plan, believing in the persona he had taken on and wearing it like a second skin. Nothing about it came easy to him, but hard on the heels of every doubt he reminded himself about why he was taking such drastic action. More importantly, who he was doing it for.

The where was the easy part. He prided himself on being one of a select number of people who knew the shelter existed. Built within easy reach of the RAF Membury airbase, the underground facility had been designed to house dignitaries in the event of an enemy attack on British soil. This was long before anybody had even conceived of a nuclear strike, but the structure was incredibly well-hidden and protected. The Ministry of Defence, who owned the land, was rumoured to have used it as a black site to house prisoners suspected of carrying out terrorist atrocities, some of whom had subsequently been renditioned to the infamous military base in Cuba. Unused for a dozen years or more, it had fallen into severe disrepair and suffered at the hands of urban explorers snaffling trophies from their finds and marking the walls with a variety of tags.

Back when he was eighteen, Lennon was first shown around the place by his uncle, who worked for the MOD. On occasion, the military or secret services made use of the house at the top of the private road, but even that had long-since been abandoned. Yet the rationale to keep the boys in the underground bunker was many-fold: it had a number of separate units in which he could conceal those he abducted; it was the kind of place with the kind of entrance few would ever stumble upon by accident; its MOD status meant that its utility services were on a maintenance schedule, which had allowed him to switch on a functioning electrical supply, provide running water and waste facilities, as well as activating the boilers to provide heat via perpetually groaning ventilation systems. Left running for months, it was a presence somebody was bound to detect. But a week or so was a risk he'd been willing to take.

Looking back, he couldn't be certain that he'd ever fully grasped the true nature of what he was being asked to do. It was as if a switch in his moral fibre had been reset, that the difference between right and wrong temporarily no longer existed. His fight had been for the greater good, and in this specific instance that meant obtaining answers. Monica had been vague about what those might be, where they might lead, the consequences for them, but had insisted that she would bear the entire burden alone if necessary.

Except now her plan had unravelled. The police had come for her, for evidence apparently secreted away by Isaac. The issue of the five hikers no longer centred on questions and answers regarding the night of a young girl's murder. It was all about a very different kind of protection; preventing Monica and himself from having any of the five testify against either of them was all that mattered.

As he finally reached the private road, Lennon's thoughts remained in constant turmoil. Fresh layers of snow crunched beneath the tyres as he sought purchase in familiar ruts along the track. By now, he was accustomed to the geographical and physical markings on either side, making it easier to keep from sliding off the trail leading up to Membury Fort.

You're not a killer, he told himself.
So what are you going to do, Jeff?

None of the five lads had any clue who he was, but they knew why they had been taken. Would the police eventually link him and Monica? Possibly. Likely, even. She would not give him up, but they had to know the men were missing, and if released, those young men would undoubtedly tell their sorry tales of woe. And it wasn't as if the detectives working the case were stupid. As much as he despised that bloody sergeant, he was a capable officer. He and his team were bound to put the pieces together at some point. Sometimes the best way to keep a secret was to remove the only people who knew about it.

Mindful of the snow and the slippery surface, he braked gently to a halt, pulled on the handbrake and switched off the engine. He'd driven to the spot more by instinct than by any rational, intelligent reasoning or observation. Earlier he'd asked himself what he had done and what was now expected of him. While she had never said as much, he had always sensed it was Monica's inclination never to allow the five young men to be free to tell anybody else about what they had seen or heard. But if that was the case, why ask him to question them, threaten them in order to obtain answers?

What do you know?
What did you see?
What did you hear?
What did you do?
What have you done?

Monica needed to know what they knew. Which surely meant that if they knew nothing, they were free to go. Only, perhaps it didn't. And what they had known amounted to little, and certainly nothing about Monica's involvement in the other girl's death. Perhaps Monica had wanted to discover how much she needed to protect herself, and the only way of finding out was to grill them and let them think their salvation lay in providing truthful answers. Yet these matters were all about Monica and how it affected her. Clearly he also had to think about himself.

What did I do?

And what am I expected to do now?

The first of those questions asked of himself was clear. As for the second...

The very thought of stabbing them to death repulsed him. And even if he had a gun, he didn't think he'd be able to pull the trigger. No. No, he could not physically take a single life, let alone five of them. He'd done things lately that he'd never thought himself capable of, but that...? No. It wasn't in him. Not a physical, face-to-face act of pure violence.

The only way to see it through was to separate himself from the final consequences of his actions. Remove their drinking water for a start by turning off the water supply at the mains. And then shut down the heating system. With temperatures set to fall below freezing yet again, the lads were likely to die of exposure before the agonies of thirst took them. The physical and mental collapse brought about by hypothermia would surely complete the task he was physically unable to take on. By then he'd be miles away, telling his employers he'd had a delayed reaction to his recent loss, buying time until he learned what the police knew, what Monica had confessed to, and whether he featured as part of that confession.

And yet now that the moment was finally upon him, he asked himself how long it might take for the boys to stop breathing. And precisely how long was too long? He could not allow them to be found alive, so to be absolutely certain he might just have to consider another way after all. Something quicker. More precise. More... immediate. He did not feel capable, yet neither was he able to see himself languishing in a prison cell because he'd failed to act.

Lennon took a deep breath and opened the car door, praying that Monica had received what might well have been his last ever message to her; the text he had sent the moment he realised the police were at the college to make an arrest.

FORTY-SIX

THE POLICE ARE HERE. RUN. SAVE YOURSELF. I'LL TAKE CARE OF OUR GUESTS.

Monica Cilliers blinked a couple of times, unable to tear her eyes away from the phone screen. With no time to think or plan, only to act, she shoved back her chair with a loud screech, and was halfway to the classroom door when her English teacher looked up from his hardback copy of a Charles Dickens novel.

'Ms Cilliers?' he said, frowning over the top of his reading glasses.

The girl ignored him. As her classmates began to stir and chatter in astonishment, she reached the door, yanked it open, and then thrust herself through the opening. The moment her feet hit the corridor her mind started to function properly. Initially frantic, Cilliers swiftly came to terms with her stressful predicament.

They had found Isaac.

And having found him, they had broken him.

That had to be the reason why the police were coming for her. Which was the very reason she had elected to strike her own blows first. Cilliers believed she had convinced the detectives of Isaac's guilt, yet if that were the case, why were they here? Why had Jeff told her to make a run for it?

Confident in the spell she had cast over Isaac, Monica wondered how the police had managed to turn him against her. Surely her statement alone was not enough to corrupt him and make her young boyfriend turn his back on her? Even a pathetic creature like Isaac had to know she was simply trying to save herself by laying the blame elsewhere, and that all he had to do was keep his cool and deny it. The police had nothing to go on other than her word. No proof, no evidence. Not unless…

Muddying the waters they both swam in was, in hindsight, a perfect solution. Not only for her, but Isaac as well. If the police couldn't know for certain who did what that night, how were they going to press charges? Having Isaac handle the axe, plus her gloves and boots, was a stroke of genius. A thorough forensic examination was bound to find subtle traces of him, further increasing the doubt she had so far created in their minds. If they hadn't already been discovered, she'd make sure they were. But what if Isaac had doubted her all along? What if he had kept hold of those items? Not burned them, nor buried them, but hidden them away somewhere close to hand. Perhaps even right under her nose.

These frantic thoughts and a hundred more flashed through her mind as she fled along the corridors and staircases. Aware of the precise location of the two uniformed officers assigned to protect her, Monica hurried in the opposite direction. Out of the building by taking the rear exit. From there across the playing fields, using hurried strides but not sprinting recklessly. Along a winding footpath that snaked through the trees and then over the narrowest stretch of the Kennet via a short wooden bridge, the river water slow moving and shallow beneath her feet. A steep and ragged incline followed, leading up towards a high embankment nestled against a main road. Cilliers huffed and puffed her way through these unexpected exertions, her features contorted into a mask of fierce determination.

She was fleeing the police. Quite possibly fleeing arrest. She would do whatever it took to get away.

Landing safely on the road's dirt verge after scaling an inconsequential wire fence, Monica leaned forward with both hands resting on her knees. By this time, she was panting heavily and blowing hard, looking up at her surroundings as she considered her next move.

And then smiling as her means of escape slid into view on the street directly opposite.

*

Michael Burridge had not slept at all well and was feeling a little woolly headed. He and his wife, Phillipa, had argued over the allocation of household chores, which had resulted in him reluctantly accepting the job of driving into town to fetch some groceries while she took care of their one-year-old son who overnight had developed a chesty cough. As he allowed gravity to propel him and the family car down the driveway and onto the lane, he was immediately alarmed by the sudden and dramatic appearance of a young girl clambering over the fence on the other side of the main road onto which he was about to turn. Before he reached the junction, the girl raced across the tarmac and hurried around to his side of the car. Distress had etched itself into her every feature. The poor thing looked terrified.

'What is it?' he asked, powering down his side window. A flurry of snow blew in, momentarily obscuring his view. 'What's wrong?'

'Help me!' she cried, scrabbling with the handle of the door behind him and throwing fearful glances over her shoulder.

Burridge looked up at the girl in alarm, stunned but also panicked by her frantic behaviour. 'Tell me what's going on,' he said.

'He's after me!'

'Who is? Who's after you?' He looked beyond, back to the fence over which she had climbed. He knew the hill fell away alarmingly on the other side and could see no sign of a pursuer. He began to open his door, but she pushed it closed, screaming at him in abject fear.

'I don't know! A man. A horrible, dangerous man. Oh, please! Please just let me in.'

Thinking rapidly, he said, 'I live just here. How about I take you indoors? You'll be safe inside and we can call the police.'

'No!' Her cry was shrill this time, piercing. 'That won't stop him. He'll break in. And when he does, he'll hurt all of us. Please, just let me in and drive! Get me out of here before he comes!'

The girl's face was twisted beyond mere panic. The uniform she wore provided scant protection against the elements. Burridge reacted as he had always hoped he would in a crisis. He flicked a switch to disengage the locks, told the girl to jump in the back. She pulled on the handle, yanked the door open, threw herself onto the back seat, and slammed the door behind her.

'Go! Go! Go!' she shrieked, reacting as if the man chasing her was about to leap over the fence at any moment.

Burridge looked quickly both ways and gunned the engine. Tyres squealed and burned rubber, smoking as he pushed the car hard down the hill towards town. With a horrified look in the rear mirror, he fumbled inside his jacket and fished out a mobile phone.

'Here,' he said, passing it over his left shoulder. 'Call the police. Tell them about the man chasing you and let them know which way we're going. They'll meet us.'

And that was when he heard a soft snick and a cold steel blade pressed against the side of his neck.

'Time to slow things down,' the girl whispered in his ear. 'We don't want to attract unwanted attention.'

'What the… why… what about the man chasing you?' Burridge stammered. 'You must call the police.'

The girl huffed a scornful laugh. 'Mister,' she said. 'The police are the last people we want to see, because they'll be the ones doing the chasing.'

*

DCI Knight was still fulminating over the news that Monica Cilliers had fled the college, when DI Fox came jogging over to where she stood on the quad outside the main building.

'Just had a message over comms,' he said, gasping for breath and trying not to show it. 'Various members of staff and students spotted our girl running. Uniform tracked her route out of the grounds and sent traffic in that direction. A woman flagged them down to say that a girl matching Cilliers' description had stopped her husband and had then jumped into the back of his motor, which took off at speed down the hill towards town. She gave us the make, model, colour, and plate. They won't get far, boss.'

Knight drew both hands down her face, feeling the ache of tension in every muscle. Snow had begun to settle on the shoulders of her overcoat. She gathered herself and nodded. 'Okay. We're no use here, so let's go mobile. Get a fix on them before we reach the exit gates, Foxy. I want to know which direction to head in.'

By the time they'd raced across to Knight's car and clambered inside, DI Fox had received an update. 'You won't believe this,' he said, anger clouding his face. 'They've just poodled past the entrance to the college, heading west on the A4. Traffic spotted the motor and shot off after them.'

Without a word, Knight gunned her Audi's engine. She tore through the gates and swung the car hard to the left, ignoring the flow of traffic. Horns blared, but she paid them no attention. Gaining speed rapidly, blues and twos warning others of their fast approach, she eventually risked a look at her DI and said, 'Put us in direct touch with whichever car or cars we have pursuing them ahead of us. I want landmarks, speed, direction.'

Fox did as he was told. Within minutes, he was communicating with a traffic vehicle through his Airwave. Knight gathered from their faltering conversation that the pursuit car had Mr Burridge's Lexus in sight. They had just screamed past The Bell pub at West Overton, which meant the two detectives were a couple of miles and no more than three minutes behind. Hearing this, Knight pressed the accelerator all the way to the floor.

Flashing past Silbury Hill and then Beckhampton, before whipping along the road at more than seventy towards Cherhill Down where this had all begun, Knight wore a determined look on her face, teeth meshed together. 'We've got you, you little bitch!' she hissed, unaware of the route the girl was forcing the man to drive, but certain there was no escaping the highly skilled driver in the traffic vehicle following close behind.

FORTY-SEVEN

Chase held his breath as the vehicle made a right turn on to the private road. From behind the snow-encrusted brambles, he and Laney watched it straighten and continue sluggishly, edging forward along the exposed trail until it disappeared from view. He listened hard, the engine never once faltering as the sound gradually faded.

'Call Knight,' he said to his DC. 'Tell them to come, but this time silently and deliberately. Have them surround the area and start closing in.'

He started the Volvo, pulled out onto the lane, and followed the tracks left behind by Lennon's car. He was forced to squint, the snow still hammering down from the sky unabated, wipers brushing large clumps aside in a futile attempt to clear the windscreen. Moments later, he eased off the accelerator and allowed the SUV to make progress governed only by the automatic gearbox.

'There it is,' he said, spotting the Nissan. Its running lights were no longer on. He squeezed his eyes into tighter slits, searching for a plume of exhaust fumes. Nothing. 'I think he's already disappeared into the trees.'

Chase parked directly behind Lennon's vehicle, penning it in should the man escape their clutches. The two of them exited the SUV silently, nudging their doors closed.

'I only just got through to DI Fox,' Laney told him sourly as she hunched into her coat. 'That problem I mentioned earlier turned out to be worse than we thought. Not only must Cilliers have got wind of the arrest before making a run for it, but she also managed to get out of the grounds before carjacking somebody. Foxy and DCI Knight have joined the chase.'

He swore and kicked out at the snow beneath his feet, almost slipping in the process. After a moment, he shrugged and said, 'Sod it. There's bugger all we can do about that. Let's get after Lennon. And we'd better hurry.'

Chase gestured towards a set of footprints set deep into the chilling whiteness leading off to the right and into the fringes of the dense treeline. He began to follow and beckoned his partner to do the same.

Hurrying proved to be a relative term. Chase felt a terrible mix of emotions pressing down upon him. He and Laney had to move quickly enough and follow close enough to reach the professor before the man had a chance to hurt the boys. But at the same time, they needed to do so without attracting Lennon's attention prior to him reaching his ultimate destination. The fine balance had slender margins for error, and as his concerns deepened, he began to feel his breathing becoming laboured.

Despite the biting wind and the sub-zero temperature, Chase felt flushed. Clouds of breath preceded him as he fought to keep his gaze steady. Reasoning that Lennon couldn't be anywhere other than where his footsteps had taken him, he felt reassured that he didn't have to scan the surrounding woods. He didn't exactly fear wooded areas, but they did have the capacity to disturb him and make him feel uncomfortable in their midst. This time he paid the numerous trees and the heavy vegetation and underwood no heed, concentrating only on following in the professor's wake.

Without warning, they emerged onto a natural pathway, no more than a few feet wide but zigzagging through the wooded area up ahead for a good twenty or thirty yards. The trees either side looked threatening and impenetrable, their naked branches overlapping to such a degree that it would have been impossible to recognise the clearing from above. His eyes scoured the way ahead until he could see tread marks leading off the tunnel-like route towards a large mound of undergrowth bunched together, heavy vegetation cascading from it to form a greater barrier.

Raising a hand to point, he turned to his partner. 'He's disappeared through there,' he whispered, gathering his breath as the air he sucked in turned icy. 'Claire, I think I know what this must be; the place where those boys are being held. I think somewhere inside that lot there's a concealed entrance.'

Laney's shoulders sagged. 'Shit! Christ, I could do with a fag right about now.'

'Yeah, and I could sink a bottle or two of beer, but we're both going to have to suck it up. We'll need to be careful once we've pushed ourselves through that barricade. Are you ready for what might be waiting for us in there?'

Steam rising from her uncovered head, Laney shook it and said, 'I have absolutely no idea, cupcake. But you're not going in there without me, so I think I'm about to find out.'

FORTY-EIGHT

THE LONG DOWNHILL STRETCH between Beckhampton stables and Cherhill was wide and clear. Knight felt DI Fox stiffen by her side as she nudged the speed up to eighty, eighty-five, and then ninety. She eased her foot off the accelerator, but never once touched the brake as they sped through the tiny hamlet. But she was motivated by what she could see up ahead. She and Fox had caught up, and in the near distance she saw the traffic car hard on the heels of the jacked silver Lexus. It was all the impetus she needed to floor it again the moment they'd cleared Cherhill and its 40mph limit.

Snow that had blown through in flurries all day long had begun to cascade from the sky in a steady tumbling stream. The countryside flashed by in a blur, but Knight knew they'd soon hit the town of Calne. Driving hard and fast was off the menu along Quemerford towards the centre, and she wondered if Cilliers realised this and might look to take the back road in the direction of Devizes instead. It was all twists and turns, but they were unlikely to come to a complete standstill as they most assuredly would if they kept going along the A4.

The increasingly slick road rumbled beneath the wheels of her car. Her eyes fixed directly ahead, she suddenly spotted a pair of red lights flickering. Followed almost instantaneously by another pair. *Is there a car in front of them or are they turning?* As if in response, the Lexus jerked viciously and immediately fishtailed, yet somehow adhered to the road as it made a sharp right turn. The traffic cops stuck to their task, never more than fifty yards behind Cilliers and the poor driver she had somehow commandeered to help her flee.

Having expected the Lexus to make a right turn at the roundabout ahead, Knight realised either Cilliers or Burridge himself had made a serious error of judgement in following the road around to the left instead. They were travelling in the direction of the quarry, and while there was a way out of the labyrinth of roads they were heading towards, there were many more ways in which they might end up at a dead end.

The first bend proved to be no problem for any of them. But as Knight gained on the two vehicles ahead and they hit a second and more severe curve in the road, a jolt to her gut told her Burridge had taken it too fast for the conditions. From her angle she could see him trying to straighten but fail, and from her left she heard DI Fox cry, 'He's lost it!'

There were two ways to go off the road at that point. To the right stood a waste plant bordered by a sturdy brick wall set behind a screen of hedgerow. To the left lay a pit filled with wastewater. The Lexus overcorrected and skidded in that direction, narrowly avoiding a parked car. It hit the grassy embankment at the side of the road and took off with all four wheels in the air before splashing down into the manmade pond.

The pursuing traffic car spewed up a cloud of settling snow and gravel as it slithered to a halt on a verge running alongside the expanse of water. Knight stamped on her brake and managed to pull up short only a handful of yards behind it. Before she could apply her handbrake, the two traffic officers had decamped and were already clambering down the embankment towards the pond.

DCI Knight and DI Fox joined their colleagues barely seconds later, looking on in grim fascination as the silver saloon disappeared beneath the surface in a roiling, seething explosion of water that sent heavy ripples tearing across the otherwise still pond.

Health & Safety restrictions forbade emergency service crews who were not suitably equipped from plunging into water to save people in danger of drowning. None of the four officers present took heed, each of them wading in to the point where they could no longer stand. Then, one after the other, they ducked their heads beneath the surface and stroked down and towards the rapidly descending Lexus.

It was an impossible task.

The water was so filthy and dark that Knight could barely see her hand in front of her face. The Lexus had been driving with its automatic running lights on, but they were nowhere to be seen. She rapidly became disorientated and, having no idea in which direction she was swimming, altered her position and started to claw her way back up.

Hers was the first head to bob to the surface, and she realised immediately that she had indeed been heading a dozen or more yards to the left of where she had last seen the Lexus. Two more heads suddenly appeared close by – both traffic officers. Then, in a rush of foaming water, two more popped up, almost alongside each other. Panting hard, Knight put her head back and gasped for breath, relieved to see both Fox and the pale, shocked face of a man she did not recognise.

The car owner, Mr Burridge, had made it.

But as DCI Knight made her way out of the freezing pond water, her clothes dripping wet and clinging to her body as she gazed over her shoulder, she realised there was no sign whatsoever of Monica Cilliers.

FORTY-NINE

'What do you think is in there?' DC Laney asked, her breathing more laboured than his. She nodded towards the area they had identified as a potential hidden access point.

'A shelter of some kind. A bunker. Below ground, thick concrete structure with steel girders and mesh running all the way through its walls and ceiling. It would explain why we were unable to see it from above and why Lennon lost his GPS signal every time he entered it. The MOD erected these places all over the country, and if you think about it, they're pretty much perfect for containing these boys.'

Nodding to himself and drawing in a deep breath, he continued on, trying to match the tread marks so as not to trample over crisp patches of snow. The sound was unmistakable, and Lennon might be close enough to hear. It felt as if it took an age to travel the short distance, but even as he approached with caution, Chase was startled by a sudden flurry of noise and motion as twigs and branches snapped as they were brushed aside, a cacophony of sound culminating in their quarry appearing from within the mass of wild undergrowth.

Chase stopped dead. Lennon staggered to a halt, coiled but unmoving. Their eyes met. It took a beat before either of them reacted, but then the professor pushed hard off his right foot and struck out through the fresh snowfall. Chase moved at the same time. As he took off in pursuit, he called back over his shoulder for

Laney to go on and find the entrance they'd been searching for, but also to wait for his return before entering.

Even as he threw out the instruction, he hesitated and started to question himself. Finding the five missing lads was of paramount importance. Rescuing them safely even more so, of course. He fought his natural instincts, which were to help his partner achieve that goal. His thoughts turned instead to continuing after Lennon. He won the mental battle. Or lost, depending on which way others might consider his actions at a later date.

Chase stumbled on, gaining ground but having to constantly avoid or battle through flapping branches that flew back at him as Lennon made his escape. He didn't bother calling out; he couldn't remember a single villain halting mid-flee in response to an order demanding they did so. Instead, he gathered his breath and used it to propel himself forwards, increasing momentum as the forested ground became less of a natural obstacle course. The professor was surprisingly nimble and agile, but Chase grew closer with each clumsy stride.

Through the trees they ran, clumps of snow driven into their faces. Chase found himself spitting every so often, his vision becoming blurred by the constant battering. He huffed and puffed, his muscles beginning to burn, but with every motion he became more enraged. That increasing fury spurred him on. No way he was giving up on this pursuit, and he knew before long they would be out of the wood, which would make his task so much easier. Already he could see the treeline thinning up ahead, patches of pure white open land laying serenely in the distance. It was just a matter of time before Lennon tired or fell, or both.

Which was the exact moment that Chase's left foot caught a root much thicker than he had anticipated. He tripped and plunged headlong to the ground, slamming face first into a bank of snow. The juddering fall forced all the air from his lungs, leaving him thrashing on the ground gasping for breath while the freezing cold snowfall did its best to fill his open mouth. He strained his neck to look up, ignoring a sharp stab of pain in his chest. The sight of Lennon increasing the space between them was all the spur he needed to regain his feet and scramble on with the chase. But he had taken no more than half a dozen paces when he realised he had damaged his ankle on the tree root, twisting it so badly that he could do nothing but hobble and curse while his suspect began to disappear into the distance.

Into the fringe. Out beyond the tree line. Going, going…

But then something Chase hadn't anticipated occurred. Lennon juddered to a grinding halt and a couple of steps later staggered before slumping to his knees. It became obvious why, even before he held up both hands behind his head, as armed officers clad in dark clothing converged on the figure, their weapons raised and ready to take care of business.

Chase wanted to collapse at that moment, his lungs on fire, a searing pain encircling his ankle in a bracelet of agony. But Laney was back the way he had come, and she was his partner. Hobbling, skipping, stumbling, Chase forced his weary frame onwards towards the concealed entrance. He brushed his way through, sweeping aside the heavy undergrowth without a thought for his own safety as it clawed at his exposed flesh. Deeper inside, he spotted another tall mound of shrubs, and as he made his way around them he came upon the opening, foliage draped either side of it like a living pair of curtains. A sturdy steel door yawned wide open, and as he approached the steps leading down into darkness, he called out for his colleague.

In response, he heard only his own voice echoing back as it bounced off the thick walls inside the structure beneath his feet.

Chase felt a desperate surge of panic rising up inside his chest. What if Lennon had not come alone? What if the bastard had a partner of his own? What if Laney had…

'I'm okay, Royston!'

Laney.

She didn't sound as if she was under any duress. In fact, his partner seemed excited. Joyous, even.

'I'm coming back up. *We're* coming back up. I've found them. Found them all. Call for help. We're going to need paramedics here.'

Almost overcome by the volume of adrenaline flooding his system, Chase dragged himself back outside where he sank to his haunches and fumbled around inside layers of clothing to find his phone. Sucking in deep breaths, eyes leaking as a result of more than mere stinging having been pummelled by the snow, he made the calls.

FIFTY

Royston Chase had been willing to make the solemn journey alone, but both Laney and May quickly volunteered to join him. Several days had passed since the events at Membury Fort. His damaged foot remained extremely tender and wrapped solidly in bandages, with the added compress of a tight elasticated support brace. He'd had to dress down and wear trainers, as his work shoes didn't fit. But he hated being a passenger, and as he only needed his right foot for the pedals, he chose to drive. A multitude of scratches and scrapes to his face were healing, though a fair few were still sore and had left unsightly marks.

The days spent navigating a crime in action, where every second was precious and the consequences of failure often disastrous, mostly passed by in a blur like a fleeting thought or distant memory. The period immediately following capture and arrest flew by faster still. Because when you had people sitting in holding cells, their custody clocks ticking down, defence solicitors and suspects' families fighting tooth and nail to prevent you from reaching the charging phase, and the CPS working hard alongside you to make your case in the most trying of circumstances, days became hours and hours mere minutes. When you were up against the clock, it never worked in your favour.

Starved of sleep, minds frazzled, anxiety levels through the roof and climbing, for police officers the interview and charging process was every bit as fraught as the chase itself. Many an investigation had withered on the vine during the custody period, resulting in suspects being bailed and set free to stalk the streets rather than remanded to a prison cell. But both Chase and Laney had found themselves massively impressed by the dedication and expertise of the Gablecross team. Every one of them had played a blinder, their combined efforts and subsequent charging decisions ultimately leading to Chase's determination to pay a visit to Grace Arnold's parents.

Greeted initially by the local FLO to whom Laney had made a phone call the previous evening, Chase was delighted to find Grace's brother sitting alongside his parents. Perhaps he'd got through to the young man after all. The anticipation inside the room was intense, but none of the detectives were inclined to milk it.

'I wanted to deliver this news in person,' Chase said, remaining on his feet together with his colleagues. 'And both Claire and Alison here chose to accompany me. We worked this case together, in addition to a whole team back in Swindon. We did so because it's our job, but also for Grace and for you, her family. Your girl deserved nothing less than our all, and I wouldn't be standing here in front of you if that wasn't what we gave.'

Chase paused for a moment to gather his thoughts, studying their expectant faces. 'As you may be aware, the police are able to detain a suspect for only twenty-four hours without charge, which includes sleep, breaks, solicitor meetings, and health checks. It's seldom enough time, and certainly nowhere near sufficient given the complexity and scale of this case. But we are allowed to apply for more time, which we did, and those applications were successful. At the conclusion, and following great debate with the Crown Prosecution Service, we eventually charged two people.'

'Two?' Mr Arnold said, surprised by the figure.

'Yes. I'll explain further in a moment. The thing is, formal charges can be a little confusing in terms of what they actually mean, so let me tell you in more basic terms where we are. Professor Jeffrey Lennon, a member of staff at Marlborough College, abducted five young hikers who camped on the hillside with Grace that night back in January. He then held them captive, made threats against them and their loved ones, before finally attempting to end their lives only minutes before his capture. He will also face a number of additional charges relating to both his conduct and his relationship with Grace's killer.'

Chase's gaze came to rest upon Mr and Mrs Arnold, who sat wedged together on the narrow settee. He kept it steady as he addressed them further. 'I realise this will be difficult to hear, but better from me than an officer detached from the case or, worse still, a member of the media. I'm sure you've heard plenty of rumours in addition to our own official statement, but I'm here to provide you with the facts. A Marlborough student by the name of Isaac Levy attempted to rape and strangle your daughter, after which he subsequently covered for the person who physically ended Grace's life. Those will be the major charges, though he, too, will have to answer a number of others put against him. Please note my use of the word "attempted". Although it is impossible for us to be completely certain, we do not believe this young man raped your daughter.'

None of the three family members uttered a single word in response, staring back at him dully. He sensed their relief, but it remained unspoken. Not knowing how much they were taking in, he gave a nod before continuing.

'Finally, I am able to confirm that Monica Cilliers, also a Marlborough College student, murdered Grace. We believe she did so in an act of pure spite and jealousy. However, as I'm sure you've read or heard, Cilliers herself was killed as she attempted to escape arrest. The Crown Prosecution Services have long-since taken the position not to prosecute the deceased, so we will not be posthumously charging the girl with the offence. Personally, I would have liked to see her stand trial, as I have no doubt she would have been convicted and received a lengthy sentence. You may think the same and feel cheated as a result, however she did lose her own life and that may be more fitting. Granted, we were unable to put her on trial and then behind bars, but that's not quite the same as her getting away with murder.'

'Will you release my sister's body to us now?' Jamie Arnold asked. 'Also, without a trial, how are we to ever know what really happened to Grace?'

Chase nodded. 'Of course. I'll make the arrangements. As for you being made aware of precisely what occurred, there will be a full coroner's inquest. You'll be able to attend if you wish. But if it's all the same to you, for the time being I am going to spare you the awful details regarding that night. I dare say there is much you still want to know, but my advice to you all is to bide your time. As and when you have questions I will answer them, but let me say this to you: nothing you learn will make you feel better. Quite the opposite, I'd suggest. If I've discovered nothing else during my time doing this job, it's that the solace you seek in knowing precisely what happened to Grace simply cannot be found. Believe me, there's only more misery waiting for you out there.'

'Did she put up a fight?' Mr Arnold asked, his face drawn and seemingly shocked at the question he had put to Chase.

Royston nodded once again. 'She did, sir. In fact, it may well be the reason why Monica Cilliers would have ended up facing a murder charge and not Isaac Levy.'

His eyes having closed, Arnold said, 'We know roughly how our daughter died, Sergeant Chase. But despite your warning, I simply have to ask you one more thing. The same question I asked you the first time you visited us.'

'No, Grace did not suffer,' Chase said. He knew exactly what the man was about to ask, because those left behind always did. 'The impact of the blows she received would have killed her almost instantaneously.'

He didn't know if that was true, and the girl had previously suffered through Levy's prolonged attack, but he did know it was what the family needed to hear. In this instance, the truth was an unwanted intruder.

'Let me be clear,' he went on. 'Grace did nothing to invite this danger upon herself. She could not have foreseen the consequences of inviting fellow hikers to camp alongside her that night. While it's true to say she was a little inebriated, we also believe she was drugged in order to ease her inhibitions and make her more compliant. At this stage we still don't know who might have done this to her, but we are pursuing the matter with the five other lads who were also on that hillside. As for any charges against them, while their behaviour was questionable, they deny any wrongdoing and claim to have had no idea that Grace had been murdered.'

'And you believe them?' Grace's brother asked, a sceptical look on his face.

'What I believe is not important at this stage. The fact is, the snowstorm that night could easily have obscured any evidence of what took place in the early hours. Enough that a casual glance would have failed to spot it or even cause any doubt. Two of the lads say they went over to say goodbye, saw that Grace's tent was empty, had a look in the distance to see if they could spot her, but in seeing nothing they went back to their mates and moved on. It's plausible. Not only that, I have to say it came across as sincere.'

'I suggest the main thing for you all to focus on here is that the person who murdered Grace has perhaps received the ultimate sentence,' Laney said, keeping her voice low and even. 'And a permanent one at that.'

'Charged doesn't always equate to being found guilty,' Mr Arnold mumbled. 'She might even have got away with it in court. Perhaps hers was a suitable punishment in that regard.'

Chase acknowledged this with a nod. 'True enough. But while we would undoubtedly have faced a *he said-she said* situation between the two students, the evidence against Monica Cilliers was overwhelming. I wouldn't be telling you she was responsible if I didn't believe it to be the case. We also believe Professor Lennon will eventually crumble and admit the truth. And the truth is that Cilliers used their relationship to coerce him into acting against his nature. She did so because she was guilty, and his affection for her made him vulnerable. We'll make that association clear in the weeks and months to come, and use the time between now and Isaac Levy's trial to uncover additional evidence against them both. We already have incriminating items surrendered by Levy, and when we and the CPS put this case together, I'm sure it will secure his conviction.'

'Can you promise us that?' Grace's father asked in a frail, distant voice. His wife had still not uttered a single word.

Chase shifted uneasily from foot to foot. 'I never have and never will make such a promise, sir. The legal system has its own flaws, and I wouldn't bet against anything. But I also have my years of experience, and they tell me the boy will be found guilty of any charges we bring against him. His actions that night not only fuelled a jealous rage, but were wholly premediated and might otherwise have led him to committing murder instead. His subsequent actions were equally indefensible. The justice system gets it right more often than you might think, Mr Arnold. I have every expectation of it doing so again this time.'

Grace's father turned his head to look at a photograph of his daughter. The room fell silent until he smiled and nodded. 'She was always our little adventurer. Started guiding when she was just four when she joined the Rainbows. Moved on up to Brownies, Guides, and kept going into the Rangers at fourteen. Grace went to every camp you can think of and loved canoeing and ziplining and abseiling. On her eighteenth birthday, she did her first parachute jump. She was a great little climber, too. There was nothing of her, really. But what she lacked in size she more than made up for in spirit and imagination. And… and courage, which she will have needed that night.'

'Grace sounds as if she enjoyed her life, Mr Arnold,' Chase said in a gentle voice. 'Sucked the marrow from it, as Thoreau would have it.'

'Oh, she did that, Sergeant. She certainly did.' His gaze switched and their eyes met. 'And she was fond of that Thoreau book, too. Particularly the continuation of the quote you just mentioned, when he goes on to say that he did not want, when he came to die, to realise that he had not lived. That just about sums up our daughter. She crammed a lot of living into her short time on earth.'

'Grace sounds like a special girl, sir.'

'That she was.' Arnold huffed a humourless laugh, which forced him to clear his throat. 'The irony is that she analysed health and safety and took on every challenge only after weighing up the potential pitfalls and their consequences. She worked and trained hard to tackle each and every one of them. But in the end, she failed to factor in the most dangerous of them all.'

'Which was?' Chase asked.

The man blinked as tears gathered in his eyes. 'Human beings, of course,' he managed to say as his voice broke and his body heaved.

They were ten minutes down the road on their way back when Alison May asked her colleagues if she had performed adequately in her first major investigation as a trainee detective. Chase regarded her in the rear-view mirror, wrinkled his face and shook his head. 'I'm sorry, Alison. To be honest, if you were a Eurovision song, you'd be getting nil points from me.'

'Sad to say, but same story here,' Laney said over her shoulder. 'If you'd just turned in that performance as an ice skater, the numbers on the cards I'd be holding up would amount to zero.'

'You just didn't stick the landing,' Chase continued.

Nodding, Laney said, 'If we were astronauts going to the moon, you'd be Michael Collins, my love.'

May blinked rapidly but said nothing. Her lips were frozen apart. Chase watched in the mirror as her chin quivered and her lips began to tremble. He nudged Laney with his elbow, unable to contain himself any longer. She turned in her seat to face their colleague. A moment later and her rigid features softened as she burst out laughing.

'You are going to have to wise up to when people are mugging you off, young lady. Now stop that snivelling, you soppy tart! I can't believe you even had to ask us. You did everything expected of you and more. Your remarks and your questions were insightful, and you didn't hold back. You played a blinder, kid.'

'Oh, you rotten bastards!' May spat, more from relief than anger. She kicked out her legs like a toddler having a tantrum. 'You two really had me going there. I thought I'd screwed up before I'd really got started.'

Through his own laughter, Chase shook his head and said, 'No, you did great. You'll be a major asset to this or any other team.'

When the joyous hubbub inside the vehicle had subsided, May leaned on the back of Chase's seat and said, 'That was nice of you to leave out the more sordid details back there.'

He sighed. 'They don't need those images inside their heads.'

'You were very careful to point out that Isaac Levy hadn't raped Grace. That was a kind touch. I mean, not only do we not know that for sure, but if one of those five bastards drugged the poor girl, then she was effectively raped by all of them.'

'I understand that. But once again, I think that family can go the rest of their lives without knowing that kind of detail, don't you?'

'Absolutely. You reckon one of them did it, Sarge? Slip something into her drink, I mean.'

'I don't know about Royston,' Laney muttered, turning her face away to stare out of the side window. 'But I'd definitely prefer to cling to that notion rather than think of Grace willingly indulging in a five-way fuckathon.'

Chase winced. 'Nice imagery, Claire. If my appetite wasn't already spoiled, it is now. But in answer to your question, Alison, I do believe that's what happened. I doubt we'll ever know for certain, not unless one of those arseholes coughs to it. In every major investigation, there are always a few loose ends that we can't tie up in a neat and pretty bow. This is one of them. We have no forensics, no witnesses – at least none willing to speak up. The boys were questioned about it, but each of them has so far denied the allegation. Sadly, like I say, unless conscience gets the better of one of them, we have to let it drop.'

The three lapsed into a contemplative silence, accompanied on the journey by the ghost of the young girl whose killer they had fought so hard to find, arrest, and charge. At the beginning of the case, Chase had imagined him and his team hunting for a single violent predator. But instead there had been several of one kind or another on the hillside that night. Grace had sought adventure, but instead had found only the worst that mankind has to offer.

'Maybe karma will weigh in,' Laney suggested after a while. 'Make them suffer for what they did. Perhaps have their bollocks turn to squares and fester in each corner.'

Chase nodded. 'Yeah. We can only hope so. But let's take some comfort from the fact that we'll see some justice for Grace Arnold. As for you, Alison, soak it all up. Think about it, learn from it, and remember it always. Especially our victim. I know I won't ever forget her.'

ACKNOWLEDGEMENTS

Many thanks to my police advisor, Graham Bartlett, whose own writing career is on a deserved upward trajectory – any errors are my own. Once again, I am also extremely grateful to my editor, my Facebook group members and #blissettes whose support always picks me up when I am flagging, to book bloggers everywhere, and to online book groups and their generous admins.

And to my regular bloggers, Nicki Murphy, Alyson Read, Sharon Rimmelzwaan, Nicola Parkinson, Karen Cole, Amanda Oughton, Yvonne Bastian, Liz Mistry, Donna Morfett, Sarah Hardy, Jill Burkinshaw, and Lynda Checkley, a massive thank you for your generosity and support. I'm in awe of you all.

I am also hugely grateful to two of my ARC readers for spotting critical issues that desperately needed spotting, and this book is all the better for their attention to detail (which was far superior to mine). Two large thumbs up for Mary Ryan and Ruth Murphy.

The Predators may be overdue, but I finally got here. I wish I had written the book in the Inuit language, as I'd have had so many more words for snow to choose from. I hope you enjoyed it, and perhaps we'll revisit Chase, Laney, and May again one day.

Cheers all.
Tony

UP NEXT

DI Jimmy Bliss will be back this autumn in *What Dies Inside Us*.

tony@tonyjforder.com
www.tonyjforder.com
www.linktr.ee/TonyJForder

Printed in Great Britain
by Amazon